THE ARTIST

THE ARTIST

MANU J

First published by
Papertowns Publishers
72, Vishwanath Dham Colony,
Niwaru Road, Jhotwara,
Jaipur, 302012

The Artist

ISBN Print Book - 978-93-6185-554-2

Printed in India

Critical Acclaim for The Artist

As the characters of Manu J's audacious psychological thriller blaze a bloody trail, the reader realises a searing fact: in this bleakest of bleak worlds, the darkness engulfing these twisted, scarred men and women isn't external — it's internal, a manifestation of their own sordid psyches. From Manas, a family man apparently living an ideal life — or lie? — to Alex, a young man haunted by the ghosts of his childhood, The Artist draws you into the minds of individuals who, having decided they're beyond redemption, have set out to destroy themselves and those around them. Set largely in Thiruvananthapuram, this is a chilling portrait of the role unresolved conflicts and past traumas play in misshaping human beings. A fluently written and blazingly paced thriller, Manu J's The Artist marks an impressive debut.

Dr. Shashi Tharoor,
esteemed Indian politician, accomplished author, and former diplomat

For a debutant, Manu has come up with a surprisingly cohesive narration that seamlessly weaves subdued undertones with graphic murderous violence, rendered with sickeningly artistic hues, taking the readers on a sometimes nauseatingly horrifying ride, from one end of the country to the other.

The subtle humaneness that the author has managed to integrate into at least one of his deviant protagonists pulls the readers into a tough moral dilemma as to whether to root for the character or condemn him outright for his macabre acts. The novel does get almost all its hard facts right, with well-researched procedures and descriptions included. Published by Paper Towns, it offers a solid read for genre enthusiasts and introduces a promising new writer to the literary scene.

The New Indian Express

Manu Joseph exhibits a remarkable command of fiction, weaving intricate details that captivate the reader's imagination without overwhelming the story's essence. His ability to balance these details with the overall narrative is impressive, especially for someone at this stage in their career.

Even more striking is his deep understanding of the human psyche. The character of Manas reflects a profound exploration of the human self, grappling with forces beyond his control, echoing the tragic visions found in the Mahabharata and Greek tragedies. Yet, the novel goes beyond a typical crime thriller; it offers a morally edifying experience, driven by themes of repentance and remorse. This work stands as a testament to the author's ability to craft a story that is both emotionally resonant and intellectually engaging.

Prof N. Manu Chakravarthy,
writer, film critic, cultural theorist

Acknowledgments

First and foremost, I'd like to extend my heartfelt gratitude to my wonderful wife, Maris. Despite her own busy schedule, she not only helped me find the time to translate my thoughts onto paper but also provided unwavering support while and after writing the novel. My little companion, Zane, my six-year-old son, helped me understand what it is to be a parent and has contributed more to this book than he could possibly fathom.

A special nod goes to my parents, V.K. Joseph and Annie P.C. Their unwavering support and keen insights, as they delved into the initial drafts, have been invaluable in shaping this work. Gratitude abounds for my circle of friends and family who took the time to read the book and provide their invaluable perspectives.

Finally, a big shoutout to Bangalore traffic! Who knew that bumper-to-bumper gridlock on my daily commute could be the secret ingredient for finishing a book? So, here's to you, dear traffic, for giving me the slow lane to writer's victory!

Characters

The Family

Manas – *Husband/Father*
Anuradha – *Wife/Mother*
Shruti – *Daughter*

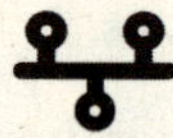

The Past

Prateek – *Manas' Friend/Brother*
Amrita – *Manas' Girlfriend*

Special Investigation Unit
(Violent Crimes)

Nasir Ali Khan – *Senior Superintendent of Police*
Sonam – *Forensic Specialist*
Akshay – *Counter Intelligence*
Avinash & Salim – *Tactical Ops*

Trigger Warning

This book has more red flags than a toxic relationship. Expect violence, deep emotional scars, mental illness, animal cruelty, and a criminal underworld you don't want to visit in real life. If you're not ready for a wild ride, maybe grab a cozy rom-com instead. You've been warned!

Prologue

Monday, April 21, 2014

No one savoured the journey anymore; it was always a mad rush to reach somewhere, and fast.

Alex drummed his fingers on the steering wheel of his blue Alto, idling on the side of the street. The streetlamp cast its amber light, bathing everyone and everything in gold. A bustling crowd, painted in honey-toned light, rushed past the window in its usual hurry to reach places. No one savoured the journey anymore; it was always a mad rush to reach somewhere and fast. Little ants scurrying to make ends meet. Blind cows meandering through life without purpose. The scratchy glass of his Timex told him it was twenty-seven minutes past seven. Almost time.

A two-storeyed building with unpainted red bricks and an occasional patch of dark green moss rose to his right. Big block letters, which had faded with age to a grungy grey, branded the building - 'Bal Bharati Public School'. Alex scanned the horde of people flowing out of the entrance, including teachers and parents after their weekly PTA meeting. *She should be here any minute now.*

A majestic, chrome metal lion figurine on the dashboard glimmered in the amber light. Lion, the king of the forest. The entire forest takes notice if a lion straightens up, fluffs out its mane, and roars. Their lean, muscular body packs enough power to knock out an elephant twice its size. But it's not the power that makes it dangerous. It was its ability to smell fear. Out of a herd of a hundred gazelles, he zeroes in on the weak with ease. Just like him.

Alex surveyed the crowd again. There was no sign of Amrita. Amrita Sharma, or Mrs Sharma, as his mother calls her, was his mother's best friend. His mother always had friends much younger than her. She was someone who rose out of poverty, fighting the good fight. But she did it all with social grace and a unique feminine charm. A true fighter and a loving mother…except when it came to her son. His lips curled into a sneer.

Alex shook the hate from his head and focused on the oncoming rush of people through the arched entrance of the school. Amrita waded through the crowd in a red dress which flew till her knees. She pirouetted with the grace of a ballet dancer to answer a call from behind, an enamoured parent hoping for one last word with the pretty teacher. She tugged the black lace shrug, which covered her delicate arms till her wrist, lower. A gust of wind tousled her hair, pulling strands over her face. She tucked them behind her ear and smiled politely at the parent, and turned back. No one would believe she was thirty-eight.

The red high heels were one of the first things that caught his attention. The way they hugged her petite feet drove butterflies down his stomach. His fetish for high heels could be traced all the way back to his childhood. But it was far from a happy memory. Each time the cane curled around his bare legs, he screamed; he screamed till he saw black spots and then complete darkness. But even louder were his mother's screams, screams of anger when she caught him playing with a high heel he found in the garbage. His ten-year-old brain had failed to comprehend the reason.

Alex woke from his reverie with a start. *Where did she go?* A moment of panic, a splutter in his heartbeat, and then he spied her walking down the road towards the bus stop at the corner. *You are slipping*. He berated himself. *Focus.*

He pulled out of the parking spot and rolled up beside her. "Hi, Mrs. Sharma."

A beautiful smile lit up her angelic face. "Alex? Where is Teresa?"

"Mom couldn't make it. She had to go to the doctor." Alex reached over and opened the door. "She didn't want her pretty friend to catch a bus back home." A smile broke out on his lips as he ran his hands through his short, messy hair.

"Oh! Aren't you a charmer?" A pink blush crept into her cheeks. "She's okay?"

"Yeah, Mom had a small cough that wasn't going away."

After a bit of struggle with her dress, she climbed into the car and closed the door. The turquoise blue beads of her necklace plunked against her full breasts. He turned the car around in a nice sweeping arc and headed back towards their houses in Dwarka Sub-City.

"Was the meeting as boring as it was in my mind?" A devilish grin grew on his handsome face.

"Even more boring than that. One of these days, somebody has to drill some sense into these people."

Silence grew as they drove on. Her milky white thighs peeked from under her red dress. It caught his attention for a second more than usual before focusing back on the road.

"I heard the internet café is doing well," she said, breaking the uncomfortable silence and pulling down her dress. The milky white hid under the red and blended into the darkness. Women had a sixth sense when it came to lecherous stares.

"The money is good, but it's the mind-numbing boredom which gets me."

"I'm sure there are ways to keep yourself busy, especially on the internet."

Alex laughed out loud. "The usual YouTube, Facebook…nothing productive."

Amrita leaned back in her seat, and the red dress started its journey up her thighs again. Alex relished the sneak peek. His eyes crept up her thighs, tearing off her clothes in his mind, one by one, as he zipped past an intersection. Out of the corner of his eyes, he saw her head turn towards him, and hesitate for a moment.

"I think… you missed the turn to my house," she said.

"We were going to your house?" He pulled up on the side of the road and killed the engine. "Mom told me to pick you up and bring you to our house."

"Oh! I'm not sure. Let me call her up and clear it right away." She fumbled for the mobile in her bag.

With the headlights gone, darkness invaded the car. Alex reached over and switched on the dashboard light. In the scant light, Amrita raised her phone close to her cheek. A ghost of a grin twitched his face.

A passing headlight blinded him for a second. The scent of her perfume waded into his nose, driving him crazy. The red leather of her high heels latched onto her creamy skin, taunting him. Her full lips dabbed with crimson red lipstick, trembled as she waited for an answer on the phone. He wanted to bite those lips off and paint her face red.

"Why does she even have a mobile phone if she is never gonna pick it up?" Her voice quivered slightly.

Alex chuckled at the comment, lightening up the mood. "Tell you what? If I don't take you home, I'll get a bashing of a lifetime. You know Mom….If it's a misunderstanding, I can always drop you home."

Amrita stared into the darkness. Her eyes darted furtively, scanning up and down the road. "But…Isn't she at the doctor's?" Her voice trembled.

Alex dismissed her concern with a wave of his hand, "She would be back home by now."

Amrita unlatched the magnetic hook on her handbag, and put away her phone. She fumbled with the lock mechanism, and managed to close the handbag on her fourth try. Her knuckles were white from clutching the handbag tightly. The acrid smell of fear filled the closed space. *This is going to be better than I thought.*

"Let me get that bag. I'll put it in the back of the car." Alex grabbed the bag out of her grasp. He twisted back with his right hand on the steering wheel, and the other extending backwards with the bag. On the way back, his hand grabbed the handle of the cricket bat lying there and in one swift motion, he brought the bat forward and whacked her on the side of the head.

Her pupils dilated, and nostrils flared in the split second she realised what was happening. A mist of blood spurt into the air and hung in the air as if time had stopped for a second. The thump of wood on bone ringed in the car. The surprise on her face was momentary before it lapsed into an unconscious serenity crowned by rivulets of blood.

PART I

CONFLUENCE

Fate is not an eagle, it creeps like a rat.
– Elizabeth Bowen

Manas

Monday, April 21, 2014

Time is the most dangerous predator in the world. You don't hear it coming until you are halfway down its throat, gasping for breath.

"Anu..." Manas called out as he pushed open the front door. He turned back and ushered his companion with an exaggerated flourish. "Ravi, come into my humble abode," Manas said, chuckling.

The dying embers of a fiery tropical sun pierced the windows and painted the living room in a deep orange palette. Long, dark shadows sprung from the furniture in the room. Two more shadows entered the fray as Ravi and Manas shuffled towards the chairs.

Bella sprinted up to Manas and jumped on his leg with a loving bark. She eyed Ravi for a second and resumed her show of affection. She must have sensed the warmth between her pack leader and the unfamiliar face. Manas loved that Labrador to death. The sight of her wheatish fur coat always brought a smile to his face.

The cream-coloured couch Ravi sunk in took a deep hue of orange in the still-bright westering sun. Manas chose the wooden rocking chair, with Bella curled up at his feet. He peered into the corridor that led to the bedroom. The hallway of happiness—as he liked to call it—had an assorted array of framed family pictures lining the walls, which led to the kitchen.

Manas rubbed the back of his neck. Did Anuradha get his message about bringing a guest over? It had been a last-minute decision. He had had a long and tiring Monday and was heading home when he bumped into Ravi in the elevator. They started talking and ended up having a pint of beer at the local pub. It was in that light buzz of alcohol that they decided to take it back to Manas' place for dinner.

Anuradha's captivating smile on her charming face washed away all his doubts. She sauntered into the living room, wearing a crimson kurta with acid-washed, baby-blue denim jeans. The last remains of daylight faintly streaked between the rails of the open window and lit up her quiet, oval face. She was just as beautiful as the day he met her.

It was her eyes that got him. Dark kohl framed her perfectly shaped doe-eyes, accentuating their ethereal beauty. Her long, curvy eyelashes beckoned him closer. He could get lost in those eyes; it happened the first time he laid eyes on her and every time after.

At thirty-eight, she had aged surprisingly well. A faint crow's feet branched out from the edges of her eyes, which deepened when she smiled. She made her way through the furniture, and handed over a cup of tea to Ravi and another one to Manas.

"Anuradha, this is Ravi," said Manas. "I've told you about him. He joined the office a few months ago."

Ravi rose to his feet from the couch and shook her hands. "Thank you, Anuradha, for ha-"

"Call me Anu. Manas talks about you all this time. I'm glad I got to meet you finally."

Ravi nodded his head, pushing his thick-framed square glasses up the bridge of his nose. "Sorry for springing this on you on short notice. I can get dinner on my way home. Just dropped by to see Manas' house and meet the Anu I've heard so much about."

"I hope nothing bad!" A quick giggle escaped her, like a ring of a bell. "You guys talk and catch up. I'll just see if dinner is ready."

Ravi's head swivelled on his neck in a near 360 degrees turn as he appraised the house.

A mahogany bookshelf rose four feet from the white tiled floor, hugging a corner of the wall. The burnt reddish brown shelf stood out like a thorn against the beige walls. The contrast, along with the mosaic of multi-coloured book covers, made for an intriguing piece of art. And right at the top of the shelf, happiness sat in a metal frame—a framed picture of Manas, Anu, Shruti, and Bella. His family.

"Well, Ravi, what do you think?"

"You, sir, have a lovely house," Ravi said with an open, friendly smile. "...And a beautiful wife and daughter."

Bella let out a short bark as if angry at being left out.

"It's the family that makes the home."

"Yes, indeed," said Ravi, "God has been kind to you."

Manas hid a smile behind his cup of tea as he took another sip. He ran the back of his fingers over his smooth, square jaw as he rocked in his chair. God always took the credit, leaving the blame for mere mortals.

"A family is only as good as the people in it," said Manas, as his face split into a wide grin, "The magical fairy who lives up there—" he pointed up towards the skies, "has little to do with it."

"Not a big fan of the man above?"

"Which one?" Manas' mouth twitched with amusement. "There are more Gods than I can count, and everyone believes they've got the right one. Any way you look at it, at least 70% of the world is doomed because they worshipped the wrong God."

Ravi cracked into hearty laughter, and Manas joined in.

"Good one, Sir," Ravi said, "But aren't all these Gods just different names of an unexplained power?"

"First of all, congrats," said Manas, extending his hand for a handshake, "You are instantly smarter than the millions in this world fighting each other in the name of religion." He sunk back into his chair and continued, "The problem I have with the concept of God is that it's propped up on crutches invented by man—Faith, Free Will, and Fate. God is a catch-all phrase for the gaps in human understanding, embodied in an untouchable shrine."

"Hmm," said Ravi.

"I know you aren't convinced. Let's do a little experiment. Let me throw arguments against God, and you counter."

Ravi nodded.

"Okay. The first and the easiest one is that of a cruel God. God is omnipresent and omnipotent, isn't he? Then why do bad things happen in the world? Why the Holocaust or the World Wars? A God who doesn't intervene, even when he has the power to?"

"Yin and Yang, Manas," Ravi said, "Good and evil are two sides of the same coin. There is always a higher purpose for what is happening. For example, the Holocaust resulted in the creation of the Jewish homeland. And both World Wars lifted the world economy out of a slump, injecting the adrenaline it needed. They were all events which seemed big to us, but were nothing on the cosmic scale. Just a brief setback for a larger good."

Manas stopped rocking the chair and leaned forward. This was why he loved Ravi's company.

"That argument, my friend, is coloured with Fate. A higher plan that we mere mortals are not aware of, a grand design invisible to us." Manas took a sip from the cup in his hand. "Okay, let's assume for one second that I go along with this. What possible higher purpose would God have for little kids who get raped or abused?"

"As you said, the grand design is not apparent to us. We are simply not capable of understanding the scale and magnanimity of it. The way I see it is that God created this world, set down his rules, and let humans live out their lives. He doesn't control every person on the planet. And God is not responsible for the vices of humans. They have—" Ravi paused for a second as a sheepish grin twisted his lips, "Free Will."

"That second one you just gave it to me in a basket," Manas chuckled. "But, you know, this Free Will thing kinda negates the purpose of being omnipotent. If I know that a child is being molested, and I do nothing to stop it, how would you judge me? I am a mere mortal, and God, if he exists, should be a better person than me. Shouldn't God be held to a tighter moral code than me?"

"Haven't you heard the phrase—'God works in mysterious ways'?"

"That translates to 'have Faith in what God is doing. It is for the best.' I think you hit the trifecta faster than I expected."

Ravi sat back on the couch, crossed his legs, and started cleaning his fingernails. Then he looked back up, with renewed energy, and asked, "How about a God who is a creator? If you look at the world, you will be amazed at how well-suited it is to humans. It has to be designed to be this perfect."

"I assume you haven't heard of the Anthropic Principle?" Manas asked.

Ravi shook his head from side to side.

"Let's see..." Manas stroked his chin as he rummaged around his brain for the right example. "You play cricket?"

"Used to, but I'm more of a football fan."

"Okay, Football it is. Imagine this. It's stoppage time of the World Cup Final, and Argentina is up by a goal. The Argentina fans go bonkers as they are about to snatch a World Cup after over two decades. But suddenly, Ozil from Germany slides into a tackle and comes up with the ball. He looks up and sees Muller sneaking a run. Without hesitation, he lobs the ball above the Argentinean defenders to Muller, but in his excitement, he puts a little too much power into the lob."

"Muller watches the ball travelling far above his head and chases after it. He checks the assistant on the line—his flag stays down. So, he pummels down the field to get to the ball.

"Romero, the Argentinean goalkeeper, realises that there are no defenders to stop the run. He makes a split-second decision and charges out to meet the ball before Muller gets to it.

"Both Muller and Romero reach the ball at the same time, collide in mid-air, and fall clumsily. But the ball squeezes through the tangled arms and legs, unharmed, rolling towards the goalpost.

"The ball rolls forward like a juggernaut through the sea of grass, each blade trying to stop the ball but failing. But an inch from the line, one brave grass stands up to the challenge and stops the ball. Shortly after, Otamendi, the Argentinean Central Back, kicks the ball out of play, and the referee blows the whistle. Argentina wins the World Cup.

"Surely the blade of grass which won Argentina the World Cup after two decades was surely a special blade of grass. Maybe it was placed there by the curator of the pitch, who was an Argentinean."

Ravi threw his head back and laughed. "I see where you are going, Sir."

Manas joined in the laughter, and added, "That's exactly my point. That blade of grass is just as ordinary as any other blade of grass in that field. It's just that it was at the right place at the right time. Just like Earth. No curator-"

Anuradha stepped into the room, parting the curtains which hid the kitchen. "Is he boring you with his philosophy?" she asked as she leaned forward to take back the cups of tea. "Did he tell you about the blade of grass bit yet?" She brushed away a strand of her dark hair away from her face.

Ravi laughed and said, "No, no. I rather enjoy it. Are you an atheist, too?"

It was her turn to laugh. "No, but not a theist either. I believe in a higher power. Call it God, or Nature, or Universe."

Anuradha caught Ravi stealing a glance at Manas. "No, he doesn't mind. He says, 'To each his own.' He doesn't mind religion as long as it doesn't create a divide."

"Religion and religious texts are not useless. They set down guidelines to live by, and at their core, they are all the same. Be it the Gita, Quran, or Bible. But people get carried away by their devotion, and interpret these books in a way that they were never intended to be. And that is where it all falls apart."

"Anyway… dinner is ready," Anuradha interjected. "Ravi, come and have a seat."

The dinner had quite a variety; browned chicken legs stacked on a white porcelain plate, reddish-orange coconut milk gravy with fish, fish fry, a few veggie side dishes, boiled rice, and chapatis. Manas scanned the chairs around the table and got stuck on the one that was empty.

"Shruti?" A wrinkle took form on his forehead.

"Out with her friends." Anuradha glanced at the clock and added,

"...And she should have been here by now…."

At that exact moment, the front door swung open with a click. The shuffling of feet, and Bella's welcoming bark confirmed it for him. "Shruti," he called out. "Dinner is ready."

"In a minute, Dad." She clambered up the stairs into her room, her sanctuary.

True to her word, she was at the table in a minute, gulping down food like it was her first meal of the day. *Ah! It was Monday. A clear Monday night.* She must be in a hurry to get back upstairs. So was Manas.

Ravi ate his food, and politely responded to Anuradha's questions. He had quite a jolly face, and an infectious laughter. The kind of laughter which instantly makes you like someone.

They had hit it off right from the moment he came over and introduced himself. He was the new Sound Engineer at the advertising firm where Manas was the Creative Director. Ravi laughed uproariously at one of Anuradha's jokes.

His face was very different when he confessed to Manas that he accidentally deleted the entire audio track for an advertisement, which was in the last stages of editing. This was a project which was behind schedule, and Manas' boss was already all over him about that. He was about to explode on the newbie when he saw his face pale as a ghost. Ravi jammed his hands in his armpits and shook uncontrollably. Manas took a few deep breaths and calmed himself down. The source material from which the audio track was mixed together was still available. So, the situation was still salvageable, but a delay was guaranteed. He took it easy on the new guy and covered for him. Ravi was in his probation period and would have lost his job if this had got out. But all Manas would get was an earful of demoralising, demeaning spew of hatred from his boss, that he was used to anyway.

"Saw the full bookshelf out in the hall," said Ravi, bringing Manas back to the present. "You read a lot?"

"Books are little slices of reality which you have never lived. Five kilometres a day to keep my body fit"—he surveyed his trim athletic body—"and a book a month to keep my mind sharp."

"Five kilometres? I tried to run once. Bought me a fresh pair of sneakers and running shorts and set the alarm for five in the morning. Four days in a row, I woke up at five, turned off the alarm.... not snoozed, but turned it off... and curled up back into bed. That was the end of that."

The table erupted in laughter. "It is hard in the beginning," said Manas. "But once you get used to it, you go through the motions without thinking."

"As if the daily runs aren't enough, he disappears every weekend to teach Krav Maga," Anuradha said, putting air quotes around the last two words.

"Krav Maga? Sounds like an item on the menu I wouldn't order."

Shruti chortled, covering her mouth to keep the food from flying off. "There goes the machismo, dad."

Manas shook his head, laughing. "It's a martial art...or rather an Israeli combat technique." He tore into a chicken leg and chewed down a mouthful. "It started about ten years back. I wanted to blow off some steam and stay fit, but I hated working out. It was so boring to lift weights for the sake of it. So, I went to the local gym, and Krav Maga was one of their courses. The trainer gave me a primer on the technique and got me hooked. Pretty soon, it became a part of my life, and now I train fifteen people."

Manas felt around and pressed delicately on the left side of his ribs, which were bruised from taking a kick in last week's sparring session. It was hard work. At 43 years old, he was no longer the young man who ducked and dove to avoid taking a hit. Maybe the closely cropped hair, broad shoulders and well-defined muscles gave an intimidating appearance, but the receding hairline with a smattering of grey hair gave him away. Even though he was fitter than an average forty-year-old, there was no escaping age. He missed the days when he could take a solid hit to his stomach and still push forward, closing the gap between him and his opponent.

Time is the most dangerous predator in the world. You don't hear it coming until you are halfway down its throat, gasping for breath.

"So, what do you do, Shruti?" Ravi asked.

Shruti plastered a polite smile on her face and said, "Astronomy and Astrophysics at Indian Institute of Space Science and Technology."

"Whoa, that's something you don't hear every day."

Manas' chest swelled up with pride as he studied Shruti. He reached for Anuradha's hands under the table. "She was in love with the great unknown right from her childhood. The theory of relativity and black holes was all she talked about by the time she was in tenth grade. So, after Higher Secondary School, we gave her a choice, and she chose this. Our little scientist." Manas beamed at Shruti.

Shruti slid down from her chair a little. "Daaad…" A light flush crept across her cheeks.

The dinner got over soon, and Shruti excused herself upstairs after a minute of formal conversation with Ravi. Bella had already settled in her corner, retired for the night, when Ravi said his last goodbyes at the door.

Anuradha closed the door and turned, bumping into Manas. He looped his hands through her midriff and pulled her close. She tried to push away his hands, but they lacked commitment.

"Not now, Manas…" she said, squirming out of his hold and walking away, flashing a smile at him.

"It's always time for…," Manas said, a naughty smile on his lips. "Listen, can you do the dishes by yourself today? Just today?"

"Yeah, yeah…. I know you are dying to get to the terrace."

Manas' face split into a wide grin. "When you are done, come up. We will be there."

~

Shruti stuck to the telescope like lovers on a moonlit night, oblivious to the world around her, lost in the cosmos. Manas still remembered the glee on her face when he gifted her the telescope.

It was a night much like today. The clear night sky spread out like a black dome with tiny sparks of brilliance. The moon took a leave of absence, letting the stars glow brighter. Shruti, Anu, and Manas had gone out for dinner and returned home late. It was Shruti's birthday, and she was irritated at Manas for giving her no presents, not even a birthday cake. She barged into the house and made a beeline for her bed when Manas called her to the terrace. She stomped her way back to the terrace, irritated at the idea of leaving her cosy bed, but stopped in her tracks at the door. It was pitch black. Manas lit a candle and fixed it on the table, spreading a dome of soft light around it. Shruti inched her way towards it. When she reached the soft yellow light, instead of a birthday cake, she found a brochure for the Indian Institute of Space Sciences and Technology.

As she was just taking it in, Manas stepped into the light and stood there with a grin on his mouth. A grin he had practised in front of the mirror hundred and thirty-two times that day.

She beamed at Manas as the realisation dawned on her. She had been dropping hints about the college she wanted to go to ever since she gave her final exams. Her face lit up like a hoarding at night as she jumped up and down on the terrace. "Best birthday gift ever!"

Manas laughed at her antics, threw his arms around her, and wished her birthday.

Shruti lifted her head from the hug and said, "Thanks a lot, Dad."

As soon as she separated from the hug, Shruti crouched by the dim candlelight, straining to read the brochure. That was when Manas pushed the telescope, mounted on a tripod, into the light.

Her jaw dropped out of the socket as her wide eyes scanned the new object. She jerked her head back and gaped at Manas, the telescope, and then back at Manas. The high-pitched shriek she let out must have made

Bella deaf. She dropped the brochure and rushed to the telescope. Her eyes twinkled in the soft candlelight.

A flash of light lit up the terrace as Anuradha captured the moment on her camera. Shruti ran up to her mother, who was waiting in the dark and hugged her in her exuberance.

There would be a handful of moments in your life that will stay with you forever, and this was one of them. Shruti's expression of pure joy was etched into his brain forever. He always carried the photograph in his wallet. It helped him stay grounded; to remember what was important.

They watched the stars into the early hours of the next morning, and that became a family tradition. Every Monday they got together as a family to watch the stars and spend time together.

An icy wind pierced his shirt and ran its tendrils through his body, driving a shiver up his spine. With a small shudder, he returned to the present. Shruti turned back, and her face lit up.

"It's beautiful today, Dad. Look there. The Scorpius is clearly visible," she said, her fingers tracing a path to the south. Her eyes twinkled like the stars she pursued.

Manas followed his daughter's fingers, and there it was, a large scorpion spread across the sky. Antares, the bright red star in the middle, blinked at him.

He widened his vision to take in the mighty canopy of luminescent stars. The sheer enormity of the universe humbled him. It always did. His memory drifted back into another Sunday night, but a cloudy day with a full moon.

The moon played hide and seek in the clouds. Shruti and Manas sat on the terrace in silence, all four eyes plastered to the cosmos. Hot wind curled around their body, warming them up and enveloping them in a faint salty fragrance. The kind of smell you would recognise if you've lived in a coastal city.

Without a preface, Shruti broke the silence. "Did you know? In the clearest of skies, you can see 2500 stars at the most."

Manas chuckled. "That solves the age-old question of how many stars are there in the sky."

"Oh, no," said Shruti, completely missing the sarcasm by a mile. "That's just about 1 in 100 billion of the stars just in our galaxy," Shruti said, wonder in her eyes.

Manas loved how Shruti got charged up when she talked about the cosmos. There was a fire in her eyes, which made her luminous, jet-black eyes pop. "Really?" he said, egging her on. "How big is our galaxy?"

"Oh, Dad... it's so big," said Shruti. "It is so big that light takes a hundred thousand years to travel across from one end to the other."

Manas let out a low whistle. "That's big!"

"Yeah.... and you know what? There are as many galaxies in the observable universe as the number of stars in our galaxy." Shruti swept her arms across the skies.

"Observable Universe?"

"Mmmhmm, the universe is like fourteen thousand billion years old. Light from anything beyond 14 thousand billion light years is yet to reach us. But even then, there are ten sextillion stars in the observable universe."

"Sextillion?"

Shruti chuckled and said," That's 10, followed by 21 zeroes."

"Phew," Manas let out a long breath of air. "That's a lot of zeroes. So, we have no idea how big the universe is?"

"Nope. Zilch. Nada," Shruti grinned. "My professor says it's infinitely large."

Infinitely large. Manas leaned back on the chair, staring into the unknown. The first human walked the earth 20,000 years ago in a universe which is 14 thousand billion years old. And humans think they matter. In the grand scale of the cosmos, we were nothing but specks of dust, irrelevant, insignificant, and inconsequential. Carl Sagan said it right - *'We are like butterflies who flutter for a day and think it is forever.'*

A warm, soft hand on his shoulders brought him back to the present. Anuradha pulled up a chair and sat beside him with a barely audible sigh. It wasn't a sigh of discomfort but of content. She slipped her hands into Manas' and leaned back as they both watched the stars together, lost in thought.

As the city dialled down into a silent slumber, nature took over the stage. The swish of a breeze and the rattle of leaves bumping into each other gained prominence.

"The silence makes you wonder, doesn't it?" Anuradha asked. "... about how alone we really are in this universe."

"There has to be somebody in this vast space who is sitting with his family right now, wondering the same thing," said Manas.

Shruti rose to her feet, folded the telescope up and put it away safely. "One of my professors told us about Fermi's paradox. He told us we were asking the wrong question. It was not 'Are we alone in the universe?' but 'Where is everyone?'. Even if we go by the most conservative estimates, there are still a hundred billion 'earth-like' planets in the universe, one million in our galaxy. Even if we consider only a 1% chance of life developing in Earth-like conditions, it still gives us a hundred thousand civilisations in our galaxy. But surely, we would have noticed at least a few of them zipping past in space."

The three of them lapsed back into a thoughtful quiet. In the silence between sounds, meaning grew.

They stayed in that cognitive cloud of silence for a long time when Manas snapped out of it.

"Whoa! It's almost twelve. What say we wrap it up?"

Shruti and Anuradha nodded solemnly. They were still lost in thought.

"You guys go ahead. I'll come in a minute," Shruti said.

Anuradha and Manas rose to their feet, straightened their clothes and headed inside. As soon as they reached the bedroom door, Manas hugged Anuradha from behind, wrapping his hands around her waist and meshing his chin in the groove between her neck and shoulder like pieces of a puzzle fitting together. Her thick tresses hung up to her mid-spine and were streaked with a few strands of grey hair. She squirmed a little before leaning back onto Manas' chest.

Manas turned her around and stroked the sharp angles of her high cheekbones. They could have been borrowed from a model. "I've missed you," he said.

He pulled her closer and leaned in till he could see himself in her eyes. Manas ran his hands over her cheeks, lifted her chin, and lightly brushed his lips against hers. Anuradha reached and closed his lips in a warm, sensuous embrace. The kiss was neither sloppy nor dry; it was just the right amount of wet. Manas melted in her mouth and let his hands roam every nook and cranny of her body. It started off on her rounder shoulders and traced a path to her hourglass-shaped hips and came to rest on the firm curve of her buttocks.

He withdrew his hands, stinging from the slap that came out of nowhere. She broke off and gazed into his eyes with child-like mischief. He saw the young girl he fell for in her deep, jet-black eyes.

"You are still a horn dog." She pushed him away, biting back a giggle.

"A horn dog who loves you."

Blood rushed into her cheeks and temples, and she turned a deep colour of red. He was amazed that even after eighteen years of marriage, she still blushed at these.

"It was a night much like this," Manas said. "Remember?"

"Clear skies, full moon, and a chilly wind blowing across. You sure knew how to get a 'yes' from a lady."

Manas chuckled. "It's been a long time since we took a trip to that hill."

"Who has got the time?" Anuradha sniggered. "But that night, I was a little unsure, you know?"

"Really?"

Anuradha nodded her head. "We used to go there all the time, but this time it was night. And after all, it was not the most popular tourist destination."

"Honestly, I was also a bit scared. But I wanted the proposal to be perfect, and this was as close to what I had in mind as possible."

Her delicately shaped mouth upturned at the thought. "It was beautiful. The starry skies, the full moon, and a single table on top of the hill; a lone candle burned bright on the table. I'll never forget that moment."

Time stood still as Manas gazed into her dark anthracite eyes, which carried maturity beyond her age. Unspoken words filled the space around them. Moments like these help you get through the drudgery of life.

The clattering of wood on concrete shattered the beauty of the moment and brought them crashing back to reality. Manas caught Anuradha's glance and rushed to the terrace from where the sound originated.

Shruti twitched on the ground, tangled between the chairs, gasping for breath. Manas rushed towards her and flung off the chairs to make room. "Anu… Quick," he shouted. He lifted Shruti's head and set it on his lap. "I'm here. Hold on," he whispered into her ears.

Her chest was blown up like a balloon, and she was still trying to breathe. Manas glanced behind and yelled," What's taking you so long?"

He laid Shruti flat on her back and found the centre of her chest with both his hands. With one sharp, swift motion, he pushed down hard. The 'whoosh' of the air escaping through her mouth was music to his ears. But the relief was temporary; Shruti gasped for air filling up her lungs, and it was back to full expansion.

Manas stroked her head. "Slowly, my dear. Short breaths."

Anuradha dashed onto the terrace, an epinephrine injector in her hand. She rammed the injector into Shruti's thighs. The effect was immediate. Shruti's throat relaxed, and the airflow restarted. The cold blue colour of her lips reversed to a warm pink.

Manas continued chest compressions until her breath normalised. He cradled her head on his lap, murmuring soft, soothing nothings into her ear; Anuradha beside him, stroking her forehead, calming her down. Soon, she relaxed, breathing in a deep lungful of air like someone who came up from drowning. Manas slid her onto Anuradha's lap and rose to his feet.

Four minutes. That was the time it took for his world to collapse. Four minutes to revive her from an asthma attack. He dreaded every living moment waiting for those four minutes.

Anuradha helped Shruti up and guided her back to her room, still panting. Manas staggered to the edge of the terrace and grabbed onto the railing. A heavy feeling in his stomach refused to melt away.

The constant fear that he would lose Shruti hung over him like a perpetual dark cloud. She carried an injector everywhere she went, but still, there would be times she wouldn't be able to get to it in time, like now. She must have tried to run inside for the injector and crashed into the chairs. *What might have happened if he didn't....?* A cold shudder whipped his spine.

Calm, measured footsteps shuffled closer. Anuradha hugged him from behind, resting her head on his back. Her warmth was a welcome break from the cold shivers rampaging his body. They stood like that for a long time, neither of them speaking, just breathing in and out.

Nature seemed to take the cue and shushed its sounds. Cold winds whispered to the trees, who shook their heads in agreement. The crickets' song ceased, as if in warning of the rumpling thunder in the distance.

The Artist

Monday, April 21, 2014

Karma is a bitch, and she'll get you one way or the other.

Alex pulled up to his house with Amrita tied up and unconscious in the passenger seat. The faded beige paint which ran all around the house was cracked and falling apart - just like the lives of its inhabitants. The neighbours were the least of his concerns. They never paid him any attention. He and his mother were stains on their freshly washed and ironed upper middle-class life. *Pretentious bastards'.*

Alex carried Amrita on his back through the garden on the side of the building to the back.

He stopped on the way and smiled at his mother. "Mom, how are you feeling? Comfortable?" He let out a short laugh. "Of course not."

Freshly dug up earth framed the old bitch's decapitated head, buried face up. Her lifeless eyes stared blankly at the sky.

"You finally 'looking up' to me now?" he said, shaking his head sideways laughing.

"Gotta go mom. Your friend is here. I'll come by later, OK? Don't go anywhere." Alex curled his lips into a sneer as he plodded onto the house, with Amrita tied and unconscious over his shoulders.

The dingy walls held a sharp contrast to the freshly cleaned white tiles of the floor. A small stream of bright red blood meandered its way out from under the closed bedroom. He put Amrita down, tied her to the chair, and stepped inside the bedroom.

A lifeless body lay on the table, blood dripping down from where the head used to be. It collected in a puddle below the table; a single stream meandered its way out through the closed door. Alex walked up to the table, appraising the work that was left.

Purple bruises circled the wrists where they were tied to the table. Bits and pieces of flesh from her neck sprayed across the top of the table, the remnants from hacking her head off. Without a head, is it even a person anymore? Or just a sack of meat? It didn't even feel like his mother anymore. *But ah! The silence.* It was music to his ears. After 29 years of incessant bickering, she finally shut up.

The bloody butcher's knife on the table brought back fond memories of his mother's last expression before he decapitated her. She had that coming.

He grabbed her legs and pushed her onto the middle of the table. The body had started to lock up; he had to finish the job faster. He picked the knife up, put on an apron and got to work.

It was unusual for him to desecrate a dead body like this. Death was something to be celebrated; it was an escape from the meaningless drudgery of life, a way to be immortalised in death. He had made sure of it. But not his mother. She deserved to be cut up into pieces and tossed into the garbage; food for fucking maggots.

He wiped off a speck of flesh from his face. Cutting up a body was messy work and time-consuming. His thoughts drifted back 20 years while muscle memory took over his hands, cutting away at the body in front of him.

A young Alex sat alone in a dark room with dusty cardboard boxes and old schoolbooks. The storeroom was the refuge of the unwanted. Every night it was the same story. At 9 o'clock, his mother would shove him into the storeroom, switch off the lights and lock the door from outside. The 10-year-old Alex would climb onto the makeshift bed in complete darkness, curl up into a foetal position, and wait for morning to come spreading light, hope. Alex wanted to reach out to the boy, pat him on the back, and tell him it was going to be OK, but he knew better. It wasn't going to change anything. Not till he was old enough to stand up for himself. But the kid never understood the 'why.' Why was he neglected and mistreated? Why didn't his mother love him like she did his sisters? Why didn't his sisters say anything?

His reverie was cut short by movement from the other room. *Ah! The guest woke up.*

Alex shrugged off his apron and wiped himself with it as he headed out into the living room, closing the bedroom door behind him. Amrita stirred in the chair, slowly opening her eyes and realising she was tied to a chair. Alex crossed the room to the music system and put on some Skrillex at full volume. Music relaxed him, but Skrillex relaxed him and drowned out the screams, both inside his mind and outside.

The wobbly base blasted from the speakers waking Amrita up completely. Her eyes burst open and darted all around the room, taking it all in and finally coming to rest on the blood seeping in from the closed bedroom.

Alex waited for it.

Confusion reigned on her face as her eyes darted furiously between the blood seeping out of the room, Alex. And her hands, which were tied to the chair.

Any moment now.

The eyes stopped dancing as her face contorted into a look of pure terror. With an extra burst of energy, she struggled against the restraints which held her to the chair.

And there it is. Sooner or later, everyone figures it out. But Alex loved this part. The change in expression. Body language is so visceral.

Amrita struggled against the knots again, but he had tied them well. A few sailor's knots he learned off the internet. She soon gave up the futile attempt and broke down, dropping her head, her body convulsing with sobs.

"Well, well, well. Look at you. So smart. Figured out the whole thing by yourselves, didn't you? No pointless questions about where you are or what is happening. I like it."

"Alex, please… Please let me go." Her eyes brimmed with tears as she pleaded, her voice trembling.. "Where is Teresa?… Oh God! What have you done?"

His body wound up tight at the mention of his mother's name. He heard his teeth grinding.

"That bitch got what was coming to her," he roared." You want to know why I did this?" he said. "YOU… You, of all people, knew what was going on in this house.

"What did you do to her?" Amrita asked.

"Underneath that dignified façade, there was an ugly monster. Do you know she used to lock me in the storeroom every night? Did she ever tell you about that?"

Amrita shook her head, tears running down her face.

"I don't know… maybe I reminded her of my father. He was an asshole who used to molest my sisters before he left, you know. But to take that out on a kid, that too your own kid? She was the devil incarnate. That's what she was."

Alex felt the tension go out of his shoulders as he let his head fall back. Sometimes venting really helps.

"So…" Amrita tried to control her sobs. "So, you killed her?" she asked, her eyes drifting towards the blood seeping under the door.

"Just couldn't handle it anymore. You would not believe the relief that came over me when I whacked that smug face off her body." An uncontrollable cackle broke out of Alex. "It was the only possible conclusion. Karma is a bitch, and she'll get you one way or the other."

Amrita tried to wipe away the terror on her face. "But why me?"

Alex chuckled and sauntered over to his bedroom and came back with a small metal box in his hands.

"You wanna see something?" Alex opened the box and took out a bunch of photographs with numbers written on the back of them- his "artworks", as he liked to call them.

The question was rhetoric. He marched straight towards her and pulled up a chair. The photograph with '#1' written on the back of it shivered in his hand and came to life.

A girl lay on a snooker table, her upper body invisible to the camera. Her legs were tied to the two ends of a cue stick, spreading her legs and planting her feet on the ground where the camera was. He traced her legs from the high heels she was wearing up through the stocking-covered legs ending with suspenders which disappeared into the darkness beneath her hiked-up dress. His recreation of the poster of the movie "Blue Velvet".

A photograph captures a moment, not just the colours and the lack of it, but the emotion too and stores it in a rectangular frame. Alex's heart thumped as the excitement of his first kill swept through his body, and his chest swelled with pride as he inspected his first 'artwork'.

Alex shoved the photograph in Amrita's face. "Meet Sakshi, a door-to-door salesgirl who came to the wrong house at the wrong time." He stressed the two drawn out wrongs.

Amrita's eyes opened wide, and her lips disfigured into an expression of distaste as she turned her head away.

"I've never told anyone this, you know. You are hearing the origin story," he said, reminiscing. "Mother was being… well, mother, and we ended up having a huge fight. As usual, after inflicting maximum damage, she just stormed out of the house."

Alex stared into the photograph in his hand. "Ever felt so angry that it paralyses you? Consumes you in its flames, blinding you with rage." Alex placed the photograph back into the box and tidied up the inside. "It was worse that day, and I needed a distraction. I put on Blue Velvet on the TV to take my mind off it and was watching it when the door rang. I went and opened the door, and there she was, standing in a black high heel, blue denim, and a black top with a flowery print. It was like she was sent for a purpose. Like God wanted me to relax and have a little fun." he chuckled. "He always took care of me."

He pulled up a chair and sat back as he went through the five photographs he had in the box, each a tribute to one of his favourite movie posters, reliving the moments. But soon, his elation slumped.

"I was on a high, perfecting my craft with each girl I came across. And I was good. I daresay the best. But like every good thing, it too came to an end." Alex leaned forward, shifting his weight in the chair. "Do you know how devastating it is for an artist to lose inspiration? My artwork became just a set of motions I go through. And staying ahead of the police became so easy that it stopped being challenging. I was on the verge of giving up on life when God threw me another bone. You."

Amrita's eyes flew open. "What are you talking about?"

"Remember the conversation we had here at my house…maybe a few weeks ago."

Amrita's face was blank.

"Let me jog your memory. You and my mother were talking nonsense, as usual, when a report about a gruesome murder came on the news. And soon the conversation turned towards murderers."

Amrita and Teresa sat around the dining table, deep in conversation. Alex turned back from the couch and said, "None of these losers come close to The Butcher of Bhalswa."

Teresa road-rolled over Alex's opinion, as usual, and said, "It's almost as if the sickos are multiplying by the day."

Amrita stared out of the window and spaced out in her thoughts. When people thought about unpleasant memories, their faces told the story through subtle changes in the facial muscles into an expression of distaste. But what Alex saw on Amrita's face was far from it. There was a degree of fondness, a degree of affection, an imperceptible uptick of the corners of her mouth.

It was intriguing enough to shrug off the insult of being ignored and probe further. "Wonder what sick motivation these guys have to kill someone," said Alex. "The Butcher killed eight people. That's a lot."

"But he's different," said Amrita. "He only killed people who have wronged the downtrodden. He was a sweet-" She broke off mid-sentence, flustered, and rose to her feet. "Teresa, shall I make some tea?"

Alex catalogued the different emotions which flashed through her face – love, longing, regret, and trepidation at having revealed too much. *Bingo!* Alex knew there was more. Amrita's encounter with The Butcher was not just from newspapers. The feelings he catalogued were of intimacy, and intimacy takes root with closeness, not by mere hearsay.

Amrita wriggled in the chair, struggling against the ropes which tied her down.

"So, you do remember," said Alex. "But it may not be entirely clear to you as to why that would matter. Not to worry… all in good time."

He dragged the chair towards Amrita and leaned forward. Her eyes flashed defiance as they dried up. She looked to be more in control as she processed the information.

"You like the movie Pulp Fiction?" Alex asked.

She turned her face away from Alex, determined not to look at him.

He grabbed her face with a free hand and pulled it back to him with force. With his face inches from hers, he saw her pupils dilate.

"When I ask you a fucking question, you reply. Do *you fucking like* Pulp Fiction?"

Amrita spat in his face. "Go to hell, you sick, twisted son of a bitch."

Alex stood up slowly, laughed, wiped away the spittle from his face, and wiped it on Amrita's red dress.

"That last part was accurate. She was a bitch, right up until I ended her life."

Alex gently placed his hand on her knees. Her creamy thighs were as soft as he thought they would be.

"I wanna show you something," said Alex as he rolled up the right arm of his T-shirt. A dark tattoo took up most of the real estate on his right upper arm. It said, "The Butcher", in dark Gothic font with the 't' fashioned after a bayonet knife. He was proud of that tattoo.

Amrita's face contorted as she shifted her gaze to the tattoo, her breasts heaving. Alex smelled her fear, and it drove him wild.

Amrita hid behind a façade of bravado, quick to mask her feelings. The façade he had seen in so many women. The façade which he loved to break down, piece by piece.

Alex closed the distance between him and Amrita in slow, measured steps, his eyes never breaking contact with hers. The constant rattling of the chair died down as she stopped struggling. An eerie calm descended upon them, leaving the heavy baseline of the music to reverberate in his heart. With each step, Amrita's body wound up tighter and tighter.

"Beautiful, isn't it?" Alex admired his tattoo in the light. "You see how the 'B' curves around the 'u'? And the 't'; what a dangerous-looking knife that is. An exquisite piece of art." He turned back toward her. "You know which Butcher it pays tribute to, right? The Butcher of Bhalswa."

Prateek

Thursday, October 5, 1995

"If there was one thing powerful than authority, it was a gesture of rebellion against it."

The street bustled with shoppers as Prateek threaded his way through the crowd. The scent of human sweat and dirt overwhelmed him. If he had not been taller than the average Indian, he would have found it hard to breathe. The cacophony of the touting shopkeepers and the hassling customers assaulted his senses when he entered the quagmire. But soon, they blended into the background as he got used to the place.

The closely spaced shops on both sides stepped on each other's toes, making the entire street look like one gigantic building, crumbling with age. A kid, barely in his teens, rushed out of a shop and erected a shade in front of it. The kind of impromptu setup, with a large sheet of cloth and a few sticks, people in India lovingly call *jugaad.*

The afternoon sun beat down on all of them without mercy. Prateek pulled up the front of his shirt, sticking to his body with perspiration. He scanned the sea of bodies behind him to find Manas - his only friend in the world. The square face and defined jawline were unmistakable in the crowd. Parting the crowd with his broad shoulders, he closed in as Prateek resumed his struggle to get through the human mosh pit.

After scores of shoves and pointed looks from people, Prateek disentangled himself from the crowded street into an alleyway. He caught his breath and waited for Manas to join him. Without much delay, Manas squeezed out between two rotund middle-aged women, exited the shopping street, and into the deserted side road.

Manas considered the patches of sweat on his grey shirt and said, "We're taking a different route next time."

Prateek nodded with upturned lips and continued down the road with Manas at his shoulders.

"How about we go for that new movie? Dilwale Dulhaniya Le Jayenge. It's Shah Rukh and Kajol." Manas glanced at him sideways.

Prateek rubbed the back of his neck with a grimace. "Nope. No Movies."

"I don't understand what kind of person doesn't like movies," Manas said with a shake of his head.

"A person who finds it a waste of-"

Aaargh!

Prateek snapped into attention. The sound came from down the road. Manas made eye contact, and they both raced down to the end of the street. The closer they got, the louder and clearer the sounds became. The screams of a boy and the shouts of a man took shape out of the din.

Around the corner, a myriad of houses rose all around, closely stacked like matchboxes. This was the residential part of the area. Off to the right side, a crowd gathered around something… or someone. They squeezed their way to the clearing in the middle.

A boy, not over ten, sprawled on the ground. Blood seeped into the dust from his right elbow, which stuck out at an odd angle. A stub of his bone peeked out from under the skin. The boy's undershirt was torn, and the exposed flesh had red, swollen belt marks. He writhed in pain, spitting out blood from his mouth; his left eye had swollen shut, and deep purple finger marks burned bright on his cheeks. A brawny man inserted his belt into the hoops of his pants a few feet from the boy, a handful of guys around him. His brow glistened with sweat, and his chest heaved with each laboured breath. With a face the colour of a tomato, he scowled at the crowd.

Prateek glared at the people around him, watching this little boy beaten up. Not one soul tried to stop it.

"What happened?" Manas asked the closest person to him.

"The kid's trouble. He stole something from that guy's wife, some knick-knack he flicked from their house. I saw him chase the kid down the street…." The man grimaced. "But he didn't have to beat him up so bad."

Manas' muscles jumped under the skin as his fists clenched. His cold, hard stare fell on the back of the man's head. The man finished putting on the belt and spat at the kid. He glowered at the crowd and was about to leave when he caught Manas glaring at him.

"Whatcha looking at, kid?" The man took a wide stance and pointed his stubby fingers at Manas.

The sturdy facade Manas put up on his face broke down as he retreated into a shell. If there was anything that Manas avoided, it was conflict. He took a couple of steps back, rubbing the back of his neck. The man, smelling retreat, took a couple of steps towards Manas.

Prateek stepped into the man's trajectory, planted his legs firmly, and stared him down. The pounding in his ears was amplified in the hushed silence of the crowd. Nobody threatened Manas when he was around.

"Walk away," he said in a calm and measured tone.

But the veiled menace in his words must have gotten through. It stopped him mid-way through his stride. Prateek saw the cogs of his brain turning to mesh together and comprehend someone standing up to him. *Typical bully.*

If there was one thing more powerful than authority, it was a gesture of rebellion against it. Drawing strength from Prateek's rebellion, people gathered around and started helping the kid. A few others dragged the man away from Prateek. Somebody called an ambulance and volunteered to take the kid to the hospital. A few leaders emerged from the crowd and took control of the situation.

Prateek felt a powerful arm directing him back the way they came from. Manas was practically pulling him away. As soon as they turned the corner back to the street, Prateek shook his hand out of Manas' hold. He picked up the pace and walked surefooted straight ahead. Out of the corner of his eyes, he caught Manas scowling at him.

Manas got ahead and stepped into Prateek's path, facing him, and held up both his hands to stop him. Prateek just stood where he was stopped glaring at Manas, his breath rushing out his nostrils. The adrenaline running through his veins strained against his skin.

"He…" Prateek swung his closed fist at a nearby wall, breaking off a bit of white powdery piece of concrete. "How can that bastard beat up a kid like that? He is just a kid."

Manas' face grew hard. "No," he said pointing at Prateek.

"The kid didn't murder anyone right?" Prateek ground his teeth, raising up his cheekbones a bit.

"I said No, Prateek."

"You think the kid deserves that?"

Manas stared down at Prateek for a second. "If you must ask, no, I don't think he deserved it. Maybe he deserves a smack on his bottoms, but breaking his arm? No. But I know what you are thinking, and I am saying no to that."

"So, you are gonna let that guy get away with this? Did you see the smug bastard? Don't you want to wipe it off that excuse he calls his face?"

Manas let out an audible sigh and looked down at an empty bottle of 7up. "You are the one who is always harping about karma. I say let karma take care of it. We are in a lot of trouble already."

"Cut the crap, Manas. I know you don't believe in karma. And Karma says the universe will pay him back, right? Aren't we part of that universe?"

"Listen to me, Prateek. Let it go."

Prateek broke eye contact and peered past Manas' shoulders. "It disgusts me that you can just stand there and let things like this happen. And to top it off, lecture me against doing something about it? The Manas I knew would be as horrified by this as I am."

Manas reached out and grabbed Prateek's shoulder. "Believe me, I hate this as much as you do, but I am just being practical. We can't stop every injustice in the world."

"I don't care. I am going to do it, with or without your help." Prateek pivoted and strode away, showing his back to Manas.

Prateek kicked at the 7up bottle, and it went scuttling across the road, the sunlight gleaming off it. He knew how to pull his strings. The bottle rolled to a stop, and so did the musical clinking. Manas would call him back.

"Ok... wait up." Manas ambled over to him, his shoulders slumped. "All right. You win. I can't let you do it alone, mainly because you'll F-it up."

A crooked smile broke out on Prateek's face. "I knew you would come around. Come on, let's go have some fun."

They turned back the way they came and reached the place where the kid was assaulted. The crowd had dispersed by then, leaving a few stragglers who didn't have anything pressing to get back to. Prateek surveyed the area and spotted the man who beat up the kid.

His stocky build and bald head were not hard to spot in a crowd. Prateek nudged Manas to get his attention and circled around to the front to get a better view. The man's thick moustache, which curled up at the end, quivered on his fat face as he guffawed at something his friend said. He drew smoke from the cigarette in his hand and swatted away a fly which was bothering him. His brown nylon shirt with floral prints was unbuttoned at the top, revealing a hairy chest. The little stunt he pulled off on the kid seemed to have no effect on him. A grating sound vibrated through his skull as Prateek crunched his teeth.

A few minutes passed, and the guy tossed the cigarette bud on the road, stomped on it with his large feet, and heaved himself down the street, waving his friend goodbye.

Manas and Prateek followed him.

"Not too close." Manas slowed down the pace. "Keep at least four bodies between him and us." Prateek nodded, fell back to Manas, and continued.

The man entered a sweet shop and went behind the counter. The board above it read -Suryakant's Sweet Shop. Prateek and Manas, without breaking their stride, sauntered into a tea shop opposite the shop.

Prateek ordered two tea and kept an eye on the man. "Suryakant. What a shitty name?"

Time went by as Prateek ordered three more rounds of tea. The sky swapped colour from sky blue to orange to purple. As the shadows got longer and darkness began its reign, Suryakant pulled down the shutter with a rattle. After locking the shop and jerking it to test it, he took the street next to the shop, going away from the main road.

Manas paid for the tea as Prateek rose and followed the man. They stuck to the dark shadows on the street to stay out of sight. As they headed deeper into the street, the more deserted it became. The low drone of the shopping street was hardly audible. And over the silence, Suryakant's happy whistling took on an ominous undertone. He took a detour into a muddy pathway, a path less taken.

Prateek peeked over the corner, taking care to stay hidden in the large shadow a nearby tree cast on the ground. Suryakant hiked, happy and whistling, along the path which snaked along the shoreline of a lake. At the end of the path was a two-storeyed house overlooking the lake.

Manas nodded at Prateek and said, "This is the place."

The Artist

Monday, April 21, 2014

Everybody breaks.

Tears flew down Amrita's cheeks as she tugged at the ropes tying her to the chair for the umpteenth time. "Please let me go, Alex. There is still a way out of this."

Alex laughed uproariously. "Why would I get out of something that is going exactly according to plan? You think I killed my mother by accident?" He dabbed the corner of his eyes with the back of his fingers.

"Ever since I figured out you knew the Butcher, an inkling of a plan took birth in my mind. The Butcher was a legend, an inspiration to many like me. But he was more than that to me; he was my guardian angel. It would mean a lot for me to meet him, and share a cup of coffee."

The music died down, setting the stage for the next track to come on. It was a playlist full of Skrillex, and it was on loop. He wasn't worried.

"You know him, right?"

"I wasn't living under a rock," said Amrita. "Everybody in the country knows him."

"Let me try that again." Alex pulled up a chair and sat in front of Amrita. "You *know* The Butcher, don't you?"

"What's there to know? He was a monster who killed over ten -"

"Not ten… It was eight." He hated when people got that wrong. Rising from the chair, Alex pivoted away from her and sauntered into the kitchen.

"That inkling of a plan that took birth in my mind floundered, and I soon realised that this was my calling, the reason I was sent to earth by the God Almighty. But that would also mean that my life as I know it had come to a crossroads," he shouted from the kitchen. "I knew you'll not give up the information willingly. And that meant that I'd have to torture it out of you. But that would mean breaking my cardinal rule. The rule that helped me stay away from the police all this time. *Not to mess with women with any kind of connection to me.*"

He picked up the knife set from the counter and cradled it in his arms. It had everything ranging from small knives used to cut apples to large ones to cut up meat. *Perfect.*

Alex headed back into the hall with the knife set in his hands. "So, it was clear that I'll be leaving Delhi and my life behind. But how can I leave everything behind without paying what's due? Mother had it coming."

Alex carefully placed the knife set onto the table right next to Amrita. "It all worked out in the end, right?" He grabbed a jug of water from the counter and gulped it down.

"I have always wondered why The Butcher just quit cold turkey. He was at the prime of his skill. He was gaining momentum, and suddenly nothing. What's that about?"

"I don't know what you are talking about," said Amrita.

"Listen, I don't want to hurt you. But if you keep this u-" Alex chuckled slightly. "Ah! Who am I kidding? I couldn't even get through the sentence. We both know that I do want to hurt you. Why don't we make it easier for both of us and just tell me what I want to know?"

"You are delusional, you know that?"

"Yes, sometimes… but not now." His mouth twitched into a wide grin. "You know, you can tell a lot about someone from just looking at them, the angle of their hands, eyes, most of all the eyes. They scream out the secrets you desperately try to hide."

Alex slid the large Chef's knife from the holder and placed it on the table, parallel to the edge. "What you are not saying, your eyes whispered in my ears." He plucked the carving knife from its stand and laid it out right next to the Chef's Knife.

"So, let's just skip all the games and get right to the part where you tell me everything about The Butcher."

She closed her eyes, took a deep breath, and slumped back onto the chair. When she opened them again, the flame of defiance had died down, but the sparkling dark brown eyes were very alert.

"Let's say for a second that I knew him. But don't insult my intelligence by telling me you'll let me go if I told you about him," she said.

"Now we are talking," said Alex, with a low chuckle of amusement. "I never said I'll let you go if you tell me what I want to know, did I?"

"Pfft... Then why the hell should I tell you anything?"

He slid the smallest knife, the paring knife, out from the set and picked the dirt and crusted blood trapped between his nails.

"You will die, that's for sure. But there are two ways you can die. A painless, swift departure from this world, like ripping off a band-aid. Or a violent tug of war between life and death in which you will want to cheat and let death win, just so that you are delivered from the excruciating pain." He looked up from his nails and held Amrita's eyes at the end of his stare.

Amrita shrunk back as fear crept back into her eyes.

Alex shook his head and pushed himself away from the table. "You're not appreciating the sacrifice I'm making here. I live for this shit. Streams of blood flowing through the fair skin... Ah! Pure ecstasy. But I am letting all that go granting you a quick death. Just tell me what you know about The Butcher."

"Go to hell, you bastard."

"Well," he took a deep breath," you've made your choice." He grabbed Amrita's dress in a bunch and, with one swift swipe of his knife, cut open the front of the dress; ripped the remaining of the dress off her body with brute force.

She sat glued to the chair, naked as she was born, tears running down her cheeks.

Kneeling in front of her, he grabbed a handful of her hair and pressed his knife into the hollow of her neck. An inkling of the familiar excitement played just out of reach. He traced the knife in between her breasts, all the way down to her belly button. The knife caught her necklace on the way, but it only offered little resistance before it gave way, scattering its beads all around. The floor danced in its turquoise glory.

"Last chance." He increased the pressure just enough to inflict pain but still not break her skin.

"Stop... Please stop...," she cried. "I knew him... I knew the Butcher."

Alex pressed on, "How?"

"He was my friend, but I had no idea that he was such a monster," she said, wiping her wet cheeks.

"Amrita, Amrita, Amrita... Do I have a stamp on my forehead which says 'Fool'?"

Alex increased the pressure on the knife, breaking her skin. A tiny stream of blood oozed out and collected in her belly button.

"Aargh!!," Amrita screamed with pain. "OK... OK. He was a very close friend," she said after catching her breath.

"I figured as much." He eased his hand holding the knife.

"Like I asked earlier, why did he quit? The police must not have caught him, or they would have made it a big deal. So, he is still alive. Where is he now?"

"I don't know," she started sobbing. "Once I found out about what he was up to, I didn't want anything to do with him. I broke off contact and haven't seen him after that."

"Just when I thought we reached an agreement." Alex shook his head from side to side. Blood throbbed in his veins as it pushed through faster and faster. He was giving this girl a chance for a swift exit from her pathetic life, and she was squandering that away.

He flipped the knife in his hand and held it like how an artist holds his brush. And he traced an 'A' on the porcelain canvas of her midriff, right above the belly button. Slow and steady strokes, strokes he had mastered over time.

Amrita screamed in pain, struggling to get away from the object causing her pain. Blood spread out of the wound, painting her stomach red.

It aroused him. He leaned forward and licked the 'A' clean. The familiar salty, metallic taste of blood. He just couldn't get enough of it.

Shallow, fast breath rocked her body, writhing in pain. He watched and waited as she regained her composition.

The transformative power of pain is unprecedented. It's just about pushing it over the threshold, and self-preservation kicks in. And when it does, there is no place for logic nor reason. Instead, just a singular focus to stop the pain or stop the person inflicting pain. It's all about the threshold; some break early, some late. But everybody breaks.

"Where is The Butcher?"

"I...," she paused to catch her breath. "I don't know. I already told you everything."

"Wrong answer," he said and proceeded to carve out a 'R' next to the 'A'.

Her eyes, white as a ghost, pleaded with him to stop. Her screams filled the room, drowning out the loud music.

But Alex was having the time of his life. The blood, the screams, the suffering; he was nearing euphoria. His vision blurred, and instead of Amrita, it was his mother tied to the chair, covered in blood. He shook his head clear, and Amrita was back. *Stay focused*, he shouted at himself.

"There are four more letters in 'Artist'. You want me to go on?"

"No.... No... Please stop... anything you want... please stop."

Everybody breaks. He tossed the knife on the table and went to the kitchen to get a glass of water. He turned off the music on his way back.

Alex gave Amrita some water and wiped her forehead." So, tell me everything." Blood dripped down her naked body onto the floor.

And she sang, sang like a parrot. She told him everything about The Butcher. She told him how they were best friends, maybe even lovers. She told him why he disappeared and where he is now.

When Amrita had told him everything, Alex rose to his feet and stretched. *This is fate*. How else could he have stumbled on the only person in the world who knows where The Butcher was? It was written in the stars. *God wants me to meet my guardian angel.* The Butcher saved him, gave purpose to his life, and showed him the way. Alex put him right next to God, and what was in front of him overwhelmed him.

He turned away from Amrita, who was recuperating and glimpsed a man standing in the shadows of the corridor leading to the kitchen. All he could see was a tall figure standing in the darkness, but he got an unshakeable feeling that he knew the man.

The cogs in his mind turned, making calculations. Five steps to the man, a knife within his reach. "Who are you?" he asked, buying time as he sized up the situation. He could take the stranger easily. And if he runs, he will just chase him down and kill him. He didn't want any snitches. He needed a few more days to make arrangements before he skips town.

"I want you to save me," the man said.

"Save you? Who the fuck *are* you, and how the fuck did you get in here?" Alex recapped his entry to the house to double-check if he had locked the doors. He did.

The man moved closer, light from the hall slowly travelling up his legs. The black trench coat and dark trousers sucked up the light that fell on it. Alex held his breath. There was something sinister in the air. The man was at arm's length. The white shirt under the trench coat was the only bright object of clothing. Alex really wanted to see the man's face, but he stopped just short.

"You know the answer to all those questions," he said. The voice was deep and booming. "I'm not your fucking teacher to spoon feed you."

"The Butcher?" asked Alex. He heard the tremble in his own voice.

The man nodded his head.

Alex fell to his knees and bowed his head. A tingle took birth at the crown of his head and travelled down his spine, and filled his entire body. His mouth took on a life of its own and was smiling so wide that it hurt him. His eyes welled up, blurring his vision.

"I… There are so many things… Always wanted to meet you... Anything..." Alex closed his eyes and breathed in. collecting his thought.

"What do you need me to do?" The Artist said.

"Come to Trivandrum, find me, and you will know what to do."

And with that, the man tracked his steps back into the shadows and dissolved into darkness. The Artist stayed on his knees for a while. His head bent down in prayer.

Ever since he found out that Amrita knew The Butcher, the purpose was dripping into the emptiness inside him. But before, it was like a wide brush, painting everything in its path in broad strokes. It had been honed to a sharp point, like a felt-tip pen. God doesn't jump out of the sky to appear before us and give us a message like he did in the Bible anymore. He does it in mysterious ways, often hard to understand. But if this was not a message from God, nothing is.

Amrita grunted with pain. It brought him back from his spiritual overture. He pivoted and charged at her with inhuman speed, grabbing the biggest knife from the table. With one graceful arc of the knife, he slit her throat; making sure her trachea, carotid artery and jugular vein are severed. Blood gurgled as she choked on it. Her face contorted with pain as she struggled for breath. But he knew it would only last a few seconds. In the absence of oxygen, the brain would fall into a coma, a peaceful death. As expected, the flexed muscles of her face relaxed into a placid calm as her eyes closed. The gasping and gurgling continued for a minute after, but she wouldn't have felt any of that. *A promise is a promise.*

~

Trivandrum. That's where he was headed. He couldn't take the train, bus, or flight. Too much paper trail. It was only a matter of time before the police figured out, he was the serial killer called The Artist. That meant only one thing. A road trip of a lifetime. A pilgrimage with a purpose.

In a sudden flash of brilliance, he remembered two girls with whom he had a standing relationship through Facebook. He invested countless hours at his Internet Café seducing these girls, and now it seems fate was urging him to collect. His rule of not picking up girls connected to him didn't stand anymore.

The mathematical and geographic symmetry of his plan appealed to him. One of them was in Mumbai, and the other was in Bangalore. A road trip to Trivandrum, with stops in Mumbai and Bangalore. The geographic lines aligned perfectly in his mind, and so did the mathematics of it. He had already killed 6, including Amrita. The Butcher had killed eight people before he disappeared. Six plus the one in Mumbai and the one in Bangalore. That makes it eight. On par with the man, he was going to visit.

Alex took out his mobile and chalked out a route to Trivandrum on Google Maps. His only regret was that he could not start the trip right away. There were a few things he needed to do, roles he needed to play before he could leave. He had to clean his house, take care of Amrita, and then act as the grieve-stricken son whose mother was brutally murdered. Buying time by deflecting suspicion. But after that, his pilgrimage starts.

Nasir

Tuesday, April 22, 2014

The present needed him more than the past.

Nasir Ali Khan sat in the passenger side of the van, eyes dead ahead, deep in thought. His eyes watered from the incessant throbbing in his head.

'*Honk*.'

Nasir threw the nastiest stare he could muster in the driver's direction. Ripping off the horn and throwing it out the window was high on his to-do list. He popped an aspirin out of the strip and gulped it down with Gatorade. A feeble attempt to appease his throat and rehydrate his body.

Never drink so much again, he promised to himself. That was the second time he made the promise this month.

He was passed out in his chair when he got the call in the early hours of the morning. It took a couple of minutes to make sense of anything, but when he got it, he was upright in his bed.

He had been on The Artist trail for quite some time now. So, when he got the call about a new victim, he wasted no time in calling up his motley crew – the members of the Special Investigations Unit (Violent Crimes). He scanned the rear-view mirror.

Sonam fidgeted with her dark auburn hair, which spread thickly on her shoulders and down her back. She curled it around her fingers and chewed on it. Her narrow eyes glanced furtively from behind her thick glasses. It's been six months, and she is still jittery every time she visits a crime scene. But he saw potential in her. She was the best crime scene investigator with forensic expertise graduating from the CBI academy. Nasir was the only crime scene investigator in the team, and with his team increasing in size, it was essential to create a backup so that he could focus on the larger picture.

Avinash, and Salim sat opposite Sonam, engaged in an animated conversation peppered with an occasional burst of laughter or low fives. In the world of tactical ops, these guys were legends. They still held so many records in the training exercises at the academy. The way they communicated when they were in an op would make you believe in telepathy. Nasir envied the connection they had; they were literally inseparable, on and off the field. In stark contrast to the bad-ass tactical ops guys, each of them were goofier than the other. They were the kind of people who would goof off before fighting a T-Rex with a pocketknife, go in, kick its ass, and come back with a few cuts and scrapes, smiling like kids with new toys.

Nasir finally focused on himself. A thin face with closely cropped hair on a balding forehead glowered at him. The thick cap of wiry black hair was fighting a losing battle against the soot grey highlights. A dark Ray-Ban shades rested on his long-crooked nose. Too much light brought back the headaches.

To his right, an inconspicuous man with a lanky frame and an ordinary face steered the van. Police would never be the first guess if you look at Akshay. His short, neatly cropped hair would probably be the only thing that betrayed him as a cop. He was just 32, but the age lines around his mouth placed him in his late thirties. Despite his appearance, his people skills and the vast network of informants he had developed as he moved up the ladder in the Crime Branch made him irreplaceable in Nasir's team. And with his face that can blend into any crowd, he aced in surveillance.

They approached Connaught Place through Barakhambra Road. A thirteen-storeyed abandoned building loomed out of the grey gloom of dawn. The incomplete building was crumbling with age.

"This is the place, right?" Nasir asked.

Akshay nodded his head.

"Salim… You ever sang in front of a crowd?" Avinash asked, glancing sideways at Sonam, suppressing a smile.

"Well, I'm glad you asked, Avinash. Yes, I have. But I did end up puking all over the front row," Salim said in a sing-song tone that brimmed with all the artificiality he could muster.

"Ah! That must have been embarrassing. Were you the same shade of green as Rookie over there?" Avinash jerked his thumb over to where Sonam was sitting.

Salim bit back a chuckle. "Well, yes. That's exactly the colour I was in. I bet rookie pukes on the crime scene in the first ten minutes."

"I'll take that bet," Avinash raised a five hundred rupee note from his pocket and held it up. "Somebody hand rookie a paper bag… you know, just in case." Avinash guffawed and slapped Sonam's back.

"-and a make-up set for after," Salim added. They exploded into a raucous laughter high, fiving each other.

"Ha Ha… very funny. Why don't you get a room, guys?" Sonam said a fake laugh on her face.

"Guys, cut it out. We are here," Nasir said as Akshay pulled up into the compound and flashed his ID. As soon as the van came to a stop, Nasir hit the ground running with his team tailing him. A couple of policemen stood guard at the entrance. Nasir strode ahead without pausing as the policemen made way for him, a puzzled acquiescence on their faces. He had that effect on people.

A crowd of policemen gathered on the far side of the corridor trampling all over the evidence. "What the hell are these guys doing?" Nasir mumbled through his clenched teeth as he closed the distance towards the crime scene. "We will be lucky if we get anything useful from here."

Amateur hour. How was he supposed to isolate the killer's fingerprints from all these other fools? Not only fingerprints, but footprints, hair, body fluids, and a hundred other things. These idiots have contaminated everything. He liked his crime scenes the way the criminal left them. They tell a much better story than the criminal himself.

They slowly made their way through the crowd to the yellow police tape. Nasir was happy that they had at least cordoned off the immediate crime scene and most of the policemen were behind it. But one policeman was posing next to the victim, clicking a selfie, grinning wide and waving to his friends who were still behind the yellow tape.

Nasir ducked under the yellow tape. His ears drummed from the blood pumping through them, and it was not because of the hangover. A visceral heat bubbled up from his stomach and exploded.

"Listen up, everyone," he shouted as he turned to face the crowd of policemen. "I want every single one of you retards out of the crime scene in *one minute*."

A hush spread among the policemen gathered.

"I don't care who you are or how involved you are in this case," Nasir continued. "As of now, you are not. And you-" he turned around and pointed at the policeman taking the selfie. "Yeah, you… with the mobile phone."

The policeman rose from the squat next to the body, his eyebrows squished together, forming a unibrow.

"What the hell do you think you are doing?" Nasir signalled him out of the crime scene with his index finger.

The policeman opened his mouth, but nothing came out.

"Were you dropped on your head as a kid? Get your sorry ass over here right now."

The policeman finally found his voice. "Who the hell are you to tell me what to do? This is my case; this is my scene." He pocketed his mobile phone and stood there, planting his legs firmly on his sides.

Nasir retrieved his badge from his khakis, held it up, fixed the policeman in a hard stare and said, "CBI, Special Investigation Unit (Violent Crimes), I am Nasir Ali Khan, Senior Superintendent of Police, and this is my team." He knew the effect his name had on people, especially the police force.

The policeman's stance relaxed a little, and he broke eye contact. The small murmuring hush of the gathered crowd reduced to a pin-drop silence.

"Aren't you supposed to salute your superior officer?" Nasir pushed on and fixed the policeman with his cold, steely gaze. The policeman shuffled his legs for a second and broke down to give him a salute.

"This is my case now. Get the hell out of my crime scene... *Now*," Nasir said with a stern, measured tone.

The crowd of policemen dwindled down to a few strays. The policeman who clicked the selfie lingered there a second more than the others but decided to slink off with his tail in between his legs.

A well-groomed policeman marched towards Nasir, an embarrassed smile on his face. Three metallic stars twinkled on his shoulder. His eyes were full of questions. The hair was cropped close to his skull, almost in a military cut.

He whip-lashed his body into a firm salute. "I apologise for his behaviour." His speech was crisp. "I had to go to the police station for some time, and things got out of hand. My name is Saket Chhetri. I am the Inspector here." He extended his right hand for a handshake.

Nasir glanced at the man for a second and turned back to gesture to his team to come over.

Saket withdrew his hand with a sheepish smile. "I'm sorry if we got off on the wrong foot here. Let me assure you that you will have the full cooperation of the Delhi Police. I've heard a lot about you, and I think you guys are doing a fantastic job, and it would be my privilege to observe your work... if you don't mind, that is."

Nasir measured him for a second. A sincere cop who admired his work. He could be useful. With a smile, he offered the handshake he had refused earlier.

"OK. Then we better get started. Ask your men guarding downstairs to stop anyone who wants to come up. If you can, try to clear the compound of your men. We would like to investigate the perimeter as well."

Saket barked out some commands over the walkie-talkie, and thrust his thumbs up in confirmation.

Nasir turned back towards his team. "Let me introduce you to these guys."

Saket held up his hands to stop Nasir. "If you don't mind, I'll take a shot at it?"

Nasir chuckled and gestured Saket to go ahead.

He pointed to Akshay and said, "Akshay Aware. Inspector, counter-intelligence and surveillance expert," Akshay nodded his head with a shy smile.

"Avinash Pandey and Salim Malik," said Saket, pointing to each one of them as he said their names, "Superintendent of Police, both. Tactical Operations, am I right?"

"You got that right, kiddo," said Salim as he pushed forward and shook Saket's hand.

"I'm... not sure who she is, though," Saket apologised as he pointed towards Sonam.

"Let me help you there," Nasir chipped in, "Sonam Lama. Fresh out of the CBI Academy, specialising in Crime Scene Investigations and Forensics."

She raised her right hand halfway and dropped it back to her side.

"Now that we got the formalities out of the way, shall we catch the bastard who did this?" Nasir asked, "Time is of the essence. Have we identified the woman yet?"

"It's only six thirty in the morning. By ten, we should be able to check for man-missing reports," said Saket.

"Akshay, I need you on this," Nasir ordered, "We need to know who the victim is. And fast."

Akshay nodded his head and headed downstairs.

"Salim and Avinash, do a perimeter check. Look for the usual and anything unusual. Tyre tracks, cigarette butts, footprints, anything." Their faces hardened, they nodded in agreement and marched downstairs.

"Sonam, take out your kit. Let's go fishing." She unpacked her kit and took out the gear.

Nasir turned to Saket. A little education never hurt anyone. "When we are at the crime scene, always walk in straight lines. That way, you know which ones our footprints and which ones are the criminals. Just stay behind Sonam and me and observe for now."

"Four by four. I'll take one and two, and you take the rest," Sonam announced.

Nasir nodded as he pulled up his protective suit. "We investigate the crime scenes in grids, so we don't miss anything," Nasir explained to Saket's confused face. "Sonam just divided the scene in a four-by-four grid and took up rows one and two."

Nasir and Sonam made their way to the yellow tape dressed in a protective suit, thick latex gloves, and paper slippers. The staged quality of the scene was a stark contrast to the dilapidated, rough, abandoned building.

The body was displayed, for lack of a better word, on a mattress which was placed close to the wall. A table lamp burned bright to the left side. A network of nylon strings held the body in position, anchored on the ceiling, where a few hooks were fixed recently. The body was propped up on her elbows, face looking ahead. The heavily made-up skin and the bright red lipstick made her seem almost alive. But the eyes were a giveaway. Dead eyes on an alive face were somehow more macabre.

The legs bent at the knee, were crossed, and the feet, wearing black leather high heels, were pointing up. Strings hooked to the ceiling held them in place. She had a half-burned cigarette in her right hand close to her chin, as if she were about to take one last puff. The left hand rested on the mattress, fingers spread and below them was a book, open and facing down. An orange pillow took up the space between her body and the mattress, her breasts resting on it. The black low-neck T-shirt revealed her ample cleavage. Purple waxy skin peeked out of the cracks in the made-up skin. Blood had seeped out, leaving a trail from the cut on her neck. A single oval pendant hung from her necklace. A silver-black gun rested on the pillow, just in front of the body, and right next to it was a brown cigarette case.

The whirring of the flash, and the clicks of the shutter, from Sonam's camera filled the room. Saket hadn't uttered a word or even moved a muscle this entire time. He turned a pale shade of green as his eyes scanned the scene but avoided the body like a ghost.

"You can take a break if you want," said Nasir, rising from the floor. The last thing he wanted was more contamination of the scene. "You haven't had anything to eat as well. We can handle this."

"Yeah… you are right. I'll grab something to eat and be right back," he said, looking at his watch.

This was just another one of the countless grisly crime scenes he had seen in his career. It was difficult at first, but you get used to it. Although admittedly, the handiwork of The Artist was usually a little too much to take in if you are new.

The team was also immune to these ghastly scenes. When you are working in Violent Crimes, you must be. It was one of the criteria when he chose them. He would pick four of five of the most gruesome photographs of the crime scenes, show them to the candidates during the interview, and ask them to describe them. Some would hand them back quickly with a pale, shaking hand. Some would make uncomfortable jokes about it. But some would describe the scene with clinical efficiency, and hand back the pictures without breaking a sweat. Those are the ones he picked.

Sonam moved in straight lines covering the area grid by grid. Every now and then, she would crouch at some place, scrutinise something, put a marker down next to it, and take photographs. The nervous girl in the back of the van was a totally different person once she donned the suit. She took a lot of photographs of the body from all angles, and then started dusting for prints. The gun, the book, the cigarette pack, the lamp; she took her time with each item at the crime scene. She picked up the book to bag it, and something slipped out from between the pages. Her face changed the moment she picked it up and read. Nasir rushed over and snatched it from her.

It was a photograph of the crime scene, taken from the head of the body, perfectly framed. This was a first for The Artist.

"The back side..." said Sonam, her voice quivered.

Nasir flipped it over, and there it was. A note penned in blood. It read:

'To The Butcher,

This is for you.

With love,
The Artist

Nasir read the first line over and over. One word jumped out at him. The Butcher. That was a name he hadn't heard in a long time. That was a name he did not want to hear. It destroyed his career, his marriage, and his life.

"...okay?" asked Sonam.

"Ah.... I'm sorry, what?"

"Are you OK," she asked again.

"Yeah... I'm fine," he lied, "It's just the headache. Can you finish up here?"

She nodded her head, biting her lips. Her soulful eyes, full of concern, lingered on him briefly before returning to the scene. Sonam took out the ultraviolet light and scanned the scene. A sudden coldness hit his core as he tried to navigate the maze of shame he had locked up in his mind years ago. Sonam severed the strings which held up the body, but *rigor mortis* had set, which kept the body up in place. Cutting the T-shirt open, she examined the body for marks, bruises, and injuries.

Nasir opened a bottle of water and drank his fill. It would have been better if it was whiskey. Nothing was right about this. Nothing.

~

As Sonam finished the examination, Nasir managed to calm himself down, regaining his composure. The present needed him more than the past.

Frantic footsteps rushed up the stairs. Saket burst into the floor and came to a stop in front of Nasir. He paused to catch his breath, bent over, and leaned on the wall. His other arm pointed back toward the way from which he had come.

"They.... found .... another....... body," he managed to say in between heavy breaths.

Nasir rose to his feet, fully alert. "Same signature? The Artist?"

"We found parts of a body…in the garbage truck parked close by… The driver called it in a little while ago."

Nasir felt his tightly wound-up body relax at the sound of that. "I, and my team's number one priority is to catch The Artist. I'm sure the Delhi Police is more than capable of handling a homicide."

"I know, Sir," said Saket. "But this is no ordinary homicide. The body is cut up into pieces, and disposed of in the garbage. We could really use some help…of course, when you are finished here…It would be huge favour, Sir."

Nasir studied Saket, an honest, eager young man. The passion in his eyes reminded him of a younger him, when the world was in black and white.

"Hmmm…okay. Let's go," Nasir said, smiling a little, and gesturing at Sonam that he was leaving.

He welcomed the distraction.

Manas

Tuesday, April 22, 2014

What do you do when your nightmares come to life?

The sun slid down the horizon, leaving a soft yellow glow in the sky. Abundant greens turned a muted orange in the twilight. The threat of rain hung over the city like a guillotine over the condemned.

Manas huffed and puffed through the empty roads; an evening run. It was unusual. He preferred his runs in the early morning, when the air was crisp, and he was less tired. But he missed his morning run that day, and he had to make up for it. *Gotta have them endorphins.*

A slow, monstrous grumbling of thunder came from deep within the dark clouds covering the sky. It was so humid that you could smell the moisture in the air. Manas picked up the pace.

Work was killing him. Sketching up an advertisement idea was the fun part of his job, but that was ruined now. It wasn't enough to be creative anymore. The client's expectations sky-rocketed, and his boss was playing to their tune. Impossible deadlines and unreasonable expectations were killing the team, one by one. One of those impossible deadlines was fast coming up, and he had no idea what to do. He had called it a day early, and headed home to get some peace of mind. And a run always helped him calm down, and would hopefully get his creative juices flowing.

He reached the gates to his home and pulled them open. A flock of birds flew across the sky, probably heading home after a day of work. Manas quickly made his way through the door, and moved toward the couch inside. As he sunk into the soft bosoms of the couch, he flicked on the television.

Bella strolled into the living room, circled the spot between Manas' legs and settled in. He reached down and ran his hands through the soft amber fur, ruffling it. The insane speed at which her tail was wagging made him laugh. She always knew how to cheer him up. He grabbed her chew toy, wagged it in front of her and threw it through the open door, outside. She dashed out the door, hot in pursuit of her chew toy.

Bella was an integral part of his support system. Moreover, Shruti and Anu adored her. Bella strutted into the room, smiling, with the toy in her mouth. He hugged her, ruffling her fur as she leaned on him.

"Stay," he said, and Bella resumed her position at his feet.

Even though he was physically home, work loomed over his shoulder like a genie controlled his master and not the other way around. Sitting in his living room with a sketch pad in his hand, he willed his mind to sketch out an idea for his client. But he knew it didn't work that way.

He had let the television blabber in the background. It helped him think.

The pretty weather girl intoned, "Heavy rains are expected to hit the southern part of Kerala and the coastal belt in the coming weeks. A depression was spotted over the Arabian Sea, and it is expected to gain in strength in the coming days...."

Manas reached for the remote and switched the channel. He didn't want anyone telling him the entire week was going to be depressing.

"Gruesome murder-rape shocks the capital," read the marquee at the bottom of the screen. He turned up the volume and sharpened his ears.

The reporter was shouting through the din, live from the scene of the crime. Or as close as he could. Police had cordoned off the area, and the reporter stood right next to the yellow police tape and yelled out the details of the murder. Manas averted his eyes as the reporter started to get graphic about the horrific murder. He focused on the remote, and zoned out the reporter. He made it a point to avoid exposure to such violence. It was one of his rules.

He was about to change it when he heard a familiar name—'Amrita Sharma.'

The name echoed in his mind. It tossed a pebble into the still water of the lake. Bright blue sky mirrored the surface of the lake, hiding the darkness under it. The pebble sunk into the darkness, silently stirring up something deep inside. Ripples glistened in the light as they scrambled away from the pebble, distorting the perfect reflection of the skies. Instead of dying out gradually, the ripples gained in size and momentum and transformed into waves as they approached the shore.

Manas froze with his finger above the 'next' button on the remote. He waited for the waves to wash over him. *The wallet; Shruti's picture inside.* He grabbed it and focused on her smiling face. The waves started to lose momentum as his breath became normal. Shruti always calmed him down.

Manas leaned towards the screen and saw a familiar face, smiling in the portrait the television channel got hold of. An apparition from another life. A bittersweet wave of melancholy washed over him. He closed his eyes and took a deep breath. Blocking out parts of his memory was something he was good at.

The news report continued attributing the murder to a serial killer who signed his work as The Artist.

The eager reporter went on without taking a breath, "In a most interesting development, we have learned that The Artist has put up the following message in a photograph left for the police: *'To The Butcher, this is for you. With love, The Artist.'* The police speculate that The Butcher mentioned is 'The Butcher of Bhalswa', and The Artist is calling out The Butcher, communicating with him. Let's take a quick recap on what we know about the Butcher of Bhalswa…."

The Butcher. This time it was not a pebble but a boulder, not a wave, but a tsunami. A single drop of sweat trickled down the scruff of his neck, down his spine. His heart strained against his rib cage, fluttering, trying to get out.

Manas had shut the door on his past eighteen years ago. But the past has a way of finding its way into the present. It usually starts with a peak through the keyhole. But before you know it, it will be breaking down the door with an axe, demanding an audience. Everything he wanted to get away from when he moved to the other end of the country would come back to haunt him.

"Stop it!" he said to himself. "This is just a coincidence. It just so happens that the only link between your past and the present gets killed. And by the pure magic of probability, a serial killer left a note to The Butcher he tried convincing himself. But there was only one problem. He didn't believe a word he just said.

"…Shruti tomorrow?" Anuradha asked.

What? When did Anu come in? How much did she hear? What was she saying? He changed the channel quickly and faced Anuradha. "I am sorry. What did you say?" he asked.

"Will you be picking up Shruti tomorrow?"

They must not know. Anuradha and Shruti belonged to another world, a world filled with happiness and innocence.

What do you do when your nightmares come to life?

"Manas…did you hear me?" Anuradha said.

"Oh… yeah, I'll pick her up," said Manas, plastering a smile on his face. "Don't worry about that."

Anuradha narrowed her eyes, and the creases on her forehead deepened. "Is everything OK?"

"Yeah, yeah, everything is fine," Manas said, turning back to the television. She usually sees right through him. Maybe if he hid his face, it would be harder for her. She shouldn't know.

"You don't look okay."

"It's just work stuff, Anu. Have a big deadline coming up."

Anuradha shot him one final lingering look, her arms tight to the body, and went inside. She had enough respect for him to trust him implicitly, but did he deserve it?

Manas rose from the couch and trudged his way to the window, Bella at his heels. Overcast weather had already spread its gloom over the neighbourhood. Children, playing in the streets, packed up their balls, stumps, and bats, and found the shelter of their homes. The motorcycles who ran the risk of getting soaked to their underwear criss-crossed their way through the traffic to reach their safe haven before the rain. The dark clouds threatened to unleash a torrential downpour any minute. It was not a question of if. It was a question of when.

Nasir

Tuesday, April 22, 2014

The illusion of safety that the law-and-order machinery uphold, was the cornerstone of any society.

Delhi zipped past his vision, most of it in a blur. She was settling into her morning routine. Adults rushing to reach their offices, and kids dragging themselves to school. The city drudged on their pristine world, ignorant of the dark underbelly and what goes on in it. Nasir had seen enough murders, enough random acts of violence to realise that no one was safe. But the illusion of safety that the law-and-order machinery upheld was the cornerstone of any society.

Saket had been yammering on about the eventful morning Delhi Police had ever since Nasir got into his jeep.

"—ever been two horrible murders so close to each other? We are stretched taut this morning," Saket said.

"Tell me about the body you found," Nasir said.

"We got a call from a garbage truck driver about plastic covers leaking blood. When our men reached and took them out."

"Of course, you took them out," said Nasir, shaking his head in disapproval. "Anyway, continue."

Saket flashed a sheepish grin. "So…we found parts of a body scattered among different garbage bags. The body has been identified as a Teresa D'Cruz. Her son Alex confirmed it."

"Any leads yet?"

"Just the one. Police dogs caught a scent, and led us to a factory."

"What factory?"

"Spices. We are questioning them as we speak," Saket said.

Nasir ran his hands through his balding head. "Hmm. Tell them they are barking up the wrong tree. Spices, especially pepper, throws off a sniff dog. Whoever has done this, must have known that."

Saket wrinkled his brow as he took in the news.

"We are here, Sir," the driver announced.

Nasir and Saket both got out of the jeep and entered the police station. As he followed Saket, he spotted a room with lone policeman standing guard. The others maintained a safe distance from the room, only allowing a few furtive glances in the direction.

They marched into the room, and the violence at display there broke his stride for a second. A faint smell of bleach tickled his nostrils. A decapitated head stared back at him from the table in the centre of the room; its purple skin was swollen to twice its size. Hands, legs, and torso occupied the slots next to it. The entire table looked like a stall at a cannibal's convention. Violent death strips every ounce of dignity from the victim.

Saket froze at the doorway, but Nasir stepped closer to the decapitated head to examine it.

"The facial trauma you see here—" Nasir pointed to the purple swelling, disfiguring the face.

Saket took a step closer to get a better look, but kept a distance.

"You have to come closer, Saket," said Nasir, gesturing him closer. "We have to look past the gore for the truth. If you want to work with Violent Crimes, you will have to get used to this."

He took a couple of timid steps towards the body.

"Okay, now...do you see the purple swelling?"

Saket gulped hard, and nodded.

"Those bruises to the face, they were made when she was still alive. The perpetrator wanted to depersonalise her. Strip her of her identity."

"To make it harder to identify the victim?" Saket asked.

"No, not quite...This is more psychological than logical. Maybe the perp hated her. I have a feeling that the act of decapitation was more than just convenience. He must have done it way before he cut up the body into pieces. He must have done it out of hate."

Saket cocked his head to a side and narrowed his eyebrows. "Why do you say that?"

"Experience."

Nasir fished out a pair of surgical gloves from his bag and pulled them on. He handed over another pair to Saket and gestured him to do the same.

Nasir stepped closer and lifted the head from the table to study the wound of separation. He asked Saket to do the same with the arms.

"You see the colour difference? The arm wound is more purple than the head wound."

Saket nodded, and dropped the arm back to the table as soon as possible.

"That means that a lot more blood drained when he cut off the head than the arms."

"So, the decapitation was done during the murder, but the rest was an afterthought?" Saket asked.

Nasir nodded in agreement. "Absolutely. Now look at the torso. You see those multiple stab wounds?"

Saket tiptoed closer to the torso.

"That's what pathologists call a 'Pattern of Rage' for obvious reasons. This, along with the decapitation of the head and disfiguration of the face, tells me this was a hate crime. And the good thing about a hate crime is that it is almost always committed by somebody who knows the victim."

Saket stripped off the gloves, pulled out a notepad, and pen and started taking notes.

Nasir picked up the head, and ran his fingers over the dark bruise marks along the neck. "See these ligature marks. You can see them in the shape of fingers. I'd wait for an autopsy to confirm, but my hunch is that the cause of death is asphyxiation. The perp strangled her to death with his bare hands. This is so obviously an emotional kill."

Nasir returned the head to the table, and took off his gloves.

"No coming to the perp, he—"

"He? How did you know it was a man?" Saket asked.

"Just an educated guess. The size of the fingers from the ligature marks, and the fact that you need quite a bit of strength to strangle a person."

Saket jotted down some more notes.

"I'm guessing, after the initial emotional outburst, he must have regained control, and then proceeded to cut up the body. And the cuts are not random. He did not just get an axe and hacked everything to pieces. The cuts are made at logical separations—the arms, legs, etc. Shows that the perp was emotionally and mentally stable while cutting up the body and disposing it."

Nasir pivoted, and strode out of the room with Saket on tow.

"So, to summarise, we are looking for an emotionally and mentally stable, intelligent man who knew the victim in person."

Saket started at Nasir with his mouth agape. "That was surreal."

Nasir chuckled. "Behavioural profiling, my friend, is a science. And you should not shy away from observing every minute detail, no matter how grisly the crime scene is."

"There is one thing that puzzled me," Nasir added, "Why did the body smell of bleach?" He conjured the best fish hook he could in his eyes and asked, "You guys didn't clean it by any chance, did you?"

Saket let out a hearty laughter. "No, Sir. We are not that bad."

Nasir suppressed a gurgle of laughter.

"There is one thing that has been puzzling us," said Saket. "We found a turquoise bead in one of the garbage bags. We questioned a few friends and family, and none of them knew about such a necklace."

Nasir rubbed his forehead. "Definitely strange and worth looking into. But the first thing you should find is the crime scene. The perp must have killed her at some place. You might get a lot more from there."

Saket nodded obediently. "Thanks a lot. You've been a big help. I'm headed to the victim's house now. Can I drop you back after that?"

Nasir answered with a nod, and headed towards the jeep.

~

The jeep stopped in front of a house battling the onslaught of time. It was the kind of house which hid in plain sight. The door to the house was obscured by the angle at which the door was built. The overgrown plants in the garden covered the front and side of the house. A lot of well-wishers gathered in clusters, whispering to each other. Silence permeated the atmosphere amplifying the gloom that settled around the house. Saket led the way inside the house.

The strong bleach smell was the first thing Nasir noted as he entered the room. The white tiles on the floor were white, unlike the rest of the house.

While Nasir was wondering about it, a six feet tall man with a lean, athletic body hobbled out from inside the house. His short, messy hair fell across his large forehead. A casual beard gave definition to his square jaw. His small, thin mouth was perfectly positioned on his handsome face.

"My condolences, Mr Alex," Saket said, shaking his hand. "Right time to talk?"

Alex lifted his red, watery eyes, and nodded his head.

"I know you've already given your statements, but do you mind telling me what happened?" Saket asked. "How did you discover the body?"

At the word 'body,' Alex covered his face with his hands, and a quake shook his shoulders.

"We can come back later, Mr Alex," offered Saket.

Alex signalled to give him a minute as the tremors subsided. When it finally stopped, Alex took a deep gulp of air and wiped his eyes with the back of his left hand.

"I own an internet café nearby. Yesterday morning, I left Mom here and went to the café. Barcelona was playing Athletico Bilbao at night and so I spent the night at the café. When I came back in the morning, Mom....

she wasn't there. I called all her friends and checked all the places she might have gone. When I didn't find her, I went to the police."

"Did you notice anything unusual?" Nasir asked.

Alex's eyebrows gathered as he tried to think. "The gate and the door to the house were open. But that's about it."

"Were there any signs of struggle? Any items missing?" Saket asked.

"Nah, everything was where it was supposed to be, and nothing is missing."

"Did you clean the room recently, Mr Alex?" Nasir asked.

Alex scratched his cheek through the sparse beard. "No...Why do you ask?" he asked, his voice unsure.

Nasir smiled at him to ease his mind. "It's just that I found the tiles a little too clean when compared to your walls. And then there is that bleach smell."

"Yeah...That's what that was? I thought it was coming from the toilet."

Alex's phone rang, with a bouncy guitar riff, in his left pocket and he took it out to look at the screen. "I have to take this. Is there anything else I can help you with, officers?"

"Yeah...Is it okay if we just look around the house?" Nasir asked. Saket shot him a confused look.

"Anything you need, officers, just nail the bastard that did this to my Mom."

"Thank you for your cooperation," said Saket with a slight dip of his head. "We will be in contact."

Alex plodded back into the house, talking on the phone.

Saket turned to face Nasir with a deep burrow between his eyebrows, and asked, "You have a theory?"

Yes, he did have a theory, Nasir thought. Alex was not home the whole day. The killer could have gotten into the house, killed Teresa, taken his time with her, and left before Alex returned. The body and the house both reeked of the acrid bleach smell. That can't be a coincidence. If there was something 22 years in the force had taught him, it was that there were no coincidences.

"Sort of. I'll be right back," Nasir said as he strode out of the house and to the car. He came back with his forensic kit.

"Can you close the doors and curtains, Saket?"

Nasir appraised the room. "Still too much light."

He pulled out an insulation tape and sealed the door. He closed the windows and blocked the light with black paper on the glass. The room grew dark. He unscrewed his Luminol spray and started spraying it at the places where the bleach smell was the strongest.

"What are we looking for?" asked Saket from a dark corner of the room.

"Wait for it," quipped Nasir.

"I don't see any—"

"There," Nasir said.

The ground began to glow a faint blue luminescence.

"That's Luminol," Nasir explained, "You can wash off a blood stain, scrub it, bleach it, but hit it with Luminol and they will glow like ghosts."

"Oh, yeah," said Saket, "They told us about that during training. But I've never seen it in use."

Nasir sprayed more and more areas with Luminol. After a few minutes, a bluish glow bathed the room, a scene straight out of a fairy tale.

Nasir rose to his feet, and turned to Saket. In the soft luminescence, he saw Saket's silhouette outlined by the bluish glow. His eyes looked out of the darkness, burning bright with excitement.

"This is your crime scene," Nasir said.

Prateek

Friday, October 6, 1995

The darkness between the stars. The unsung heroes of the night. Without them, there were no stars. Without them, there was no night. And without night, there was no day.

Sun clocked out for the day, leaving the last few strands of light to take a deep orange hue. Shadows of the rickety wooden stalls that lined the street grew longer by the minute. Colours that painted the street turned from sunny yellow to orange. With the shops turning their lights and neon boards on, vibrant, unnatural colours entered the mix, giving an ethereal feel to the place.

Prateek and Manas camped out in the tea shop opposite Suryakant's shop. The light from the bright green neon sign hit the tea glass in his hand, refracted, and presented in a pattern fit for a kaleidoscope.

Motion across the street snatched the attention away from the kaleidoscope. Suryakant climbed out from behind the counter and handed over something to the kid who worked there. He was giving directions to the kid, pointing to the shutter.

Manas met Prateek's gaze and nodded. Suryakant was calling it a day. They stood up, paid the tea shop, and crossed over to the other side of the street. Suryakant was picking up his belongings as they passed the store and slipped into the street next to it. A couple of minutes of brisk walk and they reached the spot they recced and agreed upon—a bend in the road along the side of the lake. They would see him coming from a distance.

And then they waited. The orange sky brought out a beautiful hue in the lake water, but soon, it turned dark, and the water was black. A light fog cast its misty curtain over them.

Around the bend in the road, a small flashlight danced in the darkness. *That was him.* Manas pulled out a sweet box he had bought earlier that day from his pocket and planted himself on the edge of the lake in total darkness. Prateek waited on the side, close enough to reach Manas in a heartbeat but out of sight.

As the tiny light danced closer, Manas lit a matchstick. In total darkness, the matchstick burned with vigour throwing its light all around in a brief flash. Suryakant's footsteps faltered. Manas guarded the flame against the wind, and passed the flame over to a torch, which in turn burned brightly. He drove the torch into the ground and rose to his feet.

"Who's there?" Suryakanth asked.

Manas' shadow danced with Suryakant as he swaggered towards him. In the wavering orange light, Suryakant's scrunched up face danced their way into confusion. The dim-witted expression stayed on his face till Manas was close enough for him to see the sweet box in Manas' hand – it said Suryakant's Sweet Shop.

Manas opened the box, picked up a Rasgulla and bit into it. "Mmmm. You do make good sweets." The sweet syrup trickled down the sides of his mouth. He wiped them up and licked his fingers. "I didn't pay for this box, you know? That makes me a thief, doesn't it?"

The big man put two and two together; his eyes grew cold, hard. The uncertain light of the torch magnified the vein that was popping on Suryakant's head.

"Silence?" Manas picked up another rasgulla and stuffed it down his throat. "Don't you want to wrap your hands around my neck and choke me to death? Or do you wanna beat me up, break my hands and leave me here? Oh, wait. You only do that to children."

Suryakant took a step towards Manas, making himself big. "Why don't you bugger off?"

"I thought you were a man of action," said Manas. He dropped his shoulders and shook his head slowly from side to side. "Yesterday, you were all about the action when you beat up that helpless little kid. Now you want to talk?"

Suryakant's face turned ashen as his eyes flitted to each side. "You don't know what that little miscreant did." There was nothing but darkness all around him.

"It doesn't matter," said Manas as he glanced sideways at Prateek. That was his signal.

Prateek coiled the cord of rope around his hands and rose to his feet. Three steps, and he was at Suryakant's side. Before he realised what was happening, Prateek looped the rope around his neck and pulled with both his hands. Suryakant put all his might into resisting the attempt on his life. But Prateek was stronger and in a better position. He tightened the rope across Suryakant's neck, cutting off the blood supply to the brain and air supply to the lungs until he collapsed, unconscious.

The moment Suryakant hit the ground, Manas got to work. He carried Suryakant to a nearby tree, a tree hidden in the shrubs, away from the pathway and towards the lake, and tied him to it; his face touching the tree and the body hugging it.

Prateek unsheathed his trusted scythe and sharpened it, waiting for Suryakant to wake up. The fiery light glimmered off the blade as it moved back and forth.

Suryakant woke up with a groan. The grating of metal on rock must have woken him up. With a sudden jerk, he tried to break free from the knots, which held its own. He strained his neck and peered over his shoulders to scan the surroundings. The survey came to a screeching halt when he met Prateek's gaze. His eyes slowly travelled down to Prateek's hand, where the scythe shimmered. That triggered another round of desperate struggle against the ropes.

Prateek tightened his grip on the scythe. Like a moth caught in a web, Suryakant squirmed in his bondage, and when he realised its futility, he broke down; convulsions rocked his body.

"Please..." His voice was broken, grating.

Prateek let a guttural laugh escape his mouth. "Really? Please? Tell me one reason I should listen to your 'please'. You sure as hell did not listen to that small kid pleading the same way."

"Oh, come on. You gotta understand. That little devil stole m-"

"I don't care what he stole. He deserved a spanking on his bottom, not a broken arm." Prateek resumed his slow rhythmic to and fro movements, sharpening the scythe, all the while fixing Suryakant in a cold, hard stare.

"Do you believe in karma?" Prateek asked.

Suryakant burst into another series of sobs. "Ye- Yes..."

Prateek stopped sharpening the scythe and inspected it in the light. The edges glimmered in the light from the torch.

"You've got some real bad karma. What do you think is gonna happen to you?"

"I... I don't know. Maybe I'll be reincarnated as a dog or something."

"How convenient? The problem is that I believe in a different kind of karma." Prateek walked towards Suryakant with the scythe held away from his body. "Immediate karma. It's so much more effective than having to wait for the next life to get what's coming for you."

Suryakant's eyes grew wide. "I am a very rich man. Tell me a figure, and that is yours. Just let me go."

Prateek drew the scythe above his head. "I want justice," he whispered before swinging the blade down at Suryakant's neck. The blade hit the back of Suryakant's neck and immediately broke the surface, burying it deep into his spinal cord. The scream from Suryakant's throat was loud and short lived. Blood erupted off the gash, spraying Prateek all over.

Prateek wiped off the blood on his face with the palm of his free hand. Suryakant was dead, alright. But that was just the beginning. Hacking off the head was much harder than you thought. It was so easy in the movies – one swipe and the head rolls on the floor. He remembered the first time he tried it. One strong and smooth swing of the scythe. Oh boy, was he in for a surprise? Nothing happened. He hacked at the neck again and again; blood spattering all around, pieces of flesh flying everywhere. And finally, after many strikes, when the head came off, you could hardly recognise the neck. It was so mashed up that it looked like it came out of a meat grinder. His technique improved a lot after that, but it still took him a good three swings to chop off the head.

Prateek held Suryakant's head by his hair, and with a final chop, it came loose. He tossed it into a sack and started undressing. The torch still burned bright, throwing its wavering light on the lake - the black calm lake. He dove into that darkness and washed himself off the blood. It was Manas' turn now.

Manas pushed himself off the ground he was resting on, dusted himself off and plodded onto the bloody scene. Suryakant's body was soaked in his own blood. It washed down the trunk of the tree and seeped into the ground. He untied the knots and the body plopped onto the ground. He bent over and caught hold of a leg, and dragged the body to the lake side.

The two sacks of stones they had gathered the day before were at the bottom of the lake, with the strings attached to them floating on the surface, tied to floating twigs. Manas dragged the dead body behind him as he swam to the middle of the lake and tied the ropes to the body—one to the legs and another to the torso. Manas dove underground to tie off the rope and shorten its length. He was underwater for almost a minute, but when he came back up, Suryakanth was not with him anymore. He had sunk to the abandoned depths of the pool. Karma.

Manas climbed ashore and started cleaning up the scene, trying to bring a semblance of normality to the place. Prateek floated on the dark water, gazing up at the starry blackness of space. He was always more drawn to the darkness between the stars than the twinkling dots of light. The unsung heroes of the night. Without them, there were no stars. Without them, there was no night. And without night, there was no day.

Manas and Prateek had a clear division of labour - Prateek came in for the violent part, and Manas dealt with the planning and cleaning up. It played to both their strengths. There was one more task planned for the night. But for that, the rich indigo of the sky had to make way for pitch black; the low humming of the young night had to die down into a wiser silence.

~

An occasional howl of a stray dog interrupted the silence of the night. Prateek clasped both his hands behind his head and leaned back on the bed. Manas caught a small nap on the chair. They had got back from dealing with Suryakant, took another round of showers and were waiting for the wee hours of the morning. The clock on the wall tick-tocked its way to two o'clock. Prateek shook off his drowsiness and rose to his feet.

"Manas, get up. It's time."

Manas jerked into wakefulness. He took a few seconds to reorient himself and squeezed his eyes as he got to his feet. Suppressing a yawn, he picked up a sack from the corner of the room and slung it over his shoulders.

Half an hour later, they were walking up the street leading up to their destination. Ramshackle houses, rather shacks, rose up around them. It wasn't hard to find where the kid lived. He was quite the troublemaker in the neighbourhood. This was just the latest in a long list of shenanigans under his belt.

They approached the kid's house, one among scores of similar houses all around. The blue tarpaulin spread over the roof made it stand apart from the immediate neighbours. A few multi-coloured banners covered spots on the roof where time had poked holes. A tall mango tree grew right in front of the shack, its branches spreading out and providing much-needed shade in the Delhi summers. It would be perfect, Prateek thought.

He scanned the neighbourhood. The narrow passageways between the houses were deserted; none of the houses still had a light on.

Manas handed him the sack he was carrying. Prateek reached inside and pulled out Suryakant's head by the hair. It has always fascinated him how a face loses its shape when life leaves it. It was just not the same face anymore. Somehow, it was older and younger, at the same time.

Prateek pulled out a rope from the same sack, tied it around the head and tugged it to check. The rope held firm. He glided towards a low-hanging branch of the mango tree, with rope in one hand and the head in the other. The kid would love this, he thought. With a small jump, he got the rope to loop around the branch and then pulled it down and tied the head in place.

Suryakant's head swayed in the wind, whirling around slowly. A lone macabre sentry guarding the night.

~

Prateek woke up late the next day. Weekends were the loveliest part of the week. Sleep till the sun hits your face. Play a little hide and seek by turning around and escaping the piercing rays of light. Those stolen moments of sleep were the best. He cracked open his eyes, slowly letting the bright sunlight enter. Manas snore quietly beside him, his mouth ajar. Prateek dragged himself up and pulled Manas along with him. Manas' mother must have left for work already. He lumbered onto the front porch and picked up the newspaper.

The headline of the paper read - *'The Butcher: A Ruthless Killer or a Vigilante with a heart?'*

"Manas, we made the front page again," Prateek shouted, his eyes riveted to the article as he made his way inside.

Manas glowered at him. "You know I don't give a damn, right?"

Manas was never a morning person. Prateek let the grumpy old man be and devoured the report like he was starving for days. "I'll read it out for you. Hold on."

He unfurled the newspaper, folded it back to fit in one hand and started reading:

"*Delhi had been on the edge ever since it was rocked with the series of murders, which the police have admitted being the work of a serial killer. 'The Butcher of Bhalswa' who gained his name by the decapitated head he leaves as a calling card, struck again yesterday.*"

Prateek felt an exhilarating warmth radiating through his body.

"*The latest in a series of three gruesome murders is a shopkeeper named Suryakant.*"

He skimmed over a few lines naming the previous victims and continued:

"*It is what has brought a whole new dimension, and our staff reporter has uncovered a possible motivation for the murders. The victims of all three murders had one thing in common. They were all, for lack of a better term, 'bad guys' and had at least one recent public appearance hurting someone, physically or mentally. One victim was seen mishandling a beggar, kicking her in her stomach, hurling her into the street. Another victim was a shopkeeper who used to mistreat his employees. He had beat up one of his employees and put him in the hospital just a day before the victim was murdered. The latest victim was seen beating up a kid and breaking his arm a day before his demise. Makes us wonder about the hazy lines that decide good from bad."*

Manas paused the intense examination of his toes and met Prateek's gaze. "Not bad, the reporter."

Prateek nodded. The report went on to deplore the inaction of the government and urge the public to raise its voice to hand over the case to the CBI. He tossed the paper aside.

Worry lines formed across Manas' forehead. "This is not good." He cleared his throat. "We need to slow it down."

Prateek winked at his best friend. "As long as we got you on point, CBI ain't gonna do shit, my man."

Nasir

Wednesday, April 23, 2014

Life is what you get when death isn't paying attention.

Nasir marched towards the conference room allotted for them at the police headquarters. The place bustled with activity. Young men in khaki uniforms sped past him in all directions; some balanced stacks of files in their hands, some took orders from a walkie-talkie, and some barked out orders through them.

As he got closer, the low rumble of hushed conversations got louder and overpowered the flurry of activity.

A deep booming voice rose above the din. "—don't piss off the boss man! It's as simple as that. Can you do that? And Nasir Ali Khan is one of the best officers in the force. He is one of the very few officers who was sent to the FBI for training in violent crimes. Serial killers especially. So, I would liste-"

Nasir rounded the corner, and Avinash stopped mid-sentence. He was talking to the policeman who was at the receiving end of Nasir's wrath in the morning; the selfie police. The arrogance on his face was long gone, but an air of defiance still stayed. Nasir acknowledged him with an imperceptible nod.

The room fell silent as he walked in. The who's who of local police, along with his team were seated around a beige oval table in the middle of the room. A white screen hung from the wall with a projector hanging from the ceiling in front of it. A group of policemen, probably not drawing enough salary to warrant a seat at the table, gathered on the far side of the screen. Saket beamed at him from the crowd with his bright, eager face.

"Good afternoon gentlemen," said Nasir, setting down a heavy file on the table. "Let's get right to it. I'm sure you all must have read the briefs we circulated about the criminal who calls himself *The Artist.* We have been on his tail for a little over four years now, with little luck, I must add. Akshay—" Nasir stepped back and ushered in Akshay into the spotlight. "—will give you an overview and get you up to speed."

Akshay stepped up to the laptop and put up a presentation on the projector. Three words filled the screen.

Manipulation. Domination. Control.

"Three words," he paused and cleared his throat, "Every violent serial offender has these three words at their core. Their every action, every word somehow ties back to one or all these words. The Artist is no different. He pops up once a year, on average, to make his mark and disappear. The body count has reached five now."

He pointed the clicker at the screen and changed the slide. Five photographs appeared on the screen—four of them on the left side, and one on the right.

Nasir studied the photographs from oldest to newest, from left to right. All young girls cut down at the prime of their lives. Lives which could have been saved. He let out a heavy sigh.

"He targets young women, typically 17-29, dark hair, and chic," Akshay continued, "One unique identifier is that all of these women were wearing high heels while they were abducted. All the previous victims fit this profile perfectly, except Amrita. Our latest one."

He paused for effect.

"And because of this uniqueness, we think there is something important here."

Nasir cleared his throat as he swung in his swivel chair to face his colleagues. "It is rare for a serial killer to break character unless there is a significant motivation to. And we are after that motivation, that deviation from the norm, that outlier to help us close in on him."

"Can't it be a copycat killer? I'm sure the public knows about *The Artist*," An officer with a thick moustache and sharp narrow eyes asked. "Someone else passing off the murder as a work of a serial killer?"

"Excellent. This was the exact same question we also asked ourselves earlier in the day. But it was immediately ruled out and you will see why." Nasir motioned Akshay to continue.

"We believe that The Artist is a man, aged 17-29," Akshay said. "Serial killers rarely venture outside their age group when picking their victims."

"That is just a conjecture, right?" the same officer drilled. "We can't know for sure. It might be an old man, in his late forties as well."

"Well, yes. You are right. But it is a statistically significant conclusion to make. The FBI has meticulously recorded every case they have encountered and came up with the statistically significant conclusion. We have studied countless serial killer cases from around the world and found this to be true. If you ask me if it is impossible that The Artist can be a forty-year-old, I will say no. But the probability of that happening is very less."

The officer offered a perfunctory nod in acknowledgement.

Akshay pressed the clicker again, and the screen changed to close-up shots of the victim's necks.

"Now coming to his *modus operandi*, he rapes or has consensual sex with the victim, strangles them into unconsciousness, cuts them up at different places, and eventually kills them. A lust murderer, in short."

The entire room broke into an almost collective hushed whisper.

"Now comes the sick part," Akshay pressed on. "He dresses up the body, puts on makeup, and sets up a scene resembling a famous Hollywood movie poster."

"Holy shit! Is he crazy?", the selfie policeman asked.

Nasir glowered at the policeman until he started to fluster. He had an abrasive edge that had to be polished.

"He is not crazy in the normal sense of the word, but he is neither normal." Nasir gestured Akshay to skip a slide. Close-up shots of the naked bodies of the victims filled the screen.

"We usually place lust murderers on a spectrum from organised to disorganised," Nasir continued, "The organised offenders tend to be educated, intelligent, aware of law enforcement, narcissistic, controlled, and prepared. They have no regard for social norms. These guys are methodical and cunning and generally leave a clean crime scene. And they love themselves and love to read about them. Anything from media reports to police reports. The disorganised offenders tend to suffer from some mental illness like psychosis. Impulse is their friend and motivator. These guys usually use a blitz attack to subdue the victim and murder them and often mutilate a body post-mortem. Socially inept loners."

Nasir got to his feet and strode over to the screen.

"The meticulous pre and post-murder planning indicates an organised personality." Nasir reached up to the white screen to point out the different cuts shown in the photographs. "On the other hand, body mutilation, as you see here, is a sign of a disorganised personality. But if you observe closely, the cuts on the victim's bodies have an order to it. They are not all random; there is a purpose to the chaos. We think it's a by-product of Erotophonophilia - a mental condition in which individuals derive sexual pleasure and arousal from murdering someone. So, based on these evidences, we placed him closer to the organised personality in the spectrum, which makes him more dangerous and harder to catch."

Nasir's footsteps rang loud and clear as he strode back to his seat. Akshay cleared his throat and pointed to the screen. He had switched it back to the slide they were on, only now there were red arrows pointing to the dark purple bruise marks all along the neck of the victim.

"As I was saying...Notice the ligature marks on the neck. The killer's finger marks around the neck show death by strangulation. If you notice closely, you can see that the victims were strangulated from the front and not behind. This is only possible if the killer is already in close proximity to the victim. He may be a smooth talker, possibly handsome and very comfortable with women. Again, underpinning his classification as an organised personality."

"Any motive yet? Do we know why or how he is choosing his victims?" Saket asked from the back of the room.

Akshay glanced at Nasir.

"We do not know how he is choosing his victims," Nasir chipped in, "It can be as random as him hitting up a conversation with a girl on the street. We have tried to find a connection, something common between the victims and have drawn blank till now. But we do have a theory on his motivation; or rather his psychological disposition."

Nasir laid a finger on his temple, trying to gather his thoughts. The psychological profile was hard to go down for many people. "We think he has an unconscious anger towards women. You can see it in the aggression he displays in his M. O, *modus operandi*. Poor treatment from a lover, wife or even mother may have formed the seeds of his hatred. And looking at the lust murder and the subsequent dressing up of the victims and displaying them as 'artworks,' we think he sees women as mere sexual objects he conquers. Traditionally such personalities come out of a dysfunctional childhood—an absent or abusive parent, or both. An absent father, physically or emotionally, seems highly likely as the absence of a male role model is evident in the behaviour."

Akshay leaned against the wall right next to the screen and folded his hands.

"The bodies we have discovered were spread out geographically in Delhi and NCR; and not close to where the victim was last seen," Nasir added, "So, he must have planned the place to display the body well in advance and then travelled all over Delhi with a body in his vehicle. That kind of audacity comes from an illusion of grandeur about himself, a feeling that he is a class above the rest of us and he is untouchable."

The selfie policeman spoke up from behind the crowd. "None of this is gonna help us catch the guy. What a load of cra—"

"From 17 million people in Delhi, we have come down to the people aged 17-29, who owns a vehicle and an absent father," Nasir cut in, fixing the policeman in a stare that would freeze the Indian Ocean, "That must amount to something, don't it?"

The selfie policeman shrunk back into the crowd, hiding behind others around him.

"Usually, the psych profile along with the forensics, lead us to a very small list of suspects," said Nasir, facing the rest of the audience around him, "But unfortunately, The Artist has been very careful, and we have not had much luck forensic-wise. Even then, the psych profile helps us understand him, predict his moves, or gives us clues on how he would react to a situation. So, no. This is not a *load of crap*, as my friend opined."

Akshay continued, "Now coming back to our latest victim. Delhi Police have identified her as Amrita Sharma, a 38-year-old school teacher. She was last seen at a parent-teacher meeting at her school. Eyewitnesses recall her wearing a red dress with high heels. She checks off on all items on the list except for the age bracket. But the similarities stop there, as we will see now."

Nasir sunk into his chair and leaned back with his hands behind his head. Life is what you get when death isn't paying attention. When that sneaky bastard takes notice, you are done. When Amrita woke up that day, she had no idea that it was going to be her last. Did she have regrets in life? Were there incomplete deeds she left behind? Death doesn't care. That sneaky bastard just wants to ruin lives, unsuspecting lives.

The clattering of a lot of pens brought Nasir back into the room. Sonam had risen to her feet and knocked over a set of pens on the floor. A flush spread on her cheeks to match the peach shirt she was wearing. She dropped to the floor to pick up the pens rolling on the floor; or maybe just to hide her embarrassment.

She composed herself and rose to her feet to face the audience. Her red, full-lipped mouth curved upwards in a magnetic smile. She wasn't tall, but she held herself like a queen.

"I'm sorry about that," she said, brushing back a strand of auburn hair which fell over her face, "There was a question about the possibility of a copycat killer earlier, right?"

She waddled over to Akshay, with her arm outstretched. Akshay got the message and handed over the clicker to her.

Nasir sniggered inside. Grace was not one of her qualities.

Sonam operated the clicker and the next slide came into view. A sudden silence fell over the room as the screen filled with a full-screen image of the photograph The Artist left behind. A couple of high-ranking policemen checked the time on their watch when it was displayed prominently just above the screen. Few others turned to each other to talk about something they suddenly remembered. It wasn't an easy image to look at, even for seasoned police officers.

"This is the photograph he left for us this time," Sonam said, "Our in-house movie enthusiast, Salim, has identified this as the imitation of the poster for the 1994 movie—Pulp Fiction."

The clicker clicked loudly in the room. The image shrunk to make space for the actual movie poster.

"In many ways, The Artist is an artist. The level of detailing and scrupulous planning he carries out to best replicate the poster requires dedication and perseverance. And like any artist, if you study the artwork, you can see the unique brush strokes that makes the artist. One look at the crime scene, and we knew this was The Artist. No copycat would be able to do this."

Sonam changed the images on the screen and said, "Now let's take a closer look." The screen now showed a close-up shot of Amrita's neck.

"There is a deep incised wound of the lateral and anterior neck, transecting both carotids and—"

"Err... In English so that the rest of us can understand?" Avinash asked.

Her mouth pulled into a sour grin. At that moment, she embodied the grin emoji perfectly. "Let me restart. There is a deep wound across her neck, starting from one side and extending all the way to the other. It has severed the major arteries and her windpipe. The medical examiner has certified that this was the case of death. This is a direct deviation from The Artist's M.O."

Nasir fought a knot in his belly. This was bothering him. The Artist was a strangler. Probably even derived some pleasure in watching the lights going out of his victims' eyes. *Why would he switch his M.O.?*

The screen showed a couple of other photographs as well—a close-up shot of the head, and another one of her abdomen.

"We discovered a wound in the left frontal portion of her head," Sonam continued, now in control of the room, "The wound was inflicted with a blunt object. Upon closer inspection, we found particles of wood. The wound was cleaned, and blood wiped off, presumably by the killer for his artwork—"

"Can it be that it was a pre-existing wound?" a policeman who managed to still look at the screen asked.

"No. The wound is fresh," Sonam replied, "The early infiltration of neutrophil cells places the wound less than twelve hours from the discovery of the body and collection of samples. It couldn't have happened before the P.T.A. meeting."

She pointed to the photograph of the victim's abdomen. "Here you can see the letters 'A' and 'R' carved into her abdomen. The increased free levels of histamine and serotonin led us to believe that these were antemortem wounds..." she glanced at Avinash with a sheepish grin, and continued," wounds that were inflicted before her death. The relative values of serotonin and histamine to the control samples place these wounds 15-60 minutes before death."

"So, she was tortured?" Nasir asked.

"Yes, ligature marks indicate she was tied to a chair," Sonam said.

"Sexual assault?"

Sonam shook her head from side to side. "Nothing to indicate that. No semen, no bruises."

"Hmmm..." said Nasir, running his hands through his balding head, "Strange. Very Strange."

"What's even more strange is the note he left behind," Akshay said.

Nasir offered a distracted nod. The Artist was getting more confident; cockier even. It was the first time he left a note. But why? This last victim was baffling him. A feeling deep inside his gut told him that there was something special about it. Serial offenders rarely alter their M.O. They have vain pretensions about what they do, and they spend their time perfecting their craft, making it better and cleaner. Why would The Artist be any different? And why didn't he rape or have sexual intercourse? What did he cut his victim's throat when he was used to strangulating? And why...why would he leave a note to the Butcher? Nasir felt his heart thumping against his ribs. Nothing made sense.

"Sonam....Any luck with the forensics? Or is it the same old story?" Akshay asked.

She shook her head from side to side. "As usual, the scene of the crime is clean. He must be wiping the place down and vacuuming it before he leaves."

Nasir slammed his hands down on the table. The hollow sound of wood echoed in the silence. He never left anything. Not even fingerprints.

"Salim, any luck on the perimeter check?"

"The perimeter is covered in footprints and tyre tracks. Couldn't glean any information out of that mess," Salim said.

Nasir leapt to his feet and marched up to the front of the room.

"So, this is what we have to work with. I understand that we have the full cooperation of the Delhi Police. I'd like to ask you all to keep an eye out for anything suspicious and give us a ring any time without hesitation. Thank you all."

The room was on their feet almost in unison as it erupted into a ruckus with scores of conversations, overlapping into an unintelligible drone. Slowly, they made their way out, leaving a few who decided to hang back.

Nasir paced the room, his hands tied behind his back, eyes following the ridges of the chocolate brown carpet, and his mind wandering the realm of dead girls. He came to an abrupt stop near Sonam, grabbed the evidence bags and absently went through them, hoping against hope for a breakthrough. Something to point them in the right direction.

The black gun they found at the scene was obviously a fake plastic one. No way to track those. There was a book in the next bag—'Sin on Wheels.' The Artist sure had a sense of irony. The cover showed a girl, dressed provocatively in a half-open white shirt, tucked into red, striped pants. She exposed quite a bit of cleavage and stood leaning against the door of an R.V. One of those pulp fiction novels that used to be published dime a dozen.

The next bag had nothing but a small turquoise object. No, a turquoise bead. An electric flash went through his head; millions of neurons fired in sequence to pass on the information, making the connection. His heart stood still for a moment.

"This...?" he asked Sonam. "Where did you find it?"

"Yeah... Even I thought it was weird. It was stuck in her hair, behind her head. Checked with eyewitnesses at school, and they confirmed that she was wearing a turquoise necklace the last time they saw her. It must have broken during the struggle..."

Nasir didn't hear the rest. His mind was travelling at the speed of light as he scanned the room.

Saket stood in a corner of the room with a wrinkle on his forehead and eyes unfocused. Just the man he wanted now. Nasir called Saket over and handed him the bead.

Saket turned the evidence bag over in his hands, narrowing his eyes; almost squinting. And just like that, the squint relaxed, his brows arched up. That was proof enough for Nasir; his suspicion confirmed.

"This is the same—" Saket asked.

"Yes, it is." Nasir beamed at him.

"That means—"

"Yes."

Sonam stared at both with her mouth hanging out. "What are you guys talking about?"

By that time, the rest of the team had also gathered around, probably to check out what the fuss was all about.

Nasir explained to the team how he had gone to help Saket on another case and how they found the exact same bead with the other body.

"So, The Artist is involved in the other one too?" Avinash asked.

Nasir nodded an affirmative and added, "At least, there is a very strong possibility that it is."

Saket picked up Amrita's portrait from the table and examined it. "You know...ever since you said the name of the victim, it was bothering me. The name sounded so familiar. I had collected a list of Teresa's friends for questioning. I have a sinking feeling that one of those names was a Sharma. Just hold on a second." Saket pulled out his mobile from his pocket and dialled.

Nasir didn't like this. He didn't like this one bit. The profile for The Artist was already stretched thin. If The Artist was involved in Teresa's murder, then it raises more questions than it answers. But as always, there was a silver lining. If The Artist had in fact, killed Teresa, that means he had finally slipped up. That was a crime of passion and in crimes of passion, the criminal loses objectivity; makes mistakes. And he already knew that Teresa's killer was somebody known to the victim. This might be the biggest breakthrough they have got since they started down the rabbit hole.

Saket got off the phone and smiled. "Guess who Teresa's best friend was?"

The Artist

Friday, April 25, 2014

The interplay of the rich and the poor was the engine that drove Mumbai.

Alex left the stolen, black Swift in the parking lot and promenaded out into the organised chaos called Mumbai. The city was in high gear; the maddening traffic, the turbulent flux of people, the incessant honking, and the relentless rumble of human voices.

The large dome of the CST terminal imposed on his vision, the Statue of Progress on top, reaching to the skies. Much like Mumbai, the terminal building was also a potpourri of architectural influences. You got the stained glasses and gargoyles of a cathedral, Victorian towers, Italian marble, arches, and eccentric floor plans of Indian palaces. It was a treat for sore eyes.

A local train had just arrived. The disembarking passengers surged out of the terminal, through the passageways, squished together into one gigantic beast, and spilled and spread over to the roads, disappearing into the cracks of Mumbai.

A commotion and a subsequent altercation across the road drew his attention. In the mayhem ensuing the arrival of the local train, a cycle rickshaw seemed to have hit a Bentley and both the drivers were going at it like dogs. This interplay of the rich and the poor was the engine that drove Mumbai. The affluent life, blatant consumerism, and Bollywood serves as a beacon of light, of hope, to which migrants from around the country flock. And they work hard to make it in Mumbai, in turn making her tick, which in turn enables the rich to maintain their lifestyle.

Alex whipped out his mobile to check the time and slowed down subsequently. He had a few more minutes to spare. A couple of touches here and there on the screen of the mobile, and he was staring at a youthful, exuberant face. Payal's profile picture on Facebook was alive with energy, much like her. She peered over her shoulders with a cocky smile, her one hand holding up the curtain of straight dark hair which fell behind her. The picture oozed the sensual, dusky charm that only Bengali girls could pull off. Alex swiped left and scrolled through all the photos she had put in over time. Most of them were her with her friends in different clubs in and around Mumbai; each of them chicer than the other. These photos, along with her numerous check-ins at different clubs, was why he noticed her in the beginning. Alex made the first move and they started talking. Soon the relationship graduated from Facebook to Skype, to mobile phones.

He pocketed the mobile, crossed the road at the signal, and bounced towards Sir JJ College of Architecture—Payal was a student there.

In stark contrast to the hustle and bustle of Mumbai, a calm quietness drowned the campus. Trees sheltered the ground, saving it from the sweltering sunlight. Beautiful graffiti covered the walls which stuck out of the foliage. Alex found her lecture room and stationed himself under a nearby tree.

In a couple of minutes, the lecture hall vacated, and Payal stepped out along with a few of her friends. A white tank top with a spaghetti strap revealed her dusky arms and a hit of cleavage. A blue denim hugged her long legs ending in white high heels. She was much better in person than all the photos he had seen of her. Alex got to his feet, set his hair, and strode over to her.

"Hi *payalgoescrazy*," Alex said, using her Skype username to get her attention.

She stopped in her tracks, turned her head back, and let out a shriek of joy.

"Oh my god! Alex?" A beautiful smile lit up her face. "Is that really you?" she said, with a hand on her chest.

Alex smiled slightly. "I was just in town and I thought I'll come and surprise you."

"Awesome! I did not imagine us meeting for the first time like this." Payal giggled. "How long are you in town?"

"I'll leave tomorrow morning—"

"Perfect. Let's do something tonight, Alex. And don't give me any excuses," she said putting both her hands on her hips.

He laughed and said, "Alright, how about we head up to Blue Frog tonight? Our first real date." He raised his eyebrows.

Payal beamed at the suggestion, "It's a date and you have my number. What say we meet at nine at the club?"

Alex nodded.

"So excited for tonight," said Payal, "Our first date." A childish giggle escaped her. "Listen, I have to run now. Gotta stuff myself with some food and head right back to stupid class. See you at ten? Don't be late." She ran to catch up with her friends, who were waiting a few steps ahead. Alex traced her rear end swaying back and forth as she sashayed away.

Alex pedalled the brakes as he pulled up in front of the Blue Frog. A valet rushed out to meet him, with a card to note down the number plate. But he accelerated away and parked his car a bit far from the club; in one of the many residential layouts up ahead. Leaving a paper trail was the last thing he wanted to do.

A swanky crowd gathered around the entrance waiting to get into the place. Payal stood out like a lone black tulip in a host of white ones. A body hugging, little black dress wrapped around Payal; a lace covered 'V' shaped cut, down the middle, to her navel. Alex took in her breasts, through the middle of the 'V' down to her navel. Her long and shapely legs ended in black leather high heels. The entire apparition stirred up a hurricane in his mind.

Alex tugged on the baseball cap he had on, and stepped into her line of vision and smiled.

Payal's eyes sparkled as she closed the distance between them and offered a brief hug.

He studied her up and down and said, "Whoa! You look... amazing."

Her cheeks reddened as she fiddled with the strap of her bag. "Come on, let's go inside."

Music blasted out of the club every time the door opened to let someone in. Alex took her arms and headed inside the club.

The club looked straight out of a science fiction movie. The room resembled a beehive but with round holes with tables in them and a dance floor in the centre. Dimly lit interiors and psychedelic bluish-purple lights gave it an other-worldly demeanour. The blast of electronic music from the powerful speakers took him by surprise. Each drop of the bass reverberated inside his body.

They headed over to the bar and ordered a Jim Beam on the rocks and a Pina Colada.

Payal tucked a strand of hair, which was hanging out of place, securely behind her ears. "What's with the cap, Alex? Are you hiding a bald patch under there?" she asked with a wink in her smile.

Alex chuckled. "Maybe I do. Or maybe, it's part of the attire."

"Aha! It's for 'style' is it? Then, might as well put on shades as well. I'll take you around the club like a blind person."

Alex put on a 'fake-hurt' face for a second and laughed as he took a sip of Jim Beam.

"I am so glad to finally meet you in person, you know? I used to... Nah, you'll think I'm silly." She dipped her chin with a hint of a smile.

"Oh, come on. I came all this way for you. I deserve to know all embarrassing things you used to do."

"But you didn't come here to meet me, remember?" Payal asked, with a naughty quirk on her mouth, "You were just in town, weren't you?"

Alex threw back his head and laughed. It was liberating to laugh so freely. He rarely got the occasion. The bartender served them the drinks they ordered, and he slid the pina colada in her direction.

"To tell you the truth. I am on my way to Trivandrum. But took a detour and came to Mumbai just to meet you."

Payal smiled with an air of pleasure. "Aww... that's so sweet."

"Now tell me." Alex took a sip of his Jim Beam on the rocks.

"Well..." Payal eyed the light orange drink. "I used to fantasise you being here...with me."

Alex conjured up a fishhook on his brows. "Really?" he said, drawing out the syllables. "Were you in your bedroom, alone and under the sheets when you fantasised about me?"

Payal blushed profusely and fiddled with the pineapple garnishing. "Shut up!" She slapped Alex's hand with a coy smile on her face.

They enjoyed the loud music in silence for a few minutes, and moved into a table when it cleared.

"Till when do I have you for the night?" Alex asked as he settled in next to Payal.

"Oh... I don't know as long as you want. Told my roommate not to wait up. So, quit worrying and let's just make the most of it."

Alex caressed the flanks of her arm as he reached and cupped her hands in his.

"I wish you could stay longer," Payal said with a bitter smile.

"Didn't you, like literally, just finish saying that we should make the most of it?" Alex grinned wide. "Quit moping around, and let's get on the dance floor."

He pulled her up and they made their way to the dance floor in the middle.

It was so crowded that you could not see the dance floor. The DJ played Tiesto, and the crowd was one step away from euphoria. The psychedelic lights made them feel like dancing under the Northern Lights, but the air wasn't that fresh. But the energy was infectious. Payal blended right in and started pumping her fists in the air, letting the music flow through her.

Alex watched her in the bluish light, tracing the contours of her body swaying with the music. He was not a dancer and basically stuck to the two-step. But there was no escaping the spirit of a crowd chanting and dancing to music. Gloria Estefan was right. '*The rhythm is gonna get you.*' As the DJ took them to a new high, Payal turned around gyrated her bottom, grinding on him. Alex put his arms around her and closed his eyes. He breathed in her sweet scent, sweat and perfume intermingled, and started moving with her, their bodies in sync.

Alex opened his eyes and spied a tall, well built, man in a black trench coat, passing behind the crowd, along the periphery of the dance floor. *The Butcher*. What was he doing here?

He stopped moving and straightened up. *Yes.* There was a reason he came here, and he was forgetting that, losing himself to Payal, and the music. And the Butcher was there to remind him of his purpose.

Payal noticed his stiff body and gestured the classic 'what happened' with her hands. Alex smiled, and shouted into her ears, "Time for another round of drinks. Be right back."

Stumbling his way through the crowd, he reached the bar and hailed the bartender.

"Jim Beam on the rocks, make it a double. And a pina colada, light on the cream, heavy on the rum."

Alex retrieved the crushed sedatives from his pocket and slid it in the pina colada. He made his way to their table and unloaded the drinks.

Payal was still on the dancefloor, grooving to the music; but was also fending off a guy in a sky-blue shirt. It was obvious from the way he moved that he was inebriated. He got up from the table, pushed through the crowd and reached Payal.

"Hey, let's move to the table," Alex whispered in her ear.

Payal's eyes shined, locked on the source of her relief. She squeezed towards Alex and the table, but the guy blocked her way, doing the '*balle balle*' dance. She wrinkled her nose, trying to pass him on either side, but he was having none of that.

Alex felt his muscles quiver. There wasn't time for this nonsense. He came up from behind, grabbed the guy's shoulder, and against his resistance, just moved him to the side so that Payal could get past him.

The guy's shoulders tensed up as he turned around, flaring his nostrils. Alex clenched his fists at his sides, and fixed the guy in a cold hard stare. He knew the effect of a 6'3" guy shooting daggers with his stare. The guy froze and then slinked off and blended into the crowd.

"That guy gave you any trouble?" Alex asked as soon as they settled into the table.

"Nothing new. Happens too often for my liking." Payal pulled her drink closer with a minute shake of her head and downed half the glass.

"But it felt nice to have my own protector." She glanced up with her glassy eyes, a content smile played at the corners of her mouth.

She leaned against Alex, her head resting on his shoulders. Alex wrapped her in his arms and stayed like that for a few minutes, listening to her rhythmic breathing.

"So, tell me, Alex. Why are you going to Trivandrum?"

"To help out a friend in a sticky situation."

Payal lifted her head to look at Alex. "You are a nice guy, aren't you?"

"Well, of course, I am, babe," Alex replied with a sly wink. He disentangled himself from Payal and grabbed his drink.

"All my friends are such ass-holes. They are there when the sun is up, but the moment it gets dark, I'm all alone fending off the evils of the night," Payal said, as she met Alex's eyes and smiled, "That's why I like you, Alex. You are there for me, even when the light is dim." She swayed a little and held the table for support.

Alex emptied his drink into his mouth, slid the glass away from him, and held Payal, "Somebody had too much to drink."

A gurgle of laughter came out of Payal. "You know me..."

Alex rose to his feet, pulling Payal along with him. "Come on, let's get out of here."

He looped her arms around his shoulders, held her by her hips, and made their way to the entrance. A Page 3 couple, dressed to kill, waltzed in the entrance door, and came up opposite. They glanced at Alex and his companion with concern in their eyes. Alex smiled politely and added, "Taking her home. Had a little too much to drink."

The sedative was taking effect. Payal leaned on him more and more every second. Once outside the club, Alex half-carried, and half-dragged her to his car. He stashed her in the passenger seat, wrapped the seat belt around her, and gave her a kiss on her cheeks.

"Where are we going?" Payal asked, her voice slurry, "Not to hostel."

Alex smiled warmly. "You are not going to your hostel. Just get some rest and sleep it off, okay?"

Payal drifted off, her eyes too heavy to stay open. He straightened out of the passenger side, closed the door, and walked around to the driver side. That's when he heard the *thud thud* of a few footsteps rushing up at him from behind.

The hair on his arms tingled, in a classic 'spidey sense' way. He peeked over his shoulders to find a few guys running up the street; one of them was the guy who was harassing Payal in the club. The intensity and purpose in their steps tipped him of their intentions. His muscles wound up at the sight of an iron rod in one of the guy's hands. But you don't show your cards right at the beginning.

Alex lazily glanced at the oncoming party and said, "Fuck off," over his shoulders. He didn't have time to deal with this. The sedatives would only keep Payal down for so long.

"Take a hike, boy," the leader said, "We don't give two fucks about you. Where is the girl?"

Alex turned back to face them, and planted his feet a foot apart, lowering his centre of gravity. Three guys, one bulky, one tall, and another short; the tall one had a weapon. This could get messy.

"Drop this now, and you can still walk away," Alex said with as much menace he could pour into a sentence.

But it just seemed to deflect off the machismo of the three knuckleheads. And to make matters worse, the tall guy, with the rod in his hand, charged at him with the metal weapon held above his head. As he reached within striking distance, he brought the rod straight down on Alex's head. Alex side-stepped the hit, pivoting on his right foot. He caught hold of the back of the assailant mid-pivot and in one swooping motion, egged him on his trajectory to the side of the car. The tall guy rammed into the metal frame of the car door and dented it. As he recoiled from the hit to his head, Alex grabbed his right hand, locked it in his armpit, and brought down his hands in a classic karate chop to the hands holding the rod. It clattered onto the street, accompanied by a scream of pain.

A flash of red out of the corner of his eyes caught his attention. The second friend, the short one, came at him with a wide right hook. Alex ducked under the punch and thrust his right elbow into the guy's groin. The hit connected, and the short guy crumbled into a heap of meat, wailing in pain. Alex swung his foot into a sharp kick to the ribs of the man writhing on the ground as he surveyed the scene. The leader hung back, his eyes wide.

Alex took a step towards him, when something big rammed into him in full force. His feet went flying off the ground as he was propelled backwards to the car and pinned to it. The tall guy was back on his feet holding Alex up to the car. The leader noticed the opportunity and closed in on him. Alex struggled to break the vice-like grip on his body. If they double teamed him, he was a dead man. His hands wriggled for more room and caught hold of the tall guy's finger. Without wasting any time, Alex twisted it back until he heard a satisfying crack. The tall guy screamed in agony, letting Alex go.

The moment his feet landed on the ground, he pivoted and checked for the leader, charging at him. The violence seemed to have put the brakes on him. *Good. Time to turn it up a notch.*

Alex circled the heavy man, like a predator, waiting to strike. adrenaline coursing through his veins; his senses at peak.

"You really messed up, *boy*," Alex said, drawing out the last word. His right foot surged forward like a battering ram, crashing into the side of the heavy man's head. The lights went out of his eyes in an instant as he collapsed onto the hard asphalt.

Alex fixed the leader in a hard stare. "Whaddya waiting for? Wanna run back to mommy and cry now?"

The taunt hit where it was supposed to, the sweet spot between patriarchy and machismo. There was no way he was going back up now. It was a matter of his honour now. *Stupid Fuck!*

The bulky leader minced forward, one step at a time. He tried a left jab which Alex slipped easily. Alex stayed light on his feet, circling the assailant, waiting for a mistake. A couple more missed jabs, and the guy lost patience. *Typical.* He swung at Alex with a huge right cross, his entire body weight behind it. *Big mistake.* Alex stepped inside the swing, guarding his face against the cross with his left hand, bent at the elbow and up close to his face. He absorbed the punch with his left hand, straightened it and locked the assailant's punching arm under his. Without skipping a beat, Alex opened his right palm and thrust it up at the man's nostrils. A sickening crunch followed by an eruption of blood from the man's nose told him that it did the trick. The nasal bone had broken and pushed back into the skull. Alex let go of the man, and he fell to his knees, holding his nose, bewildered by the blood.

Alex scanned the street up and down. Nothing. He hadn't attracted any attention and he wanted to keep it like that. Neither did he want eyewitnesses of him leaving the scene with Payal. Alex rushed back to his car, and broke off the long, metal antenna on top.

The leader was still on his knees, dazed by the blood on his hands. The tall guy was still out cold and the short one writhing in pain. Alex closed the distance to the leader in a few steps and before he could react, clamped his hand over his mouth. With clinical efficiency, he thrust the strong end of the antenna in between the ribs, puncturing the lungs; multiple times. The man squirmed his hands, struggling to break free. Without wasting any time, Alex thrust the bloody antenna into the man's neck. It pierced its way through the jugular, all the way into the vocal cord and out the other side. Blood sprayed out like water from a fire hydrant. He quickly repeated the same with the other two on the ground. With the punctured lungs and jugular, they would die quickly. And the punctured vocal cords made sure they did that silently.

There was blood everywhere. Blood dripped from his face onto his clothes, which were already soaked with blood. He needed to change and get out of the scene as soon as possible. Alex rushed towards the car to get a change of clothes from the back seat, but his stride was cut short by a white, pallid face looking out from inside the car. Eyes white as a ghost and mouth agape. Payal was wide awake and terrified of what she had seen. He must have miscalculated the dosage of the sedative.

It was not what he would have preferred, but there was no other choice. Alex picked up the metal rod from the ground. In one smooth motion, he opened the passenger side door and swung the rod at her head. It connected and knocked her out instantly. Blood trickled down the side of her head as she sunk back into the seat.

He leaned on the car to catch his breath. This was supposed to be a smooth exit, but it went south quickly. But there was still time to make it right. Or as right as it can be made now.

Alex pulled out a few tissues from the box on the car's dash and wiped his face and hands off the blood. He circled to the far side of the car and stripped down to his underwear, leaving the bloody clothes on the floor. The bag on the back seat was stuffed with his clothes. He picked up a clean pair of shirt and pants and changed into them.

Payal was still unconscious from the whack to the head. Alex tied her up, taped her mouth, and slung her over his shoulders. He shoved her into the trunk of the car, tied her up, and covered her with a black cloth. The three idiots laid motionless in their puddles of blood. He had to get out of there before somebody spotted him or his car.

Alex climbed into the car and pulled out of the deserted side road, leaving the scene of carnage behind him. He recited a small prayer to the Holy Trinity for getting him through this ordeal safe and sound. As he rounded the corner to get into the main road, he saw a police jeep parked down the road. His heart jumped up into his throat as he took his foot off the pedal on instinct. He hated Murphy's law that very second. But there was no other way around it. He can't turn back now; it was as good as yelling out that he was guilty. He placed his foot back on the accelerator.

As he neared the police jeep, a policeman lumbered onto the road from behind the jeep and hailed him down.

Alex slowed down and stopped next to the policeman. "Yes, officer?" Alex asked, conjuring up the sweetest smile he could.

"What are you doing here so late?" The policeman stroked the thick moustache on his full face.

"Just came out of the club over there, Sir. Got a call from home asking me to come fast."

The policeman leaned on the open window and said, "Son, I have seen punks like you for ten years. And have heard all variations of that excuse you just said. So, cut the crap and show me your papers."

Alex pulled out a thousand rupee note from his pocket and held it between his fingers. "Is this paper enough? I'm in a little hurry."

The policeman noticed the dent on the side, and narrowed his eyes.

"Damn, bikers. One of them banged into me on the side at a signal," Alex complained, still holding the thousand rupees note up.

The policeman studied him long and hard, his brows scrunched together.

Alex drummed the fingers on his other hand on the steering wheel, and controlled his breath. Though he had wiped down the car briefly, it would not pass a thorough check. And then there was Payal in the trunk.

After ten seconds, which felt like an eternity, the policeman caved in and snatched the thousand rupees note from Alex's hand.

"Thank you, Sir," Alex said with a smile.

The policeman offered him an imperceptible nod as acknowledgement as Alex shifted gears into the first and pulled away. He was just accelerating enough to shift out of first, when the policeman hailed him from behind. Alex stopped the car and turned back to see the policeman raising his arm and walking towards the car.

What now? Alex thought. Putting his hands inside his bag, he searched until his hands met the cold steel of the knife. Grabbing the handle of the knife, he unlocked the door and stuck his head out. The policeman went straight for the trunk of the car. Alex tightened his grip on the knife's handle and stepped out of the car, slowly making his way to the back of the car.

The policeman grabbed the handle of the trunk door and shoved it down. It closed with a click. "Your trunk was not locked," the policeman said.

Alex hid the knife behind his hand and thanked the policeman profusely. He took a deep breath as the policeman waddled his way back to his jeep. *That was close.*

Prateek

Saturday, December 2, 1995

*Religion is a looking glass. When you put that on,
you see Hindus, Muslims, and Christians. Take a step back,
throw away the glasses and look again; you start to see people.*

Their waiter was someone who believed in the conservation of energy. Not the law of Physics, but the conservation of his own energy. With the least number of movements possible, he shuffled over to their table and stood, with half-open eyes, awaiting their order. His short, stubby nose was grossly inadequate on his full face. Drops of perspiration decorated the generous space between his nose and slender lips. The bright red necktie strained under the weight of his generous under-chin as he sputtered out the specials of the day.

Amrita's eyebrows scrunched together in concentration but relaxed half-way through the waiter's breathless rant. She grabbed a fork from the table and play-acted stabbing herself in the stomach. Manas focused on the waiter, and nodded his head at all the right moments.

Manas loved deciphering things which confounded an average brain. At the end of the breathless chant, the waiter reverted to his low-energy consumption mode, and shuffled back with a promise to come back for the order.

Manas turned to the table with a snigger and translated the series of sounds the waiter just made. Amrita's mouth formed a perfect 'O' as Manas rattled the specials, one by one.

"One of these days, you've got to tell me how you do that," said Amrita, her eyes wide.

Manas fish hooked his eyebrow and shrugged his shoulders. "Well…" he paused, "It's a gift, you know. I would have taught you this, but I'm not sure you meet the pre-requisite."

"Oh, really?" Amrita slapped the top of Manas' head. "And what might that be, your highness?"

"Nothing much. It's just basically just one rule. You gotta be *awesome*, like me."

"Okay, Mr. Awesome. Then why did you take four months to ask me out?" Amrita's teeth gleamed in a grin.

The cocky swagger Manas was swirling in, shrivelled up as he broke into an embarrassed smile, "I…I was making you sweat." He grinned like a sheep.

"Yeah, right…" Amrita rolled her eyes and bit her lips to stifle a smile. "Let's order then." Amrita scanned the hotel for the waiter and gestured him to come over.

"You?" Manas asked Prateek.

"Na…not really hungry. Will go in half on a cup of coffee with you."

Manas shrugged in a 'have-it-your-own-way' manner as he turned back to Amrita.

The waiter dragged himself over to the table and planted himself on the floor with a pen and a slip of paper in his hand; almost like he was annoyed at the kids who made him spend energy he was trying to conserve.

"One Chicken Biriyani, a Chicken Tikka Masala, and three Rotis." Manas counted off the items on his fingers.

Amrita took a break from memorising the menu to look up, and said, "And two coffees."

The waiter nodded and headed off to the kitchen to relay the order, leaving Manas, Amrita and the misfit. Prateek browsed the colourful marquee of vehicles through the half-open window. *What am I doing here?* Manas and Amrita talked in hushed tones, barely even looking in his direction. *Third wheel.*

"…lecherous stares. Sometimes it's just overwhelming." Amrita's eyes were glassier than usual.

Prateek sharpened his ears, and focused on the conversation. He had never seen Amrita so vulnerable. She was this bold, effervescent girl who hung out with more boys than girls. He had never seen her in this light.

"Maybe you wanna take it as a compliment. Men appreciate beauty," said Manas, with a wan smile.

Amrita shook her head. "There is a difference, Manas. No matter how hard you hide it, you can see the intentions in their eyes," Amrita's voice choked, "The world is so unfair."

Prateek pursed his lips, and studied the sky-blue denim, hugging Amrita's long legs. *You dress like a whore, you get treated like a whore.*

Manas wrinkled his forehead, and held Amrita's hand. "I know, but this is our world, and sometimes we have to play by the rules and keep fighting the fight."

"What rules, Manas? Girls should not wear anything but *saree* and *churidars*? Should they not talk to boys? And God forbid, if someone is doing these things, they must be 'easy.' I'm tired of these rules, Manas. Is it a big sin to want to look good? I wear nice clothes for me, and my confidence."

Who are you kidding? You wear them to get attention. Prateek reached for a toothpick and started digging around in his mouth.

"I'm just as vulnerable as the next girl. Just because I care less for the social constructs or rules as you call them, doesn't mean I'm made of stone," Amrita dipped her eyes and looked at her hands, intertwined with Manas, "Sometimes, I can practically see them undressing me with their eyes as I approach, mentally raping me over and over. And when I'm close enough, the catcalling starts."

"We have an entire generation who grew up on catcalling, stalking heroes of Bollywood who finally got the girl. Bollywood might have moved on, but the social acceptance that it gave for eve-teasing hasn't. But I think it'll also change, slowly."

"It still doesn't help me, sitting here and now." A single teardrop meandered its way around her slender nose.

Manas circled his arms around her, tentatively, and she leaned into him.

Prateek turned away, disgusted. *Slut.*

The waiter hobbled towards them, the dishes precariously balanced on his forearm. Manas and Amrita parted from their embrace. Amrita shuffled through her white handbag with tangerine polka dots until she found her hand kerchief. She wiped her face, careful not to smear her mascara. And with a last sniffle, she composed herself into the Amrita Prateek knew.

The waiter deftly retrieved all the dishes, spread them across the table, and cleared the area. Manas and Amrita moved on to happier subjects as they finished their meal. Prateek followed the rectangular patch of light, which came in through the open window, slowly creeping up to his feet, warming them up.

At the end of their meal, Amrita rose to her feet, waved goodbye to Manas, and strode off, her head held high, and her shield back up. Prateek observed the men around her leering at her and looked away, disgusted. Maybe she was telling the truth...or maybe she deserves it.

~

Prateek scoured the newspaper, munching on some onion pakoda Manas' mother made for them, for anything related to The Butcher. He had been extra careful in following the news since a couple of days ago, a headline caught his attention. It said the CBI was 'tightening the noose'— whatever that meant.

Manas lay flat on his bed, staring at the ceiling. Prateek could literally see his brain working, every cog turning at the right time, burrowing ridges along his forehead.

Suddenly, he rose to a sitting position, doing somewhat of an abdominal crunch and said, "We need to talk."

Prateek nodded. He knew this was coming.

"We need to—or rather you need to slow down, or this will not end well, Prateek."

Prateek flashed a wide grin. "As long as you are—"

"Cut the crap, Prateek. I'm serious, and I'm not talking about the CBI closing in on us. I'm worried about a much bigger problem," Manas rose to his feet and paced up and down the room, "You."

"Lately, we are getting frivolous in our...endeavours. I'm saying we because a part of the responsibility lies with me. After all, I did agree to go along with it. But the instigator has always been you. It used to take a lot more to make you want to kill somebody, man."

"No, that's not t—"

"I am not done," Manas cut in, "When we started out, we did it because the dice were loaded in favour of the wicked, and we were just trying to tilt the balance, make the world a better place, one grain of sand at a time." He stopped the incessant up and down movement and glanced at Prateek. There was pain and anger in his eyes. "Lately, I'm struggling to find a meaning, man. A purpose to what we are doing."

"Oh, come on. Even now, we only kill people who I think...we think deserve it."

"That's just it, isn't it? Who you think or I think? It kinda got me thinking, you know? People have different moral compasses, which point in different directions, and at different intensities. How do we know for sure that what we are doing is right? How do you even define 'right'?" Manas sat down on the bed and leaned forward, his gaze glued to the abstract designs on the floor. "Take you and me for example. We had our moral compasses aligned when we started out. But I can feel them drifting apart. When you said we should do something about that prominent eve-teaser, I went along with it. Did I think it was necessary to kill him? No. But still, I went along because I could convince myself that the world was a better place without him. When you told me about the guy who stole from the temple coffer, I was on the fence. I knew what he did was technically wrong, but did removing him from the world make it a better place? No. He probably stole from the coffers to feed his children. But I went along with it, convincing myself that stealing is bad. I know it sounds flimsy, but I was grabbing at straws to keep my sanity."

"But wasn't he taking it away from the poor that the money from the coffers benefits?" Prateek felt his breath becoming short and fast.

Manas shook his head in disappointment. "We can argue all day about how he himself was poor or how the money from the coffers doesn't go to the poor. But that's not what I want to do." Manas picked up the crumbled bed sheet and started folding it.

"Do you know when it really hit me? Remember when you came up to me, veins all popping, blind rage in your eyes, and explained how you want to kill a guy who displaced a *Murti*? A *Murti* which just popped up one day on the side of the road, and people started worshipping it. He didn't even throw it away or something like that. He just moved it to a place where it became less of a nuisance to the occupants of the street. But you saw it as a Muslim trying to disrupt the Hindu way of life. Whichever way I spun it, I could never see how killing that guy would make the world a better place. Despite that, you somehow convinced me to go along with it." The ends of the sheet were slipping from Manas' hands, again and again. He hurled the bed sheet into the corner for the room. "I was hand twisted into following your compass when mine screamed bloody murder."

"He had no right to touch the deity." Prateek's eyes darkened.

"You are just not getting it, are you?" Manas leapt to his feet, "Your moral compass said he deserved to die; mine didn't. You even said you wanted to kill a guy who spat on the street. Spat on the street, Prateek. If that is your criteria, you would be killing half the population."

"If we don't respect our country, then who will? The country which nurtured you, gave you everything you have, and you spit on it?"

"I'm not saying it's okay to spit on the streets. But is it serious enough to kill a guy? Thankfully, I nipped that in its bud. But that is more the exception than the rule. Nowadays, we do things you want; what you feel is right. I feel like I'm losing control over my free will." He started pacing the room again. "And you....I'm telling this as your best friend...not just because of this incident, but many...Religion is a looking glass. When you put that on, you see Hindus, Muslims, and Christians. Take a step back, throw away the glasses and look again; you start to see people."

Prateek studied the small crevices between his nails. He knew better than to continue this discussion. This has always been the sore point between them. Manas lived in a utopia where there was no religion, no countries, and peace grew on trees. In the real world, religion unites people. Christians united across Europe, against the Muslim invasion, for the Crusades. He just wished Hindus showed the same unity when they were faced with the same situation. How different the country would have been?

A ring from Manas' mobile phone interrupted his thoughts.

Manas stepped out of the room, lingering at the door for a second. "Hey, Amrita…"

It's that whore again. What does Manas see in her anyway? She drinks, smokes, and goes clubbing dressed like a whore. Might as well be a whore. Manas deserved so much better.

Manas came back into the room, closing the door behind him.

Prateek wanted to diffuse the situation. "Amrita?" he asked, with a wry smile on his face, "What does she want? Oh, wait. I know that. You."

There was a suspicious line at the corner of Manas' mouth, a hint of a smile. "She just wanted to ask if I want to go to a club with her this weekend."

Prateek swallowed hard. "You guys slept together yet?"

"I wish," said Manas, chuckling, "Not that kind of girl."

"Not what it looks to me," Prateek muttered under his breath, which came out to be a little louder than he intended. He quickly peeked at Manas' face to see if he heard that. Too late.

"Do you have a problem with her?" Manas asked, folding his arms, taking up a wide stance.

Prateek let out a deep sigh, and said, "No, no. It's just that...never mind."

"Spill it."

"Hmmm…I feel she is not right for you."

Manas' eyebrows gathered. "Explain," he enunciated the word with crystal clarity.

"She is not a good girl, Manas. She drinks, smokes, and has a blatant disregard for our culture."

Manas' nostrils flared, and lips pulled back, baring his teeth. "To hell with your damn culture. Just what is this Indian culture you are so proud of? Is it the culture of suppression of basic human desires? A society that demonises sex and makes it taboo until the point where the sexual frustration explodes into a culture of rape? Or is it the culture of nauseating patriarchy? A culture where the majority of women don't even call their husbands by name. A culture where they are reduced to meek caretakers of the home."

Prateek dunked the last pakoda in the green chutney and gobbled it up. "The glorious Indian culture has been well documented in the ancient books, and it has none of what you just said."

"All our ancient scriptures have sex as an ever-prevalent theme, all our literature talks about liquor and hookah. Hell, Kamasutra came from India."

"But she is a girl, Manas. She is supposed to be pure. They are not supposed to drink and parade around promiscuously. That's the curse of the western culture creeping into ours."

"Oh, so Indian men can drink, smoke, sleep around, and it's all 'approved' by the Indian culture, but women should stay inside and cook?"

Prateek felt the tingling of sweat forming on his arms, and the automatic grinding of his teeth. "You're missing the point. India has a rich cultural heritage, and anybody who disrespects that is guilty in my mind. The man who spat on the street, he spat on our mother nation. Would you stand by and let someone spit on your mother? Amrita smokes, drinks, and goes partying where she can run her loose morals amok. And that's worse than spitting on your mother."

Manas stopped mid-step and considered Prateek, with a furrow between his brows. "You wanted to kill the man who spat on the street."

Prateek rubbed the inside of his thumb with the index finger. "You have no idea how much."

Manas stared down Prateek for a long time. The faint hum of the ceiling fan dominated the room.

"Don't you dare," he said as he stormed out of the room, slamming the door so hard that it shook from its hinges.

Nasir

Saturday, April 26, 2014

Silence has always been a companion of death, across the world. Whether it was eerie or peaceful was always left to the beholder of the experience.

The night was on its dying gasp, giving birth to a new day. The early birds started to announce their presence with a chirp here, and there. Nasir stood rooted to the ground in front of a tall, gritty metal gate guarding a verdant sprawl of 54 acres in the eastern edge of Malabar Hills. Pockmarks of rust detailed the fading alabaster white paint on the gate. A sign that read "This is Holy Land. Do not spit" hung on the gate. A couple of men, dressed in pure white robes and trousers complete with a white *pagdi*, untangled the chain keeping the gate closed.

In the wee hours of the night, Nasir had gotten the news of The Artist striking again. He had promptly woken up the team and caught the earliest flight to Mumbai. He was still trying to come to terms with what had happened. It was unlike The Artist to make his appearance so frequently. Nasir fully expected him to go into hibernation after his double kill.

The loud clatter of metal on metal grabbed back his attention to what was in front of him. The gates swung open with a creak.

Salim approached Nasir from behind. "So...we are going in?"

"Well, what do you think?" Nasir said, waving his hands to the open gates.

"The DGP did tell us to wait."

"His Highness can get up at his own pace, pull on his stiff uniform, have a quick breakfast, and make his appearance whenever he damn well pleases," said Nasir, marching towards the open gates, "We didn't fly out in the middle of the night to wait for anyone. You know how important time is."

People from faiths other than Zoroastrianism were strongly discouraged from entering the compound of Dakhma, The Tower of Silence. He had rung up half of Mumbai from the slumbers of early morning sleep to secure the permission to enter the final resting place of Parsis. Even then, it was restricted- no vehicles, just Nasir and his team, along with two

Parsi policemen. The white-robed gentlemen were *khandias*, the resident caretakers of the place.

One of the two *khandias* entered a decrepit two-roomed quarters at the foot of the hill while the other waited for them with a disarming smile on his face.

Nasir led the team up the slope and shook the hands of the gentleman. "I know it's early, but thanks a lot for helping us this morning. What should I call you?"

"Kersi Kohla," said the *khandia*, "You can call me Kersi. Try to keep your voice down," he whispered as he started up a narrow path up the hill.

They followed Kersi up the slope in a single file, with Nasir leading them. The eastern sky had begun to sliver and shine by now. But not much made it through the dense vegetation that grew all around them. Nobody uttered a word. A cold sense of calm descended upon them.

Silence has always been a companion of death across the world. Whether it was eerie or peaceful was always left to the beholder of the experience. Humans were always afraid of death and the places associated with it, making up stories which their volatile minds conjured. Even here, wind rustling through the trees or an out-of-place shadow is enough to create ghost stories.

Purity, both physical and spiritual, is a concept Zoroastrians hold close to their hearts. And that extends to death as well. They do not want to desecrate the four elements of the world - air, water, earth, and fire - with their dead. That ruled out cremation, burial at sea, or a grave. In one final act of charity, they leave their dead in elevated solid granite platforms open to the sun. The birds of the flesh, like vultures, will strip the flesh from the body in a few hours, and then the *nussesalars* will move the skeletons into a central pit designed for this purpose.

If you face it head-on, the chilling images of vultures tearing out flesh from human bodies might disconcert you. But take a side turn and really see it, and you will appreciate the thought behind it. Man, who came from nature, is returning to nature, an almost poetic end to life. There was also equality in the ritual; every division of class, and wealth disappeared. There were no fancy graves or elaborate cremation, just a humbling realisation that none of that matters when you move on from this life.

Nasir scanned the surroundings as a faint putrid smell wafted up his nose.

Kersi turned around and whispered as if he read Nasir's mind, "No vultures nowadays. So, the bodies, they...they just decompose or dry out.

We have kept concentrated mixtures of flowers in several pots, but it's quite useless. We, *khandias*, hardly notice nowadays. You guys got the masks?"

Nasir nodded as he strapped on a mask, and saw that the others had done the same. Their destination, a grey, granite tower, emerged from in between the foliage.

"Kersi, will you be guiding us inside the Tower of Silence, or will a *nussesalar* join us?"

"Nussesalar?" Sonam asked, tilting her head to a side.

"Well, we *khandias* carry the body up until the *Dakhma* and *nussesalars* take them in and handle the rest of the process," Kersi explained. He faced Nasir and continued, "Nowadays, the boundary is quite blurry. I can guide you inside as well."

Nasir straightened up and gestured for his team to gather around. "You know the drill, Sonam. The crime scene is up the Tower of Silence. Kersi will guide us there.." Nasir dipped his head slightly towards Kersi. "Kersi, once you show us the body, do you need to stay there? Or can you help Avinash and Salim do a perimeter check?"

Kersi glanced at Avinash and Salim with a nod.

"Salim, Avinash, if you can spare Akshay after the initial recce, I would like him to connect with the local police and get as much information about this as possible."

And with that final piece of instruction, Sonam and Nasir donned the protective gear and made their way up the stairs to the top of the tower, with Kersi in the lead. He opened the door at the top of the stairs, and what lay beyond was difficult to take in, even for professionals like Nasir and Sonam.

Three layers of concentric slabs were laid out around a central pit. A few bodies lay on the slabs in varying stages of decay and dehydration. Kersi had told them on the way up the stairs about how they have installed solar panels to dry out the body in the absence of vultures. But even then, the *khandiyas* had to move the body multiple times to make sure the body dehydrated uniformly. A process that used to take a few hours with the vultures now took days. It was worse during the monsoons.

But the body they wanted to find wasn't hard to find; it was off to the left of the entrance, close to the wall.

The body sprawled on its back; legs raised and resting on the wall, almost perpendicular to the body. The left leg partially crossed over the right in a subtle, sexy way. The head turned slightly to the left, as if she were monitoring the entrance to the *dakhma*. Both arms rested on the ground, above the head, facing upwards, like a sleeping baby.

The rosy fingers of dawn clawed their way up the pale skies. Sonam veered off to cordon off an area around the body as Nasir inched closer. Kersi took his leave.

The theme of the 'artwork' was red. The blood red lingerie on the body stood out in a grimy concrete structure. As he got closer, he saw the translucent nylon strings hooked to nails on the wall, holding the body in position. The red high heel on her right leg was nailed to the wall with the nylon string holding the left leg in place over the right. Another string held the knee in place; a subtle touch to make the body position seem more natural. Red stockings extended from the tip of her legs all the way down to her mid-thighs, where it was connected to a garter belt; the red suspenders wound its way through her dusky skin like rills of blood. The bra was so inadequate that her ample bosoms jutted out in a massive cleavage.

Death had truly conquered her body, draining all the blood leaving a pale ghost-like aura to the body. A few long incisions on her chest broke the smooth exposed skin of the victim. Dark, purple bruises adorned her neck, like a necklace. The eyes were hazy, almost white; it, along with the grisly environment, gave her a sinister presence. Chills shot down Nasir's spine as he averted eye contact.

The Artist had regressed to his old ways. Nasir was toying with the thought that The Artist was somehow evolving by the way he deviated from the pattern, but this crushed it and flicked it into an unused corner of his mind. In its place, another thought rose up. The deviations witnessed in Amrita, and Teresa became all the more significant. Nasir was convinced that they held the key to finding The Artist.

Sonam flew around the body like a butterfly flapping around a flower; only she was clicking photographs and bagging evidence instead of sucking on nectar. She was the complete package; smart, beautiful, and funny. Many times, he had caught her peering at him from behind thick glasses; her eyes filled with admiration. He could not but wonder if there was something more than an admiration in those stolen glances. But such thoughts were brushed aside as soon as they cropped up. Even though he would have loved it, why would a 26-year-old want to be with a 40-year-old divorcee?

Sonam froze mid-step on her way around the body and turned her head towards him, like a gazelle perking up her head when she heard the predator. Nasir quickly averted his eyes and studied the slabs laid on in concentric circles around him.

"Sir..." her small true voice called him.

Nasir composed his face as best as he could and met her gaze. "Yes, you done?"

Sonam nodded affirmatively. "...There are round ovular bruises on the anterior and lateral neck. Preliminary inspection suggests broken Hyoid bone. Manual strangulation must be the cause of death. Let the medical examiner confirm it. Defensive marks on her hands indicate a rape."

Nasir moved closer to the body and knelt beside it. The bruises on the victim's neck were peculiar. "He strangled her with one hand," Nasir exclaimed. "That's a first, isn't it? He is growing confident."

"Yes, there are four oval bruises on the left side and one on the right," Sonam said, as she knelt close to Nasir and examined the neck again. "Looks like he is left-handed."

Nasir redistributed his weight on both his legs and leaned back into a crouch. "Sure looks like it. It takes quite a bit of force to strangle a person, and unless he is ambidextrous, he must have used his strong hand." He checked the scruff of the neck and hair. "There is no debris on her back side."

Sonam gawked at him with a slight tilt of her head.

Nasir climbed to his feet, straightening his old back. "She wasn't raped and killed here in the Tower of Silence, or in the woods surrounding it. No debris matches either of those places. Maybe he used his car or someplace else. That is our crime scene. I doubt we will get much from here except for the body."

They went through the motions to clear out the grid space around the body, bagged a few samples from the body and climbed down the stairs. Avinash and Salim leaned against a nearby tree in a heated discussion. Kersi looked on with interest.

Nasir strode over to them and asked, "Anything interesting?"

Both of them stopped mid-sentence, and whipped their bodies into a tight salute.

Nasir acknowledged them with a slight nod. Salute was a sign of respect, not a statutory mandate. And gestures of respect should be used sparingly. But these two were policemen through and through.

Salim smiled a strange little smile. "There are three things we should be thankful for," he said, as he started counting them off on his fingers, "One. The Parsis for keeping this place hush-hush. No one comes around here and hence no contamination. Two. You. 'Cause you made sure we were the first on the scene. And Three. Spontaneous Mumbai rains."

Nasir stepped closer and let the words tumble out of him. "So, you did find something!"

Salim bounced from foot to foot. "Yes, we did. We got his footprints in the wet mud and it was leading up and back from the tower."

"Could it be one of these guys?" Nasir pointed towards Kersi.

"No, sir." Kersi shook his head. Nasir was afraid it would fly off his neck. "None of us wear boots. We are all sandal-kinda-guys."

The barrel which made up his chest grew bigger. "And the best thing is, the footprints were clear enough to take the five toe length measurements."

"That's amazing," Nasir said. "And?"

"He is six feet two inches, plus or minus two inches." Salim's high, strong cheek bones spread out into a wide grin.

"Awesome. That puts him in the narrow two percent of the population." Sonam beamed. "But how?"

"Analytics." Nasir ran his hands over the smoothly-shaven chin. "There was a study done by the Forensic Department of Kasturba Medical College back in 2012. It proposed a predictive model to calculate the height of a person from the footprint measurements. We just took it and enhanced the model with a newer analytical model to improve the accuracy." He faced Salim. "You used the model for males, right?"

Salim nodded in agreement.

"Perfect." Nasir slapped both Avinash and Salim on their backs. Even though they had an idea that The Artist was a big man, this was more specific. Something they could use to filter out suspects.

"Wait...We got more," said Avinash, with all the swagger in the world. "We measured the depth of the impression. It was too deep for a man of his height and weight. And there were no other footprints." He pulled out a kerchief from his pocket, unfurled, and folded it back, nice and neat. "It's obvious that the girl was not murdered here. He carried her in there."

Sonam strutted up to Avinash with a dead-pan face, and placed a hand on his back. "Yeah...about that. We kinda figured that out already."

Salim brushed off Sonam's hand off his friend's back, and scowled at her. "Anyway, what did our guy leave for us this time? Show me the photographs."

Sonam bit her lip to stifle the grin as she pulled out the camera from her bag. She turned it on and scrolled through the photos she took on the on-camera display. Avinash and Salim huddled around her to inspect them.

"This was an easy one," said Nasir. "Even I recognise the 'Girl in Red' from *The Matrix*"

Kersi led the way back with the rest of the entourage in tow. At the foot of the hill, he bid farewell, and Nasir thanked him again for all the help; the rest continued down and out of the compound.

A bunch of policemen gathered in front of the gate, with the DGP in the middle. Akshay, and the two Parsi policemen who had accompanied them were already part of the huddle. When Akshay saw them coming out of the compound, he broke off from the crowd and joined Nasir.

"Ah...cosying up to the DGP, I see." Nasir arched his eyebrows to accentuate the friendly jab.

"Oh, come on, cut it out. I've smoothed things over with the DGP. All you need to do is smile, shake his hand, and not antagonise him further."

"Ha-ha. All right. Let's go meet His Highness," Nasir said.

Abhay Kurundkar was a balding man, which made his small face smaller than what it actually is. The thick moustache seemed stifled by the large nose and wide lips. The Director General of Police leaned on his bullet-proof black Scorpio, a Ray-Ban shades hung from his belt.

The crowd of policemen parted to give way for Nasir as he strode up to the DGP, and shook his hands and exchanged pleasantries.

"Thanks a lot for the support Mumbai police have given us. Did you get details about the victim? I know it is still early, but as I told you before, it is really important to get as much information as soon as possible. The killer is still at large, and we both do not want him to strike again."

Abhay Kurundkar gestured to a policeman behind him, who promptly came forward and recited excerpts from a report in his hand. "Victim's name was Payal Seth, only daughter. A student of Sir J.J. College of Architecture. Last known location is Blue Frog, according to her parents' statement. Their statement says that she went over there to meet a few of her friends."

"I'll be damned if the kid was telling the truth," said Abhay Kurundkar, "Did we check with her friends?"

"We had to wake up a lot of people early in the morning, but none of her usual crowd was with her last night. They all were soundly asleep at home, or at the hostel. A couple of friends did tell us that they saw her talking to some guy they didn't recognise at noon. We will be calling them to the office to get a sketch done. From what we have gathered from her friends, she has a large digital footprint spread across a multitude of social media platforms. And she spent quite a lot of time online, either on her mobile or on her computer."

"Kids these days, I tell you." Abhay Kurundkar shook his head in disapproval. "We will let you know as soon as we know more, Akshay."

Nasir summoned a ghost of a smile. "Thank you again for all the support." And they parted with a final handshake, hoping they would never have to meet again. Nasir marched towards the jeep with the rest of the team following him.

"Blue Frog?" asked Akshay.

Nasir replied with a curt nod and marched to the jeep.

"Always wanted to go clubbing with you guys," Avinash whispered to the rest to the team, making devil horns with his fingers.

Salim covered his face with his palm, shaking his head, and followed Nasir.

~

The Jeep turned into the lane leading to Blue Frog, and stopped at a sundry group of civilians and policemen gathered on one side of the road. Nasir ran his hands over his balding head and swept off the beads of perspiration on them. There was something in his gut screaming at him to sit up and take notice. Without asking, Akshay swung close to the crowd, stuck out his neck through the window and asked, "What's going on here?"

"Some guys got whacked," a kid who was barely out of his teens replied. He was giddy with excitement.

Nasir believed in something he called an 'Ether Tranquillity' theory. Ether was the fabric which was interwoven through every living and non-living thing in the universe. It is the air we breathe, the tea we drink, and even in the woman we make love to. In equilibrium, Ether is as calm as a pristine lake in the wee hours of the morning. Good deeds slide off the surface of Ether, without breaking water. But evil deeds are messy. They make a ripple, a splash, a wave—depending on how evil the act is.

Once the Ether is turbulent, it makes it harder for good deeds to slide off, but it makes evil deeds a lot easier to commit. Many a time, there will be ripples connected by a single source moving about in the Ether, stirring it up in multiple places. Therefore, if left unchecked, evil has a habit of snowballing through Ether and ending up in total and complete annihilation.

Herein comes the 'Enforcers,' like him, who preserve the Ether and always struggle to keep the ripples in check. He had realised long before that it was the source of the ripples rather than the ripples themselves that he had to take care of. If he makes a few ripples himself along the way, so be it; you can't catch the fish without muddying up the water. These 'whacked' guys sure caused a ripple, and it had to come from the same source."

"Akshay, you take Sonam and head on over to the Blue Frog. I want every minute of last night reviewed. Salim, Avinash, you're with me."

And with that, Nasir stepped out of the jeep and elbowed his way through the crowd to the inner periphery. He whipped out his badge and flashed it at the policeman as he ducked under the yellow tape and onto the clearing in the middle. There were three bodies scattered over a small area, covered with white sheets; blood seeped through them in big red splotches.

A few policemen stood guard, keeping the crowd at bay, swatting away the selfie-clickers, and making way for the imminent ambulance. An older and larger policeman stood in the middle, obviously in charge. His eyes peered from a face pockmarked by scars, brimming with suspicion. He noticed Nasir's incursion and walked over to him, stepping over two out of three bodies along the way. The buttons on his shirt threatened to pop off from the strain his pot belly was putting them through.

Nasir handed him his badge. "Can I see the body?"

The policeman narrowed his already narrow eyes and inspected the badge. "CBI? Mumbai Police can handle this."

Nasir gritted his teeth, closed his eyes, and took a deep breath. When he opened his eyes, he saw Avinash jumping in front of him.

"*Arrey Baba*....This is your case, and we have no jurisdiction here," said Avinash, with a hand on the policeman's shoulder, "We just want to see the bodies, if it is not too much. I mean what harm can happen from us just seeing the bodies?"

The policeman regarded Avinash, and then Nasir for a few seconds, and then turned around and ordered the constable to remove the cloth covering the bodies.

Nasir nodded in the policeman's direction, acknowledging his favour, and stepped closer to the bodies. He knelt beside one of the closest bodies, a man, probably in his early twenties. A sky-blue shirt with blood all over it covered his torso. His nose was broken, dried blood covered his face. Nasir picked up a stick from the ground and pushed the head to the other side. There was a small puncture wound on both sides of his neck.

Nasir rose to his feet and checked the other bodies. They also had a similar story, except a few extra injuries here and there.

"Even if the assault was not intentional, their deaths were," Nasir said to Salim, "The killer punctured the lung and their jugular veins and left them to die. A slow and suffocating, but silent death."

"What are you thinking? Our guy?"

"Maybe. This sure has the malice I expect from him."

"Let's say this is our guy. What do you think happened here?"

"These three unlucky bastards were at the wrong place, wrong time. They must have seen our man kidnapping the girl, and tried to stop him."

"But Payal...our victim, went to meet The Artist. Why would he kidnap her? The girl would just walk out with him."

"Ah... All we know is that the victim went out to meet a mystery guy. Need not be The Artist. He could have just pick up the girl at random like the countless times he has done before."

Salim pressed his lips, draining them of its colour. He was about to counter when Avinash's booming voice cut him off.

"The blue shirt was the son of a local politician, or so they tell me." Avinash pointed behind his shoulders at the group of policemen he was chatting up. "Local politicians are dime a dozen. But what was interesting is that there was a vehicle standing next to the body."

"Eyewitness?" Nasir asked.

Avinash shook his head. "Rains. It rained yesterday and there was a dry patch right next to the bodies. They think it's a hatchback."

"Burn marks? From the tyres." Nasir scanned the asphalt all around. "He would be in a hurry to get away from the scene after murder"

Salim shook his head.

"Well, this was not his first rodeo, which brings me back to what we were discussing, Salim. Let's say we go with the assumption that these guys were killed by The Artist. There are two theories here. One. The Artist just seemed to be in the Blue Frog, saw the pretty girl, decided to take her home, and drugged or forced her into his car. These guys see him, and try to stop him. He kills them and gets away. Two. The victim came to the club to meet The Artist, he takes the girl back to his car, these guys mess with him or the girl, and he killed them."

"But it's not like him to make a mess," Avinash said.

"Have you seen the cold-blooded execution of these men? This was something The Artist could never have planned for. But when he was presented with the situation, he reacted with clinical efficiency and complete lack of apathy."

Nasir scanned the crowd, his gaze eventually settling on the policeman in charge, who was talking to another officer and occasionally glancing in his direction. After a brief animated exchange, they started towards him.

A thick moustache quivered on a full set of cheeks as the new policeman made his way towards Nasir. A slow and unsure gait, like putting one foot in front of the other, took tremendous effort.

"I couldn't help but overhear," the pot-bellied policeman who was in charge said, "You are Nasir Ali Khan, right?" He laughed uncomfortably. "I'm sorry if I was rude earlier, but you know how it is…Heard about the homicide this morning from a colleague. The girl was last seen at Blue

Frog around the corner, isn't it? Think there is a connection?" He didn't wait for an answer as he nodded his head towards the other policeman. "Anyways, Hemant here, was telling me about something. I thought you will be interested, but it's strictly off the record... ah... you know."

"So.... Um...." Hemant counted the ridges on his fingers. "OK. Last night when I was patrolling the area, I saw a car come out of this lane. I....I stopped the car as it was coming out of a No-Parking zone and...um...I asked for papers." His ears turned apple red. "He gave me an excuse for not having papers and handed me a....um...a thousand rupee note."

Nasir ran his hands over his forehead. Frustration bubbled deep inside his gut. This fool may have had The Artist in his sights, with the girl, and let him go for a thousand bucks. "When did this happen?"

"At around 11:30."

"Hatchback?"

"Yes, a black Swift, with a 'Baby on Board' sticker on the back. Actually, I remember the license plate."

A hint of a smile tugged at the corners of Nasir's mouth. "Really?"

The policeman scratched his head, looking downwards and said, "Umm....I have a photographic memory. When I stopped him again...to close the trunk of the car, I got a pretty good look at the number plate."

Look who turned out to be better than a lump of human waste in a uniform, Nasir thought. "Did you get a good look at him?"

"Um....It was night and his face was mostly in the shadows....But he was a tall guy, that I remember."

"Can you do me a favour and describe the guy, as much as you can to a sketch artist?...We can get the guy here, right Salim?"

Salim nodded as he fished out his mobile phone from his pocket. Hemant squirmed where he stood, fidgeting with his cap.

Nasir smiled broadly at Hemant, and rested a hand on his shoulder. "We will have a totally different story about how you came across the guy, don't worry."

"Thank you, Sir." Hemant flashed a relieved smile. "I'll be around here, and if you can't find me, just use the walkie." He began to turn away but stopped mid-turn. "There is one more thing...The car had a dent on the left-hand side. Don't know if it is important, but I thought I'll say."

Nasir's ears perked up. "Hold on. A dent? How big was it?"

"I don't know...um...may be ten centimetres across the diameter. Didn't look like a normal vehicle bump dent."

"Avinash, one of the guys had an injury smack on top of the head. Maybe?"

"Possible," said Avinash.

Nasir shook Hemant's hand with a big smile on his face. He almost forgave Hemant's misstep on the wrong side of the law. "Thanks a lot. We'll get you when the sketch artist comes."

A familiar rumble of a jeep turned his attention up the road, towards Blue Frog. Their jeep stopped close to the gathering, and Sonam shot out of it like a bullet, smiling like an idiot. Akshay was his usual muted self, but his eyes burned with excitement.

Before Nasir could say anything, Sonam blurted out, "The Artist, we found him."

"What?"

Akshay gave Sonam a look that said, "What the hell are you talking about?"

"Okay…" Sonam said, less enthusiastically. "We didn't find The Artist, but we got him on tape, though."

Nasir felt his stomach fall ten feet. He shook his head from side to side and faced Akshay. "Tell me."

"We scoured the footage and found Payal with a guy," Akshay said.

"The mystery friend," Salim said.

Akshay nodded and continued, "We didn't get a clear shot of his face. The lighting was dim, and the angle of the camera was bad, and he had a baseball cap on to hide his face. But he was a tall man...not bulky, but tall and well built. We have him leave with the girl at 11:14 pm from the club."

"So, we know the same guy who the victim went to meet took her to the car willingly," Nasir said. "But from here, there are two possibilities. Either this guy is *The Artist* and he killed these chaps and took the victim in the car, or *The Artist* jumped the mystery guy, killed him and his friends and made off with the victim."

Akshay surveyed the bodies strewn about the street. "None of them are as tall as the guy. I think we can rule out the latter."

Out of the blue, Sonam gasped. "This is that guy, Akshay. Look at the blue shirt," she said, pointing towards one of the bodies.

"Oh, yeah...this is that guy," Akshay said. He explained for the rest of the blank faces. "When we were searching the tapes, we found this guy harassing the victim."

"That settles it," said Nasir, "Unless by a freak of nature *The Artist* just happened to hail down the car of this mystery friend, who killed these guys, and happened to find the victim in the car, and then proceeded to kidnap her, we can safely assume our initial theory about the sequence of events is right."

"Car?" asked Sonam.

Nasir quickly caught them up on what transpired when they were at the Blue Frog.

"That's brilliant!" said Akshay, "Let me call up the office and put an alert out for the car."

"Salim, can you get the sketch artist over here?" asked Nasir.

A smile crept up Nasir's face, slow and steady. After years in pursuit, he finally felt like they were a step ahead of *The Artist*.

Anuradha

Saturday, April 26, 2014

You are the lone star in my hopelessly dark universe from the moment I met you. You gave me purpose; you gave me hope.

A drop of rain left a coin sized wet patch on the windscreen of her car. Anuradha's mild OCD made her reach for the wiper lever, but she stopped herself. That would only make it worse, smearing the water across the dust covered glass. The gloomy sky had been on the verge of breaking down into a downpour all week. The stifling humidity made everything a hundred times worse.

Shruti angled her head towards the skies, probably studying the clouds, from the comfort of the air-conditioned car. Manas used to pick her up every day, but today as Anuradha was about to end a very long day at office, Shruti called her up and complained that Manas didn't pick her up, again. It was the third time this week that she had to drive all the way across town and pick Shruti up from college. As far as she could remember, Manas hadn't missed picking Shruti up after college. And even in the rare occasions when he had to, he would call her and ask her to pick her up.

Anuradha pulled into the garage and turned off the ignition. The engine shuddered for a moment and died down into silence. Shruti dashed out of the vehicle the moment it stopped as if there was a ticking bomb in it. Maybe there was.

Anuradha took the narrow passageway along the side of the house to the front door, pausing midway only to hear the satisfying chirp of the car lock and then continuing. The first thing she saw as she entered the house was Manas glued to the television, Bella asleep at his feet. Shruti must have gone straight upstairs and found refuge in her room. Nowadays, she spent so much time in her room that Anuradha was afraid she would turn into a hermit.

Anuradha made her way to the key holder and hung the car keys. "I picked up Shruti." The car keys jingled on the holder. Bella raised her head, regarded Anuradha for a second, and went back to sleep. As expected, Manas was oblivious to the outside world.

The reporter sputtered out words like bullets out of an AK-47; no break, no pause for punctuation, just a continuous barrage of words about a serial killer - the latest 'breaking news'. Every single news channel in the country pounced on this story like hyenas on a carcass. Anuradha understood why the news channels were obsessed with it. But why Manas was obsessed about it was beyond her. He had not left the news channels ever since the news about the killer first surfaced.

In the beginning, he was subtle about it. He used to change the channel when somebody came and make small talk to mask his interest. But now he was way past it.

Anuradha stepped closer to him and tousled his strong, black hair. "When did you come back?"

The physical contact seemed to bring him back to earth for a second when he turned around and focused his eyes on her. He smiled wanly, nodded his head at her, and went back to the television. Anuradha felt her forehead wrinkling into worry lines. She needed to talk to him.

She made her way to the bedroom to change. It was almost ritualistic, the way she changed out of her clothes and wiped the make-up off her face; a ritual which marks her transition from work-life to family-life.

There was something going on with Manas. He seemed aloof, always with a frown on his forehead. She had tried to talk to him a couple of days before, but he brushed it aside, telling her it was work pressure.

Anuradha wiped the last of the mascara off her eyes and started changing out of her clothes.

Manas was her best friend and vice versa. It was them against the world. It had been like that from the time they got married. Her parents were against marrying somebody from 'North India', but they got through it together. But now, she didn't understand why he was trying to fend her off using flimsy excuses and trying to deal with whatever he was going through alone.

Anuradha turned the faucet to the right. The shock of a million cold icicles hitting her body drove everything out of her mind. *Damn it!* She turned the faucet back to shut off the shower. The switch was supposed to be towards the tap and not the shower. There was a bit of the old Manas still in there. He always left the switch towards the shower. She turned on the hot water faucet and mixed it with the cold water to make the temperature right.

Manas told her everything. That was one of the foundations on which their relationship was built. She turned on the shower. Droplets of warm water hit her face, condensed together, and rolled down her body, washing away the tiredness with it.

Everything. Everything except his past. Manas had told her that he grew up in an orphanage in Lucknow and that there was so much suffering there that he didn't want to talk about it. Something about that story didn't ring true to her, but she let it go. She, honestly, didn't care. It was the present she fell in love with. It was the loving husband, the caring father, and the person with a heart of gold she fell in love with. And that was all that mattered to her.

Anuradha could have stayed in the shower forever, letting the water run through her, washing away all her worries, all the doubts and regrets, and being one with the water. She had always thought of herself as somebody who was more comfortable in water than land. She felt more at home in a swimming pool than on a running track. But there was a life she had to get back to, a husband whom she had to talk to.

She turned off the shower, reluctantly, and stepped out of the bathroom, a towel wrapped around her hair, and another one around her body.

Anuradha hated seeing Manas struggle like this. Maybe what was bothering him was something from his past. She could not find any other reason for him not to share it with her. But she wished he would. She wanted to help him carry some of that weight. Every time Manas looked at her, under the glaze of pretence, there was a man trapped inside, trying to scream, trying to tell her something.

She got dressed, and came to the living room.

"Shruti...." she yelled up the stairs, "Time to take Bella for her walk."

Shruti plodded her way down the stairs, a mild scowl on her pretty face. Bella heard her coming down the stairs and propelled herself towards the foot of the stairs; her wagging tail acting as the rotor. Shruti bent down and ruffled her fur, gave her a hug, and clipped on the leash. And with a final scowl in Anuradha's way, she walked out of the house. *Teenage girls*, she thought.

Manas was still in his own world, engrossed by the 'developing story'. He had switched to another channel who claimed they had new information. She walked up to him and placed his hands on his cheeks.

"Manas..."

He swivelled in the couch to look at her with the same unfocused eyes she saw before. She studied the face of the man she loved as he came back to reality.

Manas' kind eyes had an unexplained ferociousness in them. It had always unsettled her and gave her a sense of security. A long, thin, Greek nose led her gaze down from the eyes to his generous mouth, framed by a well-defined jaw. The confident masculinity which got her attention the first time was still lurking behind somewhere.

"I wanna talk to you about something..." she said, prying the remote from his hands and turning the television off.

Manas straightened up like a flag post. "Is there a problem?"

"No, no. Nothing is wrong, dear...I just...I wanted to talk about you."

"Oh..." Manas let his body relax as he slumped back onto the couch. "I'm fine, Anu. It's just work—"

Anuradha reached out and covered his mouth with her fingers. His breath warmed her wet, cold hand. "Let's be honest. I need you to know that I love you, and I will always love you, no matter what... But right now, I need you to be honest with me. What's bothering you?"

Manas traced the lines on the couch with his fingers. The second hand of the clock advanced with the marching drums of tick-tock. Anuradha walked around the couch and cuddled up next to Manas.

"I don't know if you know this about me, but I live in the present and worry about the future. The past is something that shapes a man, but what a man becomes manifests itself in the present." She took his hands in hers. The rough calluses chafed her skin; they reassured her. "We have not talked a lot about your past because I was in love with your present, and wanted to be with your future. That story about the orphanage...I know it was a lie—"

"Anu, no, I—"

Anuradha smiled reassuringly. "I know, and it's okay. I've always known. I know you don't like talking about it, and I'm fine with not knowing. Even now, I am not asking you to tell me....but I hate to see you like this. I just wish I could share the weight you carry around on your shoulders. But I know you, and I also know you will never let me."

She let go of his hands and stared deep into his eyes. "But you have to tell me this...Is there something to be worried about? Is our future safe?"

Manas met her gaze with his old, tired eyes. But a fire burned beneath the surface. She could see the turmoil in them, the confusion, the fear. They all mixed together, muddying up the eyes. Even in the cloudiness, his love for her and Shruti stood out, like a diamond in the rough. And as she observed those eyes which made her fall for him, the clouds started to dissipate. The confusion, the fear, they started melting away until his eyes became clear as the water from a spring. And there was only one thing left in those clear eyes. Love.

He took her hand and squeezed it tight. It was warm and comforting as a hot cup of coffee on a cold, early morning. The night had fallen, and they sat in the dark silence for a few seconds.

"I'm sorry it had to be this way. But yes, something from my past has come back to haunt me." Manas closed his eyes and took a deep breath. "Then again, I may be overreacting. Maybe there is nothing to worry about...But if there is, I am not sure if I am strong enough to deal with it."

"You don't have to do this alone, Manas. You know I'll support you, no matter what."

Manas reached out and tucked a strand of her hair under her ears. "You are the lone star in my hopelessly dark universe from the moment I met you. You gave me purpose; you gave me hope. You gave me Shruti. You, Anu, are more important to me than you've ever imagined."

Manas rose to his feet and made his way to the window, his hands tied behind his back. He peered into the night, into the unknown. The faint fluorescent light from the streetlamp pulsated off his jaw as it moved under his skin, clenching.

"Sometimes our mind finds connections in places where none exist and weave a story making us the heroes. And sometimes it soothes us by telling us that whatever we fear is just the work of a paranoid mind. But, either way, I will take care of it."

The ominous undertone in the last sentence unnerved Anuradha. A flash of lightning painted the room white for a brief second. And in that brief second, she saw something in his face. Something primal. Something that she didn't recognise. The monstrous thunder that followed closely rattled the window glass in its sill.

Nasir

Saturday, April 26, 2014

Sometimes you have to empty a cup to fill it;
wipe the board and start all over.

The chair stifled his spine and poked at his buttocks. Nasir rose and stretched, flexing his muscles, earning a satisfying pop. *Why are hotel chairs so uncomfortable?* The fluffy white pillows and the soft feathery bed called out to him with a promise of comfort. He sunk into the soft cotton and let it envelop his aching, forty-four-year-old back and cradle his weary head.

Akshay had gotten a call late afternoon from Bangalore. Another girl was raped, killed, and displayed in a grotesque fashion which has now become synonymous with *The Artist*. They flew down here immediately, went straight to the crime scene, and then checked into a hotel for the night.

The Artist seemed to be a man on a mission. He was raking up kills faster than a hooker scoring on a Friday night. What used to be once in a year, had elevated to one in a day. And what used to be in and around Delhi, had become across state lines. One day he is in Delhi, the next day in Mumbai, and yet again in Bangalore. Where are you now?

Nasir reached for his mobile on the bed, and dialled Saket.

"Anything?" Nasir asked.

"Not yet, sir. We are still questioning people close to Teresa, but nothing has turned up till—"

"Keep looking." Nasir flung his phone on the bed, which bounced off and crashed onto the floor.

Every girl *The Artist* kills says goodbye to the world, and moves into Nasir's heart, weighing it down with remorse, and eventually finds their way into his nightmares to haunt him. Calling these girls 'victims' didn't do a lot of good but maybe they helped keep his sanity. They were all girls with dreams and hopes, which got shattered way too early. And here he was lying in the comfort of the hotel room.

Disgusted with himself, he scrambled stiffly to his feet and lumbered over to the table. It was overrun with a haphazard arrangement of printed papers, crime scene photographs, maps with marker lines criss-crossing, and post-it notes with illegible scribbling. He rummaged through the mess and retrieved a heavy, yellow file with The Artist labelled on it with huge black letters. The file was getting heavier by the day.

Nasir retrieved the report for today's victim, and he tossed the file aside. Nivedita Rathore —one more inhabitant in his already crowded heart, one more star in his contorted nightmares. He plucked out the photograph that was pinned to the first page. A cosy, single-storey house nested in a compound flush with greenery. Koramangala was supposed to be one of the safest neighbourhoods in Bangalore.

Flipping to the next page, he went over the report for the sixth time that night.

"The assailant forced entry by breaking the glass of the back window. The conchoidal lines on the thickness of the glass were emanating from a point of impact on the outside."

The glass was broken from the outside, and not in the struggle afterwards. So that must have been his entry point.

"Telephone lines were found severed. A bloody iPod was discovered in the kitchen. Blood spatter on the kitchen walls—"

Nasir drifted into Nivedita's house, reconstructing the crime in his head.

Nivedita bounced to the music on her iPod, reaching for the butter on the shelf to spread on her toast. A tall, dark figure broke in the window and climbed in. As he crept closer to her, brandishing an iron rod, Nasir wanted to warn her. But she was dancing to the music, unaware of the imminent danger. *The Artist* swung the weapon in a nice wide arc hitting on the side of her head. The sickening crunch of her skull breaking in reverberated in the silence of the house. Blood sprayed all over the white kitchen walls in a neat, directed spatter. Light went out of her eyes and she collapsed onto the floor, blood seeping from her head into a puddle near her head.

The Artist scooped her up in his arms and carried her to the living room, blood dripping from her head forming a trail. He grunted as he put her down on the beige carpet covering the living room. Crimson spread into the beige like drops of ink in a glass of water. *The Artist* struggled to take off her shorts and panties, rolling them up in the process. He tossed them aside as he unbuckled his belt, took off his pants, and proceeded to rape her. Nasir turned his head away.

When the throaty grunts subsided, Nasir looked back. *The Artist* was not there, but Nivedita was lying on the floor, naked and unconscious.

He wanted her to wake up and run for her life, but she just laid there, motionless, but breathing. The Artist came back from the kitchen, with a large kitchen knife in one hand and a glass of water on the other. The kitchen knife glinted in the sunlight when he took a gulp of water from the glass. He knelt on top of her and sprinkled some water on her face. She was slowly making her way to consciousness when *The Artist* made his first incision on her right upper arm. Her eyes flew open, but her screams were short-lived as he clamped her mouth with his other hand. Securing her arms under his knees and her mouth with one hand, *The Artist* continued to make multiple wounds on her torso, arms, and legs. Blood flowed freely from the wounds down Nivedita's bare, naked body and seeped into the carpet. The girl drifted back into unconsciousness as the crimson flow of blood spread on the beige carpet like a high tide creeping up on the shore.

The blood aroused *The Artist*, and he raped her again. This time Nasir forced himself to watch. He deserved the torture; he deserved the pain. When The Artist decided it was enough fun for the day, he closed his large hands around her neck and squeezed the life out of her. When the last of the light had left Nivedita, *The Artist* picked her up and carried her to the bedroom. But Nasir stayed in the living room, his eyes fixated on the place where Nivedita laid a moment before, too numb to move. The blood stain on the carpet was in the shape of her body, spread-eagled. A bloody angel in full flight.

"Purple bruises on the anterior and lateral neck. Multiple wounds on the torso. There was a lack of livor mortis (lividity) indicating that the victim bled to death…"

Nasir tossed the report into the pile of unmanageable mess on the table. A photograph of the body, how The Artist left it, slid out from the folder. Nivedita's dead eyes accused him of incompetence. It was marked 'Striptease - Demi Moore' below the photograph.

He picked up the sketch they developed of *The Artist* from Hemant's description. Hemant remembered the body type, the height, his build, and even the shape of his face, but not the facial features; it was lost in the interplay of light and darkness. A man with a hollow face stood proudly on the canvas, mocking Nasir, staying just out of reach.

Nasir had enough. He gathered all the sheets of papers and files strewn across the table and shoved it into the yellow file marked The Artist and tossed it aside.

He turned around and made a beeline for his trusted Glenfiddich to make himself a drink. The brown liquid poured from the bottle and sparkled as it passed over the ice cubes in the glass. Swirling around the glass, Nasir made his way back to the uncomfortable chair and took a sip. His gut told him that he had everything to nail the bastard, but somehow, he always seemed just out of reach. He and his team had been in a mad dash across country ever since it started. And in that constant state of turmoil, he hadn't gotten anytime to just take a step back and think through the new evidence. The only time he had was the short flights between the cities. Not much thinking can be done in between the take-off and landing, with snack breaks in between, but whenever he started to think, he always zeroed in on Teresa and Amrita—the two outliers. They had to be the key. He ran his hands through his sweaty forehead and wondered if the air condition was working. There was just too much running through his mind. Sometimes you have to empty a cup to fill it; wipe the board and start all over. And right now, Glenfiddich just wouldn't do the trick.

Nasir reached under the bed for his bag and searched for his special pouch. It had a place reserved in his bag wherever he went. He grabbed the cold, metal box and opened it. A zip-lock bag, a lighter, and a stack of rolling paper occupied the space inside. As he opened the zip-lock bag, the dried leaves inside emanated an all familiar, earthy, herbal aroma. Reaching into the pouch with his nimble fingers, he took out some marijuana, enough for a joint. It crumbled in his hands as he crushed it into a paper.

Nasir started smoking up in his self-destructive downward spiral phase of life, right after 'The Butcher of Bhalswa' disappeared without a trace. Drinking till it's dark, smoking up till it's light, and passing out was his routine. Even though he snapped out of that phase, both the habits stayed with him, although under control. Now it was one or two pegs, occasionally, and a blunt once a month.

Weaning off alcohol was one of the toughest things he had to do in his life. A lot of literature and studies about the adverse effect of alcohol on your body, and supportive friends made it possible. But cutting down marijuana was never a problem. He could stop and start smoking up as and when he wanted because there was no physical addition. And none of the literature had anything bad to say about the physical effects of marijuana. So, he figured, might as well keep the habit.

But after he got his life on track, he realised that the euphoria of the high was so good that he ended up spending a lot of time smoking up. And when you have a full life running, you realise time is one of the most expensive commodities. One of the primary reasons he didn't think of another marriage is time. He could spend that much more time into making the world a better place. And this expensive commodity was getting increasingly utilised by marijuana, and therefore he decided to cut down.

Nasir sifted through the crushed dope to separate the stem and seeds from the crushed leaves.

The stigma of marijuana amused him. Studies had proven that it was less dangerous and addictive than alcohol or tobacco, but still illegal. The masses always feared the unknown. Cannabis has always been clubbed with other hard drugs like cocaine or heroin under the common umbrella of drugs, which is where cannabis gets most of its bad name. Even in the eyes of the law, cannabis is as bad as cocaine, which is one of the major reasons for the surge in cocaine and heroin in the country. There is a lot more profit to be had in cocaine or heroin, but the same risk as cannabis. Simple economics made sure all the dealers switched to hard drugs and started pushing them through peddlers.

He folded a piece of a visiting card into a roach, pulled out a rolling paper from the black OCB pouch and started rolling the joint.

Getting high on weed was a chance to unwind and just think. The turbo-charged neurons fired faster and better to make lightning-fast mind maps. Not just your thought process, but everything was better when you are high; the music was sweeter, its tone clearer; food was tastier, jokes were funnier. Even your senses were enhanced. It was like hitting the 'HD' button on life.

But marijuana had one special effect on him. When he dozes off after getting high, it opens a channel between his conscious and sub-conscious through dreams. It had helped him out many times when he was just stuck with an investigation.

Nasir finished off the joint by twisting the end into a bunch and lightly roasting it under the flame. Without much ado, he lit up the joint and sucked on it. The smoky tendrils tunnelled its way into his lungs and then diffused into his blood and started the journey up to his brain. The effect was almost immediate; his muscles relaxed, and his mind expanded. A couple more drags and he was lost in the ebb and flow of the high.

Music from two rooms down the corridor entered his room without knocking. A sharp ray of light from the streetlight pierced into the room through a gap in the curtain. Dust particles bobbed in the spotlight, dancing to the tune of 'Roop Tera Mastana.' Nasir regarded the joint. It had two more hits left, but he was already high enough. His eyes were heavy, his body motionless. He took one last drag, but held back the smoke in his mouth, formed an 'o' with his mouth and pushed the smoke out of his mouth, in short bursts. Smoke rings darted out of his mouth, dissipating as it meshed with the air, morphed into abstract shapes. The smoke shapes played hide and seek with him. Every now and then a shape jumped out of the smoke but disappeared as soon as Nasir noticed. He drifted into sleep playing the game and failing miserably at it.

A gust of damp wind raced through the maze of empty streets. The black asphalt and the white line down the middle extended as far as the eye could see in both directions. It was not raining, but the tarmac was wet; it glistened a dark shade of red. Nasir glanced up at the sky; it was an unnatural shade of deep red, almost blood red. Street lamps flickered casting light and shadows on the brick-walls of the buildings that lines the street. On both sides of the street, giant billboards of movie posters rose above the buildings, silhouetted against the red sky. They were not the original posters, but the 'artworks' that The Artist left for him—'Pulp Fiction', 'Blue Velvet', 'Strip Tease', and many more.

Nasir tottered down the street and turned the corner. The Artist stood tall at the end of the street, a Van Gogh mask on his face, his left ear cut-off. Blood dripped on to the street from the stub of his ear and splattered in exquisite patterns around him. Teresa stood right next to The Artist and were talking animatedly. That was when The Artist unsheathed a samurai sword.

Nasir felt his pulse quicken. The red sky cast its strange light on the blade, giving it an ominous red glow. *No! Stop*.

Words were stuck in Teresa's mouth as her eyes fixated on the glowing sword. She tracked the glowing sword all the way through its smooth trajectory, cutting through the air with a slight whizz, until it severed her head. The silence was deafening. Nasir's lips curled into a scream, but only more silence came out. Her head slid off her neck, and rolled towards Nasir, blood spraying in all directions like a fire wheel chakra on Diwali.

The body was still standing, as though nothing had happened. The Artist swiped the blade on Teresa's clothes, sheathed it, and walked away. Nasir tore his eyes away from the rolling head and followed The Artist. He shouldn't let him get away. Not this time.

The street went on straight ahead until it dissolved into the horizon in a shimmering blood-red glow. Dank plaster on the buildings that framed the street were going green with mould. Four blocks down the street, a girl crossed the street and planted herself in the middle of the road. A dark silhouette against a red canvas. Nasir broke into a run, hurtling towards them. He had to warn her, he had to save her. But The Artist glided through the street towards her in a pace which Nasir could not keep up.

When she was three blocks from Nasir, her face became clearer. *Amrita.* The Artist and Amrita exchanged pleasantries and started talking. *Why was she acting normal?* The man had a mask on and was dripping blood from his ear.

Two blocks away. Nasir was getting out of breath, but he didn't care. All that mattered was to save Amrita.

Amrita laughed at something The Artist said. But she didn't see the metallic gleam of the knife in The Artist's hands. She didn't know how dangerous he was.

One block away. Nasir's legs ached from the full run, but he was almost there. That was when The Artist turned to him, staring right at him. His eyes glowed from underneath the mask as in invisible barrier stopped Nasir's mad dash and pushed him back, throwing him two feet into the air.

Nasir landed face first on the pavement, the rough cement scraping his face; blood crumbled from the exposed flesh. He brushed aside the pain, picked himself off the pavement and spat out some blood. He tried to yell out a warning, but nothing came out.

As he started to run towards Amrita again, The Artist sliced her neck with the serrated edge of the hunting knife. Blood squirted off her neck like water from a fire hose, bathing The Artist in blood. Amrita met Nasir's gaze, and staggered a few steps in his direction before collapsing.

Nasir skidded to a stop near her and knelt near her; he didn't mind soaking his pants in blood. This was his fault. He clutched his head and buried it between his knees. *This is not happening. Not again.*

Silence descended on him again. The howling of the wind and the rustle of a newspaper tumbling down the street was all there was. A lone door caught wind and banged against the wall in chaotic booms. The Artist was stationed exactly where he was earlier, but he was not dripping blood anymore. Shadows hid his face, but an unlit cigarette protruded from his mouth. The lighter in his left hand sparked and caught fire. He shielded the flame with his right hand and bent over to light the cigarette. The tip of the cigarette burned a crimson orange, irradiating a faint glow on his mask.

The Artist shoved the lighter back into his left pocket. The rectangular outline of the lighter bulged from his pocket. Out of the blue, a bouncy guitar riff pierced the silence. The rectangular outline began to vibrate and grow in size. It grew larger until it was the size of a mobile phone. Nasir knew that ringtone; he had heard it before. The Artist dug into his pocket and pulled out the mobile. He unmasked his face and brought the phone to his cheek. In the faint luminescent light of the mobile phone, Nasir saw his face. It was Alex. Alex D'Cruz. With a poof, the empty streets were gone, so were the red skies. He relived the day at Teresa's house. Alex took a call and excused himself from the conversation. He took out his phone from his left pocket.

Alex was left-handed.

Nasir threw open his eyes, his heart thumping in his chest, his mind racing. Alex. How did he miss him? He was over 6 feet tall, aged 27, and left-handed. When he had gone to Teresa's house, Alex was in charge. There was no father. He fit the bill perfectly. Amrita was Teresa's best friend and by extension would be on talking terms with Alex.

Something clicked in his brain. Alex had mentioned he owned an internet cafe. Nasir rose to his feet, grabbed his laptop from the table and sat on the edge of the bed. He opened the laptop and pressed the power button. The blank screen stared back at him. Nasir struggled to keep his focus on the computer, but his lingering high wasn't agreeing. After what seemed like an eternity, the windows logo faded into the screen. Red, Green, Yellow, and Blue filled in the four windows (Is that what it was supposed to be?) of the logo. Nasir wasn't sure if it was the high, but these colours were subtly pulsating one by one. He got lost in the psychedelic dance of the Windows logo, but the trance was broken when his desktop appeared on the screen. Firing up the browser, Nasir googled 'Payal Seth' and got hits in Facebook and Twitter. With a few clicks, Nasir was scouring the friends list on both the social media websites. Bingo. Alex was on her Facebook friends list—her 'mystery friend'. Running purely on instincts, Nasir clicked on Alex's name and navigated to the Facebook profile. And there in his friend's list was Nivedita Rathore.

Without wasting a second, he dialled Saket. He answered the phone with a mouth full of food.

"Is Alex D'cruz still in Delhi?" Nasir blurted out.

"Oh, sir. I'm sorry, I was having din—"

"Cut to the matter. Is he there or not?"

"He left a few days ago for some—"

"Be specific. How many days?"

"Two days."

Nasir flung the phone on his bed and rushed outside. Akshay's room was right next to his, but it took a moment to figure out. But once he figured it out, he barged in. Instead of Akshay sleeping on the bed, his entire team was gathered there, relaxing after a series of long days with well-deserved glasses of liquor.

The jovial banter in the room came to a screeching halt as everyone turned their attention to the frantic old man in the room. "Alex is left-handed," Nasir blurted out. "Alex is left-handed."

There was concern in Sonam's eyes; alarm in Akshay's and amusement in Avinash's and Salim's. Nasir took a deep breath and calmed himself down.

"Alex is The Artist," said Nasir as he flopped down on the nearest empty chair.

The effect of those four words was instantaneous. All four of them rose to their feet in tandem.

"What?" asked Sonam with those big, wide eyes.

Akshay's mouth hung loose as if it fell off the socket. Salim and Avinash high-fived in happiness.

Nasir took another deep breath, gathered his wits, and explained to them what he figured out. Akshay's face lit up with happiness and Sonam beamed at Nasir; a proud gleam in her eyes.

Their celebration was interrupted by a ringtone from Akshay's phone. He excused himself to attend it while the team waited with bated breath. Late night calls to Akshay meant one of two things—good news or bad news.

A wide smile grew on his face—an expression that is as rare on his face as a crow flying upside down.

"Guess what? His car was spotted entering Trivandrum."

Manas

Sunday, April 27, 2014

Fear is something that is biologically wired into us over billions of years of evolution. Courage on the other hand is anti-evolutionary.

Shruti skipped down the stairs, dressed in a knee-length, black skirt, and a white T-shirt. Big black letters were stamped on the T-shirt: 'Consciousness: That annoying time between naps.' *Where do these kids get all this?* Her ponytail bounced up and down, in and out of the evening sunlight. The burgundy highlights caught fire under the brilliant evening sun. Her white high heels tapped out a happy rhythm on the floor.

"Mom, I'm going out," she yelled into the kitchen as she headed for the door.

"Where are you going?" Manas asked, turning away from the television.

"Told you guys earlier, na? Going for a movie and then hang out after." Shruti rummaged her bag for something.

"Uh-huh...And you will be back by?"

"Hmmm...I don't know, Dad. I'll be a little late-"

"No, you will not," Manas said. "You will be back in your room by ten."

"By ten?" Shruti's eyebrows furrowed and mouth opened in a perfect circle. "Dad, come on, you can't do this. I'll be back around eleven or twelve, as usual."

"You heard me. Ten means ten," Manas said, turning back to the television, and effectively ending the conversation.

Shruti hovered around the front door for a couple more seconds and then opened the door to leave.

"Be safe, kiddo," Manas called after her, "And you better pick up my calls ASAP."

He followed her through the window, till she went out of sight. A pair of comforting hands hugged him from behind. Anuradha whispered in his ear, "She'll be fine. She has stayed out late before."

Manas met her beautiful, kohl framed, eyes. "It's not like before, and you know..."

"Hmmm...you said it might not be anything."

All his senses, including the sixth, urged him to lock Anuradha and Shruti inside the house and stand guard. Maybe he was being paranoid. It may be nothing. There wasn't any mention of The Butcher in any of the murders after the first one. Maybe it was just a freak coincidence.

Something in the kitchen made a whooshing sound, and Anuradha rushed inside, leaving Manas in front of the television. He dreaded the news channel ever since he saw Amrita's dead eyes in it. But like a moth to a flame, he was drawn to it, a self-aware moth that was headed towards annihilation. Manas switched the channel to the news. And plastered across the top quarter of the screen in big bold white letters on a red background was the headline he was dreading.

"The Artist strikes again in Bangalore."

From the left half of the rest of the screen, the reporter leaned forward on his desk, spewing out gory details of the latest murder. But what caught his attention was the right half, which was a map of India. Delhi, Mumbai, and Bangalore pulsed in red, with numbers indicating the sequence of murders. His eyes traced the path, connecting the dots. *One. Delhi. Two. Mumbai. Three. Bangalore.* But his eyes didn't stop there, they trailed further south where Trivandrum was.

Blood swooshed through his ears, throbbing at his eardrums. Manas switched off the television and scrambled to his feet. The walls of the room were closing in; he had to get out. And he did.

The evening sun struggled to reach Earth through the dark clouds spread across the sky. A streak of lightning split the sky in half and disappeared. Booming thunder followed seconds apart. The afterburn glowed when he blinked his eyes. He pushed open the gate and let his legs take him forward. There was no destination in his mind, but as long as it took him away from where he was, he didn't care.

A single drop of rain landed on his temple and trickled down the crook of his eyebrow to his eyes. Another drop splashed on his left arm. Powerful gusts of wind swayed the tree tops, not just the monolithic pseudo-trees like the coconut, but the mighty, sprawling hardwood trees as well.

It took only a few seconds for the rain to pick up the pace. Manas cast his gaze up towards the grey sky, squinting to keep the water out of his eyes.

There was no middle ground when dealing with a thunderstorm. Either face it head on, get drenched until you reach a safe place indoors, or run away as far as possible; far enough that the storm won't reach you. People who try to wait out the storm under puny umbrellas or store fronts are gonna get wet and they are not going anywhere either.

Heavy downpour drenched him to the bone, but he didn't care; he marched on, only not sure where he was headed.

People looked at him like he is a mad man. *Who would walk in this rain, that too, without an umbrella?* But for Manas, getting wet was the least of his problems. Rainwater gushed over his eyes, blurring his vision. It blurred his future as well. The future of the life he had built with his sweat and blood over the last twenty years.

Twenty years was a lot of time; enough to carve out a new life and settle into it. The shadow of his past peeked over his shoulders for the first few years. But slowly and steadily, it faded away. Soon enough, he met Anuradha, fell in love, and had an angel; he was happy with his new life. A life worth spending the rest of his time in. But now, the strings that held his life together were slipping through his fingers.

Manas toyed with the idea of going to the police and coming clean. They could offer protection, if not for him, at least for Anu and Shruti. But there were two problems with that.

If he just walks into a police station and tells them the truth, they will just laugh at him. Even if he proved what he was telling was the truth, they would not take the threat seriously until they had done their own investigation. It might be too late by the time they realise the truth.

Secondly, going to the police would effectively destroy the life he had built. How would he face Anuradha after she knows everything? How would Shruti feel when she sees her Dad dragged around by the police on national television? There has to be another way.

Manas looked up and realised he was at an intersection. The road towards his left led back to his house and the road to his right went on and on.

He could disappear, move to another city, build a new life, and start over. Wouldn't that be kinder than putting his loved ones through this ordeal? He could get another job, pass off his ideas as others, and stay under the radar. The usual drill. But would that guarantee Anu and Shruti's safety? What if the storm hits them and he was not there to shield them from it? Moreover, did he really want a life without Anu and Shruti? What would be the point of something like that?

The sun gave up trying to shine through the dark clouds, and hung up his boots for the day. The black clouds seamed with lightning flashes. The wind tore at the trees, creaking and swaying under its weight. Darkness engulfed the street. No streetlights, nor vehicles.

Shruti and Anuradha, he had to keep them safe. He knew he was capable of doing that, but at what cost?

A flash of lightning lit up the street for a fraction of a second. And in that short-lived flash, a familiar figure stood across the street, smiling. Manas wiped the water away from his eyes, and scanned the darkness. Nothing. *Am I losing my mind?*

Cold hands of fear grabbed his heart, squeezing it tight till he was not able to breathe. He shook his head clear. This was not the time to panic. How could he keep his loved ones safe when he himself was afraid? He was not the same skinny boy who stood by meekly when his uncle….

Thud! Thud!

Manas shuddered and chased away the memory as soon as it popped into his mind.

He was afraid.

Fear is something that is biologically wired into us over billions of years of evolution. Courage, on the other hand, is anti-evolutionary. Fear protects us, but courage protects something bigger than us. It may be a family, a society, or even the world.

And right now, to protect his family, he needed to subdue his fear, shove it into a dark corner of his mind and do what needed to be done,

A bolt of lightning charged its way across the sky, leaving a jagged path of gleaming white. Raindrops cascaded onto his face, stinging his skin. Manas pulled out his wallet, sheltered it from the rain with his body, and opened it. Shruti's happy and surprised face beamed at him from one of the photographs he had in his wallet. In another photograph, Anuradha smiled at him coyly in a pink dress. Hot tears mixed with the rain as it streamed down his eyes. Seeing their faces, those smiles, he felt an unexplained clarity. He would do anything, go to any lengths to protect them, protect those smiles. He had to.

Manas shoved the wallet back in his pocket and turned left - the road back home.

The Artist

Sunday, April 27, 2014

Some say it's about the journey, and some say it's about the destination. But for him, it was the purpose.

Time ceased to exist when you were on the road. Especially if you haven't slept for four days. The sun tries to hit you from different angles, and at night, the headlights take over. After a while, night and day blend together into a series of blinding assaults of light.

The black asphalt threaded its way through pockets of civilisation as he reached closer and closer to his destination. Some say it's about the journey, and some say it's about the destination. But for him, it was the purpose. He enjoyed the journey, and he was excited about the destination; what made him tick was the purpose.

Johnny Page caressed the guitar as the intro to Stairway to Heaven played through the stereo. Goosebumps ran down his spine.

God chose a different palette to colour each state of the county and the bold gradients which transitioned across state borders when different palettes merged were exquisite. One of the most interesting ones was at the Tamil Nadu-Kerala border. The dusty browns of the barren land blended into a celebration of emerald greens of the lush flora. And it was a sharp gradient.

He drove through five states, and none were as different from the others as Kerala. If India were a beach, Kerala would be the charming, little shack, filled to the seam with people. The bar, the restaurant, and the temporary shelters outside—all were as happy and content as the other. A place which the locals, tourists, and travellers call home.

Greenery framed the black tarmac, almost continuously, broken only by clusters of shops on both sides of the road, beautiful, sloped-roof houses, and an occasional hoarding advertising jewellery. Alex drove for a couple more hours before he heard the lady in the Google Maps say, "Your destination is on your right."

The Road Transport Office appeared only for those who went looking for it. The old, decrepit office slept in a mid-afternoon slumber; but it was just eleven in the morning. Alex parked his car up front and strolled right up to an empty counter. A middle-aged man stooped behind it, playing Candy Crush on his smart phone, adjusting the thick, black, square-rimmed glasses every now and then.

"Good Morning." Alex flashed an earnest smile at the man, hoping for a warm reception. But all he got was a cold, apathetic upturned face of the man behind the counter.

"Yes?" the man said, without moving a muscle on his face.

"Listen, Sir," Alex started, plugging in a 'Sir' to sweeten the ask. "I'm in huge trouble. On my way back from Bangalore...my wallet...you know... somebody pinched it. Most of my money, debit cards, credit cards, licence, everything gone with it. Just got some emergency cash with me."

"This is not the police station." The man looked down and swiped on his screen. The jingle of candy being crushed filled the silence.

Dissatisfaction ploughed Alex's brow. He took a deep breath and continued, "I know, Sir. But I want to apply for a duplicate licence."

Without lifting his focus from the mobile screen, the man pulled out a large form from under the counter, and slid it through the hole in the glass wall to Alex.

He glanced at the form and then back at the man. With a sheepish grin, he said, "Errr.... this is where you should help me out. You see....I... don't remember my licence number. Is there any way you can help me out there?"

The man lifted a finger to ask him to wait as he crushed some more candy. When the jingles fell silent, he placed the smartphone down and looked up at Alex. He narrowed his eyes, scanning him from top to bottom. "You have to fill out the form," he said, shaking his head.

"Oh! Come on, sir. I know you can help me out. It's really urgent."

The man picked up the smartphone and started his game again. Alex surreptitiously removed a two thousand rupees note from his pocket and slid it across the table to the man.

"Will this help?" Alex asked. Money opened doors everywhere.

The man slid a yellow candy to place and got some kind of bonus because the phone went crazy with jingles like he hit the jackpot. He looked up and tucked the magenta note into his pocket. "What's your name?"

"Manas Mitra," Alex answered with a relieved smile.

"Date of Birth?"

"Aug 28, 1971." It took him two minutes to pull that information off Manas' Facebook page.

Alex drummed his fingers on the glass as the man poured over the screen of his computer with the same interest he had for his mobile screen.

A series of clickety-clacks and the man looked up with a smile.

"Got it," he said and rattled off the number to Alex, which he promptly jotted down in the application form.

"You are a life saver!" Alex said. "I'll just be back with the form and the necessary documents. You'll be here, right?"

"Somebody will be there at the counter." The man said before returning to his game.

Alex flew down the stairs and got into his car. It was easier than he thought it would be.

With a few taps and swipes on his mobile phone, he opened the Kerala Motor Vehicles Department website. Alex clicked on one of the online applications, keyed in the Licence number along with the date of birth and clicked 'Go.'

A pair of dark eyes peered out from a square-shaped head with strong black hair, neatly trimmed. A young Manas, Alex presumed, stared defiantly out from the mobile screen. To the right of the photograph, Alex found what he was looking for. The permanent address.

With that minor victory, Alex decided to call it a day. He had four days of sleep to catch up on and he needed it for the days ahead. They would be busy and tiring.

He started the car, put it in gear, drove to the Railway Station and rented a small room in one of the hundreds of inconspicuous lodges which sprung out from every nook and cranny of the area. Throwing his luggage into a corner, he collapsed on to the bed. The old and unyielding mattress had a musty smell. But he was beyond caring. Within the next minute, he slipped off into sleep.

Alex found himself in a vast, colourless field under a grey sky. All around him towering trees with their twisted branches clawed the sky. He was alone, cold wind biting into his ten-year old skin. In the distance, three figures hovered between earth and sky: his mother and two sisters, dressed in flowing white gowns, bathed in a soft yellow light.

Alex ran towards them, but as he approached closer, the ground turned into quicksand, dragging him in deeper. He struggled to get free, but the more he struggled, the deeper he sank. His mother and sisters, oblivious to his struggles, flew away into the light.

As he sank deeper into the sand, the world became darker, hopeless. As his face went under, sand began entering his ears and nose. When he opened his mouth to scream, sand rushed inside his mouth too. The lights went out all at once when his eyes went under. And then, terror. Absolute and complete terror attacked him and he woke up with a start.

He grabbed a bottle of water and drank all of it, gasping for air, and wiping sweat from his face. This nightmare wasn't particularly more disturbing than the ones he usually got. Nightmares were part of his nightly routine, just like brushing his teeth. Years of nightmares had taught him how to handle them as well. When he closed his eyes again to go back to sleep, he imaged a different ending to the nightmare, something happier, and willed his mind to take the bait and convert a nightmare into a dream.

He quickly re-wrote the ending of the nightmare and made it such a way that just before he sunk into the quicksand completely, a figure, clad in black with a low riding hat, pulled him out and turned him onto a path with an effervescent light at the end of it; something which radiates hope. And with it, he drifted off into a dreamless slumber.

Prateek

Tuesday, January 3, 1996

Screams are only as good as the person who hears it.

Amrita fiddled with the knot at the bottom of her white shirt. The top three buttons of her shawl-collared shirt hung loose, tantalising the world with a hint of cleavage through the black camisole inside. The cigarette in her long, slender fingers burned bright as she sucked on it. The dark smoke she exhaled swirled around the car and mixed with her perfume before getting drafted out of the half-cracked window. It suffocated Prateek.

Out of his peripheral vision, Prateek noticed Amrita swivelling her head to face him. If she had something to ask him, let her. He focused on the road ahead, with a little too much concentration.

Amrita tossed the cigarette out the window. "Are we there yet?"

"Almost…" he said, with a sweet smile.

When two people are as close as he and Manas, it was practically impossible to get away from each other. It took days of planning, and a lot of lying to get away from Manas. The lying made Prateek feel bad about himself, but it was all for Manas.

Prateek spotted the gritty, brown heap of rusted metal sheets from a distance—that was the landmark. He eased his foot off the accelerator and took a turn at the corner into an unused mud road, leaving the last of civilisation on the main road. Soon enough, a building loomed in front of them. Back when it was fully operational, the plant must have been bustling with uniformed workers, but stray dogs and the homeless occupy the space now. Prateek pulled up to the side of the building, hidden from plain sight.

Amrita's lips quirked sideways into a naughty smile. "Looks abandoned…" She cocked her head to the side and narrowed her eyes. "Hmmm….Wonder why you brought me here?"

"If I told you, how would it be a surprise? But I can guarantee you one thing. It's not what you think." Prateek climbed out of the car and stretched his cramped legs. *Stupid bimbo had no idea what was coming for her.* He leaned into the window of the car and flashed an enticing smile at her. "Well...what are you waiting for?"

Amrita climbed out of the car, and gathered her eyebrows. "A gentleman is supposed to open the door for the girl, you know."

Prateek bit down on a few retorts his brain suggested, smiled at her apologetically, and rounded the car over to her side. With a flourish, he bowed, and offered her his elbows. That brought a smile to her face.

They strolled inside the building; her arms looped through his elbows. Prateek paused at the threshold of the abandoned warehouse for his eyes to adjust to the sudden change in luminance.

As his vision cleared, he took in the scene inside the abandoned factory. Time stood still. The accumulated dust between the gear teeth was thick enough to stop light from passing through. A few abandoned machinery, which were heavy enough to resist the pilferage stood tall in the dust. Different artifacts, both from the time the plant was active and recent times, were strewn over the ground, in a haphazard manner. But there was an order even in that randomness. *This would be perfect.* Prateek felt around in the bag he was holding; the furrows of the rope around which his hands wrapped around reassured him, He took a deep breath, inhaling the musty scent of time. It was going to be a beautiful day.

Amrita disentangled from him, darted to the middle of the empty space, and spread-eagled her arms, facing up. "Yoooooohooooo…"

The shout ricocheted off the walls and travelled back as a hollow version of the original. Amrita cackled with a child-like energy; her eyes lit up.

She stopped laughing and faced him. "This is amazing, Manas."

Manas? Prateek glanced behind him. There was nobody there. As Amrita gazed at him, he realised she was talking to him and got the names mixed up. He wished for a mirror to double check his poker face for cracks. A drop of sweat condensed on his temple and hung over his right eyebrow, threatening to spill over to his eyes.

His poker face must have been good because Amrita stepped closer, shrugged with a coy smile on her face, and said, "Now, out with the surprise already. Can't wait."

Prateek realised he was holding his breath. "Close your eyes..." he said, slowly deflating his puffed-up chest.

"I'm waiting," she said in a sing song voice.

Prateek unzipped his bag. The ratchety sound echoed in the hollow space and Amrita slightly cracked one of her eyes to peek. He quickly hid the bag behind his body. "No peeking..."

She giggled and closed her eyes again.

He searched for the end of the rope inside the bag and pulled it out, untangling it. Prateek looped it around his shoulders like a snake lying in wait for its prey.

"Remember....no peeking," Prateek said, as he circled Amrita on the balls of his feet, like a tiger stalking his prey. The fruity scent of her conditioner waded into his nose.

This was the part that he loved.

He coiled the rope around both his hands leaving a short portion of it between them. With an abrupt motion, he reached over her head and looped the rope back over her neck. The jerky resistance from Amrita was easily dealt with as she collapsed into an unconscious heap on the ground in less than a minute. Without missing a beat, he uncoiled the rope from his hands and fastened her hands behind her back and legs together.

Prateek scanned the room for a place to tie her down. A rusty red column that held up the dilapidated roof was two feet away. He heaved her onto his back, with a grunt and tied her to the metal column.

"Let's see you get out of this with your slutty charm, bitch." Prateek spat; his spittle landed on Amrita's cheeks.

Prateek sauntered over to his bag and emptied its contents onto the floor. The need for subtlety was long gone. The dying evening light bounced off the scythe and cast its shimmery orange band on the wall. Prateek picked it up along with the sharpening stone, and set to work. The grating sound of stone on metal was as soothing as a lullaby. Amrita was still unconscious. *Good.*

~

It took almost ten minutes for Amrita to come back around. Her kohl-lined eyes opened, and a small sliver of white peeked out. Wrinkles furrowed her forehead as her brain tried to comprehend where she was, and what happened to her.

Prateek stopped sharpening the scythe, and set it aside.

Within a few moments, realisation dawned on her. Her eyes flew open, and she jerked in her tied-up position.

"Like clockwork!" said Prateek, laughing. His hollow laugh echoed in the empty warehouse.

Amrita searched for the source of the sound and zoned in on Prateek. Her eyebrows squished together. "What..." She bit her lip. "What is all this?"

Prateek stole a quick glance behind his shoulders to make sure he was alone. "This is judgement day. Today you answer for all your sins."

Her burrow lines deepened as both her eyebrows joined. "What? Untie me."

"That's right. Today you answer for all your whoring, smoking, and drinking. You are a fucking disgrace to Indian women."

Amrita glanced around as if looking for answers. "Why are you saying all this? Enough is enough. Untie me now."

Prateek reached for his scythe and brought it into her full view in all its shimmering glory. "You think this is still a game?"

Amrita's eyes jumped out of their sockets, unblinking. Her breath caught midway in her throat. She tried to scream but couldn't.

Prateek swaggered over to her, slinging the scythe over his shoulders. "Screams are only as good as the person who hears it. I wouldn't bother getting that voice back; cause there is no one around."

Amrita froze for a second and then broke down into a series of uncontrollable sobs. Prateek neither had the time nor the patience for silliness. He swung his scythe down.

Swoosh!

The metal cut the air in a downward motion and severed the rope, which tied her to the metal column. It was a distraction, and after all, where was she gonna run?

He grabbed hold a bunch of her hair at the base of her neck and forced her to kneel down. A deftly placed foot and his body weight held her there.

Amrita gasped for breath, recovering from a series of sobs, and a guttural scream escaped her throat. Prateek's mouth twitched with amusement. That was what terror sounded like. Men or women, big or small, sophisticated or naïve, no matter who it is, terror has the same language.

He raised the scythe above his head for a true strike to the base of her neck and swung down hard. The blade cut through air with a whizzing sound and closed down the gap to the target—her neck. In the gleaming metal, whizzing through the air in front of his eyes, Prateek glimpsed a shadow. The blade came to a screeching halt touching the skin of her neck, breaking it; a drop of blood oozed out and rolled off her neck towards the ground.

While Prateek was puzzling about the blade, an insurmountable force hit Prateek squarely on his chest. He cartwheeled awkwardly through the air and landed on his back, hitting his head on the metal column to which Amrita was tied to. A sharp pain shot through his body, blinding him. When his vision cleared up, a man was staring down at him. His long, thin, Greek nose quivered in the square-shaped head; his well-defined jaw clenched. Manas was rage personified. Prateek had never seen him this livid.

"How dare you?" Manas' voice hovered a fine line between a scream and a roar. There was anguish and indignation in that.

Prateek scrambled to his feet, instantly discarding the notion of retaliating. For the first time in his life, Manas scared him.

"I'm sorry..." Prateek put up his hands, palms facing outward. "But it just had to be done. You...you just don't see it yet. This is all for you."

The vein on Manas' temple throbbed. "No, I fucking, do not see it," he said, "And unless I see it, you don't move a muscle. You ask me before doing anything. That's how it has been, and that's how it will be."

Anger bubbled up inside Prateek. "You don't speak for me, you little shit. Before I came into your life, you were a miserable little boy, too wimpy to even raise your voice against your own uncle."

Manas cringed at the mention of his uncle.

"I made you who you are. I helped you stand up for yourself, had your back the whole time. And now you...your wimpy ass thinks you can control me?" Prateek laughed maniacally; it echoed in the empty warehouse doubling and tripling upon itself.

Manas grew quiet. The blood which had rushed to his face started to redistribute. "You know what? I may have needed you back then, but I don't anymore..." His eyes focused on something behind Prateek. "I don't need him anymore," he echoed.

His face hardened with resolve, with defiance. "You are out of control, Prateek. You are addicted to violence. It's not about helping the little guy anymore but satisfying your blood thirst. All this… it stops now."

Prateek chuckled with derision. "It's cute that you think you can control me."

"Get this through your thick, dumb skull. You need me, and not the other way around. You wouldn't last a fucking day without me holding your hand like a fucking baby. The CBI is no joke."

Manas was right. He was the brains of the operation. But he couldn't let go of the control now. Not when he was so close to taking over. He put on his poker face, which split into a wide grin, and said, "You can go fuck yourself. I need you as much as a plant needs to shit."

Colour rushed back to Manas' face. His eyes widened, showing more white. "That's it," he roared, "That's just, fucking, it. I'm done. We are done." He enunciated every syllable of the last sentence.

Prateek scoffed. "You can't do that. You think you can get rid of me?"

Manas turned his back on Prateek and walked towards Amrita, who was sobbing on the floor. "Watch me." He paused and glanced back. "And just so you know...I'm letting you go just because we were friends, brothers. But...if I see you here when I turn back, I will tear you to pieces with my bare hands." And with that, he staggered towards Amrita, never looking back once.

Prateek stood rooted to the spot, frozen in time. His entire world crumbled around him. Manas was his life and without him, there was no Prateek. He stared at the back of Manas' head, hoping he would turn back, even for a second.

But Manas never did. He helped Amrita up. She recoiled from him at first, but as the trauma cleared, she stopped struggling.

Prateek gaped at them as Manas, and Amrita talked. They talked for hours; all the while, Prateek stood at the same spot, unable to move, hoping, praying for a something from Manas. But nothing. It was as though he didn't exist. Amrita's face was a cocktail of emotions, transitioning from one to another as both Manas and Amrita talked. Shock, repulsion, love, and finally, understanding. Manas hugged her as she cried her heart out in his arms.

Prateek finally understood. This was it. It was really over. He lumbered out of the warehouse into the light and walked—walked till he didn't know where he was, and what he was doing. He walked till he faded into the light.

Sonam

Sunday, April 27, 2014

You have to run with the boys and still be a girl.
It was hard work, but she had gotten used to it.

Sonam blinked away the weariness from her eyes. The 'spot your bag' game was about to start at the airport. She had been on the verge of turning in last night when Nasir barged into the room with crazy, red eyes and announced his breakthrough. And soon after, Akshay got the call about Alex's car. The flurry of activity that followed didn't agree with her body which was already shutting down after two drinks. The night went down the hill from that point.

She had never felt the hassle of air travel until the day before. On paper, you get a lot of free time during travel, but you are never free at any point in time. The travel always looms over your consciousness like a black cloud. When you are done checking in, you stand in a queue for security clearance. Once that is done, you get into a mind-numbing wait for boarding, checking the watch and the gate every ten minutes. You would think you can sleep on board, but no. Even at four in the morning, there had to be snacks. And once the snacks were done, they came to collect it, and by that time it was time for the descent.

To sum up, not an inkling of sleep last night. She was relieved when the captain announced that they would be landing in Trivandrum shortly. Those who loved tongue twisters called it Thiruvananthapuram.

Biting down on a wide yawn, Sonam observed the 'men' in her team lined up, ready to pluck the luggage from the conveyor belt. If they thought that she was a weak, little thing, why not milk it for all it's worth?

Out of the corner of her groggy eyes, she caught Nasir stealing a glance at her. Suddenly she was conscious of her frayed hair sticking up at odd angles, dark circles which must have made an appearance after last night, and early morning grumpiness. She must have looked like a bum.

"Err... Let me go to the washroom and freshen up. You guys can manage this right?" she asked pointing towards the luggage belt.

Salim grunted a yes and Nasir nodded, without turning. Nobody, except Akshay, had gotten any sleep last night. Akshay could sleep standing in a moving bus and he wasn't going to let an airplane ride ruin his sleep.

Sonam dashed to the washroom, pocketed her thick glasses, and splashed cold water on her face. It gave her heart a much-needed jump start. Out came her mobile make up set; a swoop of a hairbrush here, a touch of lipstick there, and five minutes later she was as good as new.

She had perfected the art of minimal make-up with maximum efficiency when she was in college. Always the last to wake up, she hardly had enough time to wash her face before rushing to class. But on the other hand, she had an insatiable desire to look good. All that practice came in handy, cause in her line of work it was hard to hold on to her femininity and still be taken seriously. She had to run with the boys and still be a girl. It was hard work, but she had gotten used to it.

She took a step back, and evaluated her five-minute job. The lighting and mirrors in airports were always so flattering. Her auburn hair spread thickly on her shoulders and disappeared down her back. Nothing sticking up at odd angles anymore. The best feature on her face was her pouty, full-lipped mouth which brimmed with colour. The dimples on her rosy cheeks were a close second.

She had caught Nasir stealing glances at her for some time now, but he had not shown any interest other than that. Was it because of her broad, slightly tip-tilted nose? She thought it was cute as a button, but you never know.

Sonam shoved the mini make-up kit into her handbag, and exited the washroom. It was Avinash who spotted her first. He nudged Salim, and both of them gaped at her, their mouth half open and eyes zigzagging between her and the washroom.

"You guys have a salon in there as well?" Salim asked, flicking his thumb towards the washroom.

"Shut up," Sonam said, suppressing a smile.

Nasir talked animatedly on the phone, pacing up and down the luggage belt. Sonam wondered why she found him attractive. A wiry hawk-like man, a badly preserved 44, was not her type. His arms, that looked like they had been squeezed out of tubes, were moving frantically as he was trying to get his point across to the man on the other end of the line.

A thick cap of wiry, black hair with soot grey highlights hugged the oval-shaped head. A hawk-like nose extended down and ended in an umbrella of black, short hair which sheltered his thin mouth. Luminous jet-black eyes glimmered on a deeply tanned, red-brown skin. A narrow jaw with rounded shoulders and a thin waist did not scream authority, but his presence was intimidating.

After much deliberation, Sonam decided it was the eyes. Those dark, watchful eyes that missed nothing; they were the hook. His brilliant understanding of the criminal mind was the line, and his unassuming manner was the sinker. Her gaze traced the contour of his nose and rested on the ridge where his Ray-Ban's trenched. It was then that he dropped the phone to his pocket and glanced at her. As quickly as she can, she averted her gaze to Akshay, who was standing beside Nasir. Heat rushed up to her cheeks, and she hoped to God that it didn't show.

Akshay stood next to Nasir with a thousand-yard stare. Sonam always thought Akshay was in love with Nasir. His drooping eyes set in deep shadowed sockets always seemed to shimmer when Nasir talked to him. He worshipped Nasir and the ground he walked on. Sometimes he reminded her of the pug who followed the boy everywhere he went in that commercial. A giggle escaped her when she pictured Akshay, but his long narrow head with a thin unassuming face was replaced with the pug's.

Nasir announced that the pickup from the Commissioner's office was there. Avinash and Salim had already grabbed all their luggage and stacked it onto a trolley. Nasir led the way out from the terminal, with Akshay closely behind, pushing the trolley with luggage.

Soon enough, they were all packed, neatly, in an Innova. Nasir rode in the passenger's seat, with the driver. Akshay, Avinash and Salim lined up along the middle row which left Sonam in the back seat, with the luggage.

Great! Where was the chivalry now? thought Sonam.

"So, boss...What's the plan?" Akshay asked.

Nasir turned slightly towards them, revealing his gorgeous profile. "As of now, it's pretty simple. We know he is here, and we use local police to spread the net and hope he falls into that."

"Hope he falls into that?" Avinash asked. "That sounds more like a prayer than a plan, boss."

Nasir laughed mirthlessly. "I guess it is. What can I say? This is the best we have now."

"If we can stop him from taking one more life, I'd be more than willing to pray for it," Akshay said.

"All of you are pessimists. At least now we are slightly ahead of the game," Sonam chipped in. "He has no idea we are here, and that we are on his trail. We should also look into the connection with The Butcher."

The car descended into a sudden silence as Nasir's face hardened.

"Definitely," Nasir said. He turned back towards the driver and said, "Can you pull over next to that tea shop for a second?" He glanced back at no one in particular. "Anybody else need a black tea?"

Akshay nodded, and they both got out when the SUV stopped.

Sonam nudged Salim from behind. "Listen, what is the deal with Nasir and The Butcher?

Avinash turned back, his piggy eyes with pockets under them shouted his love for alcohol. "Ah!... I was wondering why you brought up that name. It's a touchy topic for the boss."

"I'm sure you've read about 'The Butcher of Bhalswa' in your days at the academy," said Salim.

"Uh-huh," she nodded.

"What you might not have read about is that the CBI officer who was investigating the case was none other than our boss."

"What?!...Why isn't that even mentioned anywhere?"

"Asok Sir redacted it out. You know...considering the situation. It would have been a constant reminder of what happened," said Avinash.

Sonam's eyes flew open. "Asok Tiwari? The Director of CBI?"

Avinash guffawed. "Yes, the same guy. But he wasn't the director yet back then. He is a good friend of Nasir, and a mentor. Boss practically owes his life to that man."

The Director of CBI as a mentor. Must be nice.

"You've read the books, and you know what happens, right?" asked Avinash. "It was like The Butcher woke up one day, and decided that's it. It stopped as abruptly as that. Almost as if he just disappeared into thin air."

"Every officer in Law Enforcement will have that one case—the one that got away." Salim drew in a deep breath. "It was The Butcher for him. It grew from a mission to passion and soon slipped into obsession. Putting everything else on hold, he went after him. But when The Butcher disappeared, the trail was as cold as a damp January Delhi morning."

"Bottom line is, boss, didn't take it so well," Avinash said, "He hit the bottle pretty hard, trying to drown out reality."

Salim nodded. "There were times when he would stay under for days on end, or so the rumour goes."

"Eventually, he lost the respect of the force." Avinash let out a tired laughter. "Became the cliched loser drunk cop."

"The whole fiasco also pushed his marriage into a tailspin from which it never recovered," said Salim. He added as an afterthought, "Can't blame the wife. When all you see of your husband is a stranger carrying him inside the house, drunk and smelling of alcohol, you get tired…Maybe she didn't recognize the man in her bed anymore."

"This went on till Asok Sir came into the picture. Nobody knows what happened, but the story goes like this...In one rare coincidence, Asok Sir walked into a bar with some of his friends and saw Nasir passed out at the table. He recognized Nasir – he was one of the rising stars in the force and the Butcher case gave him more visibility. Asok Sir took Nasir home, threw him under the shower, and then talked to him all night. Nobody knows what they talked about, but from the very next day, Nasir was a very different man.

"Asok Sir practically dragged him back from fading into oblivion, put him in therapy, and brought him back to life. Nasir agreed to everything, including therapy, but he had one condition. He wanted to devote his life to keeping serial killers off the street. He didn't want another Butcher. Not only did Asok Sir agree, but he also took a personal interest in Nasir to make sure he was trained the proper way, and equipped to handle his mission. He personally recommended Nasir to be sent to the U. S to train with the F.B.I. That's how the Special Crimes division started off.

"Initially, it was a single officer division, with just Nasir holding the fort. But as Nasir matured and started recruiting, me and Salim joined the team. Then Akshay joined, followed by Deepak Nair—the forensic expert before you."

Sonam let out a long breath of air and leaned back against the luggage. "Quite a story. What happened to my predecessor? I know he asked to be transferred out of the unit"

Salim chuckled. "Not everyone can do what we do. Especially the forensic expert, looking at crime scenes, all day long. I guess Deepak got burned out with all the cruelty in the world. When his wife delivered a baby girl, he decided to take a step back. He talked to Nasir, and put in a transfer request."

"... are more than ready to give us all the assistance we need," Nasir's voice drifted in as he, and Akshay came back. They got in the SUV and it resumed its journey.

Nasir turned back, his mood vastly improved. A shot of tea does that to people. "Kerala Police doesn't want a murder on their soil and they will help us avoid that. But in the off chance something happens, I've asked them to preserve the crime scene for us. So, I say we put out an alert for the car and circulate a photograph to all police stations."

"We should just put out a wanted lookout in the newspapers and television," said Salim.

Akshay straightened up, alarmed. "No. That would just give away our element of surprise. We want him to be careless."

Nasir nodded. "Akshay's right." Akshay positively beamed with happiness. "We should keep it under the radar. Akshay, get in touch with the counter-intelligence wing, and tap into their network. Avinash, Salim... look around and pick out some officers and keep them on call. We might need them. And Sonam, you take the lead on Forensics, if something comes up. If not, just tail me. I could use some help."

"Let me get some shut eye," Nasir said, straightening and facing forward, "I suggest you guys get some sleep as well. Now we wait."

The Artist

Tuesday, April 29, 2014

*Sometimes when the thing you want is within reach,
your hand weighs a ton.*

T*hud!*

Alex woke up with a start and looked around, his body winding up for a reaction. A frail kid flew past him on a cycle with a bundle of newspapers strapped to the back of his cycle. It took him a couple of seconds to figure out where he was.

He smacked himself on the side of his head, and sat up straight. He must have dozed off while staking out Manas' house.

Slowly as the fog cleared, it all came back to him. After collapsing on the musty bed in the lodge, he slept straight through the next day and woke up in the afternoon. Almost twenty-four hours later. His eyes were still bleary and body tired. He got something to eat to calm his rumbling stomach, made a plan for the next day, set the alarm and went straight back to sleep. The first thing he remembered after that was the annoying alarm blaring at four in the morning. He had dragged himself up, got ready, checked out of the lodge, and made his way to Manas' house.

Alex rubbed his eyes clear of the lingering sleep. Staking out a place, studying every little detail about it was an enormously boring task. A series of rhythmic, and comical horns preceded the arrival of the milkman round the corner on his moped; two large stainless-steel containers hung on both sides. He stopped in front of Manas' house, filled the bottle left out for him, and left. Alex picked up the pen and noted down the time. *6:53 am.*

An elderly couple jogged past his car a third time that morning. The neighbour's front door opened, and a man in his late thirties lumbered out, dressed in formals, still rubbing the sleep away from his eyes. He yelled something into the house and left, presumably for work. The time was 7:15 am.

The sun tried to pierce the murky clouds but, in the end, settled for a dull glow in the sky. The first sign of life from Manas' house came at

8:15 am. A young girl in a white shirt and a crimson skirt which extended just below her knees opened the gate and stepped onto the footpath. A schoolgirl on the verge of becoming an adult, no doubt. *That must be his daughter*, Alex thought.

She swung a black knapsack over her shoulder and tacked it in place. Dark hair with burgundy highlights framed her oval face and extended all the way down to her chest. Her silky hair bounced behind her as she skipped towards the corner of the street, glancing at her wrist and the street alternatively.

She came to a stop when she reached the corner, checked her watch one more time, and brushed her fringes back behind her ears; three metallic studs shined proudly along the upper part of her ears. A tempo came rumbling down the street at 8:24 am, and she hopped on. Heads swivelled as she brushed past guys at the front to her friends at the back of the bus, and Alex understood why. She was a rare mixture of innocence and beauty.

At 8:26 am, the door of the house opened again and an older woman stepped out, probably in her late thirties. She was wearing an aquamarine kurta and light grey denim pants. With a nimble twist of her wrist she glanced at her watch, got into one of the cars parked out front, and pulled out of the house.

The rest of the neighbourhood also woke up, shook off the morning slumber and headed to work, but one hatchback remained in Manas' driveway.

Manas must be inside.

This was it. This was the moment he was looking forward to the most. Sometimes when the thing you want is within reach, your hand weighs a ton. Never meet your heroes, isn't it? All he had to do was just walk into the house and meet his guardian angel, his role model, his hero. The man who filled the void left by his father, whom he had never met. But still? What if Manas isn't the man Alex thought he would be?

Alex closed his eyes, shook off the doubts, steeled his nerves, and got out of the car. He breathed in the crisp morning air, and opened his eyes.

He expected to be in the well-lit street, a few meters away from the house of the man he wanted to be while growing up. But instead, he found himself in a dark room, distinctly Victorian, complete with a fireplace. But the fire had died out; faint glowing embers were drawing their dying breaths. The centrepiece of the room was a midnight purple armchair with buttoned upholstery. A lone yellow lamp on a coffee table behind the armchair provided the only light in the dark room.

The Butcher stretched out on the armchair, a leg over the other, his head hidden in shadow.

Alex staggered closer. With each step, he relived each of his 'artworks.' That gave him strength; confidence came racing back.

He blinked, and he was back in the street, facing a closed gate in front of Manas' house. With a little shove, the black gate swung open with a faint creak.

The slow creak of the gate morphed into a deep voice. The Butcher's voice. "You made it..."

Alex drew in a sharp breath. This was it. "Yes... I promised I would," Alex said, "I have so much to tell you."

The Butcher nodded his head imperceptibly, motioning Alex to come closer.

Alex stepped closer to the couch and hesitated.

"Well, go on..." The Butcher said.

And Alex did. He told The Butcher everything. He started with the beginning and went on to recount each 'artwork,' explaining them in excruciating detail. They shared anecdotes about the ruses they used to trap their victims. They laughed about how the victims almost always begged for their life at the end. They talked about Alex, his dreams, his plans, and his purpose.

When the conversation wound down, there was a moment of silence. Alex imagined a smile on The Butcher's face, hidden in the shadows; the kind of smile a father has when his son narrates how he came in first in the race at school. Without a word, The Butcher rose to his feet and Alex closed his eyes, letting himself melt into the warm embrace.

Alex blinked again, and he was back on the porch in front of Manas' house. He leaned on the Hyundai parked on the car porch, catching his breath, orienting himself. Up ahead, there was a wooden door which marked the entry to the house. It had 'Manas Mitra' engraved on it, and just above the engraving, a bronze lion statue hung on the door. There was a button inside the roaring lion's mouth. Alex pressed it; a two-toned bell rang inside. Alex took a step back, adjusted his shirt, combed his hair with his hands, and waited for Manas.

Manas

Tuesday, April 29, 2014

If you want something, you have to take it.

Manas zig-zagged the kitchen juggling three crises as he got ready for office. The toast was getting burned at the stove, the milk threatened to spill over at any moment, and Bella or her stomach, he couldn't be sure, growled for food. It took all the acrobatic trickery he had to turn off the stove in time, saving his toast and milk, dragging around Bella, who was hanging on to his leg by the sleeve of his pants.

He took a second to admire his awesomeness in saving the day before giving into Bella's tug and heading towards her bowl to fill it with food. Just as he grabbed the yellow bag of dog food from the counter, the doorbell rang. Bella perked her head up, twitching to the side, sniffing the air, and eyed the dog food.

Manas bent down and scratched the sides of her neck. "Can you hold on for one second? Be right back.... Stay."

He strolled through the living room to the door, Bella at his heels. She never cared much for obedience. Manas turned back midway and in a final attempt, said," Bella...Stay." His arms reinforced the command with the universally recognised gesture to stop.

Bella barely glanced at him as she went ahead and stationed herself in front of the door in a typical sitting watchdog position. Manas shook his head, laughing and opened the door.

A sinewy, well-built man on the tall side of six feet greeted him with a nervous smile. Dark tendrils of short, messy hair curtained his tall forehead. The cleft chin deepened further as the man smiled, a week-old beard obscuring it partly.

"Er....Mr. Manas Mitra?" his well-marked black brows arched in question.

"Yes…" Manas dragged out the word. He didn't have time to deal with a door-to-door salesman.

"May I come in?"

Manas narrowed his eyes. "What is this about? I really don't have a lot of time." Bella must have sensed his reluctance because she let out a low growl, and got off her sitting position.

The man put up his hands in a defensive gesture, palms facing outward. "Oh! I'm sorry. I didn't give you any context." His eyes flitted between Bella and Manas. "I have come a long way to meet you, and I'll not take a lot of your time. I'll be quick, I promise." His face relaxed into an easy smile.

Manas entertained his paranoia for a moment and brushed it aside. He let the tension go out of his hands and let the door swing inward. "Okay. Come in, and please make it fast. I have to leave in half an hour."

It took a lot more convincing to get Bella to back off. She just stood across the doorway, barking and growling, eyeing the intruder with suspicious eyes. But in the end, Manas managed to get her to follow him to the living room chair, where he sat down with a hand on Bella. Her muscles flexed under his hands as she positioned herself by his side, never fully relaxed.

The man sat down on the couch opposite Manas, a dark oak coffee table in between them. He kept glancing at Bella, who lowered her head and observed him.

"So...where are you from?" asked Manas. He wanted to cut short the conversation in the beginning itself if the man was a door-to-door salesman or worse—an Amway marketer. Bella moved under his arms, and he wound his arms through her leash for safety.

The man leaned back in his chair. "Delhi." His chocolate brown eyes maintained steady eye contact.

Manas stiffened in the chair as the air around him froze. Morning sunlight pierced the room through the window blinds. But it didn't have the desired warm effect. "Delhi?" he asked, "Are you sure you got the right address?" His grip on Bella's leash relaxed a bit. She must have felt the extra room. The hair on her neck rose as she shifted her weight to her hind legs.

The man's eyes flickered between Bella, the leash, and Manas. He lowered his head and hunched his back. "This is not at all how I imagined this moment," he said with a heavy sigh. From under his waistband, a 9mm revolver appeared in his hands. The black metal gleamed in a ray of sunlight as he set the gun down on the coffee table; the barrel pointing towards Manas.

Manas grabbed the armrest of his chair. He deliberated reaching for the gun, but it was on the side nearer to the intruder. *No, wouldn't make it in time.* The soft leather of the armrest felt slippery with his sweat. "Who..."

His throat was so dry that the words rasped out of his throat. "Who are you?" Manas knew the answer to that question but didn't want to admit it.

The man smiled; it was a ghost of a smile without an ounce of happiness. "You already know that. I can see it in your eyes. The suspicion, the frantic scrambling to neutralise the situation." He chuckled. "You and I are not that different."

"You don't know me," said Manas.

"Oh, I do. I think I know you better than your wife and daughter. But I digress...I came to tell you a story. A story of a boy who grew up without a father." The Artist leaned back into the couch and crossed his legs. "The story of a boy who had lost his way but found it in the strangest way possible. I assure you...by the time I am done with the story, we wouldn't need the gun anymore."

A bead of sweat trickled down Manas' temple, over his cheekbones. He was acutely aware of the cold trail it left on the side of his head. Rushing him would not work. Mobile phone was on the dining table, a good seven feet from where he was sitting. Discreetly calling for help was also out of the question. Showing his hand too early was the last thing he wanted to do. All that was left to do was let him tell his wretched story and wait for the right moment. Manas relaxed, for the intruder's benefit, settled into the chair, and stroked Bella's golden-brown head.

A genuine smile broke out of the man's face; the chocolate in his eyes sparkled. "The story starts 29 years ago in Bhalswa. A bastard boy was born, his father skipped town before his birth. The world knew his mother to be a hardworking, loving woman who took care of her children—the boy and two elder sisters. And it was true, for most parts. She was a kind and caring mother to the two girls, the boy's sisters. But when it came to the little boy, she turned into this evil bitch who gave the worst mother in the world a run for her money." The man took a deep breath. "The boy took this as a norm, but always wondered why his mother behaved so differently with him. As he got older, it became worse. Every night his mother would lock him in a cold, dark storeroom while she and his sisters headed off to a cosy bed. Lying in that dark room, crying himself to sleep, the boy wondered what he had done wrong."

"Any theories?" the man asked Manas.

Manas shook his head.

"May be the mother blamed the boy for the father leaving? Or maybe he reminded her of his father too much that she projected the father's vices on the son?" the man suggested.

Manas shifted in his chair. The man's voice was true, resonant, and had a very nearly operatic quality. It was one of those voices that could grab attention and hold it for a long time. "I couldn't comment on something that I have no idea about."

"You know…later, the boy learned that he was locked in the room because his mother feared he would molest his sisters. Apparently, the father did." A bitter smile broke out on the man's face; it did not quite reach his eyes.

"So, as you can imagine, the boy drudged through his grey life, getting through one day at a time. And since being at home meant being with his mother, he became quite the explorer. And one day, when he was wandering around the neighbourhood, he came across something in the colourless garbage which changed his life; or nudged it in a tail spinning spiral, depending on who you ask.

"A blood red, leather, high heels.

"In his bleak excuse of a life, the shoe was a beacon of colour; a symbol of hope, but most of all a toy he loved very much. He took the shoe home and was playing with it when his mother showed up; face red and nostrils flaring. She snatched away the shoe like she snatched away everything else from his life, and he got the worst beating he had ever got that day." He rolled his tongue over his gums. "By the end of the beating, through a haze of fading consciousness, he saw his hope burning on the ground. The boy stared helplessly at the mesmerising interplay of colours—the bright yellow flames licking the red leather, turning it into black, and blending it into his grayscale world."

Manas played and replayed all the likely ends to this confrontation in his head. It always ended badly. He swallowed hard, feeling his Adam's apple bobble. The man stared deeply into space, may be reliving his memories. Was he distracted enough to sneak a move? Manas straightened his back and shifted his weight forward, firming his legs, ready to pounce.

The man, still staring into space, reached for the gun on the coffee table. He cocked the hammer, wound his fingers over the trigger, and held it against his face, the barrel pointing upwards; the black metal contrasted against his white skin. "This is not how it was supposed to happen." He stared at the ceiling fan for a couple of moments and shot off a question to no one in particular. "Are you testing me?"

When he turned his gaze back to Manas, his eyes glistened with an extra layer of liquid. "Don't make me do things I would regret. I just want to talk."

The message was loud and clear. If he wanted to kill Manas, he would have done it already. Maybe he just wanted to talk. His best play was to just relax, and listen to the story, and wing it. Manas tightened his grip on Bella's leash and sunk into his chair deeper.

The Artist lowered the gun onto his lap, the barrel towards Manas with his fingers still around the trigger. "Hmmm....where were we? Ah! The shoes. The mother never really understood what that shoe meant to him. A part of him changed when he lost his only colour in his world to an irrational fit of anger. Let's call it the *'Turning Point.'*"

"Is there a point to the story?"

"Yes, of course," the man chuckled, "You think I would waste your time if there wasn't?" He rose to his feet, the gun still trained on Manas. "Mind if I get a glass of water?" And without waiting for an answer, he moved to the kitchen.

A clink of glass, a gurgle of water, and he was back with a glass of water in his hands.

"Have you ever tried throwing pots, Manas?"

"No, never been much into pottery."

"Oh! You must try it. So much fun. I just love the process of turning the ball of soft clay into a well-formed pot. A kid's mind is also like a ball of soft clay. It is pressed, squeezed, and pulled gently upwards and outwards in the potter's wheel of time by the influences in his childhood. And as you must have guessed, the boy in our story had very questionable influences."

The Artist sipped water from the glass and set it on the coffee table as he sank into the couch, resuming his old position. "So, the '*Turning Point*' propelled him towards a spiral of decay. It started one afternoon when the boy was spending time wandering the streets in suburban Delhi. An up-town woman sashayed her way across the street, red heels on her marble feet. She, more specifically, her red shoes, caught his attention. He followed her as she threaded her way through different shops on either side of the street and then finally to the rich part of the town as she disappeared into a white, double storey house through an ornate wooden door. The flash of red sneaking through the closing door was seared into the boy's brain. He stationed himself in front of the house, waiting for a glimpse. And it soon became a daily routine. After a week of waiting around, he realised something.

"Life does not grant you freebies. It teases you with the goods and mocks at you, at your inability. Nobody has given him anything in life. If you want something, you have to take it."

Manas scoffed at the excerpt from 'Chicken Soup for Deranged Souls.' "If you want something, you work for it. People who just take it...we call them thieves."

The Artist chuckled. "That subtle distinction was lost on a fucked up eight-year-old. One day he saw that the lady didn't close the door behind her. He crept up the stairs that led to the door, and peeked in. The corridor was empty and right next to the half-open door, a splash of red. It mesmerised him, drew him into a trance. When he heard movement inside, he didn't think twice. Just grabbed the shoe and sprinted home. He never looked back, never stopped, until he closed the door of his house behind him. As he caught his breath, hugging the fruit of his illicit endeavour, he realised that the act of stealing filled his world with more colours than a paltry stroke of red. An explosion of colours which brought a new life to his grey canvas. And thus, started what the boy referred to later in life as *'The Summer of Colour.'* It started with the shoe, and pretty soon escalated to women's underwear."

"Eight-year-old, and stealing women's underwear?" Manas arched his eyebrows, and pushed the ends of his lips down. "That's quite the jump from shoe to underwear."

The man shrugged off the veiled sarcasm. "Ah!... It's not impossible. After all the boy was living with his mother, and two sisters. Women's underwear hung around the house like bats in a cave. But what triggered the switch was not that. It was that one day, when he chanced upon something exciting on one of his break-ins. As usual, he was creeping towards the shoe stand in a house. It was at the end of the corridor, and on his way there, he saw the lady of the house through the open door to the bedroom. He was mesmerized by what he saw. As the lady stripped off items of clothing, one by one, he felt strange stirrings in his pants." The man chuckled. "At first, he thought it was an ant and touched there in panic. But it wasn't an ant sting; it felt funny, funny good. It was the woman's screams that brought him back to his senses, and he bolted from the house. All through the dash back home, the boy was reliving the experience, and that 'funny feeling'." The man ran his long and slender fingers along the arm rest of the couch.

"Slippery slope," he chuckled as he reached for the glass of water. After a sip of water, he continued. "It's easy to slide down the slope, especially if you have no one to guide you. And who did the boy have? A father who left before he was born, a mother who doesn't care and turned his sisters against him, and no older brothers to show him the way; he was doomed to slide down the slope at full speed. The closest alternative he had was the vicar at the church."

He bowed down and ran his thumb through the cleft of his chin. "The boy was a devout Christian, attended masses, and confessed every week. The priest told him repeatedly that he was on a path towards the fires of hell, and unless he changed his ways, there was no redemption for him. No amount of Rosemary's would make up for his wayward lifestyle. The boy hated fire, and the fires of hell were the last thing he wanted to see. He laid down in the dark every night, praying to God for forgiveness and hoping the priest was wrong, that there was still redemption for him. It was then that God sent him a guardian angel."

Manas pinched the bridge of his nose. "Guardian Angel? God? I think you've got the wrong house. The church is down the road, my friend."

The man scratched his temple with the tip of his index finger. "When you hear Guardian Angel, what do you see? White garbed, feathery winged angels? Levitating above ground?"

"I don't usually see things that do not exist."

The man ignored the disagreement and plodded on. "I believe they come in different forms and not in the white-garbed caricature of an Angel. How do you think your chance upon people who help you when you most need it?"

"People with humanity and kindness, and not a supernatural Guardian Angel."

"OK. You believe in people, and I believe in angels. Let's leave it at that. We can discuss faith another day." The man leaned forward, set the gun on the coffee table, and flicked it. The revolver spun around the cylinder with a whirring sound. "Now, listen to this part closely. This is where it gets interesting." The revolver stopped spinning, and the barrel pointed towards Manas.

"In one of his illegal excursions, the boy sneaked into an empty house. He rummaged through the laundry and found a black lace bra, still musty from recent use. As he inhaled the intoxicating scent, he heard movement behind him. He whipped around and saw the husband staring at him, red-faced. The boy took off as the man exploded, spewing a slur of expletives. He chased the boy through the streets and soon caught up with the boy, beating him senseless..."

Manas' heart missed a beat. That sounded familiar.

"The boy woke up in a hospital, numerous bandages across his body, and his right hand in a cast. In his pain-filled solitude, he did some soul searching. He was convinced that this was God's way of telling him to stop. The sign he was looking for. His mother refused to pay the hospital bill, and he was back home the next day with a resolve to make amends to his wayward life. The boy went to sleep, determined to be a better person, but what he saw when he woke up changed his life."

Manas froze; his whole body, even his breath froze. He knew what the boy saw. Suryakant. He never forgot the names; they were seared into his consciousness. If he closed his eyes, he could still see Suryakant's head swaying from the tree, moonlight gleaming off the blood dripping from the neck. Manas squeezed his eyes tighter, forcing the vision out of his mind.

"... who cared about him. A guardian angel sent from heaven..."

Manas swallowed hard, his mouth was dry as a desert. He felt his poker face cracking.

"...God hadn't abandoned him as he thought. Instead, he sent a protector. He wasn't straying away from the path but was on the right path. It was as clear a sign from God as any. With this newfound belief in his path, the boy embarked on a journey. A journey to fulfil the will of God, guided by the path laid out by his guardian angel. And it is that journey that led me here, now." The man grabbed the glass of water from the coffee table and downed the whole glass. "You might know me as The Artist, but you can call me Alex." He extended his left hand for a handshake.

Manas toyed with the idea of owning up to the "guardian angel" role and using the influence to get ahead of the situation. But that meant having this deranged criminal around his family. And it also meant owning up to his past and he wasn't sure he wanted to know how deep that rabbit hole went.

Manas regarded the extended hand for a moment before meeting it with a firm hand. "Nice to meet you. And that was a delightful story, touching. And you know....you were right. You don't need the gun anymore." He smiled warmly. "You don't need it because, I am not the person you are looking for." It took all his effort not to wind up his body and tip Alex off about the bluff. "I hope you find him, but now my time has run out," said Manas, as he straightened up in the chair, as a precursor to standing up.

Alex bunched up his black brows, his tall forehead riddled with lines, in a disinterested frown. "Really? You're gonna play dumb? Amrita tried to play dumb, look how that turned out."

There were some words which evoked a visceral reaction every time they were uttered. 'Amrita' was one of those words for Manas. He couldn't stop the strange cocktail of rage, and heartbreak, that was unleashed in his body. It was too late by the time he realised his face had betrayed him.

A sly smile of victory broke out on Alex's face and with that the window of 'playing dumb' was shut. Manas exhaled deeply, and let the facade break down. There was no point in pursuing the current strategy. It was time to pivot. The next best play was to pacify Alex and diffuse the situation as calmly as possible.

Manas rose from his chair and tied his hands behind his back. Alex jumped for the gun and held it in his hands, ready to fire.

"I knew Amrita. I'll admit that much," said Manas, deliberately not looking at the barrel trained at him, "But The Butcher you came searching for, that's not me. Not anymore. Not for twenty years." Manas put up a brave face and turned around to meet Alex's stony stare. "Let me be absolutely clear. I do not want any trouble, nor revenge. The past is past, and I want nothing to do with that. But if you hang around here any longer, I'll be forced to call the police."

The muscles in Alex's gun-holding hand flexed; his finger moved lightly over the trigger. Manas froze, adrenaline pumping through his veins, and studied Alex; his movements, his face, looking for a way out.

Ales's face darkened, jaws clenched, and he gripped the gun tighter. His finger on the trigger hesitated. This was it. This was the moment. Manas' muscles clenched in anticipation of an immediate action.

And then a shadow fell over Alex's face. Was it sadness? Disappointment? Or was it both? Manas' muscles relaxed a bit seeing the anger on Alex's face draining out. He looked like someone who had lost his prize catch. And slowly, blood returned to the previously white knuckles as Alex relaxed his gun-holding hand. And in a sudden explosion of movement, he shot up to his legs, pushing the couch back a foot. And without a word, he rushed to the door. With his hands on the doorknob, he paused. "If you want something, you work for it," he said, echoing the lines Manas had said a while ago. "I came all this way to meet The Butcher, and I will meet him, one way or the other." He slammed the door behind him; it shook on its hinges.

Manas' hands trembled as he struggled to close the blinds on the window. What did Alex mean by that? A small voice in his mind told him that he should confess to Anuradha. But that voice lacked conviction. His perfect life seemed like a house of cards, swaying in the wind just then. An uncontrollable shiver plagued him all the way from the window till he collapsed into the chair, burying his face in his hands.

"That was pathetic." A voice spat from the shadows.

Manas jerked back from his slump; his alert eyes scanned the house. It was empty.

The Artist

Tuesday, April 29, 2014

A man who is sleeping can be woken up,
but not a man who is pretending to sleep.

Sun lashed out at earth. Black asphalt shimmered in the heat, stretching all the way till it met the sky. The mottled beige and red sections on the wall to his left zipped past him as he sped along the road parallel to the Trivandrum International Airport.

Alex had been driving around the city all day. He knew it wouldn't be as easy as walking up to Manas and demanding to see The Butcher. But maybe some part of him did or wished it would be. Alex recalled what Manas had said when he told him that life didn't give anyone freebies. "If you want something, you work for it." Exactly. That's what he was going to do.

The black steering wheel sizzled his fingers every time he shifted positions. The back of his shirt clung on to him as he cranked up the air conditioner. Because of the runway, there were no trees to save him from the onslaught of the sun, but he was happy to get a clear sky after days of gloom.

It would not happen in a few hours. What he needed to do may take days or even weeks. But this meant that he couldn't crash at the lodge he had checked in. He needed some place isolated, somewhere hidden. A bit of googling and asking people posing as tourist got him a few abandoned factories or warehouses around Trivandrum. Armed with Google Maps and the lady who lives in it, he had been scouting these places. Right now, he was on his way to the third place in the list.

Alex pulled up on the side of the road and slid his mobile phone out of his pocket. A couple of taps and swipes and the map of Trivandrum panned out on the small screen. A blue dot marked his spot. He followed the road he was on till it met the sea and took a sharp turn to run parallel to it. A pinch on the screen zoomed it out; a couple of taps layered the satellite view on top of it. There it was, nestled into the space between the sewage treatment plant and a factory. A few abandoned warehouses. He quickly dropped a marker at the location and turned-on navigation.

"Head south-east along the Palayam-Airport Road," the lady intoned in that weird voice that stressed on all the wrong syllables.

Alex shifted into first gear and pulled out of the curb with the navigation dictating the instructions as he drove. Even at full power, the air conditioner didn't stand a chance against the strong April sun. Perspiration seeped in between his shades. With one hand, he lifted the sunglasses and wiped the burning eyes with the back of his hand.

When he opened them again, The Butcher was in his passenger seat. He threw back his head into his folded arms, a hat rested low on his long, thin nose. It hid his eyes from the blinding sunlight. His taut, bony cheeks ended in a close-shaved, well-defined, jaw.

Alex ignored his guardian angel and focused on the road. He didn't want to talk to him, not after that morning. But The Butcher just relaxed on the seat until the silence became unbearable.

Alex turned his head to his side and asked, "Did you have a lot of fun this morning?"

The Butcher pushed up his hat and peered at Alex through his half-closed eyes. "You wanted a pat on the back? Did you think it would be that easy?"

Alex shook his head in negation.

"Well then?" The Butcher shrugged. "Maybe I misread you. Maybe you are not up to the task." He sunk deeper into the seat, pulling back the hat over his eyes.

"That's not fair. I agree there was a setback, but I'm back in the game. I have bits and pieces of a plan somewhere in my mind. But the only hurdle is that I need Manas to cooperate."

"Persuasion is a powerful tool," said The Butcher.

"A man who is sleeping can be woken up, but not a man who is pretending to sleep."

"You can. If you have leverage."

"Ahh… Leverage," said Alex. He stared into the space ahead. "Where am I gonna get leverage on a man I hardly know?"

The Butcher rose from his posture and faced Alex squarely. "Like I've told you before. I am not your...fucking...teacher. And if you haven't realised it already, I am nothing but a figment of your imagination, your subconscious. So, genius, I can't tell you anything you didn't know already." He threw back his head and guffawed. "So, stop whining and grow a pair."

"In 500 meters, make a left turn," the annoying lady intoned, which brought Alex to his senses. A blur of black and red jumped in front of him out of nowhere, and instinctively, he jammed the brake pedal. A guy in a red T-shirt on a black motorcycle yelled at him in passing. "That was close, huh?"

When there was no reply, Alex checked the passenger seat. It was empty.

"That was unpleasant," he muttered under his breath, trying to calm his heart into normalcy.

"Your destination is on the right," the lady announced, and he slowed down. After parking a few meters down the road, he stepped into the hot, humid summer mid-day. In the distance, the sea rumbled as it crashed onto the shore. He gulped in the salty air in deep breaths as the humid heat beat down on him. Alex whipped out the mobile to check the maps. As he oriented himself, a faint, pungent smell of garbage poked up his nostrils. 'Allāhu akbar…Allāhu akbar…Allāhu akbar…Allāhu akbar.' The Muezzin announced the noon-time prayer through the loudspeaker mounted on the minaret of a nearby mosque.

On his right, a line of trees stood guard against intruders. Alex surveyed the road; there was nobody around. He snaked his way through the trees and as he came out on the other side, a series of three warehouses rose out of the ground, at right angles to each other; forming a 'U'. The walls were merely brown, rusted metal sheets layered, one over the other. The jagged edges of the sheets stood covered in rust as a testament to time. Wires and cables, long forgotten, wound around the sides, partially holding up the structure. The rancid smell of rotten garbage assaulted his senses. This, along with the sewage treatment plant, was the olfactory equivalent of a long hair in a mouthful of food. But it was an inconvenience he would have to live with for the next few days.

There must be an unofficial garbage dump somewhere nearby, and that means an occasional garbage truck dropping off a load. But apart from that, this was perfect. A foul-smelling garbage dump, a sewage treatment plant, and a road which led nowhere—a perfect recipe for isolation.

He circled the group of warehouses, evaluating them as he picked his way through the rubble. A pack of dogs perked their heads up from their afternoon nap and browsed the intruder, giving him only a moment of their time before they went right back to sleep. The walls of the first warehouse were well on their way to rust heaven. The gaps that rust had carved out of the walls were big enough for a cow to walk through. That would not do. He needed privacy. The second and third warehouse also followed the same pilgrimage to rust heaven with whole sections of its walls missing. Alex dropped his head to the ground along with his shoulders. After finding such a nice place, it would suck if these warehouses didn't work out.

Just as he rounded the third warehouse, he saw another abandoned warehouse which he didn't see before. It was considerably smaller than the other three, and probably why he missed it in the satellite view. Lines of trees covered two sides of the building; the three larger warehouses took care of the other sides. Privacy. But the bad news was that this one looked the most rotten with the brown of rust conquering almost all of it. Alex inched his way to the closest wall and slightly tapped it, fully expecting it to come crashing down. Surprisingly, it held its own with a loud 'gong' sound. Feeling hopeful, he circled the structure inspecting the walls. They were sturdy enough with no large holes. The icing on the cake was the door he found on the fourth side. It was so positioned that it was hidden from the road by the other warehouses. It was everything that he had hoped for. and more.

He sauntered up to the door and pushed it. It held its place. Years of rust must have shut it tight. Alex never had formal training in martial arts, but YouTube videos and self-practice went a long way. He knew the technique, and his six feet three inches of muscle and bones gave him the edge. It made him better than an average fighter. Alex took two steps back, raised his right leg, and smashed the door in with a smooth kick that delivered maximum power.

Alex stepped over the low sill of the door into the large space inside. It had all the signs of no human contact for years. Different shades of rusty brown blended into beautiful, abstract paintings on the walls. The intricate pattern of the spider webs that extended from wall to wall was so exquisite that it could be the Sistine Chapel of spiders.

There was a beauty in loneliness. An order in the haphazard way the artifacts in the vast space were arranged. Big strong columns ran from the ceiling to the ground which kept the structure standing. Nature had slowly started to reclaim the space with the greenery which cropped up here and there. An opened wooden crate lay on the ground a few steps away, and right next to it was a metal shelf at the edge of collapse under its own weight. Alex peeped into the crate and saw green mould growing on whatever was inside. The foul smell made the decision easy. That needed to go immediately.

Alex used the sleeve of his shirt to keep out the foul smell and wandered deeper into the space. He grabbed one of the pillars and shook it to see its strength, instantly realising that was a dumb move. But to his relief, it didn't budge. One of the longer sides of the warehouse housed many windows, all of which were boarded up with wooden planks. He placed his hands on his hips, and stood there with his legs apart, evaluating the space. With some work, this could be perfect. It was isolated, strong enough, and inconspicuous.

Alex plugged in his earphones, put on some music, and strode over to the wooden crate. It was time to sweat.

Shruti

Tuesday, April 29, 2014

Time heals you, helps you forget.

The singer crooned over the bouncy riffs of acoustic guitar and a mellow beat, before launching into an instantly catchy chorus. Shruti got lost in the music, the lyrics. Music had a way of flowing through her, making her body move with it. It always had more control over her body than her. *I must be looking like a complete idiot singing and dancing my way down the street.*

Taylor Swift sang her heart out about sitting by the water and making rebels of a careless man's careful daughter. *Wait! My dad's not careless; he is the epitome of 'coolness.'* Out of nowhere, an image of her dad rocking a black, dusty, leather jacket with a red bandanna across his head, straddling a Harley Davidson, flashed in her mind. Shruti pressed a hand to her mouth to stifle her giggles. *Now that would be a sight to behold.*

The giggle bubbled down as fast as it appeared as her forehead wrinkled with worry lines. Dad wasn't the cool dad she knew the past few days. This was the fourth time he missed picking her up from college this week. She didn't even bother calling her mom, she just took a bus and headed home. Who needs a babysitter? She was practically an adult.

But it was not like dad to miss picking her up. It was one of those rituals they kept up through the years. Lately, he seemed jittery and overly paranoid. Her friends had dads like that, but not hers. Whatever it is, she hoped it would disappear to where it came from, leaving her old dad to her. He was a sweetheart.

Shruti kicked a loose gravel across the road. There was a unanimous agreement among her friends that she had the best dad. He would braid her hair, wait in the department store when the girls shopped, stand at the checkout line with an armful of bras, mend her broken heart, and yet possess the rugged, confident masculinity that oozed out of him without an effort. There were at least three girls in her class that had a crush on her dad. And that's just the ones she knew about.

She still remembered that night, which her stupid sixteen-year-old self thought would be her last.

Long story short, she liked a guy, and he turned out to be a first-grade jerk. Her mother had spent all afternoon mollifying her, but she ended up in a heap on the corner of the room, crying. Everything felt wrong, the whole world felt wrong.

Dad knocked on the door and in a soft voice told her he was coming in. She quickly wiped her eyes and gathered herself to face dad. But the moment she saw his kind, comforting eyes, she felt the waterworks rearing up. He said nothing, none of the usual "it'll be ok" or "it's just a heartbreak," you will get over it. Dad just took up a spot on the floor next to her. And automatically, she leaned into his arms and buried her face into his chest.

Dad curled his arms around her and just let her cry it out.

After what seemed like an eternity, Shruti drew back her head and stared at the carpet. "I...I don't think it'll be alright."

"No, it won't be." Manas ran his hands over her head in long strokes. "I am not gonna lie to you. Heartbreaks are tough. Especially the first one."

Shruti shook her head vehemently. "No Dad, you don't understand. He was the one." And with that she launched herself into another fit of sobs which rocked her body.

"I know it feels like that now, but believe me. He was not the one, simply because the one is who you end up with." Manas leaned back his head against the wall and stared at the junction of the wall and the ceiling. "I liked a girl when I was young."

Shruti perked her head up and wiped her eyes.

Dad smiled, one of those smiles that warmed your hearts in the coldest winter.

"I have not even told Mom about this. So, this stays between us, deal?" Dad extended his hand, and they shook on it as he continued. "She was a lovely girl, smart, beautiful, and so out of my league. But for some reason, I could never fathom she liked me. We hit it off quite well. So, well that I was convinced that she was the one I want to spend my life with. But I didn't. As it turned out, I had to move out of town. And back in the days, long-distance relationship was out of the question. As I sat in the train, heartbroken, do you know what my thoughts were?"

Shruti shook her head, wiping what was left for her tears on the sleeve of her T-shirt.

"Same as yours." He mocked her crying, with exaggerated motions rubbing his eyes. "Oh no! This is the end of the world. I will never love again..."

Shruti felt the ends of her lips move slightly upwards.

Dad grew serious, and a serene smile played on his generous mouth. "And you know what happened after. Time heals you, and helps you forget. I met your mother, and fell in love. And now she is my one. So, let time do its thing and keep your chin up." He poked her with his elbow and added, "When the news of your breakup spreads in school, I bet boys would be lining up for my strong, confident cutie-pie."

Shruti didn't know why, but she felt a lot better. It was like his presence calmed her, his belief in her empowered her. And just as he told, she doesn't even remember the boy's name now. Even after a year, she could talk to Dad about anything.

She pranced her way down the road, reminiscing about her Dad, and rounded the corner towards her house. A car was parked fifty meters down the street. She could never identify the make. It's not like she never tried. She made an effort to learn them to fit in her group. Rohan and Zane always went on a tangent talking about cars, and she would be lost. But no matter how much she tried, she could never develop an interest for it. But what she had an interest in was cute guys, and one of them stood next to the car, swivelling around, obviously lost.

Somebody inside her brain punched hard on her brakes, and the prancing stopped and slowed into a sashay. She couldn't look like a dork, especially not in front of cute guys. Her heart fluttered as she stole quick glances towards him. The wiry, athletic man checked two out of three in the 'tall, dark, and handsome' list. His milk-fed chiselled face had an almost Greek God perfection; ruined only by the scrunched-up eyes surveying the area. A week's growth of beard adorned his strong jaws giving him a raw sex appeal. *Why weren't the guys in her college this cute?*

He was obviously an out-of-town-er, mostly from the northern part of India. No wonder he was lost. The guy alternated between staring at a piece of paper in his hand, scrunching his nose, and scanning the area around to get his bearings. As she was playing the possibilities of having a cute guy like him in college in her mind, she noticed that the cute guy in front of her was staring right at her. Shruti brushed her fringe into place, behind her ear, as a blush crept up her cheeks. She was painfully aware that on her wheatish face, it would show up like a red button in a white dress. Fixing her gaze firmly on the wavy lines on the pavement, she followed their meandering path forward.

Just when she thought she got past the car without making a fool out of herself, out of her peripheral vision she saw the guy approaching her. Her heart jumped up her throat and refused to go back down. Was he going to talk to her? That would be a disaster. What if she didn't know the place? Or worse, what if she forgot how to speak? A wild image of her trying to mime the directions rushed into her mind.

"Excuse me…" said the guy in a beautiful voice that begged, no demanded, attention.

Shruti composed herself, rehearsed the reply a few times in her head, and put up her best poker face. "Yes?"

"Err...Can you tell me where this is?" The guy's entrancing, chocolate brown eyes twinkled as he handed her the crumbled piece of paper. "I was supposed to meet a friend there, but now his mobile phone is switched off."

The paper was damp from his sweat. "Yeah, sure. Let me see." Shruti opened the paper and deciphered the childish scribble. Another part of her brain played a montage of all the Bollywood and Hollywood 'meet-cutes' she had seen, except that the hero was the guy standing next to her and heroine was her. *Focus, Shruti. Focus.*

She breathed a sigh of relief when she realised that she knew the address on the paper. Turning to point in the general direction of the place, she said, "You take this road down there, and take a—"

Cold hands clamped her mouth from behind and hot panic crept up her legs. Before she had time to react, a firm hand circled her torso in a vice grip, pinning her arms to her side, and lifted her off her feet. Her breath rushed out of her lungs as she fought the shock off.

"*Self Defence is primarily getting over the first shock of attack,*" her father's words echoed in her mind. She did that, but by that time she was halfway to the car.

'*Go for the assailant's soft tissue and run away the first chance you get,*' Dad's words gave her direction.

Time was running out and she had to do something. If she reached the car, it's game over. She knew what to do, she practised it countless times with her dad. But real life was different.

She hooked her left leg behind the man's left leg, anchoring her to his body, and snapped her right heel back to his groin. It connected well, and the grip loosened as the man doubled over in pain. Shruti landed on her feet and pivoted right, lashing out her bony elbow to his face. The contact sent shooting pains, radiating outward, from her elbow. She winced in pain but fought through it and continued her attack with a left cross. Her fist exploded with pain as it connected squarely on his chin.

In all the drills, she did with her Dad, this was the point where he would go down. But the man didn't. His 6-foot frame just stood there hunched over, catching his breath.

What do I do? What do I do? She felt panic clawing back to her mind. She was in over her head now. In a moment of improvisation, she swiped at the man's legs to get him on the ground. But the moment she started her motion, she knew it was a mistake. She was supposed to grab him and use her hips to push him down as she was swiping at his legs. The move fizzled out and that was enough time for the man to recover.

Shruti turned and ran for her life, but the cold hands were back, and this time stronger than before. Her legs lost contact with the ground and flailed about like a ragdoll as she was dragged back towards the car. She tried to hook her legs again to stop the erratic motion, but she never got a good enough hold. The thrashing of blood in her ears consumed her senses.

The faint light of hope was getting farther and farther away as she got closer to the car. Back door of the car opened, and she was shoved inside. *Swift*. Her brain offered a useless piece of deduction, as the man grabbed a duct tape and wound it around her mouth. It was so tight that it hurt. She flailed her hands hoping it would make contact, but he expertly dodged them and tied her up with a rope.

Panic grabbed her by its claws, dragging her down. Something moved in her peripheral vision. Out of the corner of her eyes, she saw it. A boy, skirting puberty, stood outside, rooted to his spot; his mouth hanging open. A lone witness to the scuffle. Shruti squirmed in the back seat, struggling to get out of the ropes which bounded her. She pleaded to the boy with her eyes as best as she could.

The boy fished out a mobile phone from his pocket. *Yes! Call the Police!* she thought. The boy raised the mobile phone, tapped on the screen a few times, and turned the phone sideways. Shruti gaped at the boy. If her mouth were free, she was sure it would be hanging off her jaw. *The idiot was recording it.*

The man glanced at her, then followed her gaze to the boy. "Goddammit!" He double checked the knots on Shruti's hands were tight, got out of the car, and circled closer to the boy.

Shruti twisted in the back seat and shouted at the kid to run away and call the police. But the duct tape on her mouth stifled her voice to an unintelligible moan. The kid was engrossed in filming the event that he never saw the man coming until it was too late. He snatched the mobile off his hands and hurled it on the floor.

Plastic clattered on asphalt and rang through the empty street. The boy stood there staring at his hands for a second before he bolted down the street. The man took two steps in that direction, hesitated, and turned back towards the car. On his way back to the car, he stared down Shruti.

The madness in his eyes shocked her. The charmingly sweet, chocolate eyes were long gone.

After a brief minute, he came up holding a small, black, rectangle, which he broke in half and threw away—the memory card from the boy's mobile phone.

And with it, any hopes Shruti had of getting out of the situation also broke in half.

~

The car jumped and swerved in a mad dash through traffic. It slowed down after five minutes, blending into the usual hustle and bustle of regular traffic. Shruti had been trying to wiggle out of the ropes typing her down for the past ten minutes. The only thing that gave her was a bloody wrist.

She hung on to the last of her fighting spirit, her knuckles white. The black abyss of hopelessness lay waiting below. The fall looked inevitable, but she was determined to hang on for as long as possible. But her arms were heavy, they were tired.

What was this man going to do to her? Where was he taking her? What if she never sees her parents again? Would Zane miss her when she is not there anymore?

The world blurred, shapes slowly meeting and morphing into one. She knew she was crying because there was no other explanation for the unstoppable spasms that rocked her body. The last of her fingers gave way as she descended into the dark abyss.

After a minute of unstoppable crying, the man glanced back at Shruti and flashed a smile. A smile so sweet that it didn't deserve to be on such a vile man. "Listen....girl. Don't cry. I am not gonna hurt you..." After a pause, he added, "Not unless I absolutely have to."

Shruti wanted to believe that. There was no reason for him to lie to her now. Or was she grasping at straws?

"Tell you what?...I'll take off the duct tape on your mouth... Only if you promise not to scream. Can we be civil?"

The duct tape stuck to her face constricting her breath, and she wanted that to go. She nodded vigorously.

The man reached back, with one hand, and ripped off the tape in one swift motion. An instinctive scream rose from her throat which she constricted halfway through.

A satisfied grin creased his face. "Good!...I have a feeling we are gonna be good friends. Oh, sorry! Where are my manners? My name is Alex, what is yours?"

Shruti concentrated on just breathing in and out. She needed to be in control. "Sh....Shruti"

"That's a beautiful name," Alex said, "Listen, I'm sorry for all this. It's nothing personal, but it had to be done."

Alex negotiated a tight bend in a narrow road. "You know, this is a first for me as well. No, not the kidnapping. But usually when I abduct, it's much more graceful and clean than this shit show." He chuckled. "Pathetic. What a mess! The only plus was the spunk you showed. Kudos for that. You almost got away too. That would have been embarrassing." Alex shrugged and said, "This is what happens when you do things on a whim."

Shruti wasn't sure she wanted the answer to the question, but she had to ask. "What…What are you going to do with me?" Her lips trembled at the question.

Alex set his hand on the steering wheel and turned back to face her. "You play chess, Shruti?"

A few seconds of silence passed when the rumble of the engine was the only sound around.

"I took off the gag to let you talk, so that we can get to know each other. I can always put that back if you are not in the mood for it."

A bit of bile shot up at the thought of that suffocating gag. Shruti bit it back and nodded. "Yes, a bit."

Alex glanced at Shruti through the rear-view mirror, his eyes twinkling with a smile. "That's my girl. So, you know which is the most powerful piece?"

"The Queen."

"Bingo! But do you know which is the sneakiest? The Knight. You lead a move with the Queen, and while your opponent is distracted by the dominant Queen, you sneak in a Knight to finish the job. That's what a skilful chess player does. You, my dear, are my opponent's Queen. I'm gonna keep you safe for a few days as leverage." Alex's gaze roamed over her legs, lingering a moment at the red heels. "But then again, I can't promise anything. You are very tempting." He let out a guffaw that echoed in the car.

Shruti's heart skipped a beat at the last sentence. *No, Shruti. There will be no slipping down the slippery slope of self-pity. Look at the silver lining—' I'm gonna keep you safe for a few days.'* Dad raised her to be a strong, confident woman and that was what she was going to be.

A thousand pins and needles poked her as she shifted in the back seat. Her hands, tied up behind her, were going dead. "You could do a lot better if you kidnapped the mayor's daughter." She sat upright. "I'm a nobody."

Alex's eyes flicked to the mirror before he swung the car up a lane. "No, my dear. You're extremely valuable."

Shruti looked out of the window, logging every turn Alex was making. She wanted to know where we were being taken to.

Out of the blue, Alex turned around and asked, "You heard about the serial killer on the news? The Artist?"

Shruti shrugged and instantly regretted as the pins and needles came back with venom. "Who hasn't? It's all that the news anchors can talk about this past week."

Alex glanced at her in the rear-view mirror. "Well...what do you think of him?"

"First impression: A spineless coward who kills women for his cheap thrills."

Alex clutched his heart and mocked pain. "Ouch! That hurt."

Shruti's belly twisted itself into a knot. *Something wasn't right here.*

Alex laughed a mirthless laughter. "I have a confession to make. The Artist…that's me." He raised both his hands from the steering wheel. "Before you freak out and do something stupid, let me remind you that nothing changes. I am still not planning to hurt you."

Shruti's heart dropped like it weighed a ton. *What the fuck is going on? A serial killer? Isn't that just something that happens in movies?*

Her breath sped up to the tempo of a fast salsa number. The man behind the wheels was a madman. She was in a much more serious mess than she initially thought. This beautiful man is a killer, and he is mad. The combo was not good news. It was just a matter of time before he snapped, and that will be the end of the line for her. But she had to keep the charades up. Shruti closed her eyes, took a deep breath, and brought back a bit of her sass.

"Ah yes! I'm leverage. I'm valuable. Heard it all before."

"Well, you are. You are extremely valuable to your dad. Me and him have unfinished business."

The words prodded her, like a stun gun, into numbness. The Artist? Dad? Her brain struggled to reconcile these two very separate constructs into the same context. Her dad was the Creative Director at an advertising agency, a desk job if there was any. What did a serial killer have to do with him? What kind of business did this mad man had with Dad? She leaned against the frame of the door and closed her eyes. Her head hurt.

It was the periodic vibrations that caught her attention. She surveyed the inside of the car and zeroed in on the flash of light from under the driver seat. Her mobile phone. It must have slipped out of her bag when it was thrown along with her into the back of the car. She strained her neck and adjusted herself in the seat so she can read the name on the screen. Her heart leapt up in joy when she read 'Dad' on the screen.

There wasn't a lot of time. In a few seconds, the ringtone would increase to full volume and Alex would see it. Her legs crept forward, inch by inch, cupped the phone in between her feet, and pulled it out. Balancing the phone on her left leg, she tried to swipe the call button on the screen with her right leg. The phone slipped and clattered down to the floor. *Shit!*

Alex jerked back at the noise and zeroed in on the blinking phone on the floor. The change in his demeanour was swift and visceral. He swerved left, dodging a rickshaw, and pulled up to the curb. Even before the car came to a stop, he swooped down like a hawk snatching a chicken off the ground and grabbed the phone off the floor.

The last glimmer of hope was dying right in front of her eyes. She just couldn't take it anymore. The screams that erupted off her were deafening. But they just bounced off the rolled-up windows and stayed inside the car.

Alex deftly dismantled the phone, pulled out the sim card, and scattered the parts out the window. And then he turned and stared at Shruti; a cold hard stare that threw icicles of doom at her. His sweet honey-drop eyes had the madness that he deserved. Alex's jaws moved subtly, as he ground his teeth. "I thought we were friends. And friends don't snitch," he said, as he knelt on the driver seat, extended his arms back towards her, and wrapped a fresh strip of duct tape across her mouth. Alex rummaged through his bag and pulled out a black bag which he brought down Shruti's head and tightened.

The darkness was sudden and terrifying. Inability to scream confounded her terror; incessant screams that were trying to escape her mouth, vibrated inside, and tickled her. The cord which tied her hands together was an invisible jailer who kept her in check.

Thuds and slams of doors being opened and closed jolted her in the darkness. A snake-like band slithered over her. Click! The seat belt latched onto place. Again, a series of thuds and the car sputtered to a start.

Dad! Help me, she prayed. As she bounced around in the car, stripped of her senses, her ears worked double time to make sense of the world around her.

The uproarious evening traffic drowned out the car's engine with its incessant blaring horns. But soon, it died down into an eerie calm interrupted only by an occasional rumble of a passing vehicle. *They must be outside the busy city now.*

They drove in silence for the next twenty minutes and in that silence her brain went absolutely crazy. It conjured up the most horrifying images of what would happen to her in a while. From normal murder to grisly rape-murder scenarios played out in her mind. Just when she thought she would go crazy the car slowed down and rolled to a stop. There was silence outside. If she strained, she could hear a faint whisper of waves lapping up the shore.

"We are here," a cheerful voice announced as the door opened and cold fingers clasped around her arms, pulling her out of the car. The first thing she registered was the faint, putrid smell of garbage.

It was nerve wracking to walk around blind folded, without even an arm in front of her to break the fall. But the soft hands which guided her didn't make any mistakes. She came to a stop and the hands which guided her left her. A moment of panic ensued when she heard a metallic clang, and the hand was back.

A few more steps, and they came to a stop. "I'm gonna untie you for a second now. Don't be stupid, okay?" Alex said.

A tug on the cord which tied her hands, and her hands were free. But before she could realise it, Alex shoved her forward. It sent her crashing to the ground, hands flailing about to grab on to something to break the fall.

Shruti landed on her elbows; they hurt like anything. In the darkness, her hands searched for something, anything, to hold on to, anything to use against Alex. Her hands brushed against solid metal, rough to touch, but sturdy. But it was fixed to the ground. The fleeting image of smashing the rod into Alex's head disappeared without a trace.

The soft hands were back, tying her up to the metal object she so eagerly grabbed. Rusty, hard metal grazed her arms and left a cold, stinging sensation behind.

"Shruti, welcome to your home for the next few days," Alex said, as he pulled off the black bag off her head.

The gloom of the empty space which stretched in front of her matched her mood. Rusty metal columns shot up to the roof which was nothing but rusty metal sheets. She was tied to one of those columns which held up the desolate structure; her hopes of breaking off the metal rod and escaping went up in ashes.

Alex plopped down near the closest pillar and fished out a mobile and a SIM card from his pocket.

"What do you say? Shall we call your dad?" he said, with a twinkle in his eyes.

PART II

CHAOS

"Chaos was the law of nature; Order was the dream of man."

– Henry Adams

Manas

Tuesday, April 29, 2014

Echoes are not just the hollow ghosts of the sound hitting you back. Sometimes silence echoes.

Manas' fingers danced around the steering wheel as he waited for the green light. It was a bad day to begin with. Alex waltzing into his home shook him to the core. The moment he had heard about Amrita, a small alarm had rung at the back of his mind. She was the only person in the world who knew he had gone to Trivandrum. But he dismissed it as soon as it came. Unless somebody was specifically looking for him, there was no reason for Amrita to spill the information. And even if somebody did get the information that he was in Trivandrum, he had drawn comfort in the fact that finding him in Trivandrum would be like finding the proverbial needle in the haystack. But Alex just blew that comfort out of the water and knocked on his door.

Misfortune has a habit of snowballing towards a perfect storm. And, right now, it was looking that way. He had been playing different scenarios in his mind all day, battling with himself about coming clean to Anuradha. But there was no scenario where he didn't lose the life he built here. Was he overreacting? He managed to maintain the façade with his colleagues with mere grunts and nods, but a hurricane was ravaging his mind all through the day. And caught up in that hurricane, he had lost track of time and forgot to pick Shruti up from college. He remembered the cold terror that shot down his spine when he read Shruti's message telling him not to worry and that she was taking a bus home. He didn't even see the message on time, and when he called back, she didn't answer the phone. The phone was switched off.

Take a deep breath and count to ten.

One... Two... Three...

The moment he saw green, he punched the accelerator, and the car lurched to a start. It was still a good ten minutes to reach home. His anxiety was breaking at the seams. Why didn't Shruti answer his call? And why did she turn it off? It can't be coincidence that this happens the same day Alex shows up. He wanted to meet The Butcher. He wouldn't harm his family, would he?

No! You know the drill. Calm yourself down.

Start again. One... Two... Three...

A dark blur jumped into his lane, right in front of his car. Muscle memory kicked in and slammed the brakes and the screech of the tires brought his attention back to the road. The car had come to a stop in the middle of the road and in the stillness, he realised he wasn't breathing. He took a large gulp of air to calm his frantic heart down.

The rider of the bike which jumped in front of him flailed his arms in the air. Through the rolled-up windows, he looked like a mime in a circus with his silent, but exaggerated body movements. Road rage was the last thing on Manas' mind. He veered around the mime act and floored the gas. He had to get home. Stop lights didn't make him take his foot off the pedal, neither did the hard turn towards his house. He spied a few police cars up ahead and instinctively eased his foot off the gas. His mind jumped head-first to the worst possible conclusion.

No! No! No!

As he drew closer, he saw a crowd of people gathered around a few police officers. *Should he get down and check it out? But what if...* He couldn't finish the thought, as he sped away from the place to his house. *Coward*, he spat at himself.

Manas bolted out of the car as soon as he was in front of his house, leaving the car idling in the middle of the road.

"Shrutiii," he yelled, as he burst into through the front door.

Echoes are not just the hollow ghosts of the sound hitting you back. Sometimes silence echoes. Like it did in that empty house, it was more soul crushing that anything else. Shruti should have been home by now. Manas barely noticed Bella as she made her way into the hall, silently, and stared at him with concern.

Manas whipped out his mobile phone and started frantically calling all of Shruti's friends numbers, starting with 'A'.

The house of cards he built over the last decade quivered. Paint peeled off the Queen, dethroning her. The King looked on in concern as the Numbers at the bottom shook with trepidation.

With each of the phone call ending with "No uncle" or "She left straight for home," the walls shook more, the tremors got stronger. He ripped off his tie and unbuttoned the first couple of buttons on his shirt.

A fleeting image of Alex hovering at the doorway and saying, "I'll meet the Butcher no matter what." crept up his mind. The walls were closing in, suffocating him, threatening to bury him. He needed to get out. The front door stood with the promise of more space, more air. He staggered towards it.

Manas grabbed the doorknob when his mobile rang in his pocket. Without wasting a second, he grabbed the phone and answered it. Hoping against hope that it would be Shruti's beautiful voice that answered the call.

"If you want something in life, you've got to work for it," the voice said. It was hard to forget that resonant voice, that clear diction and smooth delivery. "I did my part and now it's your turn." Alex chuckled; it was a hard chuckle.

Manas wanted to shout, he wanted to cry, he wanted to beg, he wanted to kill. But most of all, he wanted to talk. His mouth was not able to shape the words he wanted from the air that was pushed out.

"I just tied your daughter up to a pole in front of me," Alex continued, "Do you still want to hide in that pathetic little hole? Or do you want to come out and play?"

"No...." Warm tears brimmed over Manas' eyes and flowed down his face. "Leave my daughter alone you bastard!"

"Temper, temper, temper" The sing-song intonation of the sentence was more suited for a kindergarten teacher, chiding a little boy. "You'll piss me off, I do something to your daughter, you'll go crazy with revenge and come after me, then I'll have to kill you....Such a big mess. Let's not get into all that, okay?

"Before we start off, I want to put your mind at ease. I didn't take your daughter for...—" Alex paused for a chuckle to pass. "—... for obvious reasons. Consider it as a shot of adrenaline to your heart to wake you up from that deep slumber you've been in for years. To make you stand up and listen."

"Alex...." Manas took a deep breath to control his breath. "Listen, I'm sorry for the way I acted earlier. I… I truly am... You have my full attention now.... just... please let my daughter go. She has nothing to do with any of this."

Alex's voice hardened. "Life is fucking unfair. Deal with it. Sometimes you expect a kind word, but you get a 'fuck you.' Only the weak cry foul. So, man up, because I know you are better than that."

Manas was in no state to 'man-up' as Alex suggested, but he decided to fake it. For Shruti's sake. He drew a few breaths and steadied his voice. "Tell me what I have to do."

A moment of silence. Manas could almost imagine the satisfied smile forming on Alex's face. "You like gambling?"

"What?"

"People say gambling is a game of chance. But it's not. It's a game of perception. A better hand doesn't win the game, a better player does." He paused for a few seconds and said, "I play Poker, Texas Hold 'Em, mostly online. You play Poker, Manas?"

"No."

"OK, here is how it works. Pay attention because this is going to be critical. The game starts when the dealer deals two cards each to all the players, face down. These are called the *'hole cards'*. Now the two players to the left of the dealer puts in the initial bets, or in poker terminology—*blinds*. This is important because this gets the action going, guarantees some money in the pot every round. As a player, you have three options each turn—*Fold*, *Call*, or *Raise*.

"*Fold* means exactly what you think it means. You withdraw and lose the round. *Call* is to match the running bet and *Raise* is to double it. So, the initial blinds start off the betting and once the round of betting is complete, the dealer deals three cards in the middle, face up. This is called the *Flop*. This kicks off another round of betting. Now the dealer deals one card each in the next two turns till there are five cards in total, face up – these are called the *Turn* and the *River*. And after each reveal there is a round of betting.

"After all, five cards are dealt in the middle, it's up to the players to make the best five hand combination with the cards in the middle and the two in their hands. Winner takes all. It's pretty simple once you start playing."

"You know why I love Texas Hold 'Em?" Alex paused for a second and continued to answer his rhetoric.

"The uncertainty. You start betting with just two cards, never knowing what the flop, the turn, or the river will be. Sometimes the hole cards tease you till the river and let you down and sometimes you have a straight flush at the flop. But the thing I love the most about Poker is that it tells you what kind of man you are playing with."

"I don't think you took my girl to play poker."

Alex laughed. It was a hollow laugh, one devoid of mirth. "Oh...but we *are* playing Poker. The hole cards are dealt, and your daughter is the blind. What are you gonna do, Manas? Fold, Call or Raise?"

"You are one demented son of a bitch. Shruti is not a poker chip. She is my daughter."

"Hmmm...Shruti, that's a beautiful name..." said Alex. "And since you are new to the game, I'll give you a tip. If you aren't sure about the hole cards, *call* and get on with it. We have the *flop*, the *turn* and the *river* coming up. We have just started the game, Manas."

Alex cleared his throat. "I have three tasks—the *flop*, the *turn* and the *river*—for you, which I'll let you know when the time comes. You can *call*, *fold*, or *raise* each task, though I strongly advise against the latter two. Folding means the game is over and Shruti...well she'll be a fine addition to my collection. Raising means you up the stakes, which will again make me re-evaluate why I shouldn't just take the money in the pot. So, I suggest just carrying out those tasks and *call* your way through the game. Since it's your first time, I'll throw in a side bet for you, you know, to make things easier. If you *call* your way through the three rounds, no matter who wins, I'll return Shruti to you, without a scratch on her body.

"But if you fold or raise, I have no guarantees about the chips in the pot. May be the poker chip gets scratched, even broken. You may well never see the poker chip again in your life. But…No, you won't risk that. Will you?

"You love the poker chip way too much for that." Alex cleared his throat. "And yeah, one more thing. Don't bother going to the police. Marking cards is considered cheating and will lead to instant disqualification. And I know I don't have to tell you what happens." Alex broke into a hearty laughter, lined with cruelty.

The mirthless laughter from the other side of the receiver rang long after the call was disconnected. A sudden tiredness gripped Manas' body as the gravity of the situation weighed him down. The mobile phone slipped from his hand and bounced on the carpeted floor.

Thud!

The muffled thud rang in the silence and echoed in his mind. His legs gave up trying to hold him up; he leaned against the door and let it guide him down to a crouch as he buried his head between his knees. Bella trotted closer and nuzzled her wet nose onto his hands, urging him to get up. But the cocoon of self-pity he crawled into was kind; there was no wrecking ball rampaging through his life, only a comforting darkness, a debilitating darkness. He could stay in there forever, just drifting in the black, floating away from life and its immediate danger.

But a familiar aroma wafted up his nose, the fruity conditioner, the lemony deodorant, and musty sweat. *Anu is here?* Manas lifted his head up with a jerk and scanned the room. He could see the back of her head, sitting in the chair in the living room.

"Anu?" he called as he crawled towards her on all four. When he didn't get a reply. He crawled faster. "Anu...? When did you get here?" he tried again. Manas got up on his feet and rushed to the chair, rounding it to face Anuradha.

She sat there quietly. A blank stare into the space ahead. A wide, red gash ran from her left shoulder to the right side of her pelvic bone; blood soaked into her white kurta, ruining its ethereal beauty.

A primal scream rose from deep within him and ripped out of his mouth. "ANU......" he screamed.

With a sudden twitch, Anuradha turned her head towards him; her empty eyes staring deep into Manas, through the flesh and into his soul. "*You* did this," she said, "*You* killed us."

"Us?" But as soon as he said those words, his eyes zeroed in on the outlines of a body under a sheet of cloth on the chair next to Anuradha's. He didn't want to look under the sheets; he knew what was under there. But still he inched closer and gingerly tugged on the sheet of cloth, bit by bit.

A bloody ear, a very familiar ear with three studs on the outer cartilage, peeked out. Manas flinched, as he backed away from the chair, tripped over the coffee table and crashed onto the floor. His body rocked with incessant sobs, uncontrollable sobs.

"S-S-Sorry," he managed to get the word out in between the sobs. "I....I never meant for this to happen, I...only...wanted....save..." Breaths were coming harder and harder to pass. Lethargy set in as the lack of breath started to show its effect. His eyes closed.

Thud!

With a sudden jolt, his eyes flew open. Maybe his brains defence mechanism kicked in, providing that one last shot of adrenaline to kick start the breathing. His lungs expanded, a breath of fresh air. Manas raised his head and opened his eyes. But Anuradha wasn't there, nor was Shruti. There were no blood stains on the beige upholstery neither.

Thud! Thud!

An all too familiar fear crept up his legs. He was not in his living room anymore. Back in the dank room in Delhi; his old house. The forearms that were joined to his palms were not built like a club, but thin pre-puberty ones. It was his thirteen-year-old forearms.

Thud! Thud! Thud!

Suddenly he knew what the sound was. Footsteps. It was a sound he had bottled up inside him for years, hoping he would never hear them again. He knew the rhythm and heaviness of the steps. His uncle climbing up the stairs.

Thud! Thud! Thud! Thud!

The footsteps were close. Close enough to be near the door to his room. Manas shrunk back to a corner and cowered in fear. The door was not locked, or rather the door didn't have a lock. Behind that door, was a creature so vile that the mere sight of him curdled his blood. It has happened before, and it's always the same.

The footsteps stopped and with a slow, menacing creak, the door came ajar. A figure shrouded in shadows blocked the meagre light of the streetlight. From the darkness, two bloodshot eyes stared at him, paralysing his every muscle. Manas wanted to close his eyes to make it stop, but he couldn't. The door opened further, and the creature stepped into the room. Manas summoned all his strength and willed his eyes shut.

Thud!

And just like that, he was back in Trivandrum; huddled up in a corner of the living room of his house. His shirt stuck to his cold, wet body. His galloping heart slowed down to a strut as he sunk into the familiarity of his house. He double checked the chairs for Anuradha and Shruti. There were not there. Figments of his crooked imagination.

"You've never let emotions get the better of you, not since *that* night." A voice that he had exiled for more than a decade spoke. Bits and pieces from *that* night flashed in his mind like an old film.

A boy, not over eighteen years, shivered in the doorway, blood dripped from his hands and soaked his shirt. The faint light from the houses across the lake framed the boy; heat rose off him, swirling in the chilly night air. A severed head, still leaking blood, plunked into the lake, splashing water all around. The boy grinned at him, his white teeth shone brightly in the face smeared with blood.

"Prateek?" A strange cocktail of emotions took form deep within Manas. Relief mixed with terror, seasoned with longing and selfishness.

"Long time no see, my brother," said Prateek.

Nasir

Tuesday, April 29, 2014

Seventeen was just too young to die.

The air conditioner whined through the old vents, pushing cold air into the conference room. Nasir stretched his back against the stiff chair. He had set up base in an empty conference room in the Office of the Commissioner of Police.

Avinash and Salim huddled over a couple of laptops, scouring the surveillance feeds from the traffic cameras around the city. The hollow clicks of their mouse echoed in the silence of the room. It was kind of a long shot, but they were desperate. Akshay had set up base in the far corner of the room where he made calls after calls like a chain-smoker. He was running the informers the Police loaned him and keeping in touch with the Counter-intelligence wing of the Kerala Police. Sonam stuck to the screen of her laptop, taking notes in a tattered writing pad. Her dark, auburn hair danced in the cold wind from the vent behind her. And along with the cool flow of air, the sweet flowery aroma, Nasir had learned to recognise as her perfume, swirled all around him. It lifted his spirits just a little from the perpetual gloom which had permeated the room for the past two days.

They had made sure every police station and informer in Trivandrum had a photograph of Alex along with details of the car. But black Swift cars were a dime a dozen. The odds of someone spotting Alex or his car was worse than hitting the lottery.

Nasir banged his fist on the table. "Damn it, it's like finding a needle in a haystack."

"Why don't we just burn the damn thing?" Sonam looked up from her laptop.

"Huh?"

A faint musk flush gathered on her cheeks as the attention of the entire room fell on her. "Well, sir. I mean…Why don't we make him come out of hiding?"

"Hmmm, interesting. Any ideas?"

Sonam leaned forward on her elbows; her dark hair flowed down her face, hiding half her face. "Alex signs his kills. So, it's not just the pleasure of killing someone, but also a narcissistic drive to claim that kill, a need to let the world know it was him. And by extension, I think it's a fair assumption that he follows the news closely, and enjoys reading about him in the paper. And lately, there has been an abundance of that. This is the channel that is open for us to influence him."

Nasir sank back in the chair which let out a creak. He stroked his chin, absently. "Yeah...But wouldn't it be too risky? What if he gets spooked and retreats back into his shell?"

"No, we want him to do the opposite. What if we throttle the media? Starve him out so that he doesn't know what is happening with the investigation. Make it seem like he is just another news that gets brushed under the carpet as soon as something else comes up."

Nasir beamed at her. She was picking up the nuances of the job. His chest filled with pride, like a teacher whose student scored a perfect exam; completely platonic, he told himself.

Akshay strode across the room from the corner he had made his home, worry lined his face. "That won't be necessary." He collapsed into a chair next to Nasir. "Just got a call about a kidnapping. Seventeen years old, dark haired."

Nasir's head snapped into attention. *Yet another girl.* A small part of him was exhilarated at the possibility of Alex slipping up. But he felt bad immediately. "And the scene?"

"Intact," Akshay said, "It happened in a residential neighbourhood and there was an eyewitness." He took a sip of water from the bottle in his hand. "The witness ran away from the scene and managed to get away to the police. He was the one who reported it. The officer in charge rushed to the spot and secured it like we told them. The abduction took place in a private road leading to three or four houses, which means the scene will be as good as fresh."

Salim jumped to his feet. "What are we waiting for?"

Nasir nodded, slowly rising to his feet. "Let's try and save this one at least. Too many have died already."

~

All the way to the crime scene, one thought kept playing over and over in Nasir's head, like that annoying advertisement that you can't stand anymore.

Seventeen was just too young to die.

He had less than 24 hours to save the girl. The Artist takes a day to savour the victim, and the body shows up in a grotesque display of his love for Cinema.

He inhaled deep and shook his head clear of those thoughts. *Not 'the girl,' 'the victim,'* he reminded himself. Getting personally attached to a case was dangerous. It clouded his judgement. Through all his years as a law enforcement officer what he realized was that one should look at the big picture. He needed to catch the criminal and saving the victim was merely collateral. If there was ever a toss-up between the criminal and the victim, he should be picking out the casket for the criminal without a second thought. A criminal, especially a serial offender, will continue to have more victims. Therefore, saving a victim by letting the criminal go is never going to break the cycle of violence. In the end, the choice came down to the current victim versus the future victims, and logic dictated that he should save the future victims.

The screech of the car brakes invaded his thoughts, putting brakes on his thought train. They had arrived. The day was putting up a last stand against the onslaught of night and darkness along with it. The compound walls burned with deep orange fire as the battle raged on. Shadows played on the paved footpaths along the square lines running through the concrete. Lush green trees and grey streetlights lined both sides of the road. *Clearly an uptown residential area in Trivandrum.* The yellow police tape that cordoned off the area was an eyesore. It didn't fit in. And neither did the khaki uniforms roaming around the place.

The team disembarked without a word; Sonam took off towards the crime scene with the kit hanging from her shoulders. Akshay veered off to the khaki uniforms, and Avinash along with Salim headed in the opposite direction, probably to check for more eyewitnesses. Everybody had the drill down on paper.

Nasir dragged himself over to the crime scene. Ever since Sonam joined, he had taken a back seat, or rather, become a mentor to her. The cordoned off area was empty for a crime scene. But then again, there was no homicide, no body, and no blood. Nasir dipped down to his knees next to a tyre track on the road; burned rubber stuck to the asphalt. He ran a finger along the road, no dust or dirt. *A very well-kept private road*, he thought. Apart from the black mark on the floor, the only other object of interest was the pieces of a mobile phone scattered strewn across the floor.

Sonam moved closer to the tyre tracks with her camera and started clicking pictures. "This does look like a Maruti Swift."

He cocked an eyebrow and asked, "When did you become an expert in tyre tracks? They don't teach that in the academy."

"Yesterday." A sheepish grin broke out on her face. "Googled it."

He rolled his eyes. 'Google' is now a verb. And here he was struggling to log into his email on the first try. Interrogating a criminal was easier than getting anything meaningful out of Google. *'Technologically challenged' old man.*

Sonam had already moved on to brushing and bagging the mobile phone parts scattered all around. A Sisyphean exercise for sure. Alex never left prints.

"Sir," Akshay's voice called him from behind.

Nasir turned around to face Akshay, and beside him was a boy, barely out of his puberty, jammed his hands into his armpits and shivered in the warm, humid evening.

"Eyewitness," Akshay said, signalling towards the boy.

The kid stood rooted to the spot, staring but not seeing. A dark bruise lined the lower corner of his lips. He looked like he would shit his pants at the drop of a hat. Nasir suspected that this would be the last time the kid would go to the police station to report a crime. Unfortunately for him, they lived in a country where the police ruffled up the person reporting the crime rather than finding the criminal.

Nasir waved to the kid and beckoned him over as he knelt with the most pleasant smile he could muster. "Hello. My name is Nasir Ali Khan. What's yours?"

The kid shifted uncomfortably on his feet as his eyes flitted everywhere though his thick-framed glasses. "Ashok."

Nasir patted him on the back "You are very brave for standing up for—"

'Shruti," Akshay filled in.

"—yes, Shruti. And calling the Police. Although it may not seem like it now, but we all are really grateful."

Ashok met Nasir's gaze, and the corners of his mouth twitched a little. "Thank you." His tone was measured, and careful. "But I didn't stand up for Shruti *chechi*." He averted his eyes to stare beyond Nasir. "I was scared. I didn't know what to do. So, I pulled out my mobile and thought if I could get him on camera, may be the police could find him."

Nasir cupped his hand on the side of Ashok's neck, tenderly, and held his face up. "I want you to understand that what you did was the right choice. It would have been just foolish if you had tried to stop the kidnapper. And don't worry about the way the police treated you. I'll make sure you go home as soon as possible, okay?"

Ashok nodded; his shivering seemed to subside.

"Now can you help us catch the bad man quickly?"

"Of course, sir. I knew Shruti *chechi*...We had never talked, but I've seen her around. She was a nice girl."

Nasir reached for Alex's photograph from inside his pocket and passed it to Ashok. "Is this the bad man who took Shruti?"

The change in Ashok's face was visceral. Nasir knew his answer before he spoke. "Yes Sir. That's him." He handed back the photograph like it burnt his fingers.

"Are you sure? Do you want to take another look?"

Ashok shook his head. "I'll never forget those eyes. Those bloodshot, crazy eyes." Ashok stared into the space between objects, into a dimension that was his own, until he came out of it with a shudder.

"Can you tell me what happened?"

"I was heading back home after school when I saw Shruti *chechi* walking towards her house on the other side of the road...which is further down the street. A car was parked, right over there." Ashok pointed towards the cordoned off area.

"What car was it?"

"A black car. A black Swift. And a man stood near the car, looking around like he was lost. As she reached him, he asked her for something and when *chechi* turned away from him to point at something...he...he grabbed her from behind and forced her into the car. On instinct I raced down the street. But as I got closer, I got scared. So, I took out my mobile phone and started recording it. It was horrible...Shruti *chechi* saw me and was trying to say something, but her mouth was gagged with duct tape. I zoomed in to understand what she was trying to tell me and so I never saw the man coming. With a sudden force, the man plucked the phone out of my hands and smashed it on the ground."

The shiver that had left Ashok, slowly returned.

"Was he wearing gloves or anything like that?" Nasir asked.

Ashok thought for a moment, probably recalling the memory, before responding. "No, he wasn't. As soon as the mobile scattered on the road, the man bent down to pick up the memory card. I didn't know what to do and so I ran. I ran and never looked back." His eyes brimmed with tears, threatening to jump down his face. "I left *chechi* with the man and ran to the police station."

Nasir put and arm around him. "You did good, kid. You did good. Don't you worry. We are going catch the bad man, okay? And he will pay for all this." He gestured Akshay to take the kid home.

Nasir rose to his feet and rubbed the bridge of his nose. It was clear that The Artist was Alex, but that didn't bring him any closer than before to catching him. He plodded back to Sonam who was just finishing up the sweep of the area.

Sonam raised her head and met his gaze. The excitement in those eyes was unmistakable and that could mean only one thing. She found something.

"We got multiple sets of fingerprints on the mobile phone. Need to check if it one of them is Alex's."

"One of them is. He wasn't wearing gloves." But he wasn't that excited. They already knew who The Artist was. "The kid identified Alex from the photograph and also placed the black swift on the scene."

"But still, this is undeniable evidence and will place him at the scene without a doubt. No way he will get out of this in court."

Nasir's face hardened. "Yeah, *if* it goes to court." Scum like Alex deserved a bullet in the head and not a state-sponsored vacation with meals. It was not like Nasir didn't believe in the course of justice, but he just didn't have the patience for it.

She seemed determined not to let Nasir's cynicism put her down. "There is one more thing, and for this you might as well kiss me."

Nasir's eyebrows shot up in a high arc as he blinked at Sonam

"Not literally." She glanced at her feet and shuffled them. "But I found footprints and bagged some dirt from it. It looked out of place. Maybe from Alex's shoes. Quite a lot of it, actually. Like a cake of dirt stuck to the shoe. And analysis—"

"—would tell us where he has been," cut in Nasir. That was great news. He pictured him hugging Sonam in his mind but dismissed it. A congratulatory hug but may be inappropriate. "How fast can we get the results?"

Sonam chewed her hair a bit. "That's the bad news. It might take as long as a week, if we put it on priority."

Nasir shook his head violently. "That's just not going to work. We hardly have 24 hours to save the girl." *No, the victim*, he reminded himself. "Overnight it to the lab and mark it as a priority. I'll try and pull some strings. You know, to get it as soon as possible."

Avinash and Salim returned from the recon empty handed, along with Akshay, and Nasir filled them on what they found out.

"Did anyone inform the parents?" Nasir asked.

"No, they are about to send a constable to inform them," Akshay said.

Nasir hated this part, but it was as much a part of his job as catching criminals. And he knew the parents would feel better if the news came from a senior officer in charge of the operation than a constable or an inspector. "Tell them to cancel the visit. We'll inform the parents."

Manas

Tuesday, April 29, 2014

Twenty-five is a tricky age. Society thrusts you into adulthood, but you lack the maturity or perspective to be one.

Manas forced the saliva in his mouth down his throat. The gurgle of gathering saliva and the gulp of his throat were the only sound that cut through the silence. Bella had retreated into another corner and curled up there.

"Aren't you happy to see me?" Prateek's voice pierced the stillness of the house. "You don't invite guests and then ignore them."

Prateek hadn't changed much since he had last seen him, except for the beard. Disarrayed tangle of dark hair still spilled over his forehead. The blue in his eyes still pierced Manas like a cold spike. A strong chin and a long, thin, Greek nose still defined his face. But instead of a clean-shaven jaw, there was a long, full beard; unbridled growth, as messy as his hair, but trimmed at the edges to give a semblance of tidiness. He stretched out on the couch, facing Manas, spread-eagling his hands, resting on the top side of the couch.

Manas huddled in the corner, shut his eyes tight and took in deep breaths. *This is just another hallucination. The chemicals in your brain is making you see things which aren't there. Calm down and open your eyes and everything will be back to normal.*

Manas counted to three in his mind and opened his eyes. The couch where Prateek sat was empty. He breathed out a huge sigh. He could not afford to lose his mind, not now. Shruti needed him. Manas climbed to his feet, holding the walls for support. He made his way to the passageway to the kitchen and turned the corner. A pair of cold, blue eyes jumped out at him from the darkness. It startled him, sending him back towards the living room, where he stumbled over the edge of the carpet and fell backwards.

A raucous laughter filled the room. "I miss messing you up like this," Prateek said.

Manas rose to his feet, heat flushing through his body, pressing up to his cheeks for an outlet. "Why are you here Prateek? Didn't I make it absolutely clear that I didn't wanna see you again?"

Prateek glided into the low light in the living room. "Still the same, aren't we? Remember how we huddled over a thick book from the library and strained our eyes in the golden light of the candle to read. The thick black book had 'Dissociative Identity Disorder' embossed on the cover in gold. That was our moment of clarity, wasn't it? We were confused as to what we were, but that book told us we were 'alters'—multiple personalities living in a same mind. It also told us how some alters take over and sideline the others into mere observers. And how there can be altercations between alters, power struggles over who gets control? But we vowed to be different, didn't we? We promised that we would always get along and never take over each other without permission. What happened to that promise, Manas?"

"Oh, come on. Cut the bull crap, Prateek. You broke it first. You were edging me out, backing me into a corner. Don't try to spin it around now." Manas turned away and shuffled towards the living room couch. The evening sun had long gone, plunging the world into darkness. "What are you doing here?"

Prateek chuckled. "You and me both know that I'll not be here if you didn't want me to be. If you didn't drop a rope down the chasm of your mind where you exiled me."

"I didn't drop you anything. And we are the only two in there."

"Okay, if you say so. Push me back down, then. You did that once, what's stopping you now?"

Manas stroked his chin, the usually smooth jaw had a two-day stubble. It felt odd. He sure as hell didn't invite Prateek. But he had a nagging suspicion that it was his subconscious, the invisible player in the arena of his mind.

"I thought as much," Prateek said. He made his way between the chairs and planted himself in one. "You need me. Shruti needs me."

A wave of white-hot rage flashed through his body as he turned to face Prateek. "Get this through your thick skull. I do not need you." He enunciated every word in the last sentence. "I am not the meek kid you knew back in Delhi, but a grown man who is capable of handling his own affairs. So, cut the crap and get the hell out."

Prateek's face morphed into a grimace, one that lingered for a while. "What happened to us, Manas? We used to be inseparable."

"You killed people, that's what happened."

"No, we killed people and all of them deserved it."

"Even Amrita? You knew how I felt about her, and about your... idiotic communal crusade to save *Bharat Mata*."

Prateek dipped his head, and watched his thumb trace random signs on his palm. "Hindsight is always twenty-twenty. I agree...that was stupid." He raised his eyes to meet Manas'. They had a genuineness that reminded Manas of the young Prateek.

"I was young and drunk on the ideas of a Hindu nation. Twenty-five is a tricky age. Society thrusts you into adulthood, but you lack the maturity or perspective to be one. I don't know if it's worth something, but I am honestly sorry about what happened...no, what I did back then." He rose to his feet, and walked over to Manas, placing a hand on his shoulder. "And I heard about Amrita. I'm sorry."

Some of the accumulated tension melted away from Manas' shoulders. "She was part of a life I left behind....along with you. Although I'm sad about Amrita, she is not my main concern now. So, just leave me alone, would you?"

Prateek retracted his hands, as if they were stung. He stepped back and turned away. "You know I love Shruti as much as you do. I was there when she held your fingers for the first time. She squeezed so hard for such a tiny person. I was there to see the unbridled joy in her face when she took her first step, and the exhilaration in her eyes when she rode the bicycle solo for the first time. I was there when she bawled like a baby on her first day at school and when you got her through her first heartbreak. She is as much my child as she is yours. And I took that rope and climbed back up to help you save her. You need help, Manas. I saw you freak the fuck out earlier."

Hot tears flushed Manas' eyes as he relived the memories of her daughter. "My little girl is with a raving lunatic who rapes and kills women and then dresses them up in some sick display. I have every right to freak out."

Prateek shook his head, looking down at his feet. "You used to be better at this that I am. Just think about it, Manas. She is perfectly safe. Alex wants you to play a game and Shruti is all he has got to make you play along. He wouldn't hurt her as long as the game goes on. We don't know why he is doing this, or what his intentions are, but what we do have is time. Time to get Shruti out before he lays a finger on her."

"Excuse me for not trusting the psychopath to behave rationally." Manas stomped across the room to the window. Rain had begun its slow tap dance on the clear window. The pitter-patter of the rain helped him concentrate. White fluorescent light bathed the empty street outside, keeping the darkness at bay. If he stood right under the streetlight, he could be unaware of the darkness lurking behind the boundary. Prateek seemed genuinely worried about Shruti and his apology seemed to be from the heart. The time away had either matured him, drove some sense into him, or made him a better actor.

Getting rid of Prateek was one of the hardest things he had done in his life and he was not sure he could do that again. Even after shoving him deep in the depths of his mind, his lingering presence haunted him for years. In the beginning, Prateek used to call out his name, but he ignored it. Soon the calls acquired a layer of veiled menace which was soon shed to reveal plain threats, all of which Manas ignored. He was determined not to let Prateek out again. The violence just had to stop. Eventually, the voices stopped as Prateek retreated into a silence which lasted more than a decade. But even through the silence, his presence was felt. And to be honest, there were times when he missed Prateek and wanted to call him out desperately. But what would happen if he came back? Prateek was a cancer which started out as a benign mole and soon spread through the body and completely took over. And you don't escape cancer twice.

"Prateek, leave me alone and climb back down the hole you came from," Manas said.

"As you wish," Prateek said with a shrug of his shoulders. "Till you call me again, brother."

And just like that he melted into thin air. Manas dragged his feet to the nearest chair and sunk into it. The subconscious usually makes better decisions than the conscious and right then he was not sure if he had made the right decision.

Knock! Knock!

Manas jerked back in his chair, startled by the sudden intrusion. It was the door; somebody was at the door. Manas picked himself off the chair, and with the last ounce of energy left, he hobbled his way to the door and peered through the peep hole.

A wiry man in an untucked, well-ironed, off-white shirt stood like a rod in front of the door with a few people around him. Some of them were in khaki uniforms, and the others were in civilian clothes, but all of them maintained a respectable distance from the man in front.

The police. They must have come to talk to him about Shruti. Manas toyed with the idea of coming clean with the police, but Alex's warning about what would happen loomed over him. And moreover, if he were to tell them that Alex contacted him after taking his daughter, eyebrows would be raised; questions would be asked of Alex's motives. That line of questioning would lead to a place where he didn't care to be in. Maybe he can just do what Alex wants and get his daughter back to him without a scratch. Or maybe he can just deal with the scumbag himself. He had dealt with worse. Back then, he had Prateek to do the dirty work. But now, he had something he never had before—the drive of a father who would do anything to protect his little girl.

No. The police mustn't know. Manas put up a facade of a man who was broken and worried for the police. It wasn't that hard as he *was* broken, and he *was* worried.

Anuradha

Tuesday, April 29, 2014

Every man needs an anchor; an anchor to root him to reality, to tether him to home.

Sometimes you get these feelings, these inexplicable feelings of dread. That something was about to happen. Anuradha swatted away those feelings all the way home from work, like an annoying fly who just wouldn't give up.

Dark clouds ganged up on the dying sun, finishing the job. The evening gloom had settled in as the city got ready for the showers. Two wheelers zipped past her, their raincoats flapping in the wind like a cape. The sky was darkly ominous as the clouds swelled to twice their normal size.

As she made her way through the traffic, she tried to figure out why she got that nagging feeling that something bad had happened. Was it because Shruti didn't call her to pick her up? That would mean Manas must have given her the ride. And Manas...he had been exceptionally silent today. No phone calls, no messages; absolute silence. Why didn't Shruti call her once she was home? She used to do it every other day. Or maybe it's just her being paranoid.

A loud crack of thunder was all the warning she had before it started raining cats and dogs. The pattering of rain on her car roof, which used to be soothing, annoyed her. She turned up the stereo hoping to drown it out.

Anuradha turned the corner into the private road which led to her house. She noticed the yellow police tape strung across the side of the road and a lone policeman standing under an umbrella, but she brushed it aside. But when she made out the outlines of a jeep parked in front of her house; she knew the feelings she was battling were not mere ramblings of her brain. Her heart fluttered in her chest, bouncing off her ribs. She didn't bother to park her car in the garage, nor did she bother to open her umbrella as she got out. It was hard to see in the heavy downpour, but she knew the way in like the back of her hand.

She stepped into the living room through the open door to find Manas leaning forward in the chair, staring into the blank space ahead. Some guys she didn't know sat around him, expressionless. A deeply tanned, wiry man seemed to be in charge and doing all the talking. They didn't see her come in.

"Manas?" she called; all her worry, all the questions, were packed into that one word.

Manas jumped and met her gaze. Those kind eyes were strained with pain. He attempted a weak smile but couldn't go through with it. The wiry man rose to his feet and dipped his head acknowledging her arrival. A black Ray Ban peeked out from his front pocket. "We will give you two sometime." And with that he strode out of the house without even a glance at Anuradha, and the two bulky cronies accompanied him.

"Where is Shruti?" she blurted out.

Manas lumbered over to her, looking anywhere but at her. "Anu.... Shruti..."

"Is she OK? Was there an accident? Just tell me, Manas."

"No, no... There was no accident, and she is okay... for now." Manas met her gaze. The soulful eyes which she fell in love with were battered and bruised with hurt. "She was taken, Shruti....kidnapped."

It was like someone grabbed a brick and smashed it across her head. It hurt her like that. It shocked her like that. It tied her tongue like that. She just stared into Manas' eyes, paralysed. It seemed like it was yesterday that she taught Shruti how to braid her hair for the first time or told her how to tell a douchebag from Prince Charming. A sob fought through the paralysis, and made it through to her mouth. And then, the dam broke down, and the sobs just kept coming. Her whole body rocked with sharp movements as she fell into Manas' embrace. She rested her head against his warm chest and cried. She cried till there were no more tears left to shed. She cried till Manas' shirt was soaked with her mascara-ridden tears. She cried till she was lost in the tears, adrift in the sea of sorrow, of despair.

The wetness on the back of her neck was what brought her back. It was only then that she noticed the mellow rise and fall of Manas' chest was rocked with jagged breaths. Was he crying? The possibility was so strange that her brain rejected it. In all the time she had known Manas, he had never cried. He was the strong anchor to which she tied herself when she was astray. Had her anchor lost his footing?

It was only then that she was able to step back from the grief that consumed her and register that the man she was holding also loved Shruti with all his heart. She knew how much Manas loved their daughter and how much he would be hurting. And just like that, she was overcome by a need to comfort him. It surprised her. She wanted to cradle his head on her chest and whisper into his ears that everything would be okay. It was as if the tables had turned and she needed to be the anchor. That's what you do in a marriage. You become what your partner can't.

Anuradha raised her head and peered into those tired, old eyes. The fire which burned in them had all but gone. "What did the Police say?"

His body stiffened. "They think it is the serial killer on the news last week."

The grotesque imagery of dead girls that the news ran, all through last week, flashed through her mind. But all the blurred heads were replaced with her daughter's. "Manas, tell me this had nothing to do with you."

"Anu—"

A knock on the door interrupted their conversation. Anuradha plucked her gaze from Manas' wilting eyes with some effort and scanned the doorway. The wiry man was back with his two henchmen, all of them wet from the unforgiving rain outside.

"Sorry to interrupt. May I?"

"Come in, Nasir," said Manas, wiping his eyes. "Have a seat." He faced Anuradha, not meeting her eyes completely. "Nasir is from the CBI. He and his team have been tracking The Artist, and they oversee this investigation."

Nasir took a seat on the couch and waited for Manas and Anuradha to join him. The two henchmen planted themselves at the doorway.

As soon as they took their seat, Nasir leaned towards them, his hands met each other in front of him, resting on his thighs. "My deepest condolences for your daughter. We are doing everything we can to get your daughter back safe and sound. But we are on a tight timeline, and it would help us a lot if you can help us with a few things."

Anuradha just nodded.

"Mr Manas, I hope you have the photograph I asked earlier. It would help us put out a notice in all the police stations." Nasir pulled out a notepad from his pocket and opened it. "Can you tell us what your daughter was wearing when she left this morning?"

Anuradha remembered Shruti rushing off to college. She was late as usual and missed her breakfast.

"A red pants and a white T-shirt with some pink flowers printed on them," Manas said. "She loved that T-shirt..." The words faltered off his mouth, unbalanced, and unsteady.

Nasir clicked open the pen in his hands and jotted down something in the notepad. "What kind of footwear was she wearing?"

A moment of silence was what tipped Anuradha off. Manas didn't know. She cleared her throat and wiped off the silent tears.

"Leather high heels."

"Colour?"

"Red."

"Hmmm." Nasir scribbled that in his notepad with a slow nod of his head. "I have already told Manas this. Shruti was taken, may be, 200 metres from here. You might have seen the police tape up the road. We have reason to believe this is the work of the serial killer we know as The Artist. But the good news is that we know who the killer is, and we believe we can catch him in the next twenty-four hours." One of the two henchmen by the doorway marched closer and handed him a pair of photos. He grabbed them and handed them to Manas. "Have you seen this man before? Or maybe the car in the other photo?"

The split-second Manas saw the photo, his face registered recognition. It was like lightning; quick to disappear, but brighter than anything else. "No." He swayed his head slowly left to right as he passed the photographs to Anuradha.

A handsome chiselled face smiled back at her from the picture. She wanted to find something sinister in his face. Something which told her he was capable of the things he had done. But instead, all she saw was a disarming boyish charm. This was not how she expected evil to look like. She handed back the photograph to Nasir with a shake of her head.

"Is there anything else I should know?" Nasir asked.

Anuradha glanced at Manas sideways.

"Yeah," said Manas. "I called Shruti's cell phone at around six. The phone rang for some time and then it got disconnected. I've been trying her after that, but...." Manas bit back a sob. "I'm sorry....I've been trying her, but I'm getting a 'switched off' message."

Nasir rested his hawk-like nose on his index finger, the rest of the fingers supporting his chin. "We know that the abduction happened at around 5:30 pm. May be the call alerted The Artist about the phone and he switched it off, dismantled it, or threw it away. He is smart enough to know cell phones can be traced. Give me her number, I'll have my team pull out the logs to get the last known location."

Just then Manas' phone vibrated on the coffee table, with the screen lighting up. He picked it up, glanced at the screen and handed it over to Anuradha with a gesture which meant 'take the call.'

'Ravi calling' lit up the screen. She swiped at the blinking call button and placed the phone against her ears.

"Hey... Manas," Ravi said.

"Ravi, this is Anu. Manas is talking to someone. Can I take a message?"

"No, no...I just....I just heard about what happened. I'm so sorry, Anu."

Anuradha bit back another onslaught of waterworks. She never knew what to say in times like these. Ravi didn't expect a reply but leaving a conversation hanging was not something she had learned to do. "Thank you for your concern," she said, awkwardly.

"We are all praying for Shruti. Just tell me if you or Manas need anything. And tell Manas to give me a call when he is free."

"Thank you, Ravi," she said, disconnecting the call.

Nasir had finished talking to Manas, gathered everything he needed, and was on his way out. She rose from the couch and made her way to the doorway.

"I'm stationing two policemen in plain clothes around the house for your protection," he said, "You need not worry, it's just a formality. The Artist usually doesn't go after the family members. But you keep an eye out for any suspicious behaviour and ring me anytime if you find something. However trivial it may seem to you, okay?"

Manas and Anuradha nodded, and Nasir marched out of the house.

Anuradha waited a few seconds after Nasir closed the door behind him to face Manas. His eyes roamed everywhere but hers. She stood with her legs apart and hands tied in front of her. "Look at me, Manas."

Manas met her gaze, his eyes heavy with shame.

"This is because of you, isn't it? Our little baby is suffering because of what you've been hiding?" Her voice broke down as tears welled up in her eyes, blurring her vision.

Manas broke eye contact and gazed out through the glass window. Rain splattered on the window coalescing into streams which split the streetlight into three. The furrows on Manas' head deepened and he nodded, ever so slightly.

Hot fury bubbled inside her. "And you chose not to share it with the police? I never thought I'd say this, but you are a coward."

Manas turned around; his eyes more watery than usual. "No, Anu. If I knew that going to the police would bring back my little girl, I would not think twice to do it. But it's not that simple. Alex...that is his name, The Artist. Alex called me and warned me that If I go to the police, he would—"

Anuradha raised her hand, palms facing outwards, stopping whatever Manas was saying. "You mean that bastard called you, and you didn't tell the police?"

Manas stepped closer and held her shoulders. "Anu, I am probably the last person you want to trust right now, but I just...just do it this one time. It's not as simple as it looks. As things are right now, she is safe, and I don't want to change that by going to the police. She is safe for now and I intend to keep it that way...by any means necessary."

Anuradha did trust him, but more than that, he loved Shruti to death. The broken man in front of her would do anything to get Shruti home safely. "Manas...."

He moved closer still and put a tentative arm around her.

Manas was hiding something, and Anuradha wasn't sure she wanted to know. But, on the other hand, she did trust him and knew that he wouldn't put himself before his family.

"Promise me you'll bring my girl back to me," Anuradha said.

The dying embers in Manas' eyes burned bright as resolve breathed fresh air into them. "I promise you, Anu. Shruti will be back home, safe and sound." The fire in his eyes fanned higher and consumed everything in there. "And Alex would regret the moment he ever thought of laying hands on my family." The muscles on his jaws flexed as he ground his teeth.

The relentless downpour continued, white noise of nature. Manas stared ahead, his eyes never focusing on anything, deep in thought. "I want you to go to your parents' place for a few days. I can't risk losing you while I get Shruti back."

"No, Manas. I can't sit on my ass doing nothing, knowing Shruti is not safe. I wanna help."

A beginning of a smile garnered the corner of his mouth. Anuradha recognised traces of the man she fell in love with. He was still in the broken man in front of her and she trusted him to the core.

"Every man needs an anchor; an anchor to root him to reality, to tether him to home," said Manas, "I need you safe so I can come home to you with our daughter. I started this. This is between me and the man who took my daughter." His voice took a sharp edge as he said, 'the man who took my daughter' and it drive chills down her spine. She had never heard Manas use that tone; never thought he was capable of that.

Anuradha sunk into his embrace; his warm, musty smell calmed her down, gave her hope.

The Artist

Wednesday, April 30, 2014

Blessed is the man who endureth temptation; for when he is tried, he shall receive the crown of life.—James 1:12

Drops of rain pounded on the half-open door, splattering into a million drops in the wind. Alex stood two steps behind the doorway, eyes closed. The damp spray of rain caressed his face and kissed him with its cold lips. The last candle had extinguished itself, drowned in its own melted wax, hours ago. He needed to go shopping again and he hated that. A loud, booming, thunder pierced the constant pattering of rain on the metal sheets. It had been pouring down for over three hours with no signs of respite.

It was almost eight and Shruti was still sleeping. He had to get her something, something she can do while she is tied up. *Do girls this age still like colouring books?* A crack of lightning split the sky and brought white flashing lightning into the dark, dingy, warehouse. The gleam off the new chain he bought to tie her up reassured him. She had bugged him incessantly until he relented and shifted the restraint from her hands to her legs. It was not hard to imagine her discomfort being tied up by her hands above her head. But that girl had some mouth on her. Sometimes he felt like he was being told what to do by the little person tied up in the room. Alex liked that in a girl—sass.

Endless lightning lit up the room as if God was doing flash photography as Alex walked the path laid out for him, like a runway model walking the ramp. He was carrying out God's will.

Another one of those flashes lit up the warehouse and reflected on Shruti's pale smooth skin. Her T-shirt had shifted during sleep and revealed her mid-riff.

Alex crept closer, taking care where he was stepping so as not to wake her. He fished out a cigarette lighter from his pocket and pressed down on the switch as he crouched down to take a closer look. A pale, yellow flame with a blue centre sprung up like magic and cast a soft light around him. He wondered if the Aphrodite of Milos—the limbless Greek marble statue of Aphrodite—had such perfect skin. It seemed to glow in the soft light, acquiring a luminescence of its own. The sharp dip of her belly button seemed deeper in the shadows. Suddenly, he was overcome with an irresistible urge to see how deep her belly button was. Alex watched as his hands developed a life of its own and moved towards the answer.

"What do you think you are doing?" A deep, hollow sound asked.

Alex's hands froze, mid-air. A dark figure, sporting a trench coat and a fedora leaned against the doorway; the spray of rain casting a halo around his outline. Water dripped from the ends of his coat.

"I... I'm...." Alex stuttered.

The Butcher had caught him red handed. *This was not part of the plan.*

"You know she is all you got, right?"

Alex nodded, his eyes tracing the outline of his own shoes in the dim light. "Old habits die hard." He looked up, grinning.

The Butcher took off the hat and straightened it, smoothing out the creases. "The only thing that is going to die hard is you because of your old habits. You know happens when you hurt Shruti, don't you? What do you think Manas will do when he understands that she is not safe with you?"

"He would come after me with all he's got."

"That's right. And I wouldn't lift a finger to save you from his wrath."

"You have no idea how hard it is for me to have a beautiful girl next to me, tied up." Even though Alex could not see The Butcher's face, he felt his accusatory stare. "But yes, I did lose my focus there," he added, hastily. Alex ran his gaze across the curvy contours of Shruti's body. "Is it wrong of me for wishing Manas screws up?" The ends of his mouth stretched in a wide grin.

"Stop wasting time, call Manas and get this thing rolling, before your box yourselves into a corner you can't get out." The Butcher sauntered inside the warehouse and dissolved into the darkness inside.

Alex pushed himself up and killed the lighter. "But I'm not ready. I need more time to plan, scope out a few places. This is a new city and I know nothing about it."

"Planning or procrastinating?" The Butcher's voice rose out of the darkness, circling him. "Sometimes the lines can be blurry. Are you scared of him?"

"Scared? No. But I respect him...or you. I'm confused. But either ways, I don't want to go in blind."

"He is a forty-year-old has been."

Alex perched on top of an askew piece of machinery, long abandoned in its state of chaos. "Maybe you are right, but I don't want to take that chance. I'll give him a call today and get it started, but probably give him an extra day to complete it. That keeps the pressure on him and gives me time to get ready. Win-win."

"Okay," the voice from the dark said. "Be careful with Shruti, or the next visit won't be this cordial."

Alex was used to these threats by now, but it still unsettled him.

The rain finally eased up reducing the overbearing pitter-patter to a mere white noise. There were a few leaks in the warehouse, but nothing major and he was glad about that. He jumped down to the ground and made his way to his rucksack, skirting outlines of obstacles along the way. *Needed to get candles*, he reminded himself. The rucksack had almost everything he needed, and the rest of his stuff was in the car parked outside. He rummaged through the contents in the rucksack and pulled out a stack of SIM cards, he had bought, pre-activated and with fake IDs. Plucking one of the covers from the bundle, he unwrapped and popped out the SIM card from the card that held it. Alex dismantled his mobile, inserted the new SIM card, and booted it back up. As the phone took its time to turn on and catch the signal, he made his way to the open doorway.

As soon as the bars began to show on the phone, he dialled Manas.

"Hello," came an unsure voice from the other side.

Alex chuckled. "Aren't you glad to hear my voice?"

There was a pause from the other side when Alex double checked the number he dialled.

"Is she okay?" Manas asked.

"Are you a man of action or a man who just asks mindless questions? Of course, she is safe. Nobody would touch the pot."

Manas was silent on the other side of the phone.

"Don't tell me you forgot already. Poker, blinds, and the flop, the turn, and the river." Alex chuckled. "You either forgot, or don't want to play; and both makes me mad. Remember, I told you I have something planned for you, didn't I? *The flop*. But you don't even want to see the cards. How will you play if you don't see the cards, Manas?"

"Stop playing games and just tell me what to do." A stoic acceptance rang in Manas' voice.

Alex stepped out of the doorway into the cool, damp air. He loved the air in Kerala just after a rain; the crisp freshness was something he never saw in Delhi. Back home, you could taste the dirt and smoke in the air. A deep breath filled his lungs. "I told you about my childhood, didn't I? My dad left before I was born, my mother hated my guts, and my sisters were scared of me...Probably from the venom my mother injected them with every night. What that left was a kid who craved for affection, for love. But there was someone who loved me unconditionally. Bagira, my dog." Alex chuckled at the name. "Yeah, Jungle Book was big back then. There was no television at home, but I, along with a lot of other kids, used to gather in a nearby barber shop to catch the cartoon. Ah, those carefree times.

"It was one of those afternoons when I saw a puppy on the side of the road, scared and lonely. His small legs moved with erratic steps as he approached me and sniffed my legs as if he trusted me completely. Babies, human or animal, are innocent like that. It is the world that corrupts them as they grow old. I fed him a biscuit I had stuffed in my pocket. And that was it, I took him home and he became mine. That brown fur coat gave me more love than my dad, mother and sisters combined.

"There is nothing like the loyalty of a dog, is there? He would die for you without a second thought. But humans...They wouldn't think twice before killing their dog if it suited them. That's how ugly we are on the inside." The Artist ran his hands through his messy curls to straighten them out. "That pesky little dog of yours, you love him?"

"It's not him, it's her," said Manas. "She is family."

"Would she die for you?"

There was a pause from the other side. "She doesn't let strangers near me or my family. But you already know that."

"She didn't like me one bit, did she?" Alex laughed out loud. "Intelligent dog, but pesky, nonetheless."

A rustle of clothes, a clink of the chain. Shruti must have woken up. *Just in time.*

"Tell me...Would you do anything to save your daughter?" Alex asked.

"Anything." Manas' voice was laced with steely resolve.

"You really should be careful using words like 'anything'. What if I tell you that I'll exchange your daughter for your wife?"

The silence from the other side spoke volumes.

Alex threw his head back and laughed. "Relax, Manas. I'm just kidding. I wouldn't do that to you. Not this early in our game." Malice seeped into his voice. "For now, I just have a small thing for you. I want the heart of that pesky dog in a bag. Simple enough?"

"What? The heart?"

"That dog got on my nerve with the barking and loyalty. I want it gone. And I want you to do it with your own hands. Look into her eyes as the life seeps out of her. The heart is just an insurance policy. You can't pass off the job to somebody and then ask for the heart to be taken out without sounding crazy."

"I'm not gonna kill Bella. She is family."

"Oh, are you folding so early in the game?"

"Wait! You can't do this."

"Watch me," Alex said. "Take a day to stew in your guilt, thicken it into a soup, and feel like the scum of the earth as you sip on it. Think about your daughter tied up here, and the dog running around with you. You think about those big puppy eyes and how they will squirm when you drain the life out of her. But when all is said and done, I want the heart day after tomorrow." Alex pulled the mobile phone away from his face.

"Wait, I wanna talk to Shruti," Manas said, a tinny voice through the speaker.

Alex placed the phone back on his ears. "You are in luck. The sleeping beauty has woken up from her long slumber. I'll give you two some time to catch up. Maybe that will motivate you enough to go through with what must be done. But don't mind if I put it on speaker phone. Wouldn't want you two to gang up on me now, would we?" He entered the warehouse, crossed over to where Shruti was tied up, and thrust the phone into her hands. "It's your Dad."

She grabbed the phone from his hand and hastily brought it up to her ears. "Daaad…" And sobs shook her body.

"I need you to be strong for me, kiddo," Manas said.

Shruti nodded her head and controlled her sobs; silent tears threatened to jump out of her eyes.

"Are you okay, Shru?"

"Yeah dad, I'm OK."

"Listen, I am going to get you out of there, you hear me? No matter what."

The corners of her mouth twitched into a small smile. "I know Dad, just hurry up—"

Alex snatched the mobile from her hand. "That's enough family rendezvous for today," he said, as he pulled the call out of speakerphone and placed the mobile on his ears. "You heard her; she is safe. So, day after tomorrow, come to the beach at 6pm."

Alex disconnected the call, dismantled the phone, and discarded the SIM card.

Shruti's lips quivered in shock, the full lower lips, so kissable. The shapely thighs merged onto the firm curve of her buttocks. And in between the red T-shirt, he sneaked a peek of the milky smoothness of her belly. Shruti narrowed her eyes and stared down Alex, readjusting her T-shirt in the process.

"Blessed is the man who endureth temptation; for when he is tried, he shall receive the crown of life.—James 1:12," Alex intoned.

Sonam

Thursday, May 1, 2014

Maybe we are not looking at the whole picture.

Akshay pushed off the chair and shot up to his feet. The chair jerked back, rolled, and hit the wall behind. "She could be out there right now, expecting someone to walk in through the door and save her. We can't be sitting counting ducks, waiting for something to happen. I know I can't." He stormed out of the room, slamming the door so hard that there were ripples in the glass of water in front of her. Sonam had never seen Akshay that angry with Nasir. *Hell*, she had never seen Akshay that angry. Period.

Nasir, who was at the receiving end of the slamming door, shuffled his feet and sank into an empty chair next to her. The uncomfortable silence spread its gloom over the room, which had become their temporary office. He slumped down and buried his face in his hands, like a balloon losing air. Sonam wanted to reach out to him, stroke his wiry black hair, and tell him it was going to be okay. She knew he wanted nothing more to find the girl and nail the bastard to the wall. On some level, even Akshay knew. It was not like they weren't trying; it was just that they didn't know what else to try. The only thing left was to wander the streets of Trivandrum looking for Shruti.

Crap!

Nasir had told the team, but mostly for the benefit of the newbie in the team, that they should never put a face or a name to victims of the crimes. It was easy till now because dead bodies and body parts didn't have a name or a personality. They were just specimens, puzzles she needed to figure out. But it was different this time. The victim was a living, breathing, human being. It didn't help that she reminded Sonam of her sister, whom she left behind at their grandparents when she left Delhi. It freaked her out that her little sister was living in a world with freaks like Alex. With her Dad and Mum dying in an accident when they were small, she was everything for her little sister, Sana.

If she were feeling this bad, she could only imagine how Akshay was feeling. He had lost his sister when she was almost seventeen; Shruti's age.

Some sick bastard raped, mutilated her, and left her for dead. But only she didn't die then. She struggled in the hospital for weeks before she could draw her final breath. Avinash had told her that it had almost been a blessing when she finally died. It was that incident which pushed Akshay into Nasir's team.

Avinash and Salim huddled together, whispering to each other. They each had a daughter in the teen ages and behind the facade of jovial bonhomie, she thought she had seen worry for their kids bubble up. This mad dash across the country, always one step behind a killer who just wouldn't stop killing, was taking a toll on the team.

There was no good news, just bodies after bodies. At least when they figured out who The Artist was, it should have been over soon. But Alex had made that difficult. He had been too careful.

Nasir drew a deep breath and straightened from his slump, wiping his hands down his face as he looked up. "We have put feelers across the city for Alex, his car, or Shruti, but that's just not enough. It is already past 24 hours and we still haven't found the body. That's an aberration and a second chance for us. I know we have gone through the evidence many times, but can we do it again? There may be something we are missing."

Sonam pushed back the chair and rose out of it. "The single biggest lead we have is the footprint. We have confirmed that the print is Alex's due to the fact that the road was freshly cleaned when the abduction happened, and that they match the previous prints we have recorded. But.... you know how that is."

"Meaning?" Salim asked.

"We have sent the sample to Central Forensic Science Laboratory in Hyderabad. I've been calling them every day and Nasir has been pulling all the right strings, but nothing. They are hiding behind red tape."

"Let's put a pin on that for now. What else do we have?" Nasir asked.

"We sent the memory stick to the Cyber Cell here to pull something from it, but no luck. That was destroyed beyond recovery," Salim said.

"We tracked Shruti's mobile from Kowdiar at 5:30 pm, the time of abduction, to Pettah, about 6-7 kms from Kowdiar," said Sonam. she cursed under her breath for using Shruti's name. "The father said he called her soon after, 5:50 pm to be exact, which matches with the journey time between two places in peak hours. His call was the last one on the call logs, as well. The phone didn't connect to the network after that, even though the IMEI number was picked up again."

"Alex must have dismantled the phone and threw it away when he found it," said Avinash. "Someone who came along later must have seen the phone and started using it for himself."

Nasir closed his eyes and creased his eyebrows. "Maybe we are asking the wrong questions." He climbed to his feet and paced the room like a caged animal. "Instead of asking where, maybe we should ask why. Alex has the girl, and he is in a safe place. So why wait? Why not just kill the girl and be done with it?"

Avinash looked up from his scribbling pad. "I don't know if it's important, but something has been bothering me for a few days. You know the father, Manas? When we went to see him to tell him the news of the kidnapping, he seemed a little strange."

"Strange how?"

"Well, for one, he was exceptionally calm for a man who just got to know his daughter was kidnapped."

Nasir nodded in head, barely skipping a stride. "Yeah, I know what you mean. But everybody doesn't wear their hearts on their sleeves. Maybe his left brain is more dominant."

Avinash glanced at Salim, sideways. "Yeah, could be. But what really bothered me was something else. It may be nothing, but when we showed him Alex's picture, I thought I saw a glitch in his well-maintained face. Can't put my finger to it thought. May be a twitch of the eyebrows or may be his eyes lingered on the photo a fraction of a second more or may be his eyes dilated quickly. But my first instinct was that he knew the man. But then he said he did not, and I thought it was odd at the time. Why would a father lie about that? But it was still bothering me. So, I talked to Salim yesterday and he said he had the same feeling but brushed it aside himself."

Nasir slowed down his pace, his eyes sharpened; like a hawk ready to swoop down on its prey. "Let me join the club. My gut also told me that Manas knew Alex."

"Maybe we are not looking at the whole picture," Sonam added.

Nasir nodded, absently. "Let's divide the team. It's not like we got a lot going now anyway. Sonam and I will do background checks on Manas and Avinash, Salim, and Akshay continue looking for the girl."

"Akshay..." Salim said.

"He'll come around." A smile grew on Nasir's face. "He will come around."

Manas

Friday, May 2, 2014

Sometimes you hold on to things not because you need it, or because it looks good, but because it holds memories.

Manas had spent the entire day on the couch, with just Bella for company. He had called up his office and put in an indefinite leave. Anuradha left for her parents' house in the morning leaving the house empty. It felt unnatural, his house. It was a place of mirth, of life. But now, death hung around, waiting to swoop down and snatch his prey. He had been procrastinating all day, waiting for some miracle which never came. Every time he looked into Bella's eyes, a little part of him died.

The clock read four, but the sky outside said six. The overcast weather was getting on his nerves. Sunny days were a thing of the past. He rose and paced the living room, limping on his now asleep leg. The footsteps echoed loudly in the empty house. Bella raised her head from her resting spot at Manas' feet and stared at him with a slant in her head.

Bella wasn't just his pet; she was an integral part of who he was. In the beginning of his transition, he used to get nightmares almost every night. There were all these repressed memories, a whole other life, which had no outlet. He could not talk about them to anyone. Even when he met Anuradha, he couldn't talk about these to her; not without telling her what a monster he had been.

Solitude and mental stress are a lethal combination and that led him to get a dog. That was Bella. She became his confidant. He could talk about anything to her without getting judged.

He was a little less lonely, but the nightmares continued. Most nights he would get out of the bed and wander the one-room apartment he was staying to recuperate. But Bella had this uncanny ability to understand when Manas was disturbed. She would silently get up from her spot, head over to Manas, and snuggle next to him. He didn't know if it was her warmth, or her furry coat, or just her presence, but it calmed him down.

After a few weeks, something truly magical started to happen. Whenever Manas was having a bad dream, Bella would push open the door, walk in, climb on to the bed, and curl up next to him, her head on top of his. This had gone a long way in making the nightmares go away. He rarely got them nowadays, and he knew it was Bella who got him through. *And now he was repaying her with a knife to her throat?*

Like always, Bella must have sensed something was wrong, and trotted over to Manas, stationing herself across his path. The warm fuzz ball looked up with a look that said - *'Is everything okay?'*

Manas felt like shit. Only a cruel madman would make him do this. If the choice were between Shruti and Bella, it would be Shruti always. She was his little girl and he had promised Anuradha that he would do anything to save her. And moreover, Bella was on the last leg of her life. She had well outgrown the normal lifespan for a dog. The old had to make way for the young. That was just how the world worked. Bella had to make room for Shruti to inherit the world.

A mechanical smurf marched out of the clock on the wall with a cymbal in his hands, clapped them at the end of his tread, and darted back into its home which showed 4:30. The clock was so out of place in the decor, but it survived multiple rounds of re-decorating the house. Sometimes you hold on to things not because you need it, or because it looks good, but because it holds memories. Every time he looked at the clock, he remembered the tantrum Shruti had thrown in the shop to get this clock. She loved those blue dwarfs, and she just had to have it. He had a hard time explaining it to Anuradha when they got home; not with Shruti giggling all through the explanation. He chuckled at the memory, at how much power that little girl had over him. Even when she had grown up, even in captivity, that little girl made him do things he never wanted to; and he was happy to do them. He had made up his mind; *he had to do it and he had to do it now.*

Manas had done his research. He googled 'most humane ways to kill a dog' and sifted through hundreds of pages on the internet describing ways to kill a dog; each of them more gruesome than the others. What was he thinking? There was no humane way of killing any animal, apart from euthanizing at a vet. The most common and clean suggestion was to use a gun, a bullet behind its ears. *In America, maybe.* Manas had no idea how to get a gun, let alone shoot it. The first time he saw a gun up close was when Alex pulled it out when he came to visit. Since that was out of the question, he tried drugs. There were a few over-the-counter drugs which would put a dog to sleep, but none of them ensures she dies. Manas had bought them nonetheless and fed her twenty minutes ago. Anything to make it painless. The sight of her lapping up the medicine without a second thought had shattered his heart into a million pieces.

But the problem of taking her life was still there. Decapitation was so gruesome that he instantly struck it off. Moreover, it hit too close to a past he was trying to avoid. He had finally zeroed in on slitting her jugular. Her sedation might cover the pain of the cut. The last moments with his dog were not going to be as pleasant as he had hoped.

Bella had settled herself in a corner, her head down on the ground. The sedatives were taking effect. Manas crossed over to the couch and collapsed onto it. "Bella.... here." A quiver in his voice didn't surprise him. Even in her slumber, she picked up the quiver and instantly equipped her 'concerned eyes' as she trotted over to him. One nimble jump and she was next to Manas on the couch—a privilege rarely allowed. A wide grin, her tongue hanging out, twisted her face into a whimsical smile. The tail wagged vigorously, smacking Manas across his face.

Manas hugged her, letting his hands brush over her furry back; her soft coat which he had washed a thousand times. She cuddled closed and licked his neck. The rough, slimy tongue felt strangely soothing.

After a brief display of affection, she curled up next to Manas on the couch, sleepy and lethargic. Within no time, she drifted off to a deep sleep. Manas ran his fingers through her light brown fur coat, ruffling them in fondness.

"I'm sorry, I guess this is the end of the road for us, Bella," said Manas. "You know I can't let him hurt my little girl. I know you wouldn't want that either." Warmth welled up in his eyes and streamed down his cheeks. "I know you'd understand." But it did little to comfort him. He sneaked his left hand under the pillow and felt the cold, hard metal of the knife. His hands found the wooden handle and closed around it.

Bella twitched in her sleep; happy rumbles rocked her body. She was off in her dream world running with her pack; a world where there is no betrayal, a world where her Alpha wouldn't hurt her.

The pillow under which his hand grasped the knife grew heavier. A ton of fluffy foam weighed down his arms, pinning it against the couch. Manas' body rocked with a shiver. Air escaped him in a staccato of forced breaths synchronised with an uncontrollable spasm in his diaphragm. The rivulets of salty tears down his cheeks made him realise he was crying, uncontrollably.

Manas let go of the knife and drew his hands back like it burned. He had never been capable of such violence. It was the whole reason Prateek came into existence. A way to cope with the necessities of life. Desire to protect his daughter won't change who he is. Who was he kidding thinking he didn't need Prateek? Manas peeked down the chasm in his mind, still debating whether he should call Prateek.

"I'm right here, brother." Prateek's voice boomed over the silence of the house.

Manas was glad that the decision was made for him as relief washed over him. But he put up a stony facade. This time he needed to be in control. It was easier said than done. It's like they say, *sometimes you have to delve deeper down the rabbit hole to come out the other side.* "Looks like I could use your help here, Prateek."

"Ah! Finally. I thought you'd never ask." A wide smile broke out on his face. "Let's get cracking, brother."

Manas raised his hand, palm facing up. "Hold on. I have a few conditions. If not, you're going right back where you came from."

The smile froze on Prateek's face and shrunk back to a grimace. "Like?"

"Manas held up his right hand and started counting off with his fingers. "One. I will always, I mean always be in control." Prateek opened his mouth to say something, but Manas raised his other hand and pointed to the raised finger. "I am not done. Two. You will listen to what I tell you. And three. You will never come out when I am with someone. Not unless I call you."

Manas extended his right hand for a handshake to seal the deal. Prateek studied the hand for a moment. Deep creases formed and smoothed out on his brows. He met the extended hand with a strong handshake. "Agreed," he said.

The toxic poison accumulated in his shoulders, weighing them down, melted away. It was like all those countless times Prateek had done the 'dirty' work for him. The familiar euphoria of escape. But while he was floundering in the euphoria, something felt odd.

"You've changed, Prateek. Just not sure for better or for worse"

Prateek cocked his head to the side, a fishhook in his eyebrows.

"You never would have agreed to those conditions without throwing a tantrum," said Manas.

"Even though I was buried deep inside, I still shared all the experiences you had Manas. Just like those moulded you into who you are today, it changed me too."

"People change on the surface, but deep inside they stay the same." Bella breathed in and out in a slow, relaxed rhythm. "I'm counting on it. You know what to do and Prateek....don't let her suffer."

Prateek nodded, tersely, as he made his way to the couch and sunk into the place Manas vacated. He stroked Bella's forehead, setting her brown fur the right way. "You know I love this dog, right?" He palmed the knife under the pillow and in one swift motion drew it across Bella's neck. "It's just that I have the balls to do what it takes."

The yelp was short and sad. It broke his heart. Unable to avert his eyes, he watched as Bella twitched in her sleep and bled out. The fluffy, golden fur didn't shine anymore. Not like it used to. Blood soaked the amber hair and it stuck to her body, making her smaller than she was. The last moments with his dog were an audition for his night terrors. And she passed with flying colours. She would join the nightly production of the filth in his mind, he was sure of that.

Blood was everywhere. It flowed out, soaked the couch cushion, and dripped to the floor. The puddle of red grew as life leeched out of Bella. Prateek wiped the blood splattered across his face with the inside of his elbows. It just smeared it across his face, like the camouflage lines soldiers wore. It seemed appropriate. They were at war. The whites of his eyes glowed in the maroon tinted face with a twinkle which drove daggers down Manas' spine.

Bella twitched until it slowed down to a stop and then silence. "The hard part is over, but there is more to do," said Manas. It was more to get Prateek to get on with it and finish the job than anything.

Prateek raised his hands and studied the rivulets of blood winding its way across his elbows. "Hard?" He shook his head. "Remember when we were kids, I used to take a knife to your toys, cut them open? This was way more fun than that."

"Glad you are enjoying it," said Manas.

Prateek missed the sarcasm completely as he wiped the knife on the couch. An impish grin made his mouth twitch. He didn't miss a beat as he slid the knife along Bella's chest. An involuntary gasp escaped Manas' mouth as Prateek dug into the open cavity with his free hand. His beloved dog was no more. Collateral damage in a war to save his daughter. He forced himself to watch the carnage. He owed her that much.

Prateek was lost in a world of his own, manoeuvring his hands through the bones guarding his treasure. He finally succeeded in getting through the bones and pulled out her heart and held it up like a prize.

Bile rose to Manas' throat, and he swallowed hard to keep his lunch down. "Put it away, Prateek. Just put it into the polythene cover and drop it into that bag over there."

Prateek nodded, suddenly plastering a sombre expression on his face. He carried the heart across the room to the polythene bag, blood dripping on to the carpet.

The puddle of blood was stagnant; little offshoots of blood spread out across the living room.

"You are done, for now, Prateek."

"You gotta get rid of the body, but you are good at that." Prateek winked at Manas; a naughty smile stretched his face.

And just like that he was gone. Manas surveyed the living room. It was a bloody mess. He was a bloody mess. Red streaks and splashes all over his hands, clothes, even face. A warm bath and lots of soap would wash all that away, but there was no soap in the world which could wash away the remorse and regret of having to kill Bella.

Manas dragged himself to the bathroom upstairs and switched on the water heater. The red LED light glowed with the promise of warmth. He stripped off his clothes, bundled them up and dunked it into a bucket of water. Straightening up, he stared at his reflection in the half-mirror above the sink. Kubrick would have been proud of the visual.

His well-groomed hair was in a disarray. They stuck to his scalp, sticky with blood; the grey highlight shaded red. Blood had splattered and smeared across his face. A two-day stubble grew on his chin like the shadow that had been cast on his almost perfect life. His club-like forearms and blunt fingers were dipped in blood. The blood on his hands was quite literal.

He turned on the faucet, making minimal contact so as not to smear blood on it. A handful of frothy water splashed on his face. In an instant, his heartbeat slowed down, and he started to think more clearly. Mammalian dive reflex, he had read somewhere. That was when the doorbell rang.

Nasir

Friday, May 2, 2014

It's the parent's duty to make sure their offspring is safe, and I, obviously, failed her.

The rusty hinges of the gate squeaked a soft sigh when Nasir pushed it open. The hot sun and the black paint conspired to punish him for disturbing their peace. Rubbing his fingers to disperse the heat that burned him, Nasir ambled into the shade of the car porch; Avinash on his heels and Salim stationed outside. The electric blue of the Hyundai i10 gleamed in the dark, but soon lost its shine as his vision adjusted.

"Let's get this over quick," said Nasir. "We got work to do." Manas' name was engraved on the wooden door with a majestic bronze sculpture of a lion hung on the wall right next to it.

Avinash climbed up the stairs and stroked the bronze lion's mane, studying it. "That's a fancy doorbell." He reached inside the roaring mouth of the sculpture and rang the bell. "Well, that was unsettling," Avinash said, with a chuckle.

"Looks like nobody is home, boss." Avinash retraced his steps down the stairs to survey the surroundings.

Nasir knelt next to the shoe rack and inventoried the items. "No, he is here. The daily wear shoe is on the rack." He stepped back out of the porch and studied the faded, blue, two storey building. The curtain fluttered in a window, upstairs, a shadow in the window.

"Somebody's upstairs and I hope for Manas' sake that it's him," Nasir said, turning back to face Avinash. His body wound up like a snake ready to strike; his right hand flew to the holster with clinical efficiency.

"Taking a bath," Manas shouted from behind the window. "Give me five minutes."

Avinash relaxed as he withdrew his hands, leaving the weapon in the holster, a sheepish grin on his face. He was not usually on the edge, but Alex had the whole team rattled.

"What say we take a breath and look around the house while we wait?" Nasir asked.

Avinash nodded his head and whistled loudly. Salim dashed inside with a hand on the gun in his holster.

"Calm down, Mr. Bond. Nothing happened," Avinash said. The crooked smile on his face brought out the red in Salim, both on his cheeks and his tongue. And they started bickering like a married couple.

Nasir waited a moment while they went at each other. They never failed to bring a smile on his face. Avinash swayed his broad, square shoulders and thrust his stubby fingers at Salim. Nasir always wondered at the dichotomy of his thick fingers and the skill at which he handles a gun. Salim spread his wide chest and well-muscled shoulders and Avinash' s fingers seemed to bounce off them. Kids, the two of them, trapped in adult bodies. "Let me know when your domestic troubles are over, OK?"

They stopped mid-sentence and turned to him with a stupid grin plastered on their faces.

"Shall we?" Not waiting for a reply, Nasir continued," I think Anuradha is not here."

Salim cocked his head to the side.

"Her footwear is missing. The only pair of women's shoes on the rack is an old, dusty pair of sandals. She didn't just go out, she packed up and moved somewhere. Maybe she didn't feel safe...you know with her daughter abducted two hundred meters down the road."

"Or she might know something that we don't," Avinash said, "Maybe she moved out of fear."

"What do you mean?" Nasir asked.

"What if Manas arranged for her daughter to be kidnapped and when Anuradha got to know, she fled the house?"

Nasir brought his hands to his face, covering it. "So, your theory is that the wife fled the house in fear, she stopped to pack an extra shoe on her way out? And that even after knowing her husband's hand in the abduction, she didn't tell the police? And that Manas arranged his daughter to be kidnapped by a serial killer from Delhi?"

Avinash squeezed his ear which had acquired a deep red. Salim guffawed at the top of his lungs. "There is a reason why you are in tactical ops and not investigation."

He tucked in his arms to the side and studied the garden along the side of the house. "May be not," Avinash said. "But I still don't trust the guy. Something is off."

"That is something I can get behind," said Nasir. "But I think he genuinely cares about his daughter and wife."

Nasir rambled along the small path that rounded the house to the second entrance to the house. A well-maintained garden exploded in a riot of colour along the path. Clusters of sunflowers waved their golden heads in the light breeze. A splash of fuchsia, which rose out of the bougainvillea's, clashed with pristine white of the Night Jasmines.

"Heard from Akshay?" Nasir turned his head slightly to accommodate Salim in his peripheral vision.

"Not a lot. All I know is that he is spending his time on the streets, building, and spreading his network. The last time I saw him, he had dark circles the size of Uttar Pradesh." Salim traced a path around his eyes with his fingers.

Nasir knelt beside a sunflower and pretended to inspect the flower. "At this rate, he will burn out soon. I hope he comes back before that."

They turned a corner and the path ended abruptly in another car porch. This one was empty, but the black sliding gate stayed shut.

Avinash let out a low whistle. "Two cars and a two-storey house in prime real estate."

"I'm guessing it's from Anuradha," Nasir said. "Manas doesn't look like he is from money. He has those middle-class lines of worry on his face, like us."

Nasir's ears perked up at the sound of the front door opening. He rose to his feet and made his way to the front of the house.

"You have a lovely garden," Nasir said, as he hopped up the stairs to the doorway.

Manas stood at the doorway and nodded, a forced smile on his face. "Thank you. My wife works hard to keep it that way." His shoulders slouched, as if they were holding up a ton. The muscles on his face were wound tight, stretching it into a pained expression. "What can I do for you, gentlemen?"

"We came to give you an update," said Nasir. "May we?" He gestured towards the door.

Manas paused for a second and then stepped aside and went inside the house. His wet hair dripped water down his back forming dark blotches on his sky-blue T-shirt.

Nasir paused mid-stride and took in the living room. It was very different from the last time he saw it. The furniture seemed to be there, but now it was all covered with large, thick blankets, or curtains; like the place was about to be painted.

"Sorry for the mess. I had one drink too many, and I lost it," Manas said, offering up an explanation for his gathered brows. "Just couldn't look at the comfort of this room when my daughter is locked up somewhere. I just lost it and went ballistic on them. Some of them broke, and some upturned." A mirthless laughter tried to escape Manas but was shut down in its infancy. "I woke up today with a huge hangover and an ever-bigger sense of guilt. It's the parents' duty to make sure their offspring is safe, and I, obviously, failed her."

Nasir studied the picture of defeat in front of him, leaning against a wall for support. It must be tough losing a daughter, even though she is not truly 'lost' yet. He roamed his eyes over the blankets, and it got stuck on a spot of red.

"Is that blood, Manas?" He squinted his eyes for a better view. The lights in the room were switched off and the sun didn't do enough to light up the place.

"I cut myself on one of the edges when I was laying waste to this place, yesterday," Manas said, a faint smile on his face.

"It must be serious if it's still bleeding today. You covered all this up this morning, right?"

Manas nodded silently.

"You should get that dressed. Can I take a look? I was a bit of a first aid instructor sometime before." Nasir fixed Manas with a cold stare.

Manas stared at the spot of blood and slowly moved his gaze back to Nasir. The shoulder, which was drooping moments ago, straightened up, spreading his broad chest. His watery eyes froze into an icy glaze as the corners of his mouth ticked upwards. "Don't worry, it was just a shallow cut. Nothing I haven't had to deal with before. But thank you for your concern, officer." And with that he pivoted and walked deeper into the dining room, gesturing to follow him. "We can sit at the dining table, for now."

Avinash shot a pointed look at Nasir. A moment of indecision, and he made up his mind to follow Manas into the room. Nasir followed the others, walking into the dining room with slow and measured steps. His brain worked overtime. There was something wrong with the guy, but he just couldn't put a finger to it.

"Where is your wife, Manas?" Nasir asked, as soon he took a seat at the dining table.

"We thought it'd be better if she stayed at her parents place for a while... you know..." Manas glanced at the young girl who waved at everyone from behind the glass of the photo frame. A much younger Manas hugged her from behind as she laughed in a way only kids can laugh.

"That's probably the best," Nasir said, as he rose to his feet. He paced the room, both arms tied behind his back. "We have focused all our resources, 24x7, to find your daughter. Normally, I don't discuss details of an ongoing investigation to civilians, but I thought you would feel better knowing that we are making progress. There are two leads that we are pursuing actively and a bunch of others brewing on the back burner. One is a soil sample we retrieved from the scene. We think it may give us a clue to the location she is being held. We have also distributed pictures of both your daughter and Alex's to all the police stations. Every exit out of the city is covered by the police, so he is not getting out. Now it's just a matter of elimination and we will zero in on the right location."

Salim cleared his throat. "Your daughter is very lucky...you know... considering the fact that The Artist doesn't wait—"

Nasir cut him off with a sharp look. *That idiot!* Manas was smart enough to catch the meaning. Nasir could see pain in his eyes. He disintegrated into the poster boy for defeat that they saw earlier.

"We traced your daughter's cell phone to its last known location," Nasir added quickly to switch the topic. "It last pinged a tower in Pettah."

That perked up Manas. He stood up and disappeared into a room across the hall. When he came back with a map in his hands, Nasir decided it was the study. Manas spread out the map of Trivandrum on the dining table and with the marker he carried in his pocket, he placed a dot on Kowdiar. "This is where Shruti was taken. Do we have an exact time?"

"It was around 5:30," offered Salim.

Nasir stopped pacing and drew closer to the spread map in the table.

Manas wrote '5:30' next to the dot on the map. He skimmed the map and found 'Pettah' and drew a circled around the place. "When was the mobile last registered on the network?"

"It was 5:52," Avinash said.

"Seems about right," Manas said. "I had called her around that time." After writing '5:52' next to the circle over pettah, Manas traced the shortest route from Kowdiar to Pettah. "But he would not have chosen this route." And he traced another route which did not touch the main roads. "This is a bit longer, but it bypasses all the major checkpoints in the city. He must have taken this route."

Nasir nodded, satisfied. Manas was sharp as a tack.

"It usually takes 15 minutes to reach Pettah from Kowdiar, but this was peak hours, wasn't it? So that means twenty minutes." Manas rolled up his eyes to the skies as they darted back and forth. "That's twenty kilometre per hour, give or take. And now if we assume that Alex reached his hideout in the next twenty minutes, he has travelled seven or eight kilometres more."

Nasir held up both his hands, stopping Manas. "Why twenty minutes? He could have taken longer to reach wherever he was going."

Manas crossed his arms and uncrossed them again. "I wouldn't think he would take the chance to drive around forever waiting for the cops to pull him over. He would have chosen a route which is as direct as possible, but still avoiding the routine inspection by the Police, to his hideout. And he has been heading towards the beach, and there is only so much land left in that direction." He drew a large circle around Pettah on the map.

Nasir narrowed his eyes and gaped at Manas. *That's bullshit.* Manas was smarter than that. The way he arrived at twenty minutes was conjecture, and nobody arrives at precise results with conjecture. But still, somehow, he arrived at twenty minutes, not half an hour or an hour, but twenty minutes exactly. It was madness unless he knew something that Nasir didn't. And in one swooping motion all the little things that bothered him came together: the blood on the sheets, the mysterious cut, his change in demeanour. But in contrast to the direction his mind was racing, there was the fact that he genuinely seemed to be concerned for his family, a loving husband, and a caring father. The whole thing threw Nasir off, but still one thing was clear—he was not looking at the complete picture.

By the time Nasir concluded, Manas had shaded in a sector on the circle which falls in the general direction towards the sea and had dubbed it the most probable area to find Alex. His jaw was set tight against his face, his gaze far off, but alert. He reminded Nasir of the athletes he saw on the television, moments before their big event. He tugged at his mobile phone, unlocked it, and snapped a picture of the map. "Thank you for your help, Manas, and we'll keep you posted. I've got to go now."

They walked out, Manas accompanying them. When they passed the living room, Nasir sneaked a look at the blood spot. *Was it a little bigger than before?* Before he had time to contemplate, he was out the door and Manas back inside the house.

Nasir walked out of the house with Avinash and Salim, in silence. But as soon as they got outside, Avinash said, "Like I told you before, something doesn't sit right with me. Did you see how he changed when you asked him about the cut?"

Nasir nodded his head, in affirmation, and turned to Salim. "Put a couple of policemen to watch him. Civilian clothes. I wanna know what he is up to."

The Artist

Friday, May 2, 2014

Time was the only truth in this crazy fucked up world.

Alex leaned back in the driver seat of his new car - a white Hyundai Santro. Manas' quaint little two-storey house loomed on the other side of the street. The Swift had outgrown its usefulness. It would have been on the police radar by now; after all, he *was* seen kidnapping a girl in the car. The whole business was a sloppy affair; he used to be a lot smoother than that. *Total lack of planning. That's what you get.*

He ditched the Swift in the beach parking lot and picked up the Santro. The car was as easily forgettable as it was easy to break into. None of that fancy immobilisers you find in the newer cars. All he needed was a thin rope, a screwdriver and the knowledge of how to tie a slipknot.

'*Pry the door open, slide in the rope, hook it around the lock and pull, voila!*' Alex remembered the YouTube video. It looked simple and when he tested it on his own car, it was simpler. The internet café he ran was also where he learned. A lot of his skills were culled out of the information highway, that is the internet. You would find most of what he was looking in Google. But for the niche skills and gory details he had to take an exit to the dirt roads of Tor and the dark web.

A police jeep rumbled past him and instinctively, he sunk into his seat. Hot boiling rage bubbled inside him. If Manas had called the police, he would pay, dearly. But reason laid its cold hands on him, cooling him down. It may not be something Manas initiated, it whispered. After all, you did kidnap his daughter. Alex chuckled. *They should ask me*. The miniature golden elephant caparison gleamed the late afternoon light of the day as it swung from the rear-view mirror, to the right and then to the left, unable to decide. Alex couldn't know for sure either.

A few minutes later, a wiry hawk of a man strode out of Manas' house with two solid blocks of human flesh at his heels. His heart spluttered, coughed, shuddered, and rumbled ahead. If Nasir is here, it means he's onto something. Alex smacked his head with his right hand. He must have slipped up somewhere. After Bangalore, he was under the radar; or so he thought. Alex thanked his lucky stars that he switched out his car before heading to Manas's house.

Alex stayed sunk in the shadows of the car till Nasir and bodyguards boarded the jeep and disappeared round the corner. The local police were merely an irritation. Something he needed to deal with since he kidnapped a girl in broad daylight. But Nasir and his team were another story. Ever since Nasir walked into one of his crime scenes, his cat-and-mouse game with the police had gotten considerably harder.

He still remembered that day. Watching the site where he displayed his artwork was something he loved doing. It helped him relive the experience, keep it alive and fresh in his mind. He was watching the local police blundering through the scene from across the street when a police jeep screeched to a halt. Nasir jumped out of the jeep before it was stationary and bounded up the stairs with purpose. Alex may have seen him only for a few seconds, but he knew there was something different about him. It was those eyes; those dark watchful eyes that missed nothing.

Alex glanced at his watch. Half-past five. A car coughed to start in Manas' front porch. *About time.* Time was the only truth in this crazy fucked up world. And he had very little respect for people who didn't respect it.

The electric blue i10 pulled out of the gate in a hurry and turned right. Alex waited till the car turned on the indicator to make the turn at the end of the road before inserting his key into its slot. A little twist of his fingers and the car came alive, surprising him. The car was in prime condition considering its age. The i10 turned left at the end of the lane and Alex sped up the lane to catch up with Manas. Just as he was about to make the turn, a white Innova zipped past the intersection cutting him off. He swore instinctively, even before slamming his leg hard on the brake. *Fucking maniacs.*

Alex caught up with the i10 and kept at least two cars between them. Close enough to keep an eye on him if he decides to get cocky, but far enough to keep him in the background. About two minutes into the tail, he picked up on something. The white Innova that almost crashed into him was sticking to Manas' car like flies on an apple. Alex stepped on the gas and swerved around another car to come up right behind the Innova, hoping to get a glimpse of the driver in his rear-view mirror. The idiot had not bothered to set the rear-view mirror and that meant he had to try the side mirrors or get up alongside the Innova. With a timely bit of subtle manoeuvring, he edged out a car on the lane to his right and positioned his Santro to catch a peek at the guy.

The idiot driver had a young, hard set, face which reeked of authority. The hair was cropped close to the skull with hard lines framing his face. He was in plain clothes, but his mind was wearing a uniform. The idiot grabbed a walkie-talkie from the passenger seat and spoke into it. *What a rookie!* Alex chuckled. Leaving a car or two between you and your target was Surveillance 101. And now the walkie-talkie? Might as well switch on the siren too.

Alex took his foot off the gas and dropped back a couple of cars and resumed his tail. After slipping into the steady stream of traffic, he fished out his mobile and dialled Manas. If this was Manas' doing. He was so going to pay for this.

"Hello..." came the response.

"Nice escort you got there, Manas."

"What? What escort?"

"Don't play coy with me. I'm talking about the police officer following you."

Manas' words sped up. "Where? I swear I had nothing to do with that. You have to—"

"Calm down," Alex said, cutting off the nervous rambling. "The white Innova right behind you."

There was a pause on the line, after which Manas' hyperventilated voice came back on. "Oh shit! oh shit! What do I do? I swear this is not me."

What do you know? He seemed genuine. A throaty laugh broke out of Alex's mouth. "Just calm down and listen to me. Can you do that?"

Alex took the silence on the other end as a 'yes'.

"It's time to show you are invested in this, Manas. Do not slow down or look back. As far as you are concerned, nothing happened. You are just going wherever you were going before. Understood? I'll call you back with a plan."

Alex revved the engine, shifted the gear higher, and passed Manas to scout ahead. He needed a plan and a place to execute it. Soon he passed a bus top with a row of cars stacked up in the parking space beside it. A seed of an idea sprouted and grew up as he slowed down. There was a single space left and it was perfect for what he had planned. Alex side-lined his car a little down the road and kept the engine running. He dialled Manas. "There is a bus stop coming up on your left and a set of cars parked beside it. Pull into the empty space over there, head to the bus stop and call back."

In the rear-view mirror, Manas made a sharp turn into the parking space. The Innova braked hard in the middle of the road confused by the sudden turn Manas took but had the good sense to roll down the road without making a scene. Manas, unfazed by the commotion, climbed out of the car and made his way to the bus stop.

He handled the situation a lot better than Alex expected. Some of the spark he had back in the days was still with him. The fool behind the wheel took a U-turn up ahead and looped back to park his car on the other side of the road. He stepped out of the car, a black Aviator shades covering his eyes, and strolled closer to the bus stop where Manas fidgeted with the strap of the bag he carried.

The phone buzzed in his pocket and Alex picked up the call. "Had fun yet?"

"He is right here with me," Manas said, his voice half whisper and half urgent. "He's at the bus stop."

Alex laughed at the way nervous words rolled off Manas in a hurry. It was not what he expected of his idol, but then again it was unfair to judge him so harshly. They only just got started. "Yeah, I see him."

Manas instinctively swivelled his head to spot Alex. "Stop acting like a chicken and just look straight ahead. Or look at the traffic held up by the stop light. The timer says 20 seconds. You are waiting for a bus, remember. But be ready to do exactly what I say when I say it, okay?"

Manas nodded, but it lacked conviction. It was evident that he was a man who was not used to taking instructions, blindly.

Alex scanned the other side of the road. Another bus stop, bustling with people who want to go the opposite way. A bus approached the stop, swaying and swerving like a vehicle with six wheels shouldn't. In about ten seconds the bus should reach the stop on the other side. The timer on the stop light on his side read 15 seconds.

"Manas, you see that bus on the other side?"

"Yes."

"You'll have to get on that bus. Not right now. When you hear a loud honk, you just dash across the road and board the bus, okay? Don't stop to look both sides like a kindergarten kid. Just do it. A leap of faith."

"Yes..." Manas said, and after a pause, "It's not like I have a choice anyway."

"You are catching on. Remember the horn."

The bus squeaked to a stop and a flux of people poured out.

"Alex?"

"Not yet."

The timer counted down to zero, and the traffic threatened to invade the clear road in front of Manas, the motorbikes leading the charge.

"The light is green, Alex."

"Wait for it."

The first motor bike was approximately a hundred meters from Manas when Alex honked his horn. It was loud and long. The idiot in the Innova jerked his head and scanned the road for the source of the honk. But Manas didn't flinch, didn't wait. He dashed across the road dodging a few motorbikes on the way and reached the other side. The bus on the other side had finished boarding people and started to pull away. Without breaking a stride, Manas shoved the mobile phone in his pocket, sprinted after the bus and jumped onto the foot board.

By the time the policeman realised what was happening, the traffic devoured the open road, cutting him off completely. Alex pulled into the traffic and disappeared into it. A wide smile grew and then stayed on his face.

He dialled Manas and waited for him to pick up the call. Manas see-sawed across Alex's expectations. One moment he was a whiny snivelling human being, but the next he showed flashes of his past glory.

Manas answered the call with a grunt.

"You are not as useless as I thought, you know? We should team up more often."

Manas brushed aside the offer and said, "Did I lose him?"

Alex felt the snub like a prick of a cactus. *Too early*, he thought. "Yeah, you lost him. Now get to the Valiyathura Pier. I'll be there."

~

The pier was alive with the happy rumbling of families spending a quiet Saturday evening. Children shrieked at the top of their lungs as they darted across the top of the pier overlooking the sea. It pierced the low chatter of mixed conversations and the incessant crashing of waves. Orange crept into the skyline, slowly, invading and infecting everything in sight with its burning hue. Alex closed his eyes, blocked out the noise, and breathed in the salty wind; it whispered sweet nothings in his ears. The waves rose and crashed against the pillars holding up the pier, spraying salty water in the air. Growing up in Delhi, the sea was always a stranger to him. But now that he got to know her well, he was sure he could sink into her embrace and get lost in. But not before he had fulfilled his purpose.

The mobile phone rang, and he picked it up at the first ring. A glance at his watch told him that Manas was right on time. "Head over to the end of the pier. I'm there."

Alex studied a man sitting at the edge of the low wall around the pier, with his legs dangling over the side. The waves threw up another salty spray in air, exasperated at the pillars of the pier blocking their journey to the shore. The continuous spray of water had drenched the man completely, but he stayed put with a fishing line in his hand. He brushed aside whatever the sea threw at him and held on to the fishing line. The man glanced back in Alex's direction and flashed him an open smile. Alex nodded back, tipping his head a little. He knew what it meant to have that kind of purpose.

Alex turned back towards the entry of the pier and spotted Manas walking up to the end of the pier. A hint of a paunch pushed against his brown T-shirt which stretched across his solid chest. The black strap of his bag wound above his right shoulder and disappeared under his left arm. The old eyes peered out from a sun-whacked face; they narrowed when he spotted Alex. Manas shifted the bag from one shoulder to the other and changed his trajectory. Muscles rippled under his T-shirt.

Alex leaned against a pillar with the beauty of the dying day behind him. He imagined it'd be a great shot in a movie, the hero against the backdrop of exquisite beauty. It didn't take long for Manas to reach him. He took up a wide stance two feet from him, with his hands tied in front of him.

A beat of silence passed before Alex said, "The cards are on the table and the bets are placed." He pointed to the bag with his face. "Is that a raise or a call?"

Manas slipped off the bag and held it out as if it was the plague. "See for yourself."

Alex took a step closer and snatched the bag from Manas. It was a blue denim messenger bag with a pink Nike logo on the outside. It had a teenage feminine charm which meant it was Shruti's. He unzipped the main compartment and reached in. The white plastic bag inside was tinted red and it was warm to touch.

"Well done, Manas. Looks like you made it through the first round. Your daughter lives longer." The man who was fishing drew in the line and at the end of it a fish wiggled to get free. A slow smile drew across his face. "And brownie points for the way you dealt with the police. That goes in your piggy bank."

Manas' tightly wound muscles visibly relaxed and the worry lines on his face eased. He stared past Alex into the sunset. The fierce orange light bounced off his eyes; they were on fire. "I hope you know you are playing a dangerous game. Shruti is the only thing that is stopping me from ripping you to pieces right here. But keep this in mind. The moment I feel she is not safe with you, you are done." He focused his eyes back on Alex;

it drilled right through to his soul. "I'll make you wish I had killed you instead."

The last sentence was uttered in an even tone without the slightest inflexion of emotion. It unnerved Alex and sent daggers down his back. He was thrilled and scared at the same time, but he showed none. "I'm a man of my word, Manas. You play by the rules and Shruti stays safe. But the moment I feel you are losing your way; all bets are off."

Alex turned his back towards Manas, staring deep into the horizon. It was a pure power play. He wanted to make sure Manas understood he didn't consider him a threat, show him that he didn't need to put his guard up around him. "I have two more tasks for you. Go home. I'll call you when the time is right."

A smile took birth on his face and grew as he ran his hands over the messenger bag.

Manas

Friday, May 2, 2014

Darkness gained mass and fluttered its wings.

Manas had to will himself not to turn back. He walked away from Alex in calm, measured steps, but a hurricane ran havoc in his mind, throwing up trees in the air, prying open roofs like a can opener. Things which should have stayed hidden, rushed out and leading the charge was Prateek.

Prateek chuckled as he kicked away a piece of rock on his path. "*You'll wish I had killed you?* Where did that come from? Sounds like something I would say."

Manas mustered up his coldest of stares and shot it across to Prateek. "And I meant it."

"I know you did. I can feel that righteous anger of yours, you know. Much stronger than the ones you had back in the days."

As soon as they were far enough from the pier, Manas pulled out his new phone from his pocket—a generic Android phone he bought a day before. A couple of taps and swipes later, he opened the app he wanted and there it was —a blue blip moving across the map of Trivandrum. "It works!" he yelled.

"Weren't you shitting bricks in the 'if he found out' hyperbole earlier? And now you're excited?"

"It's called 'sound reasoning'. You should try it." Manas hailed an auto-rickshaw.

He was never a gambling man and rightly so. In Prateek's words, *he didn't have the balls for it.* It still gave him panic attacks thinking about the consequences if his gamble fails. Though he would never admit it to Prateek, he went ahead with it only because of Prateek's confidence. Manas didn't like it. Prateek had always been able to convince Manas to go along his way.

They climbed into the auto-rickshaw and hunched over the screen of the mobile to watch the blue dot blip across the screen.

It was the day before when he and Prateek toyed with the idea of doing something rather than sitting on their asses. Going to the police was ruled out from the get go. It was clear Alex wanted to play a game, but involving the police would force his hand and he might do something rash. As long as Shruti was with him, Manas couldn't risk that. The police would also come with further complications and questions about why Alex kidnapped Shruti, why he was playing a game with Manas, and that line of questioning wouldn't end well for him. So, they ended up discussing taking things into their own hands, which came with its own risks.

Even though the idea came from Manas, he wasn't sure if it was worth the risk. But Prateek ran with it, expanded on it, and argued for it. That resulted in a debate which lasted a little over an hour, and at the end of it, they headed out to the nearest mobile phone store and bought two disposable smartphones. The rest of the night went in installing the location sharing app in both the phones and carrying out test runs. When they were convinced, it would work, both the phones were left for charging overnight.

The phones stayed on the charging wires until Manas took them out, just before leaving the house. Prateek grabbed one of Shruti's bag, turned it inside out and sliced the waterproof lining on the inside. It was a perfect place to hide the phone. He shoved the phone inside, fixed it with a double-sided tape, and stitched it back up, sealing the hidden compartment. And they were tracking that now.

They rode the rickshaw, back to the car they had left behind, in silence. The pale blue light from the mobile illuminated their faces. Prateek stretched and leaned back, closing his eyes. "You know what makes people weak?"

Manas turned off the display plunging them into darkness. No point in staring at the moving blip. He wouldn't be able to do anything unless it stops.

"You listening to me, Manas?"

Manas pushed out a long-drawn breath. He knew Prateek was baiting him with an argument they had the day before, but it hit too close to heart to let it go. So, he bit it. "I'm sure you'll tell me anyway."

"They are trapped in a web of ties," Prateek straightened up and faced Manas. "Ties to your family, friends, love, money, property....the list is endless."

Manas shook his head. "I see it as a network of lines which feed you raw energy, drawing strength and resilience from each connection, each node."

"That bridge goes both ways, brother. You might see them as positive influences, they are leeching as much energy from you as you are getting from them. They become restraints without you realising it. You become co-dependent."

"I know what you are getting at, but I refuse to be a selfish bastard. And moreover, it's these 'ties' you despise which gave me the strength to keep you locked up. I think I'll hold on to them." Manas glimpsed a fleeting darkness on Prateek's face before he turned away, ending the discussion. Manas turned the other way and let his gaze skim over the city speeding past him.

It was half past seven and the city was humming with life. Being the capital of the state, Trivandrum had a huge population of government employees. Their nine-to-five day styled the city into a laid-back sleepy town which shuts its eyes at nine. In his twenty years, he had seen a slow and steady change. The IT industry grew its roots and flourished and brought with it some young blood. It is this conflict between the old and the new that drives the city now. He could see it even in a mundane aspect of life as the daily commute. The nine-to-fivers were up and about the city when the young toiled to reach home after a hard day at work. Their days started later and ended late.

The rhythmic buzzing of his mobile shook him out of his reverie. Manas pulled out his iPhone and answered the call.

"Hey Manas, you busy?" the voice on the other end asked.

"No, Ravi. Tell me."

"Nothing....I just called to...Did you....Did the police get any information about Shruti?" He was trying his best not to pick the scabs, but it didn't work. They were open and bleeding. They were always open and bleeding and all he could do was ignore them.

"No, Ravi. Nothing yet."

Ravi was probably his only real friend in the office. He thought he had a few more, but Ravi was the only one who called him up regularly to check on things. It was hard making friends for Manas; it was hard to trust people. But with Ravi, it was really easy. In the short six months that he knew Ravi, they had become quite close. Ravi had told him a couple of times how he was deeply indebted to Manas for covering for him in a sticky situation he was in, and he had started to see Manas as an older brother.

"-heard you are on a long leave. You should come back to work. It would take your mind off things, you know," Ravi continued.

"Don't think so, Ravi. Been keeping myself busy and most definitely not suicidal if that's what you are worried about."

It wasn't that he never had that thought. But it was not the time to clock out of life, leaving his loved ones high and dry.

"Hmmm...okay. You know you can call me anytime, for anything, right? Don't even think, just call. Okay?"

Manas hummed an affirmative into the phone before disconnecting.

A few more minutes of bumpy ride and they were at the place where Manas parked his car. They got out of the auto rickshaw and made their way to the car. The moment they closed the doors, Manas whipped out his spare phone and checked the tracking app. The blue blip was stationary.

"Finally," said Prateek, who was peeking into the screen.

Manas pinched the screen to zoom in, noted the location in the map. His heart sped up. *This is it.*

~

It was half-past eight when they parked their car in a residential pocket in a largely uninhabited area. They needed the element of surprise. Manas and Prateek sneaked closer to the target, hugging the walls of the houses on the way. Melodramatic music blared from the houses as the nightly soaps led an overly dramatic lives filled with deception and adultery. If real life was not as dramatic, it more than made up for in darkness.

Soon the houses gave way to an emptiness claimed back by nature. The outline of their target loomed in the darkness. A lone streetlight cast a low bluish white glow on the building. Manas inched closer and crouched behind a half-wall, destroyed by time, and spied the building. The walls looked barely strong enough to hold up the structure. He spotted a crack in the wall on the side, large enough for a man to pass, and gestured towards it.

They stuck to the ground, as low as possible, as they made their way towards the opening. Manas hoped the incessant chirping of the crickets provided enough cover for them to silently enter the building.

The moment they entered through the crack a moment of cold panic grabbed Manas from behind. Darkness gained mass and fluttered its wings. He whipped his head around to where he spotted movement. But nothing. Imagining things was never good. Manas threw caution to wind and turned on the display of his phone. The screen threw just enough light to coerce the dark emptiness around him to take shape. Breath regained its regular rhythm as Manas chased away the demons which lived in the shadows. They were alone. He inched towards the doorway at the far end of the enclosed space and peeked outside.

A sliver of light seeped under the door of the closed room and sliced the darkness of the corridor. A low drone of voices vibrated through the still air. Manas covered the display of his phone on instinct and turned it off as he crawled his way to the closed room. His boots crunched the debris on the ground. The silent night made it seem like he was walking on crushed glass.

As he got closer, the drone of voices formed into an argument but in hushed voices. The voices were masculine and there were at least two of them. Manas inched closer and peeked inside the room through a crack in the door.

Two shapes huddled around a small candle, one much bigger than the other. The fickle flame of the candle cast shadows which flickered and danced all around the place. The assortment of items that were scattered around the two shapes slipped in and out of light. There were two heaps of wallets and bags separated with a wide margin. Manas spotted Shruti's denim bag in the heap of bags and it hit him like a bull charging at full speed.

"Alex must have thrown away the bag," Manas whispered to Prateek. "These guys are just petty thieves divvying up the day's haul." He gestured Prateek to head back. As they retreated the way they came, Manas's feet caught on something at the edge of darkness and it tumbled down with a ruckus enough to wake the dead. He froze mid-step as the silence shattered into a thousand pieces.

The scuffle of feet were the only warning Manas got before the door to the room flew open. Light flooded the dark corridor through the open corridor. Before Manas could turn back and run out of the building, the two thieves crowded in the doorway, gaping right at him.

Manas raised his hands, palms facing outwards - the universal sign of submission. "Wrong place, wrong time. I'm just gonna go." He took a couple of steps back. The shadows on the wall grew larger as the thieves stepped out onto the corridor. They reminded him of Laurel and Hardy, but they had none of the comic relief.

"So that you can go and tell Jose that we are here?" Laurel, the lanky fellow, said, waving his lanky arms around.

Manas took another step back. "Who? Jose? I honestly don't know what you are talking about."

Hardy, the big man, stepped closer, his barrel chest rising and falling with each breath. "Honestly? Well, we believe you now that you said it 'honestly'. You guys killed Shamir. He was a good boy, trying to make ends meet. You didn't think we would react?"

Manas moved his left feet back a step and leaned forward bringing up his hands in front of him. He had stumbled into a gang war and things didn't look rosy. "I don't know Jose neither Shamir. I'm not whoever you think I am, and I am just going to leave."

But the words just seemed to bounce off the aggression and not make an impact. Laurel slipped out of the doorway and flanked him through the left. If the stick-like arms and legs were not threatening, the knife, gleaning candlelight, at the end of his right hand was. Manas kept himself in constant motion, circling the attackers, so that neither of them slips out of his vision and surprise him.

Prateek leaned against the wall, a few steps away. "This is interesting. Let's see what you got."

Hardy rushed him, swinging his huge arms in a wide arc. Manas pivoted inwards, swinging left, his extended right arm deflecting the punch. But Hardy had committed too much into the punch, lost balance and teetered on the edge. Manas stepped in and caught the guy on his way down and landed a barrage of punches to the side of his face. He let go of the heavy guy with a kick to the side of the body. He crashed on to the floor, away from Manas.

Shock registered on Laurel's face as he froze with the knife hanging in the air. He shook it off and close the distance between them, swinging the knife in a wide arc in front of him. It seemed more in defence than offence, but still the knife was a threat he needed to neutralise and neutralise fast. Manas had taught this to countless students. *'Go from defending to attacking as soon as possible."*

Manas pulled out his iPhone and gripped it inside his hands, the end of the phone jutting out. The knife swayed back and forth in Laurel's right hand, tracing a protective boundary around him. Playing the waiting game was not in Manas' interest. Laurel can lunge at any second and he may or may not be able to counter it. Instead, he needed to control the fight, get inside the arc, close enough to deal with the arm and not the knife at the end of it.

Manas counted the seconds, assessed the pattern of the knife swinging back and forth, and timed his rush perfectly. A lunge inside the arc with his left hand extended to deflect and control the knife wielding arm. Laurel saw the motion and sped up the knife to get it in front of him but was too late. The arm struck the extended left arm, deflected, and rested against the side of Manas' body. Manas' left hand slammed down, wrapping around the knife wielding arm, and pulled Laurel forward. He lost his footing and teetered forward. Manas didn't let go of the arm but twisted it behind Laurel as he fell forward and slammed the butt of the phone on the wrist, repeatedly. Laurel landed on his face, the knife clattering to the floor. Manas promptly kicked it out of his reach.

"You are holding back, Manas," Prateek said. "Finish it."

Manas put up his hands in front of him again in an attacking stance and surveyed the scene. Hardy was gathering himself up, shaking off the pain. Laurel dragged himself across the floor on one hand, the other held up in the air; a grimace on his face. Laurel and Hardy exchanged a brief look as Laurel slipped into the room. In that same moment, Hardy bull rushed Manas, his broad shoulders holding up his big arms like horns. Manas realised there was no way he was dodging this, and he braced for impact. But when Hardy made contact, it had more momentum under it than Manas ever expected. He got all his air knocked out of him and felt the world move as his legs gave way. Hardy landed on top of him with a thud and Manas wondered if he had broken something.

As he was assessing the damage to his body, Hardy pulled him up to his feet in a choke; his two mammoth hands enveloping Manas' neck, front to back. He felt the pressure against his windpipe, the soft cartilages begging to give way. With the reduced air supply, he knew he wouldn't last very long. Hardy raised his knee to make contact with Manas' stomach. It was like someone drilling a hole in his torso.

"I've seen you break out of chokes like this every day. What are you waiting for?" Prateek said.

Manas brought up his legs to block the barrage of kicks that came one after the other. Some of them he blocked, but the others landed, sending shock waves through his body. Hardy's thumbs pressed down on his trachea, and it became harder and harder to breathe. Manas blacked out for a second because of the pain and the lack of air. He knew he had to act fast.

"The combined strength of your shoulder and back muscles is greater than the arm strength of the attacker. Remember?" Prateek's voice drifted over the sound of the blows.

Manas bid his time and waited for an opening. Soon, Hardy stopped the incessant kicks to Manas' torso to catch his breath. In that split second, Manas executed a set of well-rehearsed movements with clinical efficiency.

He dropped his chin and pressed against his clavicle. It released the pressure on his trachea, redirecting it towards the strong bones. At the same time, he cupped his left hand, grabbed Hardy's right arm, and coiled his right hand tight. And in one quick, forceful movement, he pivoted his body left. Using the momentum, he pulled his left hand downwards, loosening Hardy's hold on his neck, and unleashed his right hand, palms up, at Hardy's face. His neck flung back with a crack, and he staggered back a step. Manas stepped into the extra space he just created and rammed his knees into Hardy's groin, again and again, until he was on the ground, all the while holding his right arm in a lock under Manas' arms. He twisted the arm behind Hardy's back, and got on top of him, pinning him to the ground.

"No, no, no, no," Prateek tore away from the wall he was leaning on. "Finish him. If this were Alex, would you subdue him and hand him over to the police?"

He came close, crouched next to the guy on the floor and snapped his neck. A sickening crunch echoed in the room. Hardy was dead.

"What the hell?" Manas cried out. "I had it under control."

"Can you afford to keep him subdued when the other guy comes back? Like with a gun?"

"The other guy fled the scene."

"Really? Then who is that at the doorway, with a gun in his hand?"

And there he was. The lanky fellow was in the doorway, pointing a gun at Manas. His eyes darted between Manas and the guy on the floor, who laid motionless.

"What did you do to him?" The lanky guy's voice was surprisingly deep.

He took measured steps to his fallen companion. And gestured Manas to move away from him.

Manas moved away, slowly, to make sure he doesn't give the guy a reason to shoot.

Laurel trained the gun on Manas, crouched next to his friend, and shook him to see if he responds. Soon realisation must have dawned on him, and he rose to his feet. His nostrils flared, and hands trembled as he walked closer to Manas.

"This time I'll show you how it's done," said Prateek, as he took control.

The guy aimed his gun towards Prateek's chest. He might be inexperienced, but he was smart enough to know that he should aim for a larger target. None of that 'aim for the head' gusto, but cold, and pragmatic body shot.

"You killed... you killed him?" the guy asked, his voice trembling.

Three words swam across Prateek's mind - redirect, attack, and control. Manas saw them too.

"Raise your hands. I am the one with the gun here," the guy said, managing to gain a little more control over himself.

Prateek knew this was the best time to jump into action and so did Manas.

Disarm the attacker and subdue him, Manas urged Prateek.

Prateek just smirked at the words and Manas saw something flash across his face for a milli-second. He knew Prateek had other plans.

Prateek lashed out his right arm and deflected the pointed gun and at the same time turned himself to the side making himself a smaller target. Grabbing the gun and twisting it out of his way, he unleashed a barrage of punches with his left fist to the guy's face. As soon as the grip on the gun loosened a bit, Prateek twisted the gun 180 degrees backwards, breaking the assailant's finger which as inside the trigger, took away the gun from him.

That's enough, Prateek," Manas shouted.

Prateek did not waste any time to follow the disarming with another upward attack with the butt of the gun to the guy's nasal septum, inflicting a cervical shock. The lanky fellow lifted off his feet and landed with a thud on his back. Prateek jumped on top of him, with his knees on the guy's neck, applying pressure and choking him.

Manas understood Prateek wanted to kill that man. "Stop it! You made your point."

"Brother, I'm loving the Krav-Maga. See how easy it is when you don't hold back?" Prateek's face lit up with excitement as he applied more pressure on the assailant's throat.

It took all his might to break Prateek from the man and drag him off to a side.

The lanky fellow drew in a large breath followed by a series of coughs catching his breath.

"Come on. Let's go," Manas said, as he dragged Prateek out the crack they came in through and towards their car.

"You should have let me finish, Manas. If you don't have the balls to do it, at least let me do it."

"It's not about having the balls or not. It's about taking a human life, God dammit."

"I hope you preach this sermon to the psychopath who kidnapped your daughter too."

Manas felt his whole body tighten. "Maybe you are right. I don't have what it takes to follow through. But believe me, if there is a need, I would gladly let you finish it." He met Prateek's stare with an equal intensity and counted to five in his mind. One of the many techniques he had to calm himself down; keep Prateek contained all these years. Though it didn't work on the latter anymore, it calmed him down.

As the adrenaline subsided, clearing his clouded vision, it struck him like a truck coming headlong. "If the bag was here and not with Alex, it could mean that he figured out there was a mobile stitched to the bag's insides."

"Hmmm…" Prateek just nodded his head.

Air became a rare commodity. No matter how hard he tried, he was not getting enough of it. Manas held the top of the car to stay upright and leaned on it. The cold metal sent chills through his body. "What have I done?"

Manas

Friday, May 2, 2014

You are on thin ice. One step out of line will send you crashing down to the icy depths of terror.

The customer *you are trying to call is currently switched off. Please try after some time.*

The annoyingly happy lady repeated the same thing over and over again on the speaker, in all languages. Manas banged on the dining table, rattling a few glasses, and nudging along a stack of plates precariously balanced on the edge. He swiped on the screen a little harder than he had to, and the cycle started all over again. Silence, a few low beeps, and then the lady again.

Prateek threw a rolled newspaper across the room and shot up to his feet. "Fucking stop already. You're giving me a headache. He'll call you when he wants to. Isn't that how it was till now?"

The ground shook beneath him. *Or was it his body shaking?* He was not sure. "You want me to stop?" He grabbed the phone off the table and shoved it into his pocket. "Alright, I'll stop. I'll stop worrying about pissing off an emotionally unstable psychopath. I'll stop worrying about what he will do to my little girl if he finds out what we did. Shall I also stop worrying about my wife who expects me to walk into the house with Shruti? What about the fucking psychopath who tried to kill two thieves to prove a point? Instead, I'll probably start worrying about your headache. Shall we go to the doctor?" Suddenly the weight of his body seemed too much to hold up. He sunk to his knees and buried his face in his hands.

A warm, friendly hand touched his shoulder. "You know I didn't mean it like that," Prateek said. There was warmth in his voice. Something that Manas craved right then. "I love Shruti as much as you do. We are the same, remember?"

Manas breathed slowly, counting off the ups and downs of his lungs. When he finished building the facade of bravado, he rose to his feet, one hand on Prateek's shoulder. "I'm worried, Prateek. What if Alex found out about the trace and.... and...."

"We don't know for sure, right? And for argument's sake, let's assume he did find out. Even then he wouldn't hurt Shruti. Not after *'I'll make you wish I had killed you instead before killing you'* " The left side of his mouth twitched into a cocky smile. "I think you got the message through there. Without Shruti, there is no game."

"You talking about the mentally unstable serial killer? Yeah, I'd put my bets on him thinking rationally."

"We both know he is not mentally unstable. If he is composed enough not to leave any clues for the Police all this time, I think we can rule out mentally unstable from the list. But crazy, yes. But aren't we all a little bit?"

Manas's phone buzzed in his pocket before piercing the silence with the familiar iPhone ringtone. He grabbed the phone and stared at it. An unknown number. He swiped at the screen and placed the phone close to his ear.

"Man, you surprise me every time." The sound from the other end had a clarity reserved for the opera singers.

Manas drew in a sharp breath. Alex. He keeps changing the number. Manas already had 'Alex1' and 'Alex2' on his mobile.

"Cute number you pulled there with the bag." Alex's voice wavered in tone; as if he were teetering on the edge of a wall - red, hot rage on one side and the other brimming with the golden warmth of admiration.

Panic swelled up inside Manas, threatening to swallow him belly-first. He blurted out, "I'm sorr-"

"Did I say you can talk?" Alex waited a beat to make sure he wasn't going to be interrupted again. "But you showed balls and that I can appreciate. At the same time.... Just hold on a second."

A dull thud followed by Shruti's scream travelled through his ear and straight into Manas' heart. "Don't you fucking touch her," he growled.

"You are in no position to flaunt your machismo. Grovelling suits you better."

Acidic rage bubbled in his stomach, throwing up shoots of its toxic fumes up his throat. He bit them down and swallowed it back.

"When I said you can 'call or raise', I meant you can just shut the fuck up and listen to what I say. The brownie points you racked up earlier, that's gone now. All used up." Prateek let a beat go before speaking again. In the brief silence, Manas heard Shruti's silent weeping.

"Let me very clear. You are on thin ice. One step out of line will send you crashing down to the icy depths of terror. I'll make sure of it. Imagine your daughter's head delivered to your doorstep. Her pretty little face all made up, blood wiped off. Dark red lipstick would be perfect for her. A little rouge on her cheeks, you know, to bring out her cheekbones. Ah, the possibilities are endless. I'll take my time with her too. She'll brighten up your living room, don't you think?"

Alex let out a long winding sigh, as if he were living the moment in his imagination. It clawed its way down Manas' spine, leaving a cold trail behind.

"Oh, I'm sorry," Alex said, in a cheerful tone. "You spend day and night with a beautiful girl tied up to a post and you start getting fantasies. But I'm sure you won't let me have them. Spoilsport. Anyway, gotta go now. I'll call you soon with the next task. Till then, ciao."

Anuradha

Friday, May 2, 2014

Utopias are usually perfect until they aren't.

Time was a bitch when it mattered. She drags her feet when you want her to run. And when you want to hold on to a moment, she snatches it away and disappears into oblivion. Anuradha sat on the edge of the couch at her parents' house, staring at the phone in her hand. She was at this for the past forty minutes, praying, willing it to ring. But all that she could see was her own tired face in the dark screen.

She almost didn't recognise the woman staring back at her from the dark. Frizzy hair, bloodshot eyes, and permanent worry lines all over her face. The last four days had been hell for her; alone at her parents' house. Her parents had been taking care of her, consoling her. But she didn't need consolation, she needed her daughter back in her arms.

Sleep was a rare commodity, food was an obligation, and obsession a compulsion. She glanced at her daughter's photograph propped up on the coffee table next to her. Shruti peered through the glass with her carefree, infectious smile. Anuradha reached over and ran her fingers over the photograph, yearning to touch her face, one more time.

Anuradha glanced at the phone again. Still nothing more than just a dead weight. She missed Manas' comforting arms wrapped around her, melting away her worries. Ever since the.... She bit back a sob that threatened to break out. Even since what happened, she had not been able to talk to Manas. He called her every day, updated her about the investigation, asked her how she was, and warned her to be careful. But talking was more than a mere exchange of words. The dark shadow of what happened loomed over them, every second. She was the most alone she ever felt in her life. It was like she lost her husband as well to the incident.

But the last call was different. There were hints of the old spark in Manas, a flicker of hope in the emptiness of despair. It was an hour ago when she called her, as usual. He was talking to someone when she picked up the call, but he wouldn't tell her who that was. Anuradha assumed it must be someone from the part of his life he never talks about. Even though she told herself that she didn't care about his past, she had caught herself speculating what it was many times. Drug dealer? Gun for hire? White Collar crook? But as always, she boomeranged back to the answer she didn't care. Manas was a good man and that was all that mattered. She had built up a utopia in her mind where the past didn't poke its nose into someone's life. Utopias are usually perfect until they aren't.

On the phone, Manas had indicated that he had a lead on where their daughter was and that if all went according to plan, she would be home by the end of the night. But before they could actually talk, he had to cut short the conversation with a promise to call her back in an hour. She had been counting the ticks of the clock ever since.

Anuradha checked the time; it was over an hour and still no call. Her fingers drummed on the frame of Shruti's photo. The lifeless screen of her mobile irked her. She turned it on and checked the time again. *Oh! Hell with it!* Anuradha swiped up and dialled Manas.

It rang four and a half times before Manas picked up. "Manas?" Anuradha tried to control the eagerness in her voice.

The silence from the other side told her much more than a full conversation. Hope fell through the cracks of that silence, crashed, and burned in the dark abyss of misery. She grabbed the hand rest of the couch she was resting on as tight as possible. Sinking in the abyss was not an option, giving up was not an option. "Things didn't work out, huh?" Her own voice sounded unfamiliar to her. It didn't sound like the wreck she was.

"I.... I don't know what I'm doing anymore, Anu."

"Finding my daughter and bringing her home to me. That's what you are doing."

Manas took a moment to reply. "You know I'm trying."

"Try harder. You said you had a better chance of getting her safe than the police, didn't you?" Her cheeks burned as blood rushed up to her face. "You brought this on us, your past. It's time you fix it." Anuradha regretted her words the moment it was out of her mouth. Manas loved Shruti as much, if not more, as her. And she was sure Manas blamed himself for the abduction, without her picking at the scabs again.

The silence on the other side was killing her, driving a stake into her heart with each tick-tock of the clock. "Listen... I didn't mean it like that and I'm sorry." She blinked away a layer of tears, bringing into focus the smiling photograph of Shruti. "The past is always in the rear-view mirror, isn't it? Just because you don't look at the rear-view mirror doesn't mean it's still not there. I wanted to believe it was not there. It's not just you Manas, both of us are equally responsible in ignoring it, just like we are equally responsible in getting our daughter back."

"It's not your past that has come to haunt us. It's mine."

"So what? It's *our* daughter."

"No, Anu. This is my burden to bear. A parent has one fundamental responsibility - to keep their children safe."

"Stop it! You are a great father. And this is not the time to sink into self-pity and doubt. Not while our daughter is out there, alone, and scared. She needs us to be strong."

"You're right, as always." Manas let a beat go by before saying, "I will bring our baby home, whatever it takes."

It was then it hit her like a wrecking ball, flat on her stomach. The cold fingers of terror tickled her feet and grabbed her firmly. "The shot," she blurted out. "What if she gets an asthma attack, Manas?"

"Oh shit! Oh shit! The police didn't say anything about the bag... maybe it's with her. There was a shot in it." Panic laced Manas' voice.

Anuradha laboured for a breath of air. The walls closed in. "There is no 'maybe', Manas. You know what happens if she..." She couldn't complete the sentence. "Manas..."

The Artist

Saturday, May 3, 2014

This was what he was destined to do.
It gave him purpose; it gave him direction.

"Fucking dogs," Alex swore; his eyes still closed. It was still dark enough to pretend it wasn't the morning. But the dogs were at it, as they were every morning.

He heard a rustle of clothes, a shuffle against the floor, and his eyes flew open. Shruti readjusted her position to get more comfortable. "Probably you should have thought about it before you chose a dumpster to be your hideaway." The air quotes around 'hideaway' twitched the ends of his lips a bit. He was digging the spunk.

"Moving the shackles from your arms to your legs was a big mistake," Alex said, as he turned away from her, trying to catch the tail of the sleep that was slipping away. "Don't piss me off early in the morning, little girl. You don't want me grumpy." Sleep was evading him for a few days. Between The Butcher's nocturnal visits and the planning for the game, he hardly caught any sleep.

"I'm not as daft as you think I am, you know?" Shruti was obviously not done talking. "I've read the news. I know what you are."

"Then you should be scared."

"Well, I should be. But you have some other plans for me, otherwise I would have been dead already." There was a certainty to the voice. A kind of acceptance.

Alex shuffled back to face Shruti. She was leaning against the post, sitting with her back to Alex. "You are catching on. Faster than your dad, I must say."

She caught hold of the pole and rose to her feet. "What do you want with my dad?" Her hand closed into a fist and pointed towards her mouth with her thumb. But the strain in her voice betrayed the nonchalant gesture.

"There is a lot you don't know about your dad." Alex twisted to grab the bottle, which was standing near the head of his sleeping bag and tossed it to her. "But you will soon enough."

Soon enough, Alex repeated in his mind. The game was just getting interesting, and he was loving it. Manas decided to grow a spine and put up a challenge. When has the last boss in a video game ever been easy? The games that had been easy were never memorable. *Killer Croc from Arkham's Asylum, I'm looking at you.*

"I know all I want to know about my dad..." Shruti's voice trailed off, without conviction. Alex turned back away from her, to try and go back to sleep, drowning out Shruti's resonant voice to a background noise. You can't wake up someone pretending to sleep.

The sun was still in its infancy, casting a pale blue light everywhere. The pandemonium of the dogs, the incessant chatter from Shruti, and the sun lighting up the place shooed away whatever sleep he had hung on to.

Alex unzipped his sleeping bag, pulled it off, and climbed to his feet. "I'm going out to get breakfast." He eased into a full body stretch, popping his joints, and breathing new life for the new day. "You got any preference?" said Alex, stealing a sideways glance at Shruti.

"Porotta and Beef Fry," she said, digging out a piece of rock lodged behind her back. "And a sleeping bag." She threw the rock away as it clanged on to the unused machinery gathering dust at the corner.

Alex grabbed a fresh bottle of water and twisted open the lid. "This is not a staycation at the Ritz." He threw some water on his face to chase away the dying remains of sleep and strolled out of the building. The sharp clang of the metal door creased his forehead. *Be more careful*, he scolded himself. The rowdy gang of dogs trained their attention on him as he walked past them towards the road. He stared at one of them, who looked like the pack leader, and mouthed, 'Fuck you.'

A few minutes of picking his way through the garbage and bushes, he stepped on to the tarmac of the road. The morning wasn't particularly cold, but the occasional wind pierced through to tickle him with an icy finger. Trivandrum was still opening its eyes, which worked out perfect for him. With Nasir involved, he was pretty sure there was a massive manhunt out for him, and he needed every cover he can get to stay off the radar. He had thought of getting a blanket or a sleeping bag for Shruti. Not anymore. The clothes he chose were also carefully picked. No bright colours. Just the two or three shades of brown, beige, and grey. He usually paired them with one of two jeans which were not too old, and not too new.

Alex reached the shanty food stall at the corner of the street. It was a one-man operation, open from the early hours of the morning to late night. There was everything from cigarettes and tea to omelettes and dosas.

The quintessential street food joint for the less fortunate. As usual, the morning crowd of construction workers jostled and jested while grabbing an early breakfast. There were more out-of-town-ers, mostly from the northern part of India, than natives in that line of work. So, Alex made doubly sure not to speak any Hindi.

"*Chetta*," Alex called the shopkeeper. One of the very few Malayalam phrases he picked up to get by. He held up four fingers on his hand and said," Four Dosas."

The shopkeeper sent a slight nod in his direction acknowledging the order, as he juggled tea from one glass to another as if he controlled the tea in the air with his superpowers. As soon as he was done with the tea, he deftly picked up a banana leaf from the stash under his table, folded them into a cone, and tossed four dosas into it. He pulled at the string hanging from the roof and circled the folded cone with Bruce Lee speed. Chutney and Sambar were already packed in small polythene bags and kept aside. He picked a few bags and tossed it in a carry bag with the folded cone with dosas in it. The whole affair was over in less than a minute, including the payment. As Alex headed back towards his hideout, he marvelled at the efficiency of the shopkeeper.

Alex glanced at his watch. It was half-past six. Time to wake up Manas. He grabbed a new sim card from his pocket, plugged it into his phone, and dialled Manas.

"Hello," a groggy Manas croaked into the receiver.

"Rise and shine, Manas," Alex sang into the phone.

Manas mumbled something off the microphone which sounded like 'get up'.

"Stop babbling, Manas, and wake up."

"No, no... I'm up, I'm up." Manas's voice was much cleared this time around.

"Today's the big day. It's the 'Turn'. How about I deal the cards?" Alex chuckled.

Manas grunted in response.

"It's not like you have any choice anyway, not unless you want to fold and let go of the pot."

Manas' voice sharpened. "I hope my daughter is safe."

Alex spied the rising spire of a church in the distance. It had been a long time since he prayed. He altered his path towards the church. "Would you calm down? An honest dealer keeps the pot safe. Like yesterday, she had some weird asthma attack. But I jumped into action and gave her the shot in her bag. Saved her life, didn't I?"

"Asthma attack?" There was more panic in Manas' voice than usual. "Listen, she is prone to such attacks and the only way to revive her is the shot you gave her."

"It sucks that there was only one shot in the bag. But anyway... let me deal the cards right now. What I want you to do today is arson."

"Let me give you a refill for the shot."

"Are we still on that? Let it go and focus. I'm telling you how to save your daughter here."

"What if there is another asthma attack?"

"Ah! For God's sake, just let it go. Tell you what. Hear me out for now, and then we will talk about the asthma. OK?"

Alex took the silence to be yes and continued, "So, ... Arson. I want you to set a guy's house to fire."

"What the hell?" asked Manas. He took a beat and asked, "Why?"

"The why is not important. Just do what I say, OK? God! Manas, you are irritating. "Alex scanned up and down the street and crossed to the other side. "See, it's pretty simple. I pick the guy, give you the address, and you set ablaze the place."

"I don't know-", There was a pause and a scuffle which sounded like the phone changed hands. The voice that came after was sharper, a lot more menace in it, but was still Manas. "Who?"

"The name is Rajashekharan. If I give you a little background, it may motivate you. It's right up your alley, you know, profile-wise." Alex ducked into the shadows of a closed shop when he spotted a uniform down the road. "He is a local money lender, who also owns a ration disbursement centre. A typical 'bad-guy'—an army of henchmen to do his bidding, misappropriation of the ration to the local shop keepers, arm twisting the debtors into giving him their property, to name a few. He has a posh, two-storey building in Pettah—am I pronouncing that right?—where he lives with his family."

"I can't just walk up to a house full of henchmen and set it ablaze, can I? I need a day to scout the area and come up with a plan."

"Hmmm." Alex stepped back on to the road when the uniform passed him and resumed his journey to the church. "Alright. Take a day, but just one. I'll Whatsapp you the location."

"OK. Now can we talk about my daughter's asthma?"

Alex glanced up at the cross on top of the tower of the church. It loomed in front of him like a mammoth. "I'm not a doctor, you know."

"Let me give you a refill. Without it, she will die."

He cracked open the front door and peeked inside. The church was empty, and it was dark. Perfect. "That sounds a lot like your problem, Manas." Alex found a pew in a dark corner and knelt to pray.

"OK. Let me put it in a way you understand. A dealer who messes with the pot will be hunted down. Especially when you are dealing with high rollers who have the ability to make you disappear with a snap of their wrists."

"Whoa... chill out man. I was just playing with you. Of course, I want Shruti to be alive. I'll text you a location and time. Be there and gimme the shots. Jeez."

Alex put away his mobile phone and turned it silent. It was so much fun to poke the bear.

He knelt on the pew and closed his eyes in prayer. He felt himself melt away and become one with God; let yourself be a pawn in His grand scheme of things. This was what he was destined to do. It gave him purpose; it gave him direction.

A deep hollow voice broke the serene quiet of the church. "You know you're walking into a trap, right?"

Alex's eyes flew open, like the starting gates at a horse race. Early morning sunlight filtered through the stained glass of the windows, bathing the church in rich reds, blues, and greens. The Butcher hunched over on the adjacent pew, painted in a riot of colour, as opposed to the grim black. The low-riding hat was the only exception, which remained in the dark. He looked like the lead in a Pride rally.

Alex bit back a laugh. He was already on thin ice with The Butcher. "Of course," he answered, putting on a serious face. "But I can handle Manas. How difficult can it be to outthink an old 'has been'?"

"If you say so." The Butcher rose to his feet and glided towards the altar, merging into the darkness.

Nasir

Saturday, May 3, 2014

She signed up for a husband but ended up living with the ghost of a man.

Nasir leaned back in his chair; his two hands arched behind his head. It was one of those days when the weather mirrored the general mood in the room. The sombre silence in the conference room expanded and resonated with the gloom of the cloudy day. Avinash and Salim huddled in a corner, whispering to each other.

Nasir wondered if those two ever had any thoughts that they didn't share. It was a kind of camaraderie that Nasir never had with anyone, not even with his ex-wife. Ah! The ex-wife - a marriage of convenience to get his parents off his back. And he broke it off to get his wife off his back, convenience again. His only regret was that he ruined her life. She signed up for a husband but ended up living with the ghost of a man.

Sonam leaned into the laptop screen, running the risk of smashing her cute button nose in the display. Her face was scrunched up in concentration, a small wrinkle between her brows, and her slightly parted, red lips silently spelled out whatever she was reading. He caught himself wondering how she would look in a dress. But he shut it down as soon as he realised and egged his eyes to move on. It obeyed and came to rest on the empty chair beside Sonam. "That chair had been empty for days."

Sonam looked up from the laptop, closing it with one hand. "It's been four days. I'm starting to get a little worried."

Avinash rose from the huddle at the corner and strolled closer. "Don't worry, kid. To borrow a phrase from the Americans, 'This is not his first rodeo'. There have been times when we didn't see him for a month at a stretch."

Nasir nodded his head and rose to his feet. "Avinash is right. Though he may not look like it, Akshay can take care of himself. Let's get started." He marched across the room to the whiteboard, picked up a marker and uncapped it. "It's been five days guys and we are still not any closer than we were the moment we landed in the city." Nasir wrote 'Shruti' and 'Manas' on two sides of the whiteboard and underlined them. "How are we on the soil analysis, Sonam?"

Pink rushed to her porcelain cheeks as she shook her head. "I've been calling them up every day, sometimes twice a day."

Nasir nodded. "I've had a word with the concerned authorities as well. Apparently, they are swamped, but they promised they would fast track this. Keep following up." Nasir turned to Avinash and Salim. "Anything else?"

Salim cleared his throat. "Avinash and me have been coordinating with the local police who is doing door-to-door visits with Alex and Shruti's photos. We personally scoured the area Manas pointed out, but no luck."

It was a dart in the dark considering the odds of them stumbling on Alex and Shruti. He peered at the empty space below 'Shruti' on the whiteboard with a heavy heart. "Let's move on to Manas. Sonam, would you like to present the background check on Manas?"

Sonam pushed back from the table, rose to her feet, and made her way to the whiteboard. "Manas was born on 28th March 1970 at Bishop Benziger Hospital in Kollam. That's the adjacent district. The columns for mother and father in the birth certificate was left blank. I traced him to a Loyola School in Trivandrum with his school enrolment record. Studying that record, I got to know that he was raised in an orphanage in Trivandrum - Sri Chitra Home."

Avinash hooked his eyebrows. "He sure doesn't look like he was born and brought up in Kerala. He still has a faint accent when he speaks Malayalam. Definitely not a native speaker."

Sonam shrugged with a grin plastered on her face. "Hey, I'm just telling you what the documents say. He was enrolled in Loyola School in 1975. I also got his High School Certificate which says he graduated 10th grade board exams with flying colours in 1985. He also got a valid Ration Card, Passport, and a Voter ID and all of them look legit."

Nasir crinkled his brow. "Financials?"

Sonam nodded. "There I found something interesting. He has two accounts, one with SBI, Palayam branch, and the other with HDFC, Kowdiar branch. The SBI account was started in 1999 and the HDFC one in 2000. Absolutely no financial activity before that. I have sent queries to all the major banks, just to be sure. Should have the confirmation in a couple of days."

"Strange indeed," said Nasir. "When did he get the Ration Card, Passport, and Voter ID?"

Sonam bent over the desk and stretched to grab the file from where she was sitting. Nasir averted his gaze and focused on the whiteboard. She straightened with the file in her hand, turned back towards Nasir, and shuffled through the documents in it. "Ration Card was registered in 1999, Passport issued in 2000 and Voter ID in 2001."

Nasir wrote the list of documents they got in chronological order on the whiteboard.

Birth Certificate - 1970
Orphanage Enrolment - 1970
School Enrolment - 1975
High School Certificate - 1985
Ration Card - 1999
Passport - 2000
Voter ID - 2001

"Do you guys find anything wrong with this?"

Sonam leaned her body to the side, one hand on her hips and the other supporting her chin. "The order of the documents?"

"What do you mean?"

"Well... people get into the Ration Scheme before they finish their high school."

Nasir nodded. "Agreed. But it could also be because he was raised in an orphanage and didn't need ration." Nasir wrote on the board the age when Manas got each of those certificates.

Birth Certificate - 1970
Orphanage Enrolment - 1970
School Enrolment - 1975 - 5 years
High School Certificate - 1985 - 15 years
Ration Card - 1999 - 29 years
Passport - 2000 - 30 years
Voter ID - 2001 - 31 years

"This is what bothers me. Passport at thirty is OK. You really do not *need* a passport unless you are planning to travel abroad. But Ration Card at twenty-nine? It's not like he was born with a silver spoon, is he? And Voter ID at thirty-one? It's like he lived for twenty-eight years with nothing but a birth certificate and then decided he wanted to be part of the democracy."

Sonam's hands flew over her mobile phone. "There was an assembly election in Kerala in 2001."

"Hmmm.... But there were still two assembly elections, in 1996 and 1990, for which he was eligible to vote."

"It does look fishy," said Avinash. "But how does it matter if he took the passport or ration card late? He still got valid documents."

Nasir huffed out a puff of air through his nose. "You know how easy it is to fake these documents in India? There are a million different formats for Birth Certificates across India, and it is close to impossible to spot a fake among them. Grease a few hands, and a brand-new Birth certificate is yours. Grease a few more and you have your High School Certificate. And if you have both documents, getting into the Ration system is pretty straight forward."

Avinash was hell bent on playing the devil's advocate. "What about the passport?"

Nasir chuckled. "I can get you Obama's passport in a week. And we are talking about the 1990s. There were 'agents' in front of any passport office who would give you a passport for fifteen hundred bucks."

Avinash shook his head, slowly, from side to side. "You know how I feel about Manas, but this still feels weak. And if this gets out to the media, that we are looking into the father when we are nowhere close to finding the daughter, they are going to eat us alive."

"You are absolutely right," said Nasir. "This stays in this room. Avinash, you take Salim and try and dig a little at his school. Be discreet. Sonam, you should try the orphanage and see if you can get something there. And it goes without saying that all this is in parallel to..."

The door to the conference room creaked open and Akshay hobbled in and flopped onto the empty chair like nothing happened. His gaunt cheeks seemed more hollow than usual. The dark patches under his eyes and the scant stubble on his cheeks betrayed his exhaustion. A faint but pungent smell wafted in with him and settled down all around them.

Avinash was the first to respond. "Brother, you look like shit."

Akshay twisted his face into a wide grin. "Thanks," he said.

"You think this is funny, dumb ass?" Sonam's nose flared up and blood rushed to her cute little face.

The smile on Akshay's face vanished in a second and was replaced with surprise. He glanced at Avinash and said, "A little help?"

"You are on your own there, buddy." Avinash chuckled turned away, washing his metaphorical hands.

"Where were you? People were worried sick over here, you know?"

Nasir placed his hands on both her shoulders to calm her down. "So, was it worth it, Akshay?"

The corners of his mouth twitched with great effort as he nodded. "I'm sorry I walked out like that. At that moment, I was pissed off at all of you guys for doing nothing. But pretty soon, I realised that I am angry at myself more than anything; at my inaction." He shook his head, shaking off any lingering disappointment. "How did you guys deal with losing so many lives the past few days? Honestly, I think it got to me."

"I think it got everyone here," said Nasir. The rest of the room nodded in silent agreement.

Akshay reached over, grabbed the jug of water from the table, and chugged down gulps of water. "I... after the way I stormed out, I didn't want to come back without something concrete. So, I gave a call to the counter-intelligence wing of the Kerala Police. I knew you guys had spread the net over the city to catch Alex. But trolling the bottom of the sea gets you more fish. That's exactly what I told them. Altaf, a young officer in the counter-intelligence, was particularly helpful and agreed to meet me in person."

Akshay poured out a glass of water from the jug he was still holding on. "Altaf agreed to let me use his network. He had developed to track a ring of human traffickers. Although he lets me use it, he was sceptical on how helpful it would be." He took a sip of water and closed his eyes savouring the cool liquid flowing down his throat. "So, he gives me another name - Danny."

The air in the room was so still that the only sound came from Sonam's laptop, idling away.

"Danny is an information pimp. Altaf told me he was a pure businessman, with no allegiance but to himself. But he did have an extensive network of informants spanning the city. Altaf said it had better reach than any intelligence network in the city. It sounded perfect, but there was only one problem - he was a ghost."

"A ghost who, obviously, kept his distance from the authorities," Nasir said.

"Exactly," Akshay said, nodding his head. "Ghost or not, we had to track him down. So, me and Altaf scoured the city to pull out Danny from one of the cracks in the city. When it was light, we hit the major colonies and slums in the city and when night fell, we prowled the major crime hubs in the city. We met two kinds of people – the ones who didn't know Danny and the ones who were too scared to tell us. After a couple of sleepless nights, I almost bashed a guy's face in when he was holding back information."

"Thank God you didn't," said Salim. "These guys see us, law enforcement, as an outsider and they close up faster than a clam shell if they get a whiff of hostility."

Akshay tipped his head a slight nod. "Exactly what Altaf reminded me. When you have had only a couple of hours of sleep in two days, your brain doesn't work so clearly. We were almost at the verge of giving up and coming back when we heard chatter that Danny was at a bar in Palayam - that's a place in the centre of the city. We rushed over to the bar and found him there, having a drink with a bunch of his friends.

"The man has a very open and friendly face. If you saw him on the streets, you would smile at him and move on. But if you look closely, his eyes betrayed him. A wolf in sheepskin if I have ever seen one. The moment he saw Altaf, he waved a hand at his friends, who went silent. He conjured up a sweet smile on his face and waved us over. I watched that smile vanish as Altaf told him what we wanted. The moment he smelled an opportunity, he shed his facade and became the true businessman he was. 'What do I get?', he asked.

"Altaf just fixed him in a cold stare and said, 'You get to stay out of jail.' And then he explained to Danny that he had evidence that he was using his network to peddle weed. The reaction was priceless. The wolf stripped off the sheep skin, came out and realised the shepherd had an AK-47 trained on him."

Nasir smiled at the metaphor. "I'm liking this Altaf character."

"Maybe we should see if he wants to join our team," Avinash said, laughing boisterously.

"Maybe we should," said Nasir. "But anyway, go on, Akshay. Continue."

"What transpired after went like clockwork," said Akshay. "He objected at first, tried to wriggle out of it, but when he understood there was no way out, he agreed, but in return for a get-out-of-jail-free card. I handed him Alex's and Shruti's photos and punched my number into his mobile to ring me up the moment he finds them. I also told him that if I don't get results in a couple of days, the deal was off."

Sonam was visibly calmer now. "But you could have just told us what you were doing."

"Because he knew I would tell him to slow down," Nasir said, as he met Akshay's eyes and nodded.

Just then, Akshay's phone rang, and he dug it out from his jeans pocket. "It's Danny".

Manas

Saturday, May 3, 2014

Nothing is stupid until you grow out of it.

Manas white-knuckled the steering wheel as he merged into the morning traffic. His eyes kept flicking towards the rear-view mirror. The moment he read the text from Alex, he knew it was going to be a long day. *'Aiyappa's Jewellery Shop in Chalai Market. 11:00. Drop it at the baggage counter,'* read the text.

Manas glanced sideways at Prateek who sat staring out of the car in sullen silence. He raised quite a ruckus to use the drop as an opportunity to follow Alex and put an end to this. *If it would have been that easy.* After the warning last time they tried something, Manas' hands shivered every time he thought of straying way from the prescribed line of action. He had dug in and stood his ground, firmly putting an end to the discussion. A slow smile garnered at the end of his lips, savouring his small victory.

He flicked his eyes to the rear-view mirror and there the car was again - the faded white Maruti Alto. Manas spotted the car making a hurried turn to keep up with them a few turns ago, and the car was still with him. It was no surprise that he had a police tail. He just wasn't sure if it was for his protection. Either ways after the last day's fiasco, they must have changed the tail. It was a different car and driver. But the new guy was good. He always stayed two cars behind and whenever possible to his left. It was difficult to spot him, except by chance and the fact that he was actively searching for a tail.

The first item on Manas' agenda was to lose him. But he didn't have a lot of time. It was a public holiday, the Beemapally Uroos. And that meant a huge procession around the city which had an even bigger closing prayer at the Beemapally Mosque. Manas glanced at his wrist for the time. The city would come to a standstill by half-past one and it was ten already.

"Are we gonna drive around all day or are we gonna lose him?" Prateek's voice was lined with his irritation.

Manas took a sharp left turn into a less busy side road. As close to a choke point as he can think of. The brief flash of the white alto, making the turn, in the rear-view mirror was all the confirmation he needed. He down shifted his car to the third and revved up and engine, blasting his car up the empty side road. At the end of the road, he veered sharply to the right and another right immediately after, which he knew would lead back to the main road. The empty rear-view mirror told him his tail didn't expect his sudden acceleration. Without wasting any time, he took a left and disappeared into the residential criss-cross streets, eventually merging back onto the main road, and on his way towards Chalai.

"That was easy," said Prateek, breaking the silence for the first time since they got int the car.

Manas smiled and nodded his head. "Only because he wasn't expecting us to shake him off."

Prateek studied the traffic flowing around him for a second before turning back towards Manas. "Are we done talking about what we are gonna do today?"

Manas jammed the breaks at the red light and the car rolled to a stop, right in front of the Secretariat - the symbolic seat of power of the Kerala Government. Roman architecture at its best. It was as if they unrolled the Colosseum into a two-hundred-meter strip and smack in the middle of it erected a Roman Temple with its tall single pillars holding up the majestic head.

Inside the compound walls, the Government with all its administrative offices stood tall and all along the foot paths, people assembled to protest and bring it to its knees. The quintessential dichotomy of conflict which powers any democracy. A hunger strike seemed to be the most active protest of the day. A few people leaned against a makeshift bed, deflated, while the rest of their comrades shouted slogans. The red flag flapping about in the wind told him it's one of the 'left' parties.

"The people of Kerala keep the Government on a short leash, never letting it relax into incumbency. Every five years, they switch the plates to the opposing coalition. The fellows here are very much aware of their rights and they don't let you get away with much."

"You've been living here for what? Fifteen years?"

Manas studied the rhythmic up and down motion of the closed fists of the protesters. "Fifteen years making this place mine. It embraced me in its welcoming arms, making me one of hers. But sometimes I do miss Delhi. Not the place, but the people."

A dark cloud passed over Prateek's face. He peered outside the car in silence. "I've never said this to you-," he said."- but I'm sorry about what I did. Hatred can blind you to reason. And I had a lot of that back then....

you know with the whole saffron nationalistic pride. Kind of stupid if you think about it now."

"Nothing is stupid until you grow out of it."

Prateek nodded in affirmative. "The change in environment helped, too. A lot fewer stooges spewing venom over here."

"Religion and Caste doesn't have the same pull here as it has in the rest of India. People are religious, but not fanatical. Caste is still there, but it's a subtle vein which runs under the flesh and not a brand on your forehead." Manas glanced at the light which turned green and shifted the car into gear wondering whether the reform Prateek was talking about was real or just another one of his manipulations.

Either ways, it felt good to open up to Prateek. He felt like a piece of the jigsaw puzzle had been finally put into place.

"You have a good life here, Manas." Prateek fiddled with the dashboard controls to turn up the air conditioner. The sun was shining extra bright, as if to compensate for the rainy and cloudy days of past. "You say you admire the people of Kerala for their tenacity to stand up for what is right. And here you are letting Alex walk all over you and destroying the very thing that makes your life tick."

"It's not always black and white, Prateek. Maybe you'll understand if you were a father."

"I love Shruti. Right from the time she was a little bundle in your arms. Maybe I'm not a father, but I'm very well an uncle. Every time I think about her and Alex, I lose my shit. And it irks me that we are not doing anything to save her."

"You were there when Alex warned us about what he would do if we try anything else, right? With a guillotine above Shruti's head, how can you think of taking any risk."

"Not any risk, but a calculated risk. Think about it Manas. Right now, the only thing that is keeping Alex from killing Shruti is the 'game'. What happens when you finish all three tasks? Do you honestly think he will just let her go?"

Manas concentrated on a sharp manoeuvre to get around the car in front of him. He didn't want to answer it because he knew he wouldn't like it.

"Alex overplayed his hand the moment he showed us how much he was willing to let go to keep the game running. Our best chance is to find Alex while he thinks he has the leverage, but in fact he doesn't."

Manas chewed the insides of his mouth, tasting the metallic blood seeping from a small break in the skin. The plan Prateek proposed was risky, too risky and unstructured for his taste.

"It'll work," said Prateek. "But only with the old Manas by my side."

"I need to think about it." Manas pulled up to the curb and parallel parked his car. Without exchanging a word, they got out of the car with the bag in hand and stepped in to the Chalai Market.

In the early mid-day, the market reminded him of an angry teenager; loud, brimming with energy, and crass. A pot-pourri of people from all slices of life crisscrossed the narrow main street. Motorcycles, cars, and trucks honked at full volume as they zipped through the gaps in the flow of people. The narrow road ahead of them branched out into a myriad of networked lanes, shops on both sides of it. Fruits, vegetables, household items, jewellery, handicrafts, photo frames, perfumery, spices, the list just goes on. Manas had visited the market once or twice in his life, but always stuck to the main street. The side streets were reserved for people who knew what they were doing.

They ventured deeper and deeper into the labyrinth of shops, towards their destination - Aiyappas Jewellery. The salty odour of sweat mingled with the titillating aroma of spices and the sweet smell of the flowers wafted up his nose. The aroma of spices, it took him back to a Sunday evening, not so long ago.

Anuradha was in the kitchen, preparing one of her Kerala style dishes, rich in spices and coconut. The aroma that filled the house was simply mouth-watering. Shruti hung out in the kitchen watching Anuradha cook. Manas eyed her with utmost suspicion. She never hung out in the kitchen, except when she wants something, and she knew Anuradha was the easiest prey. Manas chuckled as he remembered that the charade was for a brand-new mobile. It was a good day. The chuckle shrunk back to where it came from.

But Alex took it all away. Starting with his first love, Amrita, he bulldozed his way to the foundations of his life. His daughter held hostage and his wife hiding out at her parents' place, worried and alone. On top of all that Alex made Manas bring back Prateek from the dead. Yes, there were parts of Prateek he missed. But he was more than that and you can't pick and choose what you get. *Once you let the monster out, there is no going back.*

But was there any other way? Getting his little girl safely home was his one and only priority. He thought he could do it alone, but the last few days took that belief and slapped him across his face. As difficult it was to admit, he needed Prateek; he needed his cold, no-holds-barred attitude towards violence. The only diamond in the muck was the hope that he could send Prateek back when this was over. But that hope was becoming smaller every passing second.

"Isn't this the place?" Prateek poked on Manas' shoulder, reviving him from his reverie.

Manas scanned the area and spotted the board saying, 'Aiyappas Jewellery'. A small shop snuggled in between a shop bursting with kitchen utensils and another perfumery which pushed out a cocktail of fragrances.

Shoppers attacked both sides of the road like waves of the sea, grabbing little pieces of the sand as they retreat. Manas pulled on the shoulder straps of the backpack as he elbowed his way to the opposite side of the street from the shop.

"You sure it'll work?" he asked Prateek.

A genuine smile erupted from Prateek's surprised face. He nodded vigorously. "We hide around here, wait for Alex, follow him to the hideout. Wait for dark, sneak in, and get Shruti out."

Manas bit his lip as he scanned the crowd for Alex. "Sounds too simple."

"Some of the best plans are, Manas. But we will need to improvise and there I need the old Manas." Prateek studied the surrounding buildings, evaluating each, probably, for a hiding place. "And one more thing. This is the real deal. So, don't hold me back when I'm doing what needs to be done."

Manas took a deep breath and shut out the hustle and bustle of the market. He was still not a hundred percent convinced, but he had to do something. If this goes right, all of this was over by nightfall. And he could send Prateek back to the depths of his mind and return to his life. The longer he waited, the harder it would be. But if things go wrong.... No. He couldn't afford to think about that now.

A couple more deep breaths as he counted down from five and he opened his eyes. "OK."

Sonam

Saturday, May 3, 2014

A bullet in the head is the fastest form of justice.

Sonam bounced up and down in the back of the van as it dashed through the city, jumping over potholes. Instead of the usual riot of butterflies in her stomach, she was giddy with joy. This was the first real lead they had ever since they set their foot in Trivandrum. Danny had come through with what he was tasked to do. One of his informants spotted Alex in the Chalai Market. They hardly finished the call before rushing into the van and dashing across the city to Chalai Market.

Salim, who was the first one to reach the van and thereby the driver, white-knuckled the steering wheel, swerving through the traffic. Nasir ran his hands over his balding scalp, again and again, glancing at his watch every two seconds. A tense silence filled the van as everyone was lost in their own thoughts.

A few more minutes of silence, and Salim pulled the van over to the curb. As soon as the van jerked to a stop, Nasir wiped his forehead one last time and turned back to address the team. The fire in his eyes were unmistakable.

"Guys, this is not going to be easy. I checked with the local police; Chalai market is a very large market with a myriad of crisscrossing streets filled with shops and people. But we have to find our man, no matter what." He turned to Akshay, with concern in his eyes. "Akshay, you good?"

Akshay nodded, his eyes sharp. Where he got the energy to carry on was beyond her.

"Here is the plan. We must cover a lot of area, and fast. And for that, we need to split up." He ran his gaze over Sonam for a second and said, "I don't want Sonam out there-"

"But sir I was top of the class in hand-to-hand comb-"

Nasir stopped her mid-sentence with a raised hand. "I have no doubt you can handle yourselves. But no. I need people with experience on the streets. You will be coordinating the operation from the van, the control centre."

Nasir turned to Avinash, effectively closing the conversation. "Avinash, Salim... I need to break you up. Avinash, you close in from the east end, Salim from the west end and Akshay will start from the south end. I will stay with Sonam and the van at the north side as you guys converge on us. Be methodical, cover every street and by lane, but be quick about it."

Avinash unlocked the door and stepped outside.

"If anyone spots Alex, call for backup," said Nasir. "Do not, I repeat, do not move in on your own. Just stay on him, out of sight till backup arrives. I know I don't have to tell you all this, but just to be sure we are on the same page. Once the back-up is in position, on my signal, converge on him from all sides."

"Roger that," said Salim, already in the tactical mode. "Radio check?"

A plethora of '*check*'s echoed in and around van and everybody gave a thumbs up.

"Just one more thing," Nasir added. "Shoot to kill. If you decide the situation is serious enough to pull out your gun, head and body shots only. In the heat of the moment, do not stop to decide whether to shoot him in his leg or not. I'd rather see a scumbag dead that one of you guys hurt." He let a beat pass by before continuing, "In fact, if at any point you feel he is going to get away, just shoot the damn bastard. We'll figure out the rest later."

Sonam scanned the faces of her team. She spotted determination, excitement, a touch of fear, but no surprise. Not the first time they've heard this speech. But how can everyone be fine with it? Taking a life was not their jurisdiction. That's what the judicial system is for, isn't it?

"We are just… going to kill him?"

Nasir let out a deep breath, as if he were forced to answer a stupid question from a kid. "A bullet in the head is the fastest form of justice. Despite that, if it's possible, arrest him. But just not at the risk of you guys getting hurt."

Sonam, miffed at the patronising tone, stooped down to tie her shoelaces.

"OK, everyone... Fan out," said Nasir.

The guys exited the van one by one, leaving a few minutes between them and rushed towards their positions. Avinash was the first one out, his bulky form seemed bulkier with the bulletproof vest under his plain clothes.

"Control, do you read me? Avinash's voice was clear, but tinny.

"Loud and clear," said Sonam.

Akshay, the last person to peel off, paused with one leg out of the door of the van and glanced back at Nasir, suppressing a smile. What was that about? She made a mental note to ask Nasir later.

"On my way to the east end, doing a cursory check along the way," crackled the tinny voice through the radio. "I will keep you posted. In the meantime, have I told you guys about how Salim caught half a kilo of cocaine?"

"Only like a million times," said Akshay. "You have got to get some new stories, if you are gonna keep doing this."

"Ah! Newbie, have you heard it?"

Salim groaned over the radio. "Shut it, Avinash."

Sonam was intrigued. Knowing Avinash, it was bound to be something embarrassing. She glanced at Nasir to read the room. The last thing she wanted to do was step on his toes and mess up the operation.

Nasir read her mind and chuckled. "Go Ahead, and it's OK. Avinash keeps blabbering over the radio every chance he gets. But that doesn't affect his attention on the subject, if that is what you are worried about."

Sonam stabbed at the radio button to open the line. "No, I've not. Tell me."

"Excellent choice, kiddo. So, this happened back in the days when Salim was a nobody in the Delhi police. And as any nobody in the police force, he is stuck with night duty. So, one night, as he was about to cosy up and sleep in his chair at the police station, the telephone rings on his table. He raised his head, annoyed at the ringing disturbance, and picked it up. The good Samaritan, who called, explained to him how someone was trying to break into a house across the street. And apparently, the guy was not even discreet about it.

"Salim was pissed off. It's one thing to rob a place, but being unapologetic about it? 'Not while I'm on duty', he thought, as he dragged himself into the jeep and rolled up to the location, flashing siren lights and everything. When he reached the location, he saw the perp sitting in front of the house, leaning against the door. In hindsight, the guy was too well-dressed to be a thief. But young Salim didn't have this hindsight at the time and strutted up to the guy, in full gusto. The stench of alcohol drifted into his nose -"

"Didn't you reach your position already?" broke in Salim.

Avinash chuckled. "Almost there. Don't worry, I'm pacing the story just right. So, where was I? Yeah. So, Salim walked up to the guy and asked him what the problem was. The guy was piss drunk and after many trials he managed to explain to the scary policeman that he lived in the house and was trying to get into it. Being the beacon of hope that he is, Salim offered to help the poor guy. So, he asked the guy if he had the keys to his house. The guy couldn't tell heads from tails, but somehow caught the word 'key' and said, 'you are brilliant, why didn't I think of that before?'. With that, he started rummaging his pocket for keys. Salim stood there beaming, his chest inflated with pride at helping a man and making the world just a little better.

"The guy keeps pulling out stuff from his pocket and handing it to Salim. First came some used tissues, then a wallet, a mobile phone, but no keys. He tried his blazer pocket. And out came a receipt, a key chain, but no keys, a square packet, taped over with brown packing tape, but still no keys. Salim stood there a second, with all the stuff that came out of the guy's pocket in his hands and stared at the idiot who handed over a packet of drugs to a police officer. And at that moment, he knew he was going to be promoted. The rest is history, isn't it, Salim?"

If someone's voice could be red from embarrassment, Salim's voice would have been. "Are you done now? Sonam, it was a bit more complicated than what Avinash just said."

Loud laughter filled the radio frequency. "It is exactly how Avinash said, Sonam," Akshay said.

Sonam glanced at Nasir for confirmation. The guys had pulled her legs for far too long for her to believe them completely.

Nasir chuckled and said, "It's true. Though Salim is an excellent police officer and got into the CBI on that accord, this is how he first got noticed."

"Sorry to break up the party, but I have reached my position," said Avinash.

"Me too," said Salim.

"In a minute," said Akshay.

"OK, then guys, let's start the sweep."

The Artist

Saturday, May 3, 2014

Life was better with a soundtrack. It always made it better, dig out the order in chaos.

Chalai market was chaos personified. People zipped in and out of shops like bees hunting for nectar. The cacophony of a million human voices laughing, bargaining, and fighting jarred against his mind which craved order. He pulled out his Skullcandy earphones and jammed it into his ears. The earphones hugged tightly to his ear canals, cutting out the ambient noise.

Alex pushed ahead, head down, focusing on plugging in the 3.5" jack into the socket on his phone. He dodged the approaching mass of shoppers as he tapped and swiped on the screen to get the song he wanted to listen - *Jaguar by What So Not*. The soothing female vocals drowned out the clamour and soon the heavy base infused drop blew his mind; like the thousand times it had did before.

Life was better with a soundtrack. It always made it better, dig out the order in chaos. The mundane pedesis of the crowd flitting in and out of shops transformed into a perfectly choreographed music video.

A figure, all clad in black, floated into his peripheral vision. "Don't even bother, Butcher. I know what I am doing."

The Butcher opened his mouth halfway and closed it again.

"Not gonna walk in the market and meet Manas. I got it covered." Alex chuckled to himself.

"Your funeral," the black figure said, as he faded out of Alex's vision.

The Butcher was his idol, and he adored him and all that. But that shit was getting irritating. He needed a little peace of mind and not somebody to eat his head. The heavy bass pounded on his eardrums, delivering a unique sense of calm. That was more like it. He did a quick scan to make sure there weren't any police around. Alex wanted to get out of the crowd as soon as possible because every moment he is out in the open is a moment he is testing the laws of probability. Alex stuck to the shadows along the sides and scanned the crowd for a jobless loser with questionable ethics.

His attention landed on a well-dressed guy, with a striking face. The large bulbous nose overpowered any other feature on his face. He was rooted to a spot in front of a kitchen shop, his hands folded in front of him and resting on his paunch. The man glanced at his watch and looked down the street and repeated this every two or three seconds. Not his guy. Obviously waiting for someone and not somebody who needs the cash.

Alex studied and discarded three other men when he came across the guy he was looking for. One look at him and he knew he had hit gold. He leaned against a wall next to a tea shop, sucking on a cigarette. The smoke swirled around him in an intimate affair, moving its arms all over him. A dirty grey, striped, shirt draped over him torso and a brown, tattered pants covered the rest.

Alex changed trajectory and headed towards the tea shop, training his eyes on his target. The guy tossed his cigarette to the ground, stamped on it, twisting his leg to put it out, and plodded over to the tea shop. He raised a hand to order a tea and a riot of colour collided with him. A pretty girl in a purple *salwar* and yellow *dupatta.* She briskly apologised, barely looking at the man, and walked away. The guy smirked and stared at her behind as it swayed its way across the street.

From his vantage point, Alex saw the whole thing and there was no way the girl bumped into him by accident. It amused him, piqued his curiosity. He glanced at his watch and then at the guy. There was enough time to take a detour and come around to the guy later. It was not like he was going to go anywhere. So, he decided to follow the girl's shapely behind swaying its way through the crowd. She turned a corner into a relatively empty lane and stopped, leaning against the wall. Alex shored up near a street seller, appearing to check out the T-shirts scattered on a very large, blue tarpaulin.

The girl checked up and down the street and retrieved a black wallet from her *dupatta,* took out the cash in it, and stuffed them into her bra. As she strutted back into the crowd, she tossed the wallet aside.

Alex took a conscious effort to keep his mouth closed as he realised what he just witnessed. A pickpocket? She must be the prettiest pickpocket he had ever seen. She was perfect for his purpose, he thought as he resumed tracking her through the crowd. Street smart, unethical, and needed money.

She meandered through the crowd and after a while slowed to a stop. Alex quickly scanned the direction of her gaze and spotted her next target - an unsuspecting shopper with a bulging back pocket, ripe for picking. Alex wanted to watch her work, more closely. He was fascinated by the girl.

The girl slid her hands into the side pocket of her salwar and retrieved something, palming it out of view. Once she was in position, she moved towards the man, stopping at the street shops, like a normal shopper. As she passed by the man, Alex spied a quick, fluid motion of her hands, grazing the man's back pocket and off came the wallet into her hands. *What just happened?* Alex did a double take, saw the slit in the man's back pocket, and smiled. This girl was good.

Alex decided it was time to move in and altered his direction to intercept her current one. When he reached close enough, he tapped her shoulder.

She whipped around and her beauty blew him away. The two dark pools of mischief stared at him with disdain. A gold nose ring gleamed in the mid-afternoon light on her nose. It scrunched up in a frown at the stranger who tapped her shoulder.

"Nice technique on the swipe," said Alex, mustering up the most wicked smile he could muster. "You could be a magician with such skilful hands, you know?"

"What? Mind your own business, OK?" The voice was as sweet as the girl.

Alex broke into a hearty laughter. "I am. You want to make some money?"

The girl narrowed her eyes and stared at him through the slits on her face. "You want to get the hell out of shall I shout and gather some people? They don't take kindly to men like you here."

Alex just replayed the sentence in his mind and smacked his head with an open palm. "No, no... I didn't mean that," he chuckled. "I meant I have a business proposal for you."

Her eyebrows went up at the sentence; an uneven, almost comical fishhook. "Business?"

"Yeah, you do something for me, and you get paid for it. Simple as that."

She peered at him, with eyes full of suspicion.

Alex chuckled and said, "Come, let's talk and I'll explain everything."

Manas

Saturday, May 3, 2014

Nobody can plan for the unknown. You just run with it.

Manas shifted his weight from one leg to another; a thousand pins and needles poked his feet. He had been crouching under the half-wall for a long time of the second-floor corridor overlooking the street. 'Aiyappa's Jewellery' was right across the street. His body didn't agree with what he was putting it through and was protesting vocally. *Aged and outdated*, he thought. Just like the marriage bureau he was crouching in front of. Cobwebs hugged the corners of the doors which was saturated with dust. The faded board, which was gathering rust, was wiped clean. One of the last men standing in the onslaught of the all-powerful internet brigade.

Prateek's eyes stuck to the reflection on the tinted windows of the closed office. The garbage bin in which they hid the bag brooded at them through the reflection. Prateek had not let the bin go out of sight even for a second since they started the stake out. There was a sense of determination in his eyes, a sense of purpose. Manas wasn't sure if it for Shruti's benefit or his own. *No*, those were thoughts he didn't have the luxury to have. He needed to trust Prateek. That is the only way he stands any chance at getting his daughter back.

The cotton T-shirt stuck to his back, pulling at his skin when he moved. Manas swallowed hard in an effort to calm his stomach and nerves. The logic in Prateek's arguments convinced his brain, but his heart wasn't that easily convinced.

"It's past eleven. Where is he?" Manas asked.

Prateek glanced at him sideways as he straightened up the wall he was leaning against. "Have patience. It's not like the bag is going anywhere." He dusted his hands off on his pants as he resumed his study of the stream of people passing by in the reflection on the window.

It was business as usual down in the streets. People from all walks of life collided, merged, and meshed as they formed into a large single-celled organism; slowly expanding and contracting. There was no religion, cast or gender down there, just humanity. Maybe John Lennon was inspired from such a congregation of humans to write about his utopia of a brotherhood of man with no religion, no countries and no possessions.

A flash of purple in the drab palette of a tired crowd caught Manas' attention. It moved through the crowd with ease, snaking in an out of spaces, heading straight for the jewellery store. As it got closer to the jewellery store, the pretty girl who brought the flash of colour came into focus. A pretty girl in a purple *salwar* and yellow *dupatta* moved closer to the jewellery.

Manas felt his gaze zero in on her. As he was trying to understand why, she stopped next to the bag, scanned the area, and picked it up from the garbage bin he had hidden it.

"She is stealing the bag!" he poked Prateek. He was about to jump up and scream at the thief, but Prateek's strong arm pulled him back under the half wall. Manas wanted to scream, but somehow, he couldn't. It was odd as Prateek wasn't covering his mouth.

Prateek grabbed the front of his shirt and fixed him in an even stare. "Manas, I need you to calm the fuck down and think." He loosened his grip on Manas' shirt and shook his head. "I feel we have reversed roles. Usually, I'm the one who jumps the gun, not you."

Manas took in a deep breath and counted to five. Prateek was right. He needed to get his act right. Manas replayed the approach of the girl in his mind. It was not the Brownian motion of a usual shopper, nor the faltering, uncertain one of a thief. It had purpose, it had direction. It wasn't chance that brought her.

Prateek pointed his head towards the street. "Alex might be around. We don't want to spook him, do we?"

"I doubt he is around. He is a celebrity in the law enforcement circles. A smart man like him would send somebody to pick the bag up."

"You don't say."

Manas brushed passed the sarcasm and said, "Alex will meet her to get the bag from her. And even if I am wrong, we still need the bag back. So, let's follow the girl with the bag."

"Well, then... What are we waiting for?" Prateek asked as he pushed off the ground and on to his feet.

Manas rose to his feet but froze at the top. "This complicates the plan, Prateek."

"To hell with the plan, Manas. Nobody can plan for the unknown. You just run with it." And with that, Prateek got to his feet and ran to the end of the corridor and down the steps on to the street. Manas tottered for a second, but then followed him down.

Prateek was waiting for him at the entrance to the street with a smile that said, 'I knew you would come around'. Manas hated that smile.

"You want to take point?" Prateek asked.

Manas nodded and set the course to intercept the girl. He meandered through the human obstacle course, all the while keeping the girl in his sight. Prateek hung back a few feet on the other side of the street. He knew what had to be done; they had done it countless times before - stay in the shadows, blend in, and rotate the vantage position.

The bright purple of the girl's salwar pierced through the dreary crowd of muted browns and blues. What ruse Alex must have used to get the pretty girl to do his bidding? Did she understand the risk she was in?

As he was wondering the possibilities, she turned sharply into an alley, bumped into a man, and continued her path, apologising profusely to the man. But Manas saw something that the man didn't. A flick of her wrist, a flash of black leather between the man's pocket and the girl's *dupatta* covered hand. *Pickpocket.*

"And a talented one at that," Prateek said.

Was it time to switch positions already? Manas glanced back behind his shoulders, but Prateek was not there. He was a good ten feet away but smiling at him; a twinkle in his eyes.

Panic blew its cold breath down his spine, tickling the hair follicles all the way from the lower back to the neck. *This is not good.* His identity was sacrosanct. He had always been able to keep it separate from Prateek's. But the lines were fading away the last time he banished Prateek from his life. Towards the end, Prateek was everywhere. There were no thoughts that were just Manas'. There were no corners of his mind where he could hide from Prateek. And at the very end, Prateek was strong enough to sneak around and do stuff without Manas' knowledge.

It was nothing short of a miracle that he could wrestle back control and send Prateek into exile. May be the rage at discovering Prateek almost killed Amrita helped. Manas wasn't sure he could repeat the performance. The Prateek that came back was somehow stronger, more mature. And he could feel the poison spread. It always started like this; with the lines blurring.

Manas squeezed his eyes shut, hoping to suffocate that thought. Not the time, nor the place. The girl turned into another alley and disappeared around the corner. He shoved his way through the crowd, making a beeline for the alley the girl turned into.

The moment he turned into the alley, he was hit across the face with a mouth-watering, but suffocating aroma. A plethora of scents waded up his nostrils, firing a multitude of signals to the brain. Some of them brought up images of the food items it belonged to and some other just titillated his salivary glands. He was in the food street of the Chalai market- a place where everything from Arabian *Shawarmas* to *Boti*, a spicy local cuisine of goat intestines, were up for sale. One in two buildings in the street were restaurants and the rest sold spices, vegetables, and meat. And in between the nooks and crannies of these shops, small tea shops and shacks rose up like mushrooms after a rain.

Manas spotted a bright purple flash disappearing into a narrow shop down the road. 'Malabar Spices' read the hand painted board in front of the shop. He scanned the crowd for Alex. Nothing. Training his eyes on the shop and its entrance, he blended into the crowd and floated to a Shawarma shop across the street. The smell of slow-cooked chicken made his stomach grumble.

Prateek nudged him from behind and pointed at the shop across the street. "Come, let's go in."

Manas shook his head subtly. "We stay here. Out of sight." He raised his hands and asked for a menu. A fair skinned boy with a tuft of hair jutting out from his chin ambled over and handed him a laminated menu card.

Manas studied the menu, keeping an eye on the shop across the street. His fingers moved on the laminated dance floor, tapping out a familiar rhythm as he mentally ranked the items on the menu.

Out of the corner of his eyes he caught purple and yellow streak across the entrance of the store. The girl had exited the store, thrusting her hands into her *salwar*, adjusting herself.

Prateek pushed off his back leg and started to follow her.

"She doesn't have the bag with her," said Manas as he held Prateek back with an outstretched arm.

"So, he is inside?" asked Prateek.

"Either inside, or on his way." Manas raised his hands to call the waiter over.

The boy came closer and stood with a pen and a piece of paper. "One Chicken Shawarma, plate and an Arabian Grape Juice," said Manas. The boy swivelled to relay the order, but before he could do that Manas held up a two hundred rupees note. The yellow piece of paper caught his attention.

"Want to make a quick buck?"

It sure got the boy's attention, but he looked at Manas with eyes full of suspicion.

"You see that shop over there?" asked Manas, pointing to 'Malabar Spices' across the street.

"The one after the hotel?"

"Yeah, that's the one. All you have to do is to keep an eye on the shop and tell me if a man comes out with a black bag with a pink Nike logo across its back. Easy, right?"

The boy stood with the pen and paper, contemplating the offer. He chewed the inside of his cheeks as he made mental calculations of risk and reward and when the reward won, a smile broke out on his face, and he nodded.

Manas shook the boy's hand and headed inside the shop, out of sight. "And one more thing," he called out to the boy. "Put some extra chicken on the Shawarma."

Nasir

Saturday, May 3, 2014

Fear is just an evolutionary necessity.

The air was thick in the closed van. Nasir wasn't sure if it was the humidity or the awkward silence. The high mid-day sun battled the heavy shades in the back of the van. Streaks of piercing light filtered through the battle into the van. The awkwardness was not just Nasir; it was mutual, and that made him happy. Sonam had switched on the nerd mode and hunched over her notes. A generic ballpoint pen jiggled in her neatly manicured fingers as she scribbled on the notepad. A thick pair of glasses hung over her laid back nose. In the fiery light of the sun, her dark auburn hair caught fire and danced in the slight breeze that filtered into the van through the cracks in the window.

He could stare at her for eternity, recall every small freckle and faint scars from her teenage pimples, but that wasn't enough to level the age difference between them. Nasir might have gone on, not more than, three dates ever since the divorce. And all of them because he didn't want to offend somebody who took it upon themselves to find him a mate. It was not that he didn't like women, or love their company, but he just didn't have time for them. But every now and then, a woman came along who skirted the traditional courtship and went straight to the sack. He found his pasture in such enlightened women.

But Sonam was different.

The moment she walked into the room for her interview, she had piqued his interest. The subdued air of confidence and the poise she displayed during the interview was remarkable. To storm a boy's club like the CBI and to do it with unparalleled grace was something to admire.

What started out as a casual appreciation of her talent and grace soon grew into an infatuation which reared its irritating face at the most inopportune of times; like the telemarketers peddling credit cards or personal loans. But what egged Nasir on was the nagging feeling that there was a degree of reciprocation for whatever he was feeling. There were a few times he caught her staring at him and there was always something in her eyes which he could not put his finger on. Why such a young and beautiful girl be interested in someone old enough to be her father was a question which stoked the fires of self-doubt.

Sonam scrunched her nose and pushed up her specs with a slender finger. And before he could avert his gaze, she glanced up at him, catching him in the act. In a futile attempt to salvage his dignity, he quickly diverted his gaze and thoughts to studying the teeming crowd outside. But out of the corner of the eyes, he thought he saw her smile. He resisted the temptation to confirm it and instead refocused his energy into scanning the human faces outside to catch the now familiar face of Alex.

The outline of a man with closely cropped hair and a square shaped head caught his attention. He was facing away from him, but straight broad shoulders, the rigid posture, and the way he held his head high was vaguely familiar. Nasir grabbed the door of the van and paused, contemplating whether to exit the van to get a better look. It was then the man turned to his side scanning the crowd for someone. The long, Greek nose stood out in the profile confirming his suspicion. What was Manas doing here?

Nasir twisted the door handle and with a sideways glance at Sonam said, "Stay in the Van and coordinate. I'll be right back." He stepped out into the busy street leaving a bewildered Sonam with her mouth half open. There wasn't time for an explanation. He scanned the crowd for Manas and spotted him enter the food street.

Before taking two steps in the direction, his earpiece crackled. "Rover calling basc, Rover calling base," said Akshay. "I have eyes on the target. I repeat, I have eyes on the target." His insistent voice was particularly tinny through the radio. "Doing a verification run. Stand by for confirmation."

Nasir stopped mid-stride and retraced his steps. He would figure out Manas later, but Alex was a clear and present danger. The electronics street. He brought back the map the team had memorised on the way to Chalai market. It was the street laying parallel to the food street. He rushed to the van, twisted open the door and jumped into it.

"Don't ever do that again," said Sonam, with an angry huff. "I don't even know what a verification run is, and you want me to coordinate it?"

Sonam was clearly distraught. She may have aged a couple of years in the short few minutes. Nasir chuckled at her wide eyes and held up a hand in apology. "Saw Manas out there and didn't have time to explain."

"Manas?" Sonam's mouth acquired a state of half open wonderment.

Nasir wrinkled his brow. "Strange, I know. We'll check up on that later. But now, Alex is the priority." He turned on the radio and said," Rover, this is base. Do you have confirmation?"

"Not yet. Approaching the subject."

Nasir turned to Sonam and explained, "When we spot a possible target, we do a confirmation run putting us in a face-to-face position with the target to confirm his identity. That is a verification run."

"What if the target makes you?"

"A skilled surveillance mission ensures a constant rotation of the tail so that the target doesn't get suspicious. But a lot of it depends on the person doing surveillance as well. Some people are gifted with a face that will blend them into any crowd. For e.g., Akshay."

Just then the radio crackled to life. "Base, this is rover. I have confirmation. Subject entered a building in the northern end of the electronics street. The building looks abandoned."

"Rover, commence recce. Note all exits and wait for backup. Team, you heard the man, Converge at the electronics street, northern exit. Proceed with caution."

"Mario to base. Already on the way," said Avinash.

"Luigi on the way, base," said Salim.

Nasir turned to Sonam and said, "Let's mobilise on foot. Put your earpieces and pick up the bags."

Nasir crouched in the middle of the huddle at the north exit of the electronics street. They were behind a building which blocked the view from the target building. They shrugged off the strange looks from passers-by.

"Avinash, Salim, you are up." Nasir tossed one of the duffel bags to them and passed the other to Akshay.

Salim zipped open the bag and pulled out black vests with bold white lettering across the chest -'POLICE'.

Maybe it was the years of constant threat, but the Israelis knew how to make a weapon. The black Kevlar bulged where armoured plates were inserted for extra protection. The vest was reserved for the elite of the elite special forces in the country. But Nasir had pulled on the right strings to procure it for his team. Salim and Avinash had been with him since the beginning, loyal to a fault, and he wanted to get them something that said thank you.

Avinash slotted his muscular arms through the armholes of the vest, slid it sideways into position and strapped on the Velcro side closure. Salim was already in the vest, tugging it to see if stayed in position. When it came to tactical ops, these goofballs knew how to handle themselves. They were strapping on their helmets by the time the rest of the team managed to slip into the vests.

Avinash whipped out the stock on his Heckler and Koch MP5 and pressed it against his chest, checking the rear sight of the gun. "How many exits?"

"Two on each of the two sides," Akshay said holstering his Glock 17 9mm semi-automatic pistol.

Salim angled the gun towards the ground, checked the safety position. "What about the back?" He ejected the magazine, pulled back the bolt and locked it to inspect the chamber.

"Covered all four sides on my first recon. No doors out back. The building behind is so close that there is hardly enough space for a man to walk through."

Avinash emptied the chamber of his Glock 17, slid out the magazine, and locked back the slide. "Locked and loaded," he said, with a stupid grin plastered across his face as he rammed the magazine back, released the slide, turned off the safety and holstered the weapon.

"Do you have cliches for breakfast?" asked Salim.

Nasir holstered his Glock and scanned the team. Sonam appeared smaller in the oversized vest, battling the weight of the armoured plates embedded within. She was not ready to be on a field op. And Akshay was still tired from sleepless nights.

"Three men enough to clear the building?" he asked Salim.

He exchanged a brief glance with Avinash and both nodded back. They had been with him long enough to read his mind.

"Alpha team would me Salim, Nasir and me, with me taking the point," said Avinash. "We enter through exit A and clear the rooms as we move deeper. Bravo team, that is Akshay and Sonam, cover exit B and be ready to provide backup, if necessary."

Sonam, who was paler than usual, let out a breath of relief. Nasir walked up to her and checked the vest to see if the armoured plates are in position. "If you see him coming, don't think, don't hesitate. Just shoot. OK?" She nodded her head a little too vigorously.

"Make sure the safety is off," said Salim.

Her pouty, bee-stung lips quivered a little as she pulled out the gun from her shoulder holster and flicked the safety off.

"Scared?" asked Nasir.

"A little."

"That's good. Fear is just an evolutionary necessity. Avinash and Salim must have been in hundreds of ops, and they are still scared."

Sonam let out a forced chuckle. "It sure doesn't look like it."

"We are good actors." Avinash chuckled. "You don't eliminate fear, you control it, channel it to anger, aggression. Whatever works best for you."

"In fact, fear is essential," said Salim. "The absence of fear makes you reckless."

"-and dead," chimed in Avinash. "But you'll be fine, kiddo," Avinash said. "Don't be fooled by the soft-spoken, unassuming, nobody next to you. Akshay is a straight-up bad-ass."

The dark circles under Akshay's tired eyes crinkled with a shy smile. "Why don't you guys stop wasting time and get on with it?"

Avinash nodded, briskly. "On me," he called.

Nasir fell in line as they stacked up at the entry, their MP5s out, safeties off, and pointed at the ground. Avinash took up point as the commanding officer. He stood as close to the door as possible, leaning slightly forward and knees bent in a half crouch. Turning his head slightly to the left, Avinash karate chopped the air with his hands; thick fingers pointing towards the door. Nasir nodded and broke off from the group to position himself on the other side of the closed door. He nudged the black, rusty metal door, and it wasn't locked. Avinash brought his fist up in the air and counted down; his fingers popping in the air with each count. At three, Nasir eased the door inside and stood aside to make way for the breach party. Avinash glided in on the balls of his heels, his gun pointed to the ground and finger on the trigger. He went straight to the back of the door and then swept right, clearing his side, and took up a stance facing the left. At the same time Salim stepped into the room, swept left, and stood facing the right side.

Nasir walked in backwards, facing the door they just came in, completing the interlocking fields of vision. Tactical ops were all about trust, covering your teammate's blind spots and trusting they will do the same. The mid-day sun seeped into the dimly lit enclosure. It was mostly empty, except for a few old cans of paints scattered here and there.

Avinash whispered into the radio. "Nasir, stay in position. Salim, stack up on me at the door on the right side of the room." The quiet shuffling of feet could have been easily been the rats.

"Nasir, on me," the radio crackled.

Nasir broke off from the door security detail and stepped over to line up behind Salim. It was important to present as small a target as possible to oncoming fire. Avinash inched closer to the open door, pulled out a mirror from one of the pouches in the vest, and scanned the next room.

Avinash retreated and briefed the rest of the team. "A long empty corridor with rooms on either side, ending in a set of stairs on the far end. Salim and I will clear each room as we move forward through the corridor. Nasir, you stay in the corridor and make sure no surprises jump out from the other rooms. Three rooms on each side. Salim you go left, I'll go right. On three."

As Avinash counted off the third finger, they burst into the room in a single file, but silent. Avinash lead the charge, Salim followed, and Nasir bringing up the rear end. And with the grace of a synchronised swimming team, Avinash and Salim peeled off to the right and left, leaving Nasir in the middle, training his gun down the middle of the corridor.

"Clear on the right," Avinash called in.

"Clear on the left," Salim echoed.

Salim and Avinash emerged from the rooms and criss-crossed into the opposite rooms as Nasir stepped ahead, crossing the cleared room. They repeated the exercise uneventfully, reached the end of the corridor, and gaped at the two-man wide staircase. Nasir caught a momentary glance between the two bulky men. It was how they communicated, but he wasn't privy to the language.

"What is it?" Nasir whispered.

Salim raised a finger to his mouth and gestured him to stay put. He joined Avinash who was waiting at the foot of the stairs. As soon as Salim joined him, they took up positions back-to-back, covering the 360 degrees together, and started up the stairs; one at a time. They stuck to the walls as they crept up to the landing and deployed themselves covering all the tactical angles.

"Head up the stairs," whispered Avinash through the radio. Nasir closed the distance to the stairs in a few silent steps. "Stick to the sides and check for creaks before you put your weight on it," said Salim.

With one last sweep of his rear, Nasir began the climb: one foot at a time. He found the nails that fixed the step to the frame and placed his right feet right on top of it. And with a slight change in his body weight, he applied more and more pressure on the leg, ready to pull back the moment the faintest of a creak. How did the two bulky men on the landing of the stairs make the climb easily? But he kept at it, one leg in front of the other, until he reached the landing.

Avinash pointed up the next set of stairs. "Head up there and relieve us."

Nasir rounded the corner and started the next leg of the tortuous journey up the wooden stairs. As soon as he was in position, he gave a nod, and Avinash peeled away from Salim and nimbly lunged up the stairs. To Nasir's dismay, Salim followed suit with the same nimble steps and made it upstairs in a jiffy.

The space upstairs was just like the rest of the building; forgotten, abandoned, and silent. A small corridor stretched in front of them with two rooms opening into it. The stairs took a sharp turn and continued upstairs. Salim pointed at Nasir and then to the stairs.

Nasir nodded his head and crouched at the foot of the stairs. Avinash and Salim exchanged a brief glance and veered off into the two rooms. A stream of 'clear' messages rattled the radio as they joined Nasir at the foot of the stairs.

The floor above was an open terrace. This was not looking good. They should have found Alex by now. Nasir double checked the Glock in his holster. Avinash and Salim didn't betray any such misgivings, but then again, they were trained to think 'officer-based' than 'suspect-based'. Years of tactical ops have taught them to put officer's lives first and not be overwhelmed by the pressure to get the offender as soon as possible. When they are in the proverbial 'zone', they hardly think about the suspect, rather they focused on getting through to their target in the safest way possible.

They followed the same formation they used earlier to get up the stairs. They paused at the entrance to the terrace for a couple of seconds to let their vision adjust to the full light of the midday sun. As the blurred whites resolved into shapes, Nasir saw the empty terrace. The low half-wall was almost black with dried moss. The stairs opened up into the middle of the terrace, facing the electronic street. Avinash and Salim rushed into the terrace, veering off to two sides as they swept the open space with precision. Nothing. Nasir lumbered into the terrace, with his head hanging low. He really thought they had Alex, but he seemed to have vanished into thin air. Avinash's smooth brow wrinkled with worry and Salim's eyes didn't hide his surprise.

"You sure we didn't miss him on our way up?" Nasir dropped the MP5 to let it hang by the sling around his shoulder.

Salim nodded his head and raised his hands to his ears. "Bravo team come in. Do you have eyes on the subject?"

"Negative," crackled the radio.

"Fuck!" said Avinash.

"This doesn't make sense," said Nasir. "We are sure he entered the building, and we covered the only two exits out of the building. Starting from the bottom we swept each floor. If he heard us or not, he has no way except up." He scanned the open space around him. No water tanks, or security houses. In short no place to hide out. He stepped closer to the edge and peeked over it. "No landings as well." When he turned back, he saw the building behind them. "Fuck!"

"We are fucking idiots," said Nasir as he strode towards the back side of the building. "Akshay said there was hardly any space out back because the building behind, didn't he?" His hands quivered as he touched his earpiece. "Bravo, head out into the Food street and find Alex. He has jumped over the small gap onto the adjacent building."

Avinash crouched near the edge and picked up a smoking bud of cigarette. "We've not missed him by much. It's still smoking."

"I don't think he would have stopped for a smoke if he knew we were in the building," said Salim, stepping up on the ledge. "We still have the element of surprise. Let's jump over the gap and clear the next building, top-down."

Nasir nodded in approval. "No more stealth. Storm the building, shoot on sight. It's time to finish this."

The Artist

Saturday, May 3, 2014

The road to glory would not be paved with flowers.

Alex leaned against the half-wall in an almost sitting posture and sucked in a long drag from the cigarette sticking out of his mouth. The smoke rippled through his throat with a familiar tickle and hugged his lungs, like long lost lovers. Smoking was one of those vices which was as pleasurable as it was harmful. Alex loved the warm feeling of the rough paper between his knuckles and the familiar feeling of light dizziness too much to let go of the habit.

He was lucky he stumbled on this abandoned building while scouting the place. Nasir and the police made things so much more difficult. He knew the road to glory would not be paved with flowers. But it was getting tiring; the constant vigil, looking over your shoulder for that somebody who will recognise you. This was a welcome break; to just kick back and relax until it's time to start again.

Fuelled by the light dizziness, his mind took flight in the light breeze and took home on Shruti, her innocent eyes, and sultry body. Alex shook off the thoughts. He knew where they were headed. It was becoming harder to control his urges with Shruti. Her shapely up-tilted breasts teased him in his dreams; blood dripping down them and onto his face. God, with a little help from The Butcher, had kept him clean till now, but *'how long?'* was the question.

His mobile phone rattled in his pocket; two short bursts. That was the cue. Alex tossed the half-smoked cigarette to the ground and climbed on top of the half-wall he was leaning against. A heavy gust hit him square on his face as he glanced down the gap between the two buildings. It was small enough to step over, he didn't even have to jump.

A short hop and he was balancing on the ledge of the adjacent building. Alex climbed down and headed to the opposite side, overlooking the food street. He had explicitly told the girl to be discreet in picking up the bag. Manas had grown some balls and was up to something. But judging from the way she flicked wallets, she shouldn't have any problems. When compared to the electronics street, the food street had a distinct laid-back vibe. The crowd was still thick but was meandering like a river on the plains; trying to decide which way it should go. He scanned the sea of people, especially the ones around the spice shop. Nothing. He pushed away from the ledge and headed down the stairs to the ground floor. The building housed a few shops selling kitchen utensils and a bakery on the ground floor. Alex kept his head down and acted like he belonged as he passed the shops and stepped out onto the street.

The mouth-watering aroma hit him like a bullet train and made his stomach grumble. It was literally a meat lover's paradise. He stuck to the food stalls and the crowd in front of them to make his way to the drop. Every now and then he stopped to appraise chickens slow roasting in their glass-walled furnace of hell. It helped blend in and appeased his stomach. Alex circled the shop - 'Malabar Spices'- with his eyes peeled out for Manas or the Police.

A few rounds of the place, each time swooping a little closer, told him the coast was clear. A cursory glance back towards the building he came from made his heart jump up his throat. Two men exited the building, in casual clothes, but with an unmistakable air of authority. Alex knew the older man-he would not forget his sharp, narrow eyes, nor the hawk-like nose. Nasir and the bulky crony parted the crowd as they made their way towards Alex. But their eyes roamed everywhere, searching. *Good. At least they haven't spotted me.*

Alex pivoted and made sure he had his back to them as he hastened his pace, but not so much as to draw attention. He fought the urge to knock the slow-moving idiots out of the way. As soon as he reached the drop, he scanned the inside of the shop. Clear. Alex bounded up two steps and walked right into the shop. On his way inside, he dropped the promised money on the counter and was met with a cursory nod from the shop owner. He burrowed his way to the deep corner of the shop and found a bag sitting there. He frowned at the pink Nike logo on the black bag. It was better to paint a big bull's eye on his back than carry around the bag. But he didn't have anything to hide it as well. With a short wave of dismissal, he slung it over his shoulder and headed out.

Alex stopped at the exit, and spied Nasir and his crony. They were closer than they were before, probably a hundred feet away, but still searching. His hands itched to pull up the hood, but he knew better. In hot mid-day sun, the hoodie would stick out like a sore thumb. Keeping his head down, he exited the shop and took a left, blending into the crowd. Alex maintained his steady pace, resisting the temptation to look back, and made his way to the main market alley. He stepped into the large river of human bodies and dissolved in it.

Manas

Saturday, May 3, 2014

Violence is the best power trip.

Manas tore into his shawarma; chunks of chicken squirmed out of his hold and jumped on to the table. The only food he had all day was a meagre bowl of Corn Flakes and that was just not enough. Prateek fretted in the corner, not eating anything as usual. Out of nowhere, the strongest flash of nostalgia hit him. They were inseparable in a life that was so simple; before the madness began. Prateek was his partner in all the innocent and naughty things thirteen-year-olds around the world did. No matter how much you wish for it to stay the same, life gets complicated as you grow old. When you are a kid, the world is black and white. You know something is bad and something is good. But as you grow older, the black and white world morphs into shades of grey all around; the well-marked paths and lines become blurred, and you lose your way in them. Some of those paths are bloody, and incidentally they got into a path which was the bloodiest of them all.

The skinny boy he had tasked with monitoring the spice shop parted the curtains and peeked inside. 'Sir,' he called.

That was the cue. Manas dropped the half-eaten shawarma on to the table and rose to his feet. The boy waited at the door; half hidden by the curtain he parted. Manas pulled out the two hundred rupees note from his pocket and thrust it into the open palms of the boy. He pocketed the note and pointed towards the right. That was all Manas needed. He rushed out of the shop, with Prateek at his heel.

He paused at the exit and scanned the lazy crowd, towards the right of the spice shop. It had gotten busier than earlier, probably because it was lunch time. Manas searched the crowd for the pink Nike logo, but couldn't find it. Panic knocked on the door as his breath became shallower. Did he lose-?

No, there he was. Alex was over of six feet tall and he wasn't hard to spot. A tall figure, hunching to try to blend into the average height of the crowd. Manas signalled to Prateek and they pushed through the crowd towards Alex.

"Now, this is the Manas I've known," Prateek whispered in his ears. "Taking control, just like old times."

Manas fought the urge to smile as he pushed aside an uncertain couple deciding where they wanted to have lunch. "Maybe the 'how', but most definitely not the 'why'"

"For me, the why is also the same. To help you."

"Oh, come on! You do this for yourself, Prateek. To satisfy your perverse need for power."

"Guilty as charged," said Prateek with a deep chuckle. "Ah! It's a uniquely exhilarating feeling. To have another human being at your mercy! Violence is the best power trip."

"You better reign in the power trip. This time it's different. Violence is just a means to an end and not the end in itself." Manas raised up his hand a little to signal Prateek to slow down. There were only five or six people between them, and Alex and he wanted to maintain the distance.

The continuous motion of the human beings along the street reminded him of water running along the foot paths on a rainy day. It meandered towards the main street which swallowed it like a storm drain. The raw human stench was unbearable as people crowded against him. Manas breathed in the carbon dioxide swirling all around him, and at that moment he envied Alex and his six feet frame.

They let the crowd take them forward for a while when Alex started to make his way to the left, side stepping people. Manas and Prateek followed suit, gliding to the side with as little disturbance as possible.

"He is moving out," said Manas. "The hardware street is that way."

"That's an exit, if I remember correctly," said Prateek.

"And a lot less crowded. That's gonna be a problem."

Prateek nodded as he stepped aside to let an old man pass by before making his way to the side.

Manas grunted in distaste as they turned the corner into the hardware street. There were hardly ten to fifteen people in the street. The 6"3 figure of Alex made its way up the street; his square shoulders slumped, but his back was arrow straight - the typical hunch in tall guys who feel the need to blend in.

Manas and Prateek stuck to the sides and headed straight to a shop which had a temporary shed propped up in front of it. PVC pipe joints of different shapes and sizes hung on jute strings, swaying and rotating in the occasional breeze. Manas sauntered over to a set of ladders leaning against the side of the shop and pretended to inspect them. There was an unencumbered view of the street in between the PVC pipes. Alex proceeded up the street, slowing down every now and then to check his rear. Did he know he was being followed? Or was he looking for someone else? If Alex had spotted him, he wouldn't ignore it. Must be something else. Police? Instinctively, he scanned the people in the street and coming in from the main street.

He needed to get closer or else he was going to lose him. Manas signalled Prateek to be ready as he waited for Alex to complete one of his checks. As soon as he did one, Manas rushed out of the shop and headed diagonally across the street to get behind a stack of red and white plastic chairs. He tried to hear over the blood whooshing through his ears for any sounds of commotion. When none came, he let his breath out and waited for the next opportunity. And step by step, he got closer to Alex, hiding behind obstacles, and changing the sides.

Soon enough, they were just a few feet from the end of the street. Alex was at the end of the street, carrying out one last check before exiting the market. Manas and Prateek crouched behind a set of flowerpots, stacked hip high in an intuitive, and structurally strong formation which spread the weight uniformly. The shopkeeper stared at them like they were out of their mind, but Manas was way past caring. A plump, middle-aged lady swaggered in wearing a black saree with red pattern. She admired the stack of flowerpots as she walked up the steps to the shop, but miscalculated the height and slipped and fell backwards, on top of Manas. He lost his balance and crashed into the stack of flowerpots. It swung for a second and proceeded to fall over onto the street, shattering with a loud cascading clatter. Dust swirled up around the reddish-brown pieces of burnt clay as they skittered across the street, as if they were running away from the impact.

Dammit! Manas pulled himself up from the mess and oriented himself. There was no way Alex missed it. He stole a quick glance in Alex's direction. In a moment when time stood still, he saw Alex's chocolate brown eyes trained on him. There was a mixture of surprise, admiration, joy, and anger in them. And then Alex broke eye contact, turned around and bolted towards the exit.

The Artist

Saturday, May 3, 2014

You are not leaving.

Alex dashed through the thinning crowd, shoving aside people in his path. The market exited into a slum which had the pedigree of being the underbelly of the city. A working-class colony of crumbling, blackening shacks, sheds, and small housing complexes; right in the backyard of the Secretariat, the centre of power in the state. The irony was not lost on anyone.

He glanced back to catch a blurry glimpse of Manas criss-crossing through the crowd with a speed uncharacteristic for his age. Alex didn't expect Manas to find him, not after all the precautions he took. Another check told Alex that he was closing in fast. He needed to lose him, and it would not be with speed.

A sharp turn into an alleyway put him in a direct path into the depths of the slum. The zig-zag maze of narrow pathways, barely wise enough for two people, would be perfect to lose Manas in. Alex extended an arm out to grab the corner of a building and leveraged it to turn around the corner. He never thought he would say it but, inertia was a bitch. An inopportune chuckle rose to his throat, which sunk back just as fast when he saw Manas charging at him, closer than ever. *Shit, that man can run.*

Alex worked out occasionally, but that was mainly sparring with a heavy bag or strength training. He never thought endurance training was what would save him. His lungs cried out for oxygen. Rotting, blackening shacks and sheds whizzed past him as he propelled himself headfirst along the narrow alley. Lactic acid collected in his thighs, bringing with it the familiar ache, but he powered through it.

Even though he could not see Manas, he could hear the flurry of footsteps chasing him get closer and louder. He needed to slow Manas down, he thought as he scanned his path. In that new perspective, the obstacles he side-stepped, presented themselves as opportunities. The plastic chair he jumped over, the bucket of water he swerved to avoid, all of them opportunities to slow Manas down.

Alex spied a bicycle leaning against the wall up ahead. *Perfect.* As he charged down the street, he extended his arm, grabbed the handle of the cycle, and pulled it onto the path. Alex didn't stop to check the effectiveness, nor to check what the owner of the cycle was shouting but continued down the path pulling down more obstacles behind him.

As he slowed down to make another turn into a slightly wider path, Alex glanced back and groaned. Manas leapt over the obstacles without breaking a stride, his face set with determination. *Dammit!* Shoving his irritation to the back of his mind, Alex charged down the street. The moment he looked up and took stock, he knew the turn was a mistake. The path he was on was apparently an upscale part of the slum, with solid structures and rare alleyways. Alex pushed himself to go faster, ignoring his tired feet, screaming lungs, and the cold finger down his spine. He desperately searched for an alleyway he can duck into as he leapt over a puddle of water in the middle of the road. The footsteps were closer than ever as they splashed through the water puddle. It was then Alex heard another sound, a plasticky thump.

Alex glanced back and caught a blur of blue before a plastic bucket hit him squarely on his back. It didn't weigh much, but it was enough to derail the balance of a body going full tilt. He had to slow down to regain balance, but before he had the chance to do that Manas crashed into him with an outstretched leg. Alex was not prepared for the sheer force of the kick as he tumbled onto a temporary shed made of metal sheets. It crashed down with him with a loud clatter.

The loud sound and falling metal sheets disoriented Alex for a second. He shook it off and raised his head just in time to see Manas leaping on top of him. Alex stuck out a leg, stiffened it, and redirected Manas' momentum to the side, leading into the crashed metal sheets.

It was too late to make a run for it again. Alex jumped up to his feet and adopted a fighting stance, putting some distance between him and Manas, who recovered from the crash almost instantly. He rose, shoving aside the metal sheets on top of him; dust plastered across his body, blood dripping from his right upper arm, soaking his T-shirt. Manas hardly spared a glance at the bleeding arm as he circled Alex, like a tiger toying with his prey.

A mixed cocktail of emotions played havoc with Alex's mind. Admiration for the man who shrugged off injuries that would make men younger than him weep, excitement at the prospect of meeting his match, anger at the betrayal, and a sliver of fear that he may lose.

Time slowed down as his heart pumped adrenaline all through his body. Alex turned his body sideways, in a manner typical of karate, and made himself a smaller target. Manas raised his arms up over his face, palms open and facing Alex, and tilted his head forward. His body was fluid and relaxed as he circled Alex, just out of reach.

In a fight, the first strike was very important. It sets the tone for the conflict psychologically. Alex waited for the perfect moment to launch it as he side stepped to counteract Manas' circling. He needed to buy some time.

"Your daughter is going to get a hard lesson as soon as I get back."

Heads popped out from houses and the alleys to check out the commotion; they stayed to watch the fight. Nobody tried to stop it; maybe they are used to fights.

Manas fixed him in the coldest stare Alex had ever got and said, "You are not leaving."

A group of teenage boys gathered behind Manas; they pointed at the two men facing off and giggled in a way only teenage boys can. One of them burst out laughing and Manas jerked back his head instinctively for a fraction of a second. That was all Alex needed. He kept his body sideways, extended his right arm, and lunged into a punch with the full weight of his body behind it.

Manas sidestepped the lunge, like he was expecting it, and grabbed hold of his punching arm. Without wasting a moment, he used Alex's momentum to pull him down to the floor. A loud cheer rang from the crowd as Alex landed on his face with a thud. He spit out the dust that got into his mouth and pushed himself up to his feet. *It wasn't supposed to go this way. Wasn't Manas distracted, or did he trick me into thinking he was?* Manas had circled away to maintain a distance; a fire burned in his tired old eyes.

Alex studied the grace with which Manas moved his feet; it almost seemed like he was floating. Definitely trained in some form of martial arts, and a good one at that. It was time to go old-school. Alex switched to kick boxing, a style he was much more comfortable with, and raised his arms in front of his face in a traditional boxing stance. The style suited him because of his long arms and legs, and he needed every advantage he had now.

He inched forward, occasionally jabbing the air around Manas, to use the narrow path to his advantage, and back Manas into a corner. And it was working. It was evident in Manas' uncomfortable face, eyes furtively racing up and down the street looking for a way to get out of the corner he was being circled into. He sensed an imminent move, and spotted Manas shifting his body weight to his back leg. Manas launched a kick below the waist. Alex jumped back leaving Manas to kick the air and lose his balance. Not missing a beat, Alex closed in with a roundhouse kick which landed with a thump. Manas lost his footing and landed on his back. The crowd cheered at the gladiators in the arena.

Manas recovered with surprising agility and got back to his feet, but that was all the time Alex needed to close in the gap and unleash a barrage of jabs and punches. Not giving the opponent a break to think was a sure shot way of putting him on the defensive. But Manas' defence was above par. He retreated into a complete defensive shell, blocking, and deflecting all the attacks thrown his way. Alex mixed up face and body punches, hoping to crack open the strong defence. But it was frustrating to see all the combinations he spent hours practising on a heavy bag sent back with such force. All the YouTube videos told him that mixing up body and face punches will surely open the opponent's defence. *Such bull!*

His patience was running thin. Alex stepped closer with a huge right hook, favouring power over caution, in an effort to break the stalemate. Instead of moving away and blocking the punch, as he was doing till now, Manas stepped into the punch, raising his left hand, deflecting the punch, and locking the arm under his arm pit. At the same time, his right hand shot up to Alex's face, palms open, and unleashed the energy coiled in his body.

The open palm hit him in an explosion of stars and blood, as he was taken off his feet. Gravity was not kind to Alex. The impact of landing on the paved road jolted his spine, sent shooting pain all through his body, and drove out all the air in his lungs. Alex writhed on the ground, struggling to catch his breath as warm blood filled his nose and flowed down the side of his face. At the back of his mind, a voice was telling him to get up, get away.

Alex knew he was outsmarted and outclassed. His fight-or-flight response chose the latter in self-preservation. He needed a distraction; he thought as he stuck out his hand and groped for something he could use. It closed around a hard, rectangular rock and he hurled it at Manas, lying down.

Manas

Saturday, May 3, 2014

Breathe. You do this every day. Just inhale and exhale.

"Look out," Prateek yelled.

Manas spotted a red flash heading his way and dodged it deftly. The brick flew past his face as he crashed into a group of onlookers. He disentangled from the human melee, apologising, when they pointed down the street and yelled out something. He didn't catch it, but he understood. Alex hurtled down the street away from him; toward Shruti. *No! That was not an option.*

Manas propelled himself behind Alex, shrugging off minor aches and pain. Shooting pain travelled through his bleeding arms with each swing. With each raspy breath, his lungs cried foul. *Breathe. You do this every day. Just inhale and exhale.*

Alex turned the corner at the end of the street, towards the right, and disappeared. Manas sped up to the end of the street and turned the corner. He had exited the slum and a set of railway tracks extended to both sides. Alex was a hundred feet ahead of him, running along the tracks. And up ahead a railway tunnel rose out of darkness, like the open mouth of a giant lying on the tracks.

"If he gets to the tunnel, we'll lose him," said Prateek, as he ran alongside Manas.

Manas pushed himself harder towards the running man who had his daughter. He had to catch Alex before he disappears into the tunnel.

The distance between them was closing. Ninety feet. His legs were screaming for oxygen. A dull ache pulsed and spread along the lower part of his body. Eighty feet. *'Your daughter is going to get a hard lesson as soon as I get back.'* Alex's words echoed in his mind, reverberated and amplified. Seventy feet. Alex was almost at the tunnel, and it was becoming clearer to Manas that he wouldn't be able to reach him on time. *A hard lesson. No!*

Just then, Manas heard a soft rumbling, slowly getting louder. He glanced back. No trains there. A dirge of the horn up ahead made it clear;

the train was coming from beyond the tunnel. He was pleased with the stroke of luck. With the train coming, Alex would have to stay out of the tunnel and that means he couldn't slip away in the darkness.

But to his surprise, Alex didn't slow down, didn't make a detour. Instead, he sped up and ran straight into the dark mouth of the giant. Manas had made up his mind in a split second and propelled forward. Losing Alex was not an option, train or not.

"Manas, if you didn't reach the end of the tunnel before the train comes in, you are dead meat."

"I know," Manas said as he plunged into the darkness of the tunnel.

The slow rumble of the tracks grew steadily as the train charged closer. Alex's silhouette flickered against the light at the end of the tunnel as he continued unhindered. In the sparse light, Manas took stock of the tunnel. It was narrow, barely enough to let a train pass through.

The hiss of the brakes and the clanking of the couplings came closer and closer. It drowned out the footsteps echoing in the dark tunnel. Manas put every last ounce of strength into running. The behemoth of a train appeared up ahead, charging at them at full speed. Alex was almost at the end of the tunnel, but so was the train. Manas was fifty feet from the end of the tunnel when Alex jumped out of the end of the tunnel, missing the train by a hairline.

The locomotive chugged inside the tunnel, at full speed, plunging the tunnel into darkness. On instinct Manas jumped to the side and flattened himself against the tunnel wall. It was then he recalled that the sheer force of air pulled under the train was enough to knock a grown man off his feet. Manas dropped to the ground like a bag of rice, and hugged the ground, hoping there was enough room for him under the speeding train. The clickity-clack of the wheels charged down the tracks but was drowned out by the blood swooshing around in his ear.

The train charged closer, threatening to devour everything in his path. Wind howled in his ears; a precursor to what was coming. Manas spread his fingers and dug them into the earth. He squeezed his eyes shut, flattened his face against the cool dirt, and laid there; consumed by the fear of death. The entire world shrunk to that moment, that train and that tunnel. Manas wasn't ready to die, not until Shruti was safe. A prayer rose to his lips; a prayer that wasn't directed to any God but rather a call of help to the universe. For a split second, he wondered if believing in God was a safer choice.

Shruti's infectious smile shattered the brief philosophical discourse and brought him back to the hard realities of life. The possibility that he might not see that smile killed him inside. And Anu. He would have given anything for a chance to peer into her dark anthracite eyes, lock lips on her generous, slightly parted lips.

The train reached Manas and thundered past him in a murderous rage. He hugged the ground closer, flattening his body as much as he can. The rhythmic clapping of the wheels was deafening. The howling, screaming wind filled his world.

Nothing prepares you for the sheer power of a train. The sheer might with which it sucks you under its wheels.

Manas held on for dear life for little close to a minute before the last coach brushed past him with a whoosh of air. The all-engulfing rumble that consumed his life for the last minute faded away. He stayed on the ground, motionless, for a few more seconds; waiting for the shivers that rocked his body to settle down.

He slowly climbed to his feet, holding on to the sides of the tunnel for support. A wave of nausea hit him from nowhere and he bent over and puked. As Manas wiped his mouth and straightened up, he heard footsteps behind him.

"What the hell were you thinking?" Prateek asked.

"What do you think I am doing? Getting Shruti safely back in my arms."

"By dying under a train?"

Manas turned away from Prateek and walked out of the tunnel. Alex got away. *That fucking bastard got away.*

'Your daughter is going to get a hard lesson as soon as I get back.'

NO! The air around suffocated him, bind his hands down to his side, rendering him helpless. Rage bubbled up in his gut. Rage against himself, against Alex, and against the world which dug up the past he had left behind. It rose inside him, consuming him. And just like a pressure cooker letting off a whistle, he screamed; a hard, long, guttural scream which echoed in the tunnel.

The Artist

Saturday, May 3, 2014

This is a point of no return. You have no idea who I am.

Alex turned into the foliage covered side road leading up to the abandoned warehouse he had made his hideout. The Maruti Alto jumped and rattled as he made his way through the rocky, unpaved path. With each bump, his body cried out in pain. The fight really took it out of him.

He pulled up behind a line of trees, hidden from the main road, and stopped the car. Alex reached for the bloody tissue on the dashboard and wiped his nose. Fresh blood tainted the pink tissue. The high noon sun beat down on him, mercilessly. He was still trying to extract clarity from the muddle of emotions he was feeling.

At first it was rage, unbridled rage. But it soon mixed with something on the other end of the spectrum - happiness. He was happy that his idol finally took notice. The excitement he had in facing off with him and seeing him in action was way better than reading about it in old newspapers. And then it soon turned into self-loathing. He had thought he was smart enough to catch Manas off guard. Outsmarting his idol, his guardian angel; how exciting it would have been?

"I'll make it easier for you," said the voice he was too familiar with. The Butcher stood at the entrance of the warehouse. "You are angry at him for his disrespect and at you for acting like a know-it-all jackass." It was strange how clear his voice was even when he was so far.

"Oh, good, it's the sound of reason," muttered Alex, as he exited the car and slammed it shut.

"Was that sarcasm?"

The menace in that voice sent chills down Alex's spine. "No, no. Just upset at what happened today."

"So am I. Despite multiple warnings, you fucked up."

Alex shambled towards the warehouse entrance. "I... OK, you're right. I fucked up. But it's OK. We still have a lot of moves left."

"Do you know what's happening here?" asked The Butcher with a shake of his head. "Why do you think Manas does what he wants and not do what he is told?"

Alex rattled the lock and chain he used to secure the door to the warehouse, to check if it still held its own. "I don't know. Maybe he is just bull headed."

"What did you do when he tried to find you with that phone hidden in the bag?"

Alex opened his mouth to answer but was cut off before he could say anything.

"That was rhetorical," snapped The Butcher, with some of the earlier menace creeping back into his voice. "When you found out, you called him up, congratulated him on his balls, and slightly berated him for pulling that stunt. Do you think you made him afraid for his daughter's life with that little slap?"

The silence that ensued dragged on for longer than it was comfortable. Alex glanced outside, towards the Mosque. The loudspeaker from the Mosque continued blaring out prayers and songs. They had been at it since the morning, courtesy the festival. *Thank God it's getting over today.* When he glanced back at The Butcher, he saw him glaring at him, with his hands tied behind his back.

"Wasn't that.... rhetorical too?" Alex ventured a guess.

"No, it was fucking not," The Butcher shot out. "And answer the fucking question."

"I thought it did," said Alex as he leaned against the frame of the door and stared out into the line of trees.

"The right answer to that question was 'no'." The Butcher paced like a caged lion, hands behind his back. "You think Manas fears you? Respects you? Would he have done any of this shit if he did either?"

Alex felt a familiar sensation boiling up inside him. The corners of his vision turned red.

"How does it feel to be treated like a maggot?" The Butcher stopped abruptly and faced Alex; his eyes burned from under the shadow of his low hat. "Is the great Artist afraid of Manas? He seems pretty confident that you won't lift a finger to hurt Shruti."

Alex ground his teeth and clenched his jaw so tight it hurt. "I wanted to kill that bitch so many times. Wasn't it you who stopped me?"

The Butcher sized Alex up, from head to toe., and said in a slow and deliberate diction. "Kill, yes. But I never stopped you from anything else, did I?"

Ah! It threw a light on in his brain and suddenly everything was clear. Fear was the answer. By letting Manas go unpunished for his indiscretions, he reinforced the behaviour. And now it was time for a correction. Manas needed to understand that there were consequences to his actions.

"I know what to do," said Alex, as he pulled out the key from his pocket and unlocked the door.

"Yes, you do." The Butcher glided around the corner of the warehouse and disappeared.

Alex kicked the door in, and it flew open and smashed into the wall with a loud bang. Shruti jerked back at the sudden explosion and gaped at him with pale, frightened eyes. Alex closed the door and secured it from inside. The edges of his vision blurred as red spread across his eyes. He glanced at Shruti, who shrunk back from his gaze. Her eyes roved over the red on his clothes, his face, and then fixed on his eyes. Blood drained from her face as her predicament sunk in.

He stormed across the room, pulled off his shirt and threw it into a corner. It hit the walls with a faint thud and dropped to the ground. A rhythmic drumming grew louder as if it was adding to the moment with a tasteful score. Islamic songs over the loudspeaker came closer as the closing procession of the festival travelled the streets. Alex plucked his bag off the ground and rummaged inside to find a fresh T-shirt and a new SIM card. He dismantled his phone, put in the new SIM card, and dialled Manas as he pulled the new T-shirt over his head. The rhythmic beats, shuffling feet, and the low drone of hushed conversations filled his mind space as he waited for Manas to pick up. Procession was practically in his backyard.

The phone rang a few more times before Mans picked it up. *More disrespect. What happened to picking up on the second ring?*

"Hel...." Manas cleared his throat and continued," Hello."

"You're out of get-out-of-jail cards, Manas."

"I.... I'm sorry, Alex. I don't know what I was thinking."

"Little too late for apologies, don't you think? I let you off with a small rap because I respected you. But respect is a two-way street and I don't see any coming my way. Every chance you get you undermine my authority. No more, Manas. No more."

A sinister chill spread between the gap between words. The voice that answered him was different, stronger. "You can take your veiled threats and shove it up your ass. Shruti is all you have for keeping me off your back. She is safe."

A harsh chuckle escaped Alex. "There is a lot between alive and dead. She serves my purpose even if she is barely alive."

"You wouldn't dare..."

Alex marched over to Shruti and slapped her with the back of his hand, hard. She cried out in pain and collapsed into a series of sobs. "Just remember, that's on you. That and what's about to happen. It's all on you."

"This is a point of no return, Alex. Even if you lay as much as a hand on Shruti, you are done. You have no idea who I am."

"I know exactly who you are," said Alex, as he disconnected the call.

Alex took out the SIM card and threw it out. It was becoming like second nature for him. But what he was going to do was far from it. Once he started down the familiar slippery slope of torture, it was hard to hold back; he never had to hold back. He scanned the room, especially the dark corners. No, The Butcher was nowhere to be found. But he had to be there. He would stop Alex before things got out of hand. Or at least God would. After all, everything was His plan.

Shruti cowered in fear, shrinking into a corner as far as possible from him as the chains allowed. He made his way to Shruti, with slow, measured footsteps.

"I've dreamed of this for so many days." Alex scratched his beard; the stubble had grown out into an irritating length. "Let's get you into a chair.... much more comfortable that way." He scanned the space around and spotted the chair he had got for himself. It should work.

Alex pulled up the chair and tied it to the nearest pole. "Listen, this is how it's going to go down. I'll be getting you into the chair, one way or the other. Either you struggle and I beat you up and then get you into the chair, or you come over here like a good girl. I prefer the first one, you know. So much more fun."

Shruti scrunched up her long, thin nose and spat at Alex.

Spunk turned him on, and Shruti had plenty of it. "Well, have it your way."

After a bit of struggle and a few kicks to his face, Alex got Shruti off the ground and into the chair. She squirmed against his strong arms as he tied her down.

Alex straightened up, sauntered over to his bag, and pulled out a set of knives, his set of knives. In the movies, you always see the torturer line up the tools in front of the victim to inject the fear of God in them. But that was stupid. Torturers who loved their craft never hesitated, never put on a show about it, but just savour it.

Shruti wriggled under the knots Alex tied. Alex fished out his mobile phone from his pocket, pulled up the sound recording app, and set it down close enough to capture what was about to happen. A thoughtful gift for his dear friend, Manas.

With the stage set, Alex stepped closer to Shruti and knelt beside her. Shruti's eyes widened as she tried to get out of the chair. But he had tied them real tight so that she could hardly move. Just the way he liked it.

Alex placed his hands on her thighs. Shruti went still and stopped struggling. A strange calm washed over the abandoned warehouse, like the eye of a storm. Alex eyed the red pants which covered Shruti's thighs. A few dusty brown patches, from lying on the ground, marred the perfect red. He grabbed the knife and traced the inside of her thighs all the way up with the tip of the knife. It eventually came to rest on one of the smudges.

Shruti's eyes were calm and glassy. She stared straight ahead, in a stoic acceptance. The façade of bravado never lasts. It all breaks down sooner than later, he thought as he slowly increased the pressure on the tip of the knife. She winced at the pain, but still stared straight ahead, not betraying her emotions. Alex kept on increasing the pressure, bit by bit, until the tip broke through the fabric and then the skin under it.

Blood spilt out where the knife broke the skin and seeped into the pants, cleaning up the smudges, and restoring the glorious red. Tears streamed down her eyes, and face contorted in pain, but she was still not screaming.

All the girls he had before broke down way before. At the very least show signs of weakness by now. It irritated Alex. Alex drew back the knife and slit open the pants from bottom to her upper thighs, on both legs. Shruti's lips trembled.

The white lace of her panties peeked out from under the red pants. Blood dripped down and wound its red tongue around her porcelain thighs. It captivated him and beckoned him. Alex ran his hands over the bare skin, smearing the blood all over them. It always looked better tinted in red. But it was just one leg. He needed to fix that.

Alex took one last look at the show of courage Shruti was putting up and carved out a long arc with his knife on the outside of her right thigh. Blood squirted out all along the line, spilling over to the ground and covering her legs with red. Shruti let out a primal scream as finally, the façade broke down. It was so satisfying. Once the walls come down, they never stopped screaming. Shruti screamed at the top of her lungs and it echoed in the hollow space and joined back as a chorus to her subsequent screams.

Shruti's white T-shirt had sprays of red across. He grabbed the T-shirt and cut it open completely. White lacy bra covered her sassily up-tilted breasts. It was wet and dirty from sweat and trembling with her shuddered breath. Shruti's full, lower lip quivered, recovering from the shock waves of pain that shot through her body.

Pain is the strongest of physical stimuli. It is wired so deep into the instinct for survival that no matter how well you control your mind, once you pass that pain threshold, everybody breaks. And beyond the threshold lies the world where Alex revelled in.

Sweat and dirt lined her skin; her perfectly sculpted collar bones were a sight for sore eyes. Alex traced a line above them with his knife, not too deep, leaving a trail of blood in its wake. Shruti screamed one last time before passing out. Blood gathered in the hollow of her collar bones and spilled over in rivulets meandering through and over her breasts. The white bra, which stuck to her body, acquired a deep red as blood conquered it. Alex felt stirrings in his pants, a familiar sensation from the past. This was everything he hoped for and more, the red colour, the drops of blood on her chest, the red invading her breasts. He wanted more. The knife took a detour and reached the straps of the bra.

"That's enough," said The Butcher.

Alex slid the knife under the strap of the bra and with one quick motion he cut off the strap.

"I said that's enough."

Alex paused with the knife under the other strap. The menace in The Butcher's voice rattled him.

"Stop gaping at me like a fool and bandage her up." He paused for a second and added, "Right now!"

The force of the last word broke through the haze. The mist cleared up and Alex saw what was in front of him. He took out the knife from under Shruti's bra strap and stepped back. Shruti was unconscious, half naked, and covered in blood; with more blood dripping down to a puddle from her open wounds.

Alex met The Butcher's empty stare from under the shadows of his fedora and nodded. "Just have to click a couple of photographs for Manas."

The Butcher's head made an imperceptible nod before blending back into the darkness from which he came from.

Alex grabbed his phone from the ground and stopped the recording. He played it back and revelled at the clarity of Shruti's screams. He'll have to cut off the beginning before sending it to Manas. A few quick taps brought up the camera app, and he started clicking from different angles.

Usually, he demanded the perfection of a DSLR to capture his artwork. But this was just a work-in-progress. The camera phone should do the purpose.

A few clicks in, he stopped the photography session and rushed to the first aid kit in his bag. He had refilled the supply just the day before. Within a few minutes, he managed to bandage all the wounds and stop the bleeding. Some of them may need stitches, but right now a tight bandage would have to do.

Alex was still flush from the act and in no mood to talk to Manas. He picked up his mobile phone, inserted a new SIM card, and verified the number in Whatsapp. It took a while for him to edit and make the audio clip appealing. As soon as it was done, he sent the audio clip, along with a couple of the best pictures he clicked to Manas. He typed a message:

'Despite what the pictures may suggest, Shruti is still alive. And if you want to keep her alive, you better play fair.

It's the Turn and the cards are dealt. But I'm raising the stakes for this round. Now you don't just set Rajashekharan's house on fire, you kill him before that. Call? or Raise?'

-and hit send.

Nasir

Sunday, May 4, 2014

Coincidence is the crutches of the inefficient.

The 18-year-old Glenfiddich held its head high on the tabletop like a snobby aristocrat. But that aristocrat was what saved him from the self-destructive spiral he sledded down after The Butcher got away. Along the path to recovery, he realised getting completely off alcohol was more difficult that he thought. As a compromise, he pledged to himself, that he would only drink Glenfiddich 18 and that worked. At over five thousand bucks a bottle, it controlled his alcohol consumption. And it became a permanent fixture in his overnight bags. He only used to drink when the situation really called for it, and this one fit the bill.

He lost Alex in the market, had no clue where Shruti was being held, and was baffled by the mystery that is Manas. To sum up, he screwed up, royally. A small part of him objected at the narcissistic tendency to shoulder the whole blame himself, but he shut it up with a tight slap across its face. He was responsible and there was no getting away from it.

The whiteboard behind him showed all the signs of the heated discussion he and his team had earlier in the day. Nasir just wanted to forget about all of it for a night, just one night. A sound sleep without the faces that haunted his dreams sounded too good to be true. That was the promise the snobby bottle held.

He closed his hands around the cool exterior of the bottle and poured himself a dram. The brown liquid tumbled into the glass, shimmering in the soft overhead light. Nasir twirled the drink and breathed in the whiskey's scent. The strong alcohol smell cleared his nostrils. A couple of drops of water and a light stir liberated the rest of the aroma and diluted the strong alcohol flavour. He breathed in deep and this time he got what he was looking for - the flavours of the single malt wafted into his nostrils. Loads of fruits entangled in an interplay of fragrances, with a hint of cinnamon swirling around the edge, just out of reach. Nasir stopped flirting with the drink, took a sip, and swirled it around in his mouth, breathing through his nose. The dry sherry and cinnamon with a touch of ginger washed over his palate, and along with it the warmth of the liquid.

As he sank back into the chair, savouring the single malt, he heard a knock at the door. Sonam strode in without an invitation and planted herself in a chair next to Nasir. Her pouty, bee-stung lips held a firm line beneath a broad, slightly tip-tilted nose. Nasir kept his drink aside and waited for Sonam to speak up. He knew there was something on her mind.

She grabbed a tuft of her dark auburn hair and chewed on it. "We really screwed up, didn't we?"

Nasir closed his eyes and nodded his head. "Read my mind. I was just drowning my sorrows in a bottle." He reached for the drink. "You want one?"

"No," said Sonam, shaking her head, but her gaze lingered on the sleek bottle.

"It's OK. You are off duty and so am I. Just an old man trying to forget himself." Nasir grabbed a fresh glass off the table and filled it with a small peg. "Soda? Water?"

Sonam bit her lips and then smiled. "On the rocks."

Nasir's eyebrows arched up. "My kinda girl."

A musk rose flush crept up her ivory face as she grabbed the glass from Nasir. She rose to her feet and crossed the room to the white board hanging on the far wall; the drink cradled in her hands.

Red, Blue, and Green strokes criss-crossed the white board, trying to prove their point, but ended up in utter chaos; much like the brain storming session they had earlier in the day. Everyone wore their hearts on their sleeves and the meeting turned into a blame game. It had got so out of hand that Nasir had to cut it short and send everyone back to their rooms to cool down.

Sonam stationed herself in front of the white board, right in front of Manas' name. "You know, in the beginning, I thought it was a waste of time looking into Manas." Her soft voice broke his reverie. "But now I'm not so sure..."

"Don't blame yourselves for that. I was second guessing my gut whenever it raised a flag at Manas."

Sonam turned back to face Nasir and sipped her drink. The whisky wet her lips and shimmered in the light. "You know, when I made the trip to the orphanage, I fully expected find somebody who knew Manas."

"I was hoping I could take him out of the equation, myself. We have enough troubles without Manas adding to it. When Avinash and Salim also came back empty with the school records, there was no way I could rule him out."

Sonam strolled across the room to the window and pulled back the shades. "Why was Manas at the market yesterday? Too much of a rarity to chalk it up to coincidence."

"Coincidence is the crutches of the inefficient. If there is one thing that I learned from twenty years of service, it is that there is always a better answer than coincidence." Nasir suddenly realised that he was sipping on air. "Alex kidnapping Manas' kid seems less and less random," said Nasir, refilling his glass from the bottle.

"But... I'm just having a hard time connecting the two. Alex has never been out of Delhi, more or less. Definitely not south of the Vindhyas."

"We know he has not. But what about Manas. As long as we can't verify Manas' past, we have to consider the possibility that he was not in Kerala all his life." The glass in Sonam's hand was empty. "Feel free to take as many refills as you like, OK?"

A sheepish grin broke out on her delicate face as she reached the table and poured herself another drink. "He could have been in Delhi, but not in the recent past though. We just don't know for sure." The ice cubes in her glass floated up and clinked against the glass.

"That's just what I hate about this whole thing. We don't know anything for sure. All we have are intuitions, guesses, and they are just not enough. We don't know where Shruti is, we don't know why Alex kidnapped her and not kill her." He slammed the glass on the table a little too hard. Sonam blinked at the sound. He saw concern in her eyes.

Nasir dipped his eyes and studied the contours of the tablecloth. Warmth filled up his eyes. The sheer helplessness weighed him down like an anvil. Every breath was hard, laboured, against the crushing weight of responsibility. How many more had to die because he couldn't do his job right. He closed his eyes shut, crossed his arms, and buried his head in them.

A few minutes passed in silence as he wallowed in self-pity. A cold, soothing touch on his outstretched arms broke his internal self-deprecating rant.

"It's not your fault," said a soft, angelic voice. "We all know you are doing the best you can and .... believe me it's a lot better than a lot of other best's."

Nasir wiped his eyes on his shoulders before he rose and opened his eyes. Through the haze of his watery eyes, he saw her; saw a twinkle which belonged in the stars; a darkness that belonged in deep space. The magnetic smile on her face was infectious. And in that instant, he felt better.

He was so overpowered by the porcelain beauty in front of him that he reached out and touched her face; just to see if she was real. And she was. Her ivory skin was as smooth as it was to look at. Nasir moved his hands down towards her red, full-lipped mouth. It quivered ever so lightly and parted as his hands brushed against them. He reached out and kissed those lips.

Sonam opened her lips to catch his lower lip in between them. The kiss was so warm and full that it almost breathed new life into his ageing body. He breathed in her sweet, musky scent, letting it consume him. His hands travelled across her back, probing every inch of her delicate body, all the while pulling her closer to him. Sonam cupped the back of his neck and leaned into the kiss, sucking the upper and lower lips one by one.

Nasir's hands slipped under her shirt, brushing against her mid-riff on their way up. As his hands roamed over her curves, there was nothing else on his mind. It was the clearest it had been ever since he started down the rabbit hole in pursuit of Alex. A part of him screamed that it was wrong, but somehow, it felt good, it felt right. It was the best he had felt since 1999 - ever since-

Nasir froze as a chill passed through. *1999.* It was right there on the white board all this time. He slid out his hands, broke off the kiss, and left a wide-eyed Sonam on the table as he walked to the white board like a zombie.

l Certificate - 1985 - 15 years
tion card - 1999

Somebody had erased the white board in the heated discussion earlier in the day, but not completely.

Sonam got off the table, slightly bewildered and out of breath. "What is it?"

"The earliest verified record Manas has is the Ration Card, isn't it? It was in 1999."

Sonam nodded her head, but the wrinkle in her eyebrows screamed her confusion. The red flush on her confused face refused to leave as she tried to get her breathing in control.

"You know which year The Butcher went missing?"

Her eyes grew wide as the implication of what Nasir was saying dawned on her. "No..," she gasped.

"I know it won't hold up in a court but think about it." Nasir started counting off points on his fingers. "The Butcher disappears in 1999. Manas appears in Kerala at around the same time. The Artist quoted The Butcher at the start of the journey. He kidnaps Manas' daughter. Both The Artist and The Butcher have their base in Delhi."

Disbelief danced in uncertain steps on Sonam's face; the flush was all but gone.

Nasir pressed on. "It just fits beautifully and fills in the gaps perfectly."

"Manas might be hiding something, but isn't it quite a jump to link him to The Butcher? And if it's true, then why hasn't he killed anyone after that? Serial Killers don't go cold turkey."

Nasir shook his head from side to side. "I don't know, but I got a gut feel about this. And experience has told me not to ignore my gut."

"I guess it's worth talking to Manas. Let's get the others and go talk to him tomo-"

"No. Right now." Blood whooshed through Nasir's ears in pulses. "It has to be now." He would not be able to get a moment of sleep with this hanging over his head. The rabbit hole went deeper than he thought.

Manas

Sunday, May 4, 2014

Karma. A drop of black ink, seeping and spreading through the delicate tissue of his life.

Shruti's tinny screams on repeat were an assault on the dead of the night. Manas stared at the screen of his mobile as it dimmed and turned off, but the screaming didn't stop. And when it did, the silence that followed was worse. The universe held its breath as Manas turned on the screen and it play again, for the umpteenth time. The illusion of calm was broken again with force as Shruti's screams split the night.

It was his fault. All of it. Karma. Nobody was supposed to find him in the other corner of the county. But it did and was consuming everything he had come to love; a drop of black ink, seeping and spreading through the delicate tissue of his life.

Prateek leaned back on the chair opposite, deep in thought. When his past reared its ugly face, it brought along with it an angel and a devil. But he was having a hard time deciding who was what.

The sound clip ended. It was time to replay. Manas turned on the screen and hit play. He opened the photograph Alex sent him and forced himself to look at it. He deserved it.

Prateek shot to his feet and sent the chair skittering across the hall. "Would you shut that fucking thing off?"

"I never should have listened to y-." The last word caught in his throat as shudders rocked his body.

"Look at the bright side, Manas." Prateek's voice was considerable softer. "She is still alive. Do you just want to keep listening to the clip or do you want to save her while you can?"

"What do you think I was doing till now?"

Prateek took a deep breath as he turned away from him. "I hate to admit this, but I guess we should stop trying to outsmart Alex and just do things his way."

Manas nodded his head.

Prateek turned back towards him with a smile on his face. It was a much younger Prateek, wearing an unnaturally white shirt, drenched in rain; a knife on his right hand, blood dripping from it onto the carpet. "I can help you," he said. "Just like old times." He wiped the knife on his white shirt, leaving a wide bloody trail on the pristine white.

Manas shook the vision clear, but he knew what his brain was trying to tell him. He had to put Prateek in the driving seat to do the things Alex wanted him to do. It was as easy as breathing, but there would be no coming back from it. Prateek had slowly, but steadily expanded his sphere of influence ever since he showed up. Five days, and it had already become hard to say to no to him. The ropes were slipping out of his hands. If only he would just let go, Prateek would make sure Alex gets what he wants and Shruti would be safe. But at what cost?

Unleashing a monster on the world was not something he cherished doing. But that was the reason he told himself to make him feel better. He had a much more powerful, and selfish reason. Once he let go, he was letting go of his life, Anu and Shruti along with it. There was no version of the future where he gets back to his life once he lets the monster out.

The mobile phone he discarded on the coffee table vibrated with an amplitude akin to the ringtone. He snatched it from the table and checked the number. Anu. For a split second, he toyed with the idea of coming clean. It would be such a load off his chest. But then again, there was no going back from that.

The phone vibrated in his hands, the screen lit up with Anu's photograph, looking up at him, expectantly. Manas just couldn't bring himself to swipe on the pulsating call icon. He stared at it for a couple more seconds and let the phone slip out of his hand. It bounced off the carpet and rested face down; silently blinking.

"You gonna pick that up?" Prateek took a seat and stretched his legs.

"And tell her what? That I messed up? That her daughter is being tortured by a madman?"

"Fair point," said Prateek. He leaned forward and rubbed his temples. "So, what about tomorrow?"

Tomorrow. The day Alex set for his final task. He and Prateek had gone to Rajashekharan's house earlier in the day. They canvassed the place from all angles, casually talked to some people around there, and got an idea of his daily routine. What Alex wanted was far from an easy task.

"I am not sure, Prateek. His goondas guard him and the place all the time. We would need at least a couple of days to find a suitable entry point."

"Let's not waste time talking about things we don't have. It has to be tomorrow. Can you get me near him? I'll handle the rest."

Manas knew that but getting him there was the challenge. He paced the room like a caged animal. The house was guarded 24x7 by his goondas. Servants were another complication. The only people allowed inside were the people vetted by the goondas at the entry gate. And the walls surrounding the place were high. "I don't know Manas. Let's go there tomorrow and wing it. Something might turn up or we'll improvise. By force or wit, I'll get it done. I'll get you close to him." He stopped by the window and cast a lazy glance across the silent night.

"We never used to wing it, brother. But if you say you'll get me there; I know you'll get me there," Prateek said, slapping Manas in the back.

But Manas barely registered it. He was studying an unmarked vehicle jutting out from behind a wall down the street. The second-floor window he was looking out of provided him with an excellent vantage point as he scanned the street. A man in a plain white shirt and a dark pants sauntered up the street, towards his house. Manas traced his path to his house and beyond and saw another man moving towards his house from the other side. He buried his head in the mobile phone in his hands, but his trajectory was steady. There was something amiss, but Manas was just not able to put his fingers to it. But his gut screamed foul.

At first glance, they seemed natural; just a couple of guys headed somewhere. But the man in plain shirt was too relaxed, in almost forced carefree manner. The other man was too focused on the mobile screen. But what rang his alarms was the coordination between the two seemingly strangers.

Manas pushed away from the window and stormed across the room to the window on the other side. "We may have a problem." He hid behind the wall and peeked out to scan the approach to his backyard. Two silhouettes jumped up and down over the walls, converging on his house. One of those men stepped in and out of a beam of light. The reflected light off his face caught Manas' breath. He had seen that man before. The stocky figure of the man seemed to float above the ground as he moved towards the house. He was one of the cronies who hung back when Nasir came to him the day Shruti was kidnapped.

This is bad. There was a group of policemen converging on him from all directions. A part of him argued that they might be coming to deliver updates about Shruti. That was the part of him who also argued that Amrita's death and the subsequent mention of his name was a coincidence.

If they are covering all sides, they think he is a flight risk. Panic scratched its cold, scrawny claws down his spine.

"Prateek, something is not right."

Prateek's eyebrows shot up. "What is it?"

"A group of policemen are converging on the house."

"Why?"

"Damned if I know," shot back Manas. But as he finished the sentence, it dawned on him. "They know."

"They know what?"

"They know." Manas stepped back from the window, warmth drained from his face, along with the blood. "They must have figured out who I was, who we were." He racked his brain to find the link and it clicked. "The documents. It must be that. I made them in a hurry. Damn it. I wasn't expecting a background check. And why would I? The plan was to stay under the radar and live out the rest of the days."

Prateek held up both hands in a conciliatory gesture. "Let's not overreact. Maybe they just figured out the documents were not authentic and just want to talk to you."

"Don't be daft. You don't bring five to six men to 'talk'. You don't surround the house for a document fraud."

Manas rushed to the bedroom, pulled out a knapsack and stuffed a few shirts and pants in there. "There is no time to argue. We have to get out of here." He unplugged his computer and shoved it into the bag and bounded down the stairs. "I can't take a chance. Getting caught is simply out of the question, especially with my little girl at the hands of that maniac."

Manas reached the back door of his house and pushed open the door ever so slightly. Prateek joined him at his side, a hint of fear and excitement flickering across his face.. Manas peeked outside; it was clear. The policemen coming over the walls were still a couple of houses away.

"Stay low and follow me," he told Prateek as he creaked open the door and slipped out through the smallest possible opening. He stuck to the ground, dashed towards the wall at the far right of the house and flattened himself against the concrete, crouching. Peeking around the corner, he spotted the police converging at his house from all sides.

Prateek panted beside him. "Why don't we make a break for it?"

Manas shook his head and whispered, "There may be other policemen we don't know about. And there aren't many bushes or trees to cover us either."

"What are we gonna do?" A drop of sweat glimmered on Prateek's forehead. Manas had never seen him sweat; it was strange.

"The way I see it, we got only one play. They expect me to be in the house, completely unaware of their approach. They must be counting on the element of surprise at their side. We can try hiding here and hope they pass us unnoticed and into the house."

"I don't like how unsure you are of this."

"Got a better plan?" Manas waited for a couple of seconds and added, "Didn't think so." He crawled towards a bush thick and tall enough to hide him and Prateek, and as he did, he thanked Anu for taking up gardening as a hobby. The faint rustle of leaves as he squeezed in was so soft that it wouldn't have risen above the melodramatic crescendo of the evening soap from the neighbour's house. In the dark of the night, loud ragged breathing was all he could hear, apart from the dull thud of the blood in his ears. One wrong step and the game was over.

It was subtle at first, but as time went on, the footsteps became clearer. The swish of feet over dirt, the rustle of dried leaves crushing under solid boots, the thud of heavy feet landing over the walls. When they were closer, Manas could make out two separate sets of footsteps, but still they somehow felt like one; they felt like they moved in sync. Two soft thuds announced their final jump over the wall and into his compound.

Through the curtain of leaves, he studied the two stocky men who just landed like cats. The absence of a paunch was the first thing he noticed followed by the barrel chests. They were bulky, but not fat. They were the same policemen who came with Nasir the day his life went to shit.

The crackle of the radio was loud as the crack of a whip. *'Are you in position?'* it asked. The one with broad shoulders raised his beefy arms to the radio, buckled on his shoulder and responded with a short and curt 'yes'. He had a stupid grin plastered on his face, like a kid on Christmas eve. The other policeman, who was not as bulky, nodded his head. The plump face on his round skull was dead serious.

'Go,' crackled the radio.

The first policeman glanced at the other, raise his right hand to his forehead, as if he is shielding his eyes from a non-existing sun. The other policeman nodded with an OK sign as the former drew a pistol from his belt. He cocked the gun and pointed it downwards as he stepped closer to the kitchen door. When he reached within arms distance of the door, he stood back and gently tested the lock. In response the door swung open, silently. In the light which seeped out, Manas noted the frown in his eyebrows and the hesitation in his step. But he powered on, leaving the other policeman to guard the exit.

The second policeman started sweeping the back of the house, peeking behind and under places people could hide. This is not good. He expected both of them to enter the house so that he can slip out the back. He didn't want to attack the police and make things worse for him, but he needed to get out of here.

Manas glanced at Prateek, nodded his head, and slowly exited the bush he was hiding in. He crept along the ground on the balls of his feet towards the policeman. The policeman was clearing the storeroom which had nothing but some old tools and coconuts. Manas dashed across the open ground like a cat in the night and jumped behind a low bush closer to the storeroom. He landed with a soft thud, rolled instantly to avoid sound, and came up in a crouch. Counting down from three, he waited to make sure nobody was alerted. When the door to the storeroom swung open, he paused his breathing. The policeman stepped out and rounded the storeroom to clear the sides. *Perfect.* He still had his back towards Manas.

The perfect moment to launch an attack was almost as elusive as the Loch Ness Monster. The longer he waited, the farther the policeman was going. That means more open space to cover before reaching him. But if he jumped out too early, it would alert him of an imminent danger. Even the approach was tricky. It shouldn't be too slow so that the policeman turns back and sees him coming. Neither should it be too fast that it disturbs the night too much. The slightest change in the wind might be enough to tip off a trained person.

Manas was biding his time, waiting for the right moment, when the policeman swivelled towards the bathroom. *This was it.* It was the moment he was waiting for.

Manas bounded over the bush he was hiding behind and dashed across the open space, taking care to avoid stepping on dried leaves along the way. When he was two arm lengths from the policeman, he slowed down to a crawl and stopped breathing. The right hand formed into a thin karate chop and slipped in between the policeman's jaw and neck. Muscle memory took over and extended the hand all the way across the man's neck and hooked against the left bicep. At the same time his left hand closed in on the policeman from the other side and cupped his mouth. Without giving time to react, he tightened his shoulders and applied pressure to the man's neck, cutting off his blood supply to the brain. It hardly took a few seconds for the big man to collapse into a heap of muscle on the floor.

Manas surveyed the top floor and saw a silhouette walking across the upstairs window. He needed to get out of there. Prateek joined him, as they jumped over the wall and blended into the night. While he was getting away, only one thought ran in his mind. It was over. The house of cards he built for the last decade was uprooted, chewed, and spit up by the all-consuming hurricane of his past.

PART III

CATHARSIS

Redemption can be found in hell itself if that's where you happen to be.

– Lin Jensen

Manas

Monday, May 5, 2014

He was not a monster. But there was a monster in him and there was a difference.

Manas laid flat on his back, staring at the ceiling, contouring the fan and its dusty edges. Small, irregular lumps of cotton poked him in the back. This along with the bedbugs made sure he tossed and turned all night chasing after the ever-elusive sleep. It wasn't surprising. He didn't check in to The Taj; just some dingy little lodge in one of the crevices of Thampanoor, the heart of the city. One of those places where the business picks up at night and dwindles down by sunrise.

His eyes weighed a ton from the sleepless night. But it wasn't the bed bugs, the lumps in the mattress, or the amorous shouts through the thin walls that kept him up. It was the prospect of a new day in a new world. The world as he knew shattered to a million pieces last night.

Sunlight seeped in through a crack in the window, casting a sharp bright streak across the roof. It grew and spread its light-yellow hue all over the room. The blinding light hit a corner of the roof where the most beautiful spider web shimmered and shivered. In the far corner, a moth struggled against the sticky strands, wriggling to get free. But the more it struggled, the more tangled it became. In the ill-advised attempt to free itself, it sucked itself deeper and deeper into the web, sealing its fate. Within a few minutes, the moth was so entangled in the web that it stopped struggling, resigning to its fate; waiting for the spider to come and put it out of its misery.

Manas bolted upright in his bed. That was not going to be him. He may have gotten himself tangled in the web of his past, but he was not ready to roll over and give up. Instead of fighting against the current, it was time to swim with it.

Prateek snored lightly in the bed next to him. All the reasons Manas had to keep Prateek at bay had been shattered. The second Manas decided to flee from the police, he must have confirmed their suspicion. It was just a matter of time before they would go public with it. And everybody would know what a monster he was.

'Monster he was'.

Manas really wanted to keep that sentence in the past tense. But the sharp turn his life took the past few days made it an impossible aspiration to hold on.

He was not a monster. But there was a monster in him and there was a difference. Manas had taken pride in the fact that when he recognised the monster in him, he could hold it under lock and key all these years. But now the door rattled and bulged as the monster inside flexed his muscles. All of a sudden, the lock seemed flimsy. He could feel the monster shuddering under him, willing him to let go, to show him what it can do. But a part in him kept saying, *'You can never let go. Not after what it did and knowing what it will do.'* But that voice had grown weak. And in its place another stronger voice came up, urging him to let go and save his family, his daughter.

Manas kicked the sheets off and rose to his feet. He teetered into the dingy, claustrophobic bathroom. Brownish red stains of tobacco decorated the walls and the wash basin. He gingerly held the knob of the faucet with two fingers and turned it. It creaked open and water gurgled out. Manas cupped his hands, collected some water in them, and splashed it across his face. The water hit his face and rolled off it on to the floor. It felt good, and he did it again, and again, until he was standing in a puddle of water.

The spider can go to hell.

It was time to take off the leash from Prateek. But at what cost? How can he let him loose, fully knowing what he is capable of? How many more lives would he be adding to his already heavy burden?

No. He needed a fail-safe; a way to ensure he contains whatever comes out of the Pandora's box.

A figment of a plan took root in his brain. But before he could flesh it out, he heard a creak from the cot. Prateek must be up, he thought.

Manas grabbed the towel he hung on the door last night, wiped his face, and stepped out of the bathroom. Prateek sat at the edge of the bed, well rested and fresh.

"Time to go?" Prateek climbed to his feet and moved in front of a small mirror hanging from the wall.

Manas nodded his head as he crossed the room and dumped the towel on the empty bed. "We need to talk."

Prateek stopped midway through combing his hair, cocked his head to the side and looked at Manas through the mirror. "About?" he asked.

"We used to be a good team, weren't we?

Prateek turned back to face Manas. His eyes lit up with excitement as he reminisced. “We were the best. Your meticulous planning and my ruthless execution.”

Manas chuckled sadly. “I think I lost it. None of my plans seem to work now.”

“Nah, it’s not that. All the plans we had lately has been not yours. I made you do all those, and you know I suck at that.”

“And the execution mine because I didn’t let you. Because I wanted to be in control.” Manas sat down on the bed and stared at the ground. “I want to change that.”

Prateek stepped closer. “What do you mean?”

Manas looked up at Prateek’s eager face. “I mean let’s be our old selves and teach that son of a bitch who took my daughter a lesson.”

Manas

Monday, May 5, 2014

He had been running from his past all his life and it had finally caught up.

The weather was particularly fickle in Kerala. The sunlight which threatened to burn the skin off in the morning quickly turned into a thunderstorm. Manas was happy at the first thing that had gone his way in days. The rain gave him enough cover to move around the city. He was positively sure that by now his photographs would be all around the city, if not the state.

Manas paused at the doorway of the lodge and pulled on a black raincoat which covered him from head to toe, including his backpack. He tugged his cap down to cover more of his face as he stepped out of the lodge and onto the heavy downpour. A quick scan up and down the road reassured him that there were no police in sight. But that wasn't saying much as he couldn't see what's beyond a hundred feet on either side. He strode across the road when the vehicles eased up a bit and headed straight to the bus bay on the other side of the road. Prateek followed at his heels.

There was a direct bus to Pettah in sometime as his helpful neighbour at the lodge told him. The perpetual red eyes, wild hair, and the constant stench of marijuana from his room made him a safe target to talk to. Stoners are the least bit bothered what you are up to, and overly helpful. Although it took him a little short of fifteen minutes to remember the bus number, he had kept at it until he got it. In between he had offered Manas a hit, snacked on a few sweets, offered them to Manas, and even took a large bong shot himself. As soon as he extracted himself from the friendly, neighbourhood stoner, Manas had double checked the information on Google Maps. Just to be sure.

They didn't have to wait for long for the bus to show up. As soon as the bus slowed down, they jumped onto the bus and found a seat quickly. There was not a lot of people riding it because of the heavy rain. As soon as they settled in, Mans pulled out his mobile and keyed in the location Alex had given him. It was one of the side roads which branched out from the

Airport Road which cuts through Pettah. He pinched the screen to zoom in and turned on the satellite layer.

Prateek shifted closer to get a better look. As the satellite view loaded, a myriad of old and new roofs popped up from a sea of green. But one reddish brown sloped roof dwarfed the others around it and right on top of it, the red pin of the keyed in location rested.

When compared to the other buildings around it, Rajashekharan's house was huge with a lot of space around it enclosed by compound walls. Manas zoomed in further and pointed to one of the sides where a few trees sprouted right next to the walls. "We just have to hope that one of these trees have branches overhanging the compound. This might be our best bet."

Prateek nodded his head. "What about getting in through the front door? Some excuses or disguises?"

Manas shook his head. "That's not gonna happen. A man like that must have a lot of enemies. And round-the-clock security. You can't just waltz in."

"Even if we scale the walls like you said, wouldn't the goondas notice?"

"They will." Manas stared outside through the window at the city rushing past it. "I don't like this any more than you do. But we have run out of time."

After a short and silent bus ride, they reached the Pettah Bus Stop. Manas pulled back his raincoat, closed it up, and stepped out of the bus. The rain had lightened up a bit but was strong enough for him to pass off the raincoat as a necessity and not a disguise. He set up navigation on his mobile, shoved the earphones in place.

As you would expect on a rainy Sunday morning, the streets were empty except for an occasional car cruising along, or a motorbike rushing to find some cover.

"Turn left towards Puthan Road," crooned the lady from Google Maps, and they obliged.

Manas surveyed the street, taking it all in. It was a narrow street, fifty feet across. Houses of different shapes and sizes lined both sides of the road, but the road as such was empty. A few stray dogs wandered the streets, waging their own little war. He spotted the top of Rajashekharan's house just behind a curve in the road up ahead and marched towards it.

Even though his hearing was muted by his nervous heart pumping blood right into his ear, he heard a small din from around the curve. As he got closer, he saw people gathered in front of Rajashekharan's house. Anger and indignation hung in the air with people shouting slogans, unfazed by the rain. Red flags with a sickle, hammer and a star stuck to the poles on which they hung, dripping water. Some held up placards with messages in Malayalam. Manas strained to read them; he had mastered the linguistic part of the language, but the script was still hard to read. It took some time, but he figured out what the protests were about - misappropriation of ration.

Prateek raised an eyebrow as he tried to figure out what was happening. As Manas was explaining it to Prateek, a seed of a plan took root in Manas' mind. It was still not fool proof, but with the right kind of luck, it just may work. But before doing anything, he wanted to check something first.

With a quick flick of his hand, he gestured Prateek to follow him as we took the lane which wound around the sides of the compound; the place where they had seen a few trees growing along the compound wall. *Bingo.* Just as he hoped, one of the branches from one of the trees leaned closer to the wall, making it possible to scale the wall.

They circled back to the front of the house where the protests were raging on. It wasn't a big protest, probably 15-20 men and a couple of women. The leader was a young man, in his late twenties, with fire in his eyes. Leading from the front, he shouted slogan after slogan from his heart and the others followed. A few of Rajashekharan's goons stood guard at the gate, folded hands, and wide stances. The police were conveniently absent. Emotions ran high among the crowd, but the young leader kept them under control. But the atmosphere was tense, with both sides waiting for a provocation, and neither of them giving the other side one.

Manas picked up a stone and held it against his side as he blended into the crowd, rallying the slogans, and becoming one among the crowd. The stone was heavier than he expected and was getting heavier by the minute. But he had to make a diversion. When he managed to drift to the back of the protests, he yelled in the best Malayalam he could manage, "*Poyi thulayeda Rajashekhara* (Go to hell Rajashekharan)," and hurled the stone at the goons guarding the gate.

There was a moment of pause as the stone flew across the crowd and hit a goon smack on his temple. He went down like a sack of potatoes, holding his head. And soon pandemonium broke loose as the agitated protesters took up Manas' cry and started hurling stones at the house.

The other goons rushed to their fallen co-worker and some of them called for reinforcements. A lot more goons rushed out of the house, they pushed open the gates and poured out into the crowd, smashing everyone to bits.

Manas and Prateek slipped out the back during the melee and made their way to the side of the house, with the tree.

A huge, stupid grin was plastered across Prateek's face, but Manas didn't care for it. They were only one tenth of the way there, and there were still a million things that could go wrong.

Manas scaled the tree, hung off the overhanging branch, and jumped feet first into the compound. He landed on the balls of his feet and rolled forward to absorb the momentum. Prateek followed suit, in stealth, and they both huddled behind a low bush. Manas knew they had to move and move fast. The scuffle out front won't last forever, he thought as he stripped the raincoat and hid it in the bush.

The house itself was a grand re-imagining of the traditional Kerala architecture, with verandas all around the house and multiple entrances from all sides. It was perfect. There must be an open courtyard in the middle of the house as well, Manas thought. The back entrance would be bustling with cooks and caretakers of the place. So that was out of the question. So was the front entrance. It would be too conspicuous.

Manas darted across the open space between the bush they were hiding behind and the building, with Prateek at his heel. Without missing a beat, he jumped on to the veranda and kept going straight to the ornately carved teak wood door, one of the side entrances. His heart was beating fast. If anyone saw them now, it would be game over. He crouched in front of the door and pushed it open, gently. The door offered no resistance as it swung inwards. He grabbed it and opened it just enough to peek inside.

As expected, there was an open courtyard in the middle of the space with a Tulsi plant flourishing in a raised platform. An inner veranda circled the open courtyard which served as pathways to the different rooms arranged around the courtyard. On the opposite side of the courtyard, Manas spied a staircase which headed upstairs. If Rajashekharan had a private quarters, it would be upstairs.

The courtyard was deserted, with everyone gathered out front to either watch or participate in the scuffle. Manas pushed open the door and darted across the courtyard to the foot of the stairs and paused to catch his breath. He needed to control it if he was going to hear above it.

They sneaked up the stairs, one step at a time, and paused on the landing to take stock of the situation. The stairs ended in an open area, a large carpet laid out in the middle of the room and a few furniture arranged around it. It was obviously a space which served as a living room for guests. An ornate wooden window straight ahead was the primary source of illumination, but currently most of it was blocked by a well-built man, looking outside through the window.

Manas crept up the stairs, as stealthily as he could, and made it closer to the window. The man was so engrossed in the ruckus out front. Manas slowly reached from behind and put him in a chokehold, cutting off his breath and blood. Within a few seconds, the big man collapsed and Manas guided him down to make the least bit of noise. He grabbed the rope and cloth from his backpack and tied the man up, with a cloth shoved in his mouth firmly.

"We can't leave him here," said Prateek.

Manas nodded and pushed him under the largest *diwan* in the room. The rich velvet cloth which covered the diwan extended to the floor.

There were rooms opening on both sides. The rooms on the floor were laid out like a garland around the central open courtyard. It was like one long room but broken into many sections. Like a video game with different levels to clear before the boss fight. He had to choose a side and he chose the right side, at random.

Prateek came up behind and asked, "What if there are more of these guys?"

"Highly unlikely," said Manas as he stepped into the adjacent room. "But even if there is, I'm sure we can handle-"

Manas stopped mid-sentence and gaped at the contents of the room. It was a pure display of wealth. There was no other point to the room apart from shoving the fact that he had money in the faces of his guests. The centre piece of the room was a full-length ivory tusk, with an intricately carved golden base. It held its head high in the middle of the room, a soft light burning on top of it, providing it the spotlight it deserves. The walls were lined with traditional *Kalari* weapons, but all in pure gold. Swords, armour, shields, *urumi* and knives of different sizes and shapes glimmered on the wall. Rajashekharan was wealthier than he had thought initially.

Manas shook the luxury from his mind and powered on to the next room. Some call it a den, some call it a man cave, but that was what the next room was about. A tall bar rose from a beige suede leather carpet. The liquor cabinet behind had the most exquisite collection of liquor ranging from Old Monk's, Jameson's, to Glenlivet's and Johnnie Walker Blue Label's. A leather recliner sofa rested close to the bar, with a few other chairs or diwans peppered around the space. A billiards table laid low under the sheets, with a light, which was switched off, hanging above. Quick scan of the room told him it was empty. As much as he liked to linger around, he had a job to do. So, he pushed on through and reached the other side. This was the first room he had come across with a door, and that too a closed one. He was close and he knew it.

Manas pushed the door, and it swung inward, silently. He was at the boss level. The largest room he had seen till then was big enough for a king size cot, and ornate study table, and a leather couch facing the 50-inch TV that hung on the wall. The boss sat at the study table, looking out the window, away from the door and unaware of his visitors.

"I promised you I would get you here," whispered Manas. "It's all you now, but I'm stepping out."

Manas retreated into the man cave just as silently as he came. The last thing he saw before the door closed on him was Prateek putting Rajashekharan in a headlock, with his one arm across his mouth. He didn't like what was happening inside, but it was what needed to be done.

It didn't take long before the door opened again, and Prateek stepped out. His hair matted against his skull, blood dripping from his hands onto the beige carpet. The eyes darted in his sockets with wild abandon and his mouth twitched with rapture. "It's done," he announced.

Manas bit back the bile gurgling in his mouth. There it was, their first kill in twenty years. He handed Prateek a change of clothes. Prateek was still flush from the exercise. There was a spark in his eyes; something wild inside him shook the dust off its body and rose to its feet. Manas had no idea how to tame that beast.

Prateek quickly changed out of the blood-soaked clothes and shrugged into a fresh paid of clothes.

The job was only half done and there wasn't much time left. The commotion out front had all but subsided. Manas peeked out of the nearest window and saw the goons dispersing and returning to their positions. Manas quickly unzipped his backpack and extracted a can of kerosene. He unscrewed the cap and splashed it all around as they made their way back to the staircase.

When they were at the open space near the staircase, Prateek fished out a lighter from his pocket and met Manas' eyes. What he saw in those eyes, scared Manas. But he shook it off and nodded his head and Prateek tossed the lighter into the Kerosene-soaked carpet. The whole room went up in flames as soon as the lighter hit the wet carpet.

Fire has a unique sense of fairness. It is as ruthless to the rich as it is to the poor. Orange flames rose out of the sea of fire and licked the ivory centre piece, each lick leaving a trail of black soot. The intricate carving on the base was reduced to a mere black band of burning metal. *Kalari* weapons along the walls lost the glimmer as the fire licked them dull.

Manas knew they had to move as the fire would attract a lot of attention. But Prateek stood rooted to his spot, mesmerised by the fire; a dark glaze in his eyes. Manas had to pull Prateek from where he stood and drag him to the staircase. Just as they were about to start down the stairs, Manas heard a flurry of footsteps clamouring up the stairs.

Damnit! There were too late already.

Manas quickly backtracked, pulling Prateek along with him, their way and slipped into the room on the other side of the raging fire. The footsteps rushed towards the fire and burst into a cacophony of panic. After a few seconds of panic, one of them took charge. He ordered the rest of the men to get buckets of water while he himself volunteered to get the fire extinguisher from downstairs.

Manas bid his time, counting the seconds to get out of there. It was only a matter of time before they realise someone was in the house and he had to get out before that. From behind the almirah he was hiding behind, he heard a few footsteps rushing past him and into the bathrooms. This was his chance. Manas and Prateek jumped out from behind the almirah, and darted downstairs. A quick peek down the stairs from the landing showed nobody in the courtyard. Without wasting one more second, they rushed to the side entrance, the way they came in and pulled open the door.

As soon as the door was open, Manas charged outside and bumped into a mammoth of a man, with an extinguisher in his hands. The man absorbed all the momentum Manas had with ease as he recovered from the shock of the collision. And as soon as he did, comprehension dawned on his face, he dropped the extinguisher and grabbed Manas by his neck with both hands.

Manas' training kicked in and he raised both his hands in front of him and brought them back towards his neck, grabbing the palms of the big man on the way back. And with one swift motion, he plucked the chokehold and landed a kick to the man's groin. He went down like a sack of potato. Manas stepped over the man and ran for the wall. Prateek was right behind him as they both climbed the wall, jumped onto the other side. The moment his feet hit the ground, he took off putting distance between him and the melee. But the thing he was really running away from was right at his heel, smiling at him, still giddy with happiness. He had been running from his past all his life and it had finally caught up.

Nasir

Monday, May 5, 2014

We are the gatekeepers who keep the dark from the light, and we never give up.

Sonam twisted her bangs in between her fingers as she pored over the case file. They didn't have an opportunity to talk about what happened between them. Nasir had been pole to post since last night without a moment to spare. But there seemed to have an implicit understanding between them to brush it under the carpet until things slow down.

Salim sat at the table fiddling with the oversized cervical collar he got from the hospital last night. They had found him unconscious behind Manas' house after the raid last night and rushed him to the hospital. They assured that there was no lasting injury, just a sprained neck. But they stuck him with a cervical collar, just in case.

Akshay walked in the door. His dark circles spread out from under his eyes threatening to swallow his face. Salim turned his whole body to see who was at the door, a hand holding his neck.

Nasir scanned the room; it was a full house, at least physically. It was day 13 without any results; six days since Shruti was kidnapped. And to pile it on a twenty-six-year-old case had surfaced with all its ugliness. They needed a pick-me-up, and they needed it now.

Nasir cleared his throat, more to catch the attention of the room than anything, as he rose to his feet and faced the team.

"I know things look rough right now. It's been an uphill climb ever since we started this, with nothing we can call a win." The heads which hung limply from the necks rose as they focused on Nasir. "But you all know the drill. This is just how police work is. It's not glamorous as the movies would have you believe. It's a lot of grunt work with nothing but the satisfaction that you might save a life at the end of it all. We bang our heads against a thousand doors in the hope that at least one open. And when it doesn't, we buckle up and head for the next door. We never give up." The droopy shoulders in the room straightened up. "We bleed without a second thought for people who don't give two hoots about what we do. We are the gatekeepers who keep the dark from the light, and we never give up. The eyes which stared at him grew sharp, with a new intensity in them.

"And right now, there is a mad man out there who needs to be stopped...," Nasir paused a second before continuing. "We have all seen it happen; one small piece of evidence, an overlooked fact, a subtle lie in a testimony, that's all it takes to overturn a case. And we are going to find it, no matter what. Because the buck stops with us."

By now the energy levels in the room had gone through the roof. Avinash banged his hands on the table and rose to his feet.

Akshay grabbed a copy of the case file from the table. "Let's go through the facts once again."

Sonam, who was already buried in a copy of the file, pushed up her specs, rose to her feet and marched to the drawing board. She drew a small circle, shaded it, and wrote '29th April' next to it. "Let's start with Shruti's kidnapping. Two days after we landed in Trivandrum."

She scribbled on the board with the blue marker as she spoke. "Three leads we got from the location are: the dirt we scraped off the ground, an eyewitness, and an SD card which supposedly contained a recording of the act. We have sent the dirt to the labs for analysis and haven't got back the results yet." She raised her hands in a gesture of admission. "That's on me." She put a star next to it and wrote her name next to it. "From the eyewitness, we got the make of the car and the description of the abductor which led us to Alex. The SD card was a bust. It was damaged beyond recovery." Sonam crossed out the item on the board.

"Shruti's SIM was tracked till Pettah, where it went off the grid," said Akshay.

Nasir glanced at Avinash. "Remember the time we went to see Manas?"

"Of course. It all makes so much more sense now that we know he is not who he said he was."

"Sonam, did we check the dried blood we found at Manas' place?" asked Nasir.

"The one we scraped off the living room furniture?"

"That's the one. He told us he cut himself when we saw him last."

Sonam shook her head. "That was not human blood. It was canine."

"Hmmm.... nothing is just fitting right." Nasir turned towards Salim. "When we were there, he sold us some bullshit story about Alex reaching his destination in the next twenty minutes and he deduced a possible area on the map where we could find Alex." He pulled out his mobile and searched the gallery for the snap he had taken that day.

"Even though I had dismissed it as a desperate father grabbing at straws to keep his sanity, maybe it was more," said Nasir. "What if Alex had called him after he had kidnapped his daughter?"

"Entirely possible," said Akshay. "May be that is what is different about this from The Artist's usual *modus operandi*. Maybe he wants something from Manas."

"Let's not forget about the note The Artist left after his first kill in the recent string of murders. It was made out to be a tribute to the Butcher. There is definitely something cooking between the two of them," added Nasir, still scrolling his gallery.

He finally found the snap and cast it on to the projector for everyone to see. "I know we have given this area an extra focus, but I think we should divert all our resources into this area now." It was a risky move, and he knew it. But he had to do something, and he had a good feeling about this. "I want our guys to comb through this area, look under every stone, and bring me results."

Akshay gave a sharp nod as he left the room with his phone to his cheek.

"And Sonam, get that damned report. Sit on their head, abuse them, do whatever it takes to get it. I'll deal with the consequences."

She nodded in tacit agreement.

"And Manas?" asked Salim.

"Do we have a trace on his mobile?" asked Sonam

When Avinash shook his head from side to side, it didn't come as a surprise to Nasir. Manas was smart enough to realise it can be tracked. "I have a feeling that if we catch one, we will find the other," said Nasir. "But I think we should focus on Alex. Whatever Manas had done was twenty years ago and never heard a peep out of him ever since. He is not a clear and present danger."

Akshay walked back into the room mid-sentence. "Hold that thought. The Commissioner just called me. There was a murder and arson at Pettah."

"We have much bigger fish to fry. I'm sure this can wait-"

"The victim was beheaded, and the house was set on fire," cut in Akshay.

Beheaded. It rang all kinds of alarms in Nasir's head. Beheading was the calling card of The Butcher of Bhalswa. It changed everything.

Nasir shot up to his feet. "Akshay, co-ordinate the search of the area," he barked. "And Sonam, the report. I want it yesterday. Avinash, Salim, you're with me. Where is the murder site, Akshay?"

Nasir opened the door, jumped out of the car, and slammed it shut before it came to a stop. Avinash and Salim followed closely at his heel as he strode into the house at full tilt.

Death was all over the house. People gathered around the house in groups, hushed silence prevailed. A few female voices cried out from inside the house, bereaving the departed soul. Your life is only yours till you die. Then it is inherited by the living; the memories that you left behind, the grief over the void you left. After death, you are just baggage that the people who care about you carry around.

Nasir brushed past death and rushed into the house, flashing their badges to gain entry. He hoped the police had done enough to preserve the crime scene. But then he really didn't need to examine the crime scene to know if it was The Butcher's work. A policeman standing guard in the open courtyard in the middle of the house pointed them upstairs. Nasir ducked under the yellow police line, which stretched across the bottom of the stairs barring their entry to the second floor.

A policeman stood on the landing of the stairs. His khaki uniform was freshly cleaned and pressed, the badge shining on his shoulder. "I'm Sub Inspector Sharath Raghavan," said the policeman, a smile decorating his young face. "You must be Nasir... the Commissioner told me to expect you." He launched into a salute.

Nasir nodded in acknowledgement. Obviously, a new recruit. The salutes were always too stiff and eager in the beginning. "Avinash and Salim-", said Nasir, pointing towards them, "-both in my team. Can we see the scene?"

"Of course," said Sharath. "But I must warn you, the fire might have destroyed a lot of the evidence. We have saved everything we can."

Nasir's heart pumped blood in overdrive as they climbed the rest of the stairs. All he needed to see was the body. He had seen enough of them to know The Butcher's work.

Sharath led the way through a blackened corridor; the walls and roof were charred by fire. They passed a couple of rooms, each room opening into the next and paused at the door at the end. Sharath turned to face them and said, "It… might not be easy to digest what's beyond the door. My breakfast almost jumped up my throat when I saw it."

Nasir exchanged a brief glance with Akshay and Salim, before nodding sombrely.

Sarath pushed and the door swung open. A slightly charred head hung from the ceiling, swinging slightly in the wind from the open window. It was as if somebody punched Nasir in the gut and chased all the air out. He didn't have to see anything else to be sure this was the work of The Butcher. The public display of the head of his victims was his trademark.

Nasir stepped inside. The blood splatters along the walls were charred black by the fire. But some red remained. The reds and blacks intertwined in making this into a nightmare more suited in the dreamscape than reality. He waded deeper into the dream and knelt beside the headless body and examined the cuts on the neck. The hack wounds were clean and with that the last hope that it would be a copycat impersonation went out the window. The job was not an amateur one. It needs practise to make such clean cuts, and the Butcher had much more practice than anyone else.

But one thing bothered him- the fire. It was never The Butcher's M.O. But the rest of it was. Suddenly his legs weren't strong enough to hold his weight. Avinash moved closer and offered a hand. Nasir took it gratefully and rose to his feet, biting down the bile that threatened to spill out. The quicksand he was trapped in for the last few days stirred and started gobbling him up at a faster rate. His descent into decadence at the wake of the Butcher's disappearance flashed before his eyes. A single drop of sweat collected and rolled off his temple, travelling down the side of his face, tickling him along the way.

Out of the corner of his eye, Nasir saw Sharath coming up to him, poised to ask something. However helpful it would be, it was not the time. He closed his eyes hoping he would go away. But he heard Avinash's voice instead, asking Sharath about some trivial detail and distracting him. *Thank you, Avinash.*

The shit just hit the fan and they were caught without an umbrella. Now he had not one, but two serial killers roaming around the city in some sick and twisted game of one-upmanship. The rest were just caught in the crossfire, collateral damage.

"This stops now," murmured Nasir, bolting back the way they came in. Avinash and Salim followed closely as they exited the building, jumped into the jeep, and slammed the doors shut. The tyres screeched and burned as they pulled out onto the traffic as they headed back.

Manas

Monday, May 5, 2014

Motives are not always black and white.

Manas leaned on the glass window of the bus, looking out into the empty streets. Rain had picked up again and reigned king as humanity ran for cover. He ran his hands through his forehead, feeling every burrow and bumps on it. He needed the distraction. Every time he closed his eyes, Rajashekharan's head floated around in his mind, blood dripping from all cavities. Prateek relived every excruciating detail of his adventure on the ride back. And all through that, only one thought ran through Manas' mind - What monster have I unearthed from my past?

There was a time when he had thought Prateek wanted to help him because he cared for him, for Shruti. But motives are not always black and white. While Prateek did love Shruti, she was not the complete picture.

And he could feel Prateek getting stronger by the hour. Manas recognized the pattern all too well. But last time it happened over months, or even years. There wasn't much time left before Manas would lose control.

The rain lashed out against the window, sending small vibrations up through his jawbone. The inkling of the plan which he conceived that day morning came back to his mind. It could work, but there would be no coming back from that. No happily ever after. He chuckled at his naivete. That ship had sailed long ago.

It hurt him to think about not seeing Anu again, not running his fingers through her rippling dark cloud of hair. The police must have already told Anu about him. Manas could not imagine how she must be feeling. The man she fell in love with and married was a murderer. She must be blaming herself for not seeing the signs or allowing herself to be duped by such a vile man. A sudden warmth filled his eyes. Manas wanted to talk to her; needed to. If he owed an explanation to anyone in the world, it was to Anuradha.

A quick swipe of his eyes with his fingers cleared up the blurriness. He cleared his throat and turned to Prateek. "Listen, can you do me a favour?"

"After what you pulled in there? Anything my brother. Anything."

"Well, it's nothing major. I need to talk to Anu."

"That's it? You want me to distract the police while you sneak in?"

"No, no. Going to her parents' house is suicide. The police would be staking the place out. I was thinking of giving her a call from one of the payphones on the road."

"Alright, we'll get down at the next stop, make the call, and then head back."

"Err.... Actually, I need to talk to her alone. I may never see her again, but I wanted to try and explain everything to her."

Prateek sat back and stroked his chin as he thought about it. "OK," he said, breaking the short silence. "You get down at the next stop. I'll continue. Will meet you back at the lodge?"

"Perfect, thank you, brother," said Manas, and he meant it. Manas got to his feet and signalled the conductor to stop the vehicle.

As soon as he stepped out of the bus, on instinct, he reached into his pockets for his mobile phone. But he withdrew his hands when he was startled by the unfamiliar phone in his pocket. Then it came back to him. He took out the sim and turned off his mobile phone the moment he began his run; but not before setting up an auto-forward to the new number. He needed the number as it was the only way Alex would be contacting him. He just hoped the additional layer of re-routing would buy him enough time before Nasir figures it out.

The burner phone in his pocket was his only contact into the outside world and he still needed that. Anu's phone will be tapped, and any calls, especially from him will be traced in a matter of minutes. That's why he got down well ahead of his hideout, so that even if the call is traced, he can slip out and take shelter in his dingy lodge.

Manas spied a yellow board, with PCO written on it in big block letters, across the road. Exactly what he wanted, a public telephone. He crossed over to the other side of the road, inserted a few coins into the slot, picked up the receiver and dialled Anu's number.

"Hello...," came the sweet voice after two rings. It was the best thing that had happened to him in days. The sheer emotions overwhelmed him, snapped shut his mouth.

"Hello…," asked Anu again.

Manas wanted to answer, but he had no idea what to say or where to start.

After a brief pause, Anu asked," Manas?"

The silence extended, begging to be put out of its misery. But no one spoke.

"Tell me it isn't true, Manas."

"I… I can't do that."

"Give me one reason why I shouldn't call the police right now." Anu broke into a sob. It broke Manas' heart. "How did I miss it? I should have seen the signs."

"You didn't miss anything because there wasn't anything to miss, Anu. The Manas who was with you, that wasn't an act." Manas bit his lip to arrest the slight quiver on them. "What you heard is a part of my life from which I've been fleeing when I came to Trivandrum. But it has finally caught up with me and took our daughter hostage. I am sorry, Anu. I really am."

"How could you kill all those people, Manas?"

"You deserve an explanation… I know that Anu. It's why I called you today."

"The police gave me a pretty good explanation of what you did. All the while I was listening to it, I was waiting for them to realise it was a goof up and say that my husband is not a serial killer. Even now, I was hoping you would tell me it's wrong. I don't think I can take any more today."

"All I am asking is for ten minutes. Just hear me out. I know I don't deserve it, but please."

The silence on the other end of the line gave him a tacit go-ahead.

"There is no easy way to say it, but I have what the doctors call dissociative identity disorder or multiple personality disorder. It all started back when I was a kid, and my uncle-"

Knock, Knock

Manas took a deep breath to clear out his mind and normalise the rising blood pressure. "I'm sorry, Anu. It's hard to talk about it. Let me try again. Two personalities have made my body its home - one is the man you know and the other calls himself Prateek. And what I have is a peculiar form of dissociative disorder where I physically see my other personality as a separate person. Alternate identities take form in people when they face situations which they can't handle or deal with themselves. And mine was my uncle."

Knock, Knock, Knock!

"My uncle, who used to visit home very often, had a habit of creeping into my room when everybody slept and take advantage of me. And this uncle was one of the closest relatives we had in Delhi. Everybody loved him. So, I couldn't talk about this to anyone else. And it continued for little close to a year and it was becoming unbearable. It was then that Prateek appeared for the first time.

"How the disorder manifests in me is that I can see and talk to Prateek all the time. But there are a few times when Prateek completely takes over. In such times, I would be completely disassociated from my body, somehow paralysed, helpless. But I see and hear everything."

Manas paused for a second. Anuradha had been silent all this time, and he really wanted to hear from her. But the silence stretched on when he realised it's not going to happen. "The first time Prateek took over completely, he killed my uncle. But I was okay with it. After all that man deserved it, I thought. I even helped get rid of the body and nobody found out about that. Not even the police. And after that, things got better. I was happy and I gave all that credit to Prateek. He stayed and became my friend, brother, and more."

Manas leaned on the flimsy enclosing of the phone booth which gave him an illusion of privacy. "Prateek was all but dormant all through my childhood. Apart from one or two occasions, he never took over. But he was there for me all through those years. And then I grew up and ventured out into the big bad world. That's when it started to go bad."

"That's when the murders started?" asked Anuradha.

It was comforting to hear that resonant voice. Manas closed his eyes and pictured her loving face with those kind eyes. "Yes, in a way. You know why I involve in all those NGOs? I hate people taking advantage of the downtrodden using money and power. But back then, I didn't have that clarity of thought. I saw oppression all around and had the most irresistible urge to do something about it. And we did."

"So, are you saying those people deserved it?"

"Back then, I used to believe so. Prateek always had an uncanny ability to convince me of anything. And somehow, he convinced me that killing people who abuse their power and take advantage of the poor was the only way to restore the balance. Our own sick way of 'sticking it to the man'. Once we identify the target, I would plan the whole thing and Prateek would do that actual killing."

"It was still you, Manas." Anuradha's voice was cold, but strands of warmth laid hidden beneath the clear diction.

"Yes, it was, and that is something that eats me alive every second of my life. I'm not telling you all this to justify what I've done. No. Not at all. I was as much a part of those murders as Prateek. Hell, we are the same person in the eyes of the world. But why I want to tell you all this is for you to better understand. To have closure. I think I owe you that."

"Hmmm."

"It started out well. We became really good at covering our tracks. But soon I started noticing something. Prateek was getting a lot more say in the decisions we make and most of them started to be misaligned with the way I see things. And that stirred up some issues. It soon escalated to a point when he did something that really upset me. That's when the fog cleared, and I realised that it can't go on like this. I needed to take control of my life and I did.

"I did two things. Packed up my bags and moved to the farthest place possible to turn a new leaf, away from the madness, away from the gore. And that's how I moved to Trivandrum. And at the same time, with the sheer will of mind, I exiled Prateek into a deep corner of my mind. The physical representation of Prateek was no more, but he was still in some corner of my mind. He would still talk to me, but I ignored it. It soon turned to pleading, the threats and finally outbursts of anger. I didn't have sleep for months after and I missed him dearly. But I stuck to ignoring him because I was scared what he was capable of if he comes back.

"A few months passed and one fine day, the voices were no more. All that was left was a void, I didn't know how to fill. Prateek was such an important part of my life that I started remembering him every corner I turn. That's when I met you."

Manas switched the receiver from one hand to the other. "You were an angel who walked into my life at the right time. You gave me purpose, rooted me in reality, and helped me manage my condition. I read up on all literature about my condition and figured out ways to keep it under the wraps. And then came Shruti, and by then I was a hundred percent confident that I would not see Prateek again, and that I can have a normal life. I was doing just that, and what a wonderful life we had. But all that changed when Alex paid me a visit. You may know him as The Artist."

"The same mad man who took our daughter?"

"The same. There was only one person in the world who knew I moved to Trivandrum. Just one. It was a girl I was involved with at that time, Amrita. And as luck would have it, Alex figured out where I was when he... when he killed Amrita. It was all over the news, and it shook me to the core. It was the first hint of the dark past wrapping its cold, clammy hands around me."

"That was why you were acting weird all week?"

"Yeah. I was scared shitless. And as Alex travelled across the country to Trivandrum, killing all along the way, I was losing my mind. And one day Alex knocked on our door and started talking about The Butcher and how he considered him to be his guardian angel. I didn't know what to do and so I acted like I had no idea what he was talking about. Just hoped he would go away, but instead he… he took our daughter. I guess it was his way of grabbing my attention. He called me the day Shruti was taken to let me know that she is safe and will be as long as I go along with what he says."

"You could have just told this to the police."

"I almost did. Two things stopped me. One was that Alex told me specifically not to call the police. The way I thought, if I just went along with what he had in mind, Shruti would be safe. But if he knew that I went to the police… I didn't want to take that chance. And the second is that there was no way I could have told all this to the police without letting them know who I was. And that meant letting go of you, Shruti, and the life I have here. I know it was selfish but I was not ready for that. So, I decided I'll try to handle this on my own.

"Well, not alone. The day Shruti was taken, I was freaking out when Prateek appeared; and he stayed. I tried to manage without him, Anu. I really did. But the things Alex wanted me to do…." A sob gurgled up from his stomach. "He made me kill Bella, Anu."

"What? You killed Bella?" The voice on the other end of the line caught on something. "How could you Manas? You loved that dog, we all loved her."

"It was one of the hardest thing I had to do, Anu. But it was Bella or Shruti and I chose our daughter. But I was not able to go through with it and finally, Prateek stepped in to help me."

There was a long silence at the other end. Manas could hear her shallow breaths becoming longer. He pictured her wiping the tears rolling down her eyes, and breathing deep to regain composure; like he had seen her do hundreds of times.

"This Prateek. Is he with you now?"

"No, I asked him for some privacy. Told him I want to talk to you one last time, alone."

There was a moment of silence. "What… What do you mean? One last time?" The tone of her voice changed, like some switch was thrown inside her head.

Manas breathed deep. "Let's face it, Anu. There are somethings you can't undo. There is no going back to the life we had after this. It's the end of the line for me."

Sometimes silence has more syllables than any word. And the silence which spread out over the phone at that moment was heartbreakingly sombre.

"But before I go, I want to make sure I right the wrongs I have done in my life. I'm gonna get Shruti back and leave the world a safer place for her. I can't have a maniac like Prateek roam around taking lives. But at the same time, I do need him to save our little girl. I may have figured out a way out of this dilemma, but there is no coming back from it, Anu."

"No, there must be some other way. You can talk to the police."

"I will, Anu. I'll talk to the police. But as for me, it's either a lifetime in prison, or death. There is no version of the future with you and Shruti. And that is a future I don't care to have. So, I don't really care what happens to me now, as long as you and Shruti are safe."

The silence that settled around the conversation was broken by the silent sobs from the other side of the line. It broke Manas' heart all over again. This was it. The last time he would hear her voice; the voice which gave him strength, the voice that guided him through the treacherous path of life. He felt a wave of emotion lashing out at him, breaking the fickle, strong facade he had put up for Anuradha.

"Manas," said Anuradha. "You should know the call is being traced. Get out of there."

"I know, Anu." Manas caught a sliver in his voice, betraying his emotions. "So, this is goodbye, my love. I promise I'll get our daughter safely back in your arms."

"I know you will. Just one more thing, Manas." Anuradha's voice softened. It was the voice she used on those lazy Sunday mornings, cuddling up in bed with Manas. "You are a good man, Manas. And I don't regret falling in love with you."

Hot tears streamed down Manas' face. "When I'm gone, remember me like that. And not as the monster you will see in the newspapers." He slammed the phone back on the cradle and wiped his eyes on his sleeve.

There wasn't time to linger. He had talked much longer than he intended to and had to get out of there as soon as possible. A bus passed by him, slowing down at a bump in the road. Manas ran and jumped onto the bus and boarded it. It didn't matter where it went, as long as it was away from there. He had one more call to make.

Manas got down after three stops and found another pay phone. He fished out a business card from his wallet and punched in the number.

It rang for a few seconds, and then a thin neutral voice answered.

"Hi, this is Manas."

"Manas?"

"Let's cut the crap, Nasir. I know you have people headed to the last trace location. I also know you are tracing this call right now. So, we both know I have very little time. All I am asking is ten minutes to explain myself."

There was a long silence on the line, after which Nasir replied, "Ten minutes."

Manas retold the entire story right for his childhood to the point where he was making the call to Nasir. And when he stopped, there was just silence on the line.

"Believe me when I say this," said Manas. "I don't want Prateek out in the world any more than you do. But I want to save my little girl and for that I must maintain the charade that I'm still playing Alex's game."

"Why should I believe anything you say? Now that you have your back against a corner, and now you want a way out."

"You don't have to. You said it yourself. It is only a matter of time before you catch me. And I'm not trying to negotiate my way out of this. All I am asking is for some time."

"Time to do what?"

"To save my daughter."

Nasir breathed out audibly and the words that came next were much softer. "Manas, you come in, and I promise you I will do everything in my power to save your daughter. This is the word of an honest policeman."

"That is exactly why I called you. But I can't come in yet. I am the only bait that Alex will bite, and I intend to keep it in water for as long as possible."

"Listen, we are really close to figuring out where Alex is. We are spreading the net and raking everything in. There is no need for a bait anymore."

"I'm sorry, Nasir. I know you can't guarantee my daughter's safe return. Hell, no one can. I made a promise to my wife that I would get our daughter back safely, and I intend to do just that." Manas cradled the receiver in between his neck and checked his watch. He didn't have much time left. "Listen, I have a plan to save my daughter as well as take care of the Prateek problem."

Nasir let out a hard laugh, almost a bark. "No, you aren't going to slip through my fingers one more time."

"One more time?"

"Oh, you don't know? When you were marauding your way through Delhi, I was leading the team handling your case."

"Well… I'm sorry, I had no idea. Like I told you, I didn't leave Delhi to slip through your fingers. And no, I am not going to slip through your fingers again. In fact, what I propose is the exact opposite."

"I'm listening."

"Me and Prateek are more like the brain and brawn of the entity you know as "The Butcher of Bhalswa". Without me, Prateek is just a violent psychopath who wears his heart on his sleeves. I'm going to let Prateek take the lead up until I get my daughter back and then fade away. Without me, catching Prateek is going to be as easy as catching a common thief."

"I want to trust you. Before I knew you were the Butcher of Bhalswa, you struck me as a man of your word. But now.... My men are almost there, tracing the call. Tell me why I shouldn't just let them take you."

"You do that; you catch one serial killer. But you keep me in the game. You get two."

"OK. I believe you want to save your daughter. But what guarantee do I have that you won't just take off after doing that?"

"There is no way I can convince you. I don't want to be second fiddle and be even a passive part of taking somebody's life anymore. And moreover, I want to leave the world a safer place for Shruti. I want my karma to die with me and not haunt my family." Manas glanced at his watch and scanned the area around. Nasir might be just keeping him engaged in buying some time for the police to reach his location. He needed to wrap this up fast. "To sweeten the deal, I'll throw in the address of my current hideout as well. So, it's a win-win for you. But you will have to wait for two days before moving in. I'll even keep my cell turned on, so you can track me."

"This goes against my every instinct, but yes. I'll bite. Two days. That's all you are getting. Give me your location."

Manas spied a couple of men marching onto the street and searching for something or someone. The black trousers and matching canvas shoes were a dead giveaway. "But you have to show me that I can trust you. Two of your men just reached the street. Call them off."

"OK, hold on." Nasir barked some orders on his side.

The two men converged on the phone booth. They were only fifty feet away when one of them spotted Manas and course corrected towards Manas, his eyes fierce and fixated on him. The other man pulled out a walkie-talkie from his back pocket and raised it to his mouth. After a short conversation, he called out something to the other policeman, who stopped in his tracks and reversed his course. And together both of them left the vicinity.

"Thank you," said Manas.

"Now, the address."

Manas spelt out the address of the lodge he was put up at, and when he was done, he added, "I want you to promise me that even if something happens to me, you will save my daughter."

"I promise," said Nasir.

The Artist

Tuesday, May 6, 2014

Relationships were a burden at best, but mostly a liability. The only person who wouldn't leave is you.

The sun was still yawning in his bed when Alex made his way towards the junction around the corner from the abandoned warehouse. The early morning mist settled around him, wetting his nose. It gave him the perfect excuse to cover himself with his hoodie, and he needed the excuse. It's been seven days since he abducted Shruti and that wretched kid saw the whole thing. The police machinery must be cranking extra hard trying to find him. And strangely, there hasn't been any news about "The Artist". Either the media had lost interest or Nasir is throttling the media. Either way, Alex could feel the noose tightening.

He could not get caught. Not when he was so close.

Yes, he was so close to his destiny. Things were going just as he had hoped it would. He could still feel the tangible excitement when he called Manas the day before.

The phone rang a couple of times before Manas picked up.

"Yes, it's done," barked Manas as soon as he picked up the call.

"No 'Hi', no 'Hello'?" asked Alex. "Straight to business. I like it."

"Yeah, now let's get to it. Where is my daughter?"

"Hey, hey, hey. Hold up," said Alex. "All in good time my man, all in good time. But how do I know if it is done? Is there a souvenir? Hmmm.... say, a head?"

"What? No!" said Manas and paused for a second. "If you want proof, check the newspapers. It should be plastered all over them tomorrow."

"Well, you've got a point there. I'll call you back tomorrow, then." Alex let out a short laughter before disconnecting the call.

He was not sure about Manas, but he was so excited that he couldn't sleep the whole night. The anticipation of reading about the latest Butcher murder in the papers was just too much to handle. The cherry on the cake was that this time, he orchestrated it. Unlike the times when he was just a spectator reading out old newspaper reports, he was an active participant this time. But would the media connect the dots and figure out it was the Butcher of Bhalswa? Or would the police censor it out not to spread panic? Would there be pictures? Details? So many questions swirled around his mind chasing away sleep.

At first light, he got up and headed out to get the day's newspaper, right from the distributors. And now he could make out through the haze a figure hunching by the roadside under a streetlight, sorting newspapers. He counted and divided the newspapers into different bundles, ready for the newspaper boys to deliver. Alex sauntered over to him and asked for The Hindu. "Nah! make it the Time of India," he added.

The Times of India was much better at this sort of news, he thought as he handed over a few coins to the man. Alex unfolded the newspaper and was not disappointed. The lower quarter of the front page had the news of the murder, along with a picture of the burning bungalow. It also had a call out to check the Regional section. And he was elated when he did that. There was an even bigger and more detailed coverage of the murder. But the title disappointed him a bit. Alex expected something like 'The Butcher of Bhalswa back?'. But the Butcher's name wasn't mentioned in the headlines. Maybe it's there in the content. But he didn't stop to check. Shoving the newspaper under his armpits, Alex rushed back to the abandoned warehouse.

By the time Alex reached back to the warehouse, the sun was peeking out of the misty clouds, spreading a much-needed warmth in the world. A dog sniffed a zig-zag path across the refuse, eyeing Alex now and then. He returned the stare as he fished for the keys to door in his pocket. The gang wars and loud lovemaking kept him up at night. But Shruti seemed to sleep through the ruckus like a log.

Alex threaded the key into the lock and gave it a slight twist. It clicked open and he slowly let the chain which kept the door closed go. He didn't want to wake Shruti. She had a rough couple of days. Alex had gone out to a medical shop, bought all the supplies, and dressed her wounds with the help of a few YouTube videos, but he was no doctor and she needed one. The one on her thigh was particularly difficult. It was bleeding so heavily that he had to tie a tourniquet above to stop it.

The door creaked open. Darkness reigned supreme inside the warehouse. The boarded-up windows allowed little light to come through. He crept up to his makeshift bed in the corner. In the dark, his foot caught a metal sheet which came down shattering the silence in the room.

"Fuck," muttered Alex, under his breath, as he checked to see if Shruti woke up.

"Bathroom," Shruti said, her voice still groggy from sleep. She slept a lot these days.

Alex nodded as he walked up to her. The dynamics of their relationship had changed drastically after the incident. Earlier, he could tell she despised him, but wasn't really scared of him. She had that spunk he loved in girls. But he broke her and her spirit. Now when he looked at her anthracite eyes, all he could see was fear and repulsion. Even though he was used to those looks, this one hurt him.

Shruti still wouldn't look him in the eye. Alex unlocked the chain around her leg and helped her up. He knew she was letting him do that because there was no other way. She could not lean on her leg without breaking open the wound. As she hobbled along with Alex to the makeshift bathroom behind the warehouse, he appraised her sharp and confident profile. Even in pain, she had a dignity which made you respect her. The white bandage on her collar peeked out of the blue T-shirt Alex had bought for her. The T-shirt, pant and even brassiere she wore was destroyed beyond use.

As he observed Shruti get into the makeshift enclosure to do her business, an unfamiliar emotion washed over him. Remorse? No, couldn't be.

"Careful," came the now familiar voice of The Butcher. He leaned against a misaligned piece of machinery. The morning rays of the sun kissing his feet.

"I don't think she can walk properly, let alone run away. Then there is the locked door."

"I was talking about your feelings for the girl."

"Feelings? What feelings?" Alex crossed his arms to face The Butcher. "She is just the means to an end. Leverage."

"If you say so. But just keep in mind the long game."

"Hmmm.... I've been thinking," said Alex. "Is that necessary?"

"Absolutely. Manas will be never be where we want him to be without that."

"He could," said Alex, but it wasn't even convincing to him.

"Destiny is made by choice, not chance," said The Butcher, as he faded away from the dark from which he came.

Alex nodded, silently. He knew it was right, but something in his mind was nagging him. Did he care about the girl? She did remind him of his little sister, with whom he had long since lost contact when she married and moved out of Delhi. As kids, they were really close. But the constant barrage of poison from their mother distanced them. She must have realised it when she grew up, but by then the relationship was long but broken. As soon as she got married, she moved out and never looked back. Another life his mother dear ruined.

No. He shook his head to clear his train of thought. He couldn't get attached to the girl. Relationships were a burden at best, but mostly a liability. The only person who wouldn't leave is you.

Alex shook out the newspaper and started reading the article. The entire article had just one line about the Butcher. He threw the newspaper on the floor. It skidded across the space into a corner. *One fucking line.* That too a speculation that this might be linked to the Butcher. The police statement was that this was a copycat murder. *Fucking pussies.* They don't even have the balls to admit the truth. The Butcher was back. Alex brought him back.

But the job was far from done. He pulled out the phone, pulled it apart to insert the new sim, and dialled the new number Manas had given him.

He picked up the call and barked," Happy?"

"Very," said Alex. "Not your finest, but still a thorough job."

"Cut the crap. Let's talk about my daughter. Where is she?"

"Hold on. Did I not explain the rules of the game before? There is one more round left. The River."

Manas let out a deep sigh. "Whatever it is, it's between you and me. Let her go and I'll do anything you say."

A bittersweet smile formed on Alex's lips. It was empowering to see a legend coming down on his knees in front of you. But at the same time, he felt bad for Manas. God works in mysterious ways, and he chose Alex do what was necessary. The path to glory was rocky and full of thorns. "It doesn't work like that, and you know it. You are doing everything I say *because* I have Shruti."

"One more."

"I think it's time we met again."

"Alright. Where do I come?"

Alex laughed out loud. It felt as harsh on his throat as it sounded out loud. "Not so easy. This is your last task. The last round. Find me and come take Shruti with you."

"What? If police with all its resources couldn't find you the whole last week, how am I supposed to do that?"

"You have something the police don't. Motivation." And with that Alex disconnected the call and shoved the mobile into his pocket. Shruti climbed out from the makeshift bathroom, holding the walls for support. Alex held out a hand for her to grab onto.

Manas

Tuesday, May 6, 2014

You can't outrun your past. You just can't.

Manas held on to the mobile long after the line was disconnected, staring at the brightly lit screen. His stomach dropped hard. The last task was close to impossible. It was the very thing he tried to do many times before he gave up and toed the line. The phone slipped out of his hands and bounced on the floor before coming to rest, face down.

"What happened?" Prateek asked.

Manas's legs moved, with a robotic conviction, and led him to the bed where he sunk down. "He wants us to find him and take Shruti back."

A short happy laugh escaped Prateek. "That's great news. Isn't that an open license to go after him and bring him down?"

"It's something we tried and failed at."

"I know. But that was when I was making the plans. But you do know where he is, don't you?"

The map of Trivandrum with a circle drawn on it flashed in Manas' mind. "No. I know which area he might be in. There is a difference."

Prateek sat right next to Manas and leaned back, supporting his weight on the two arms extended backwards. "Hmmm... Is there a time limit?"

"Not explicitly. But I'm sure he would lose his patience in a couple of days and after that...." Manas blinked away the warmth from his eyes.

"Cut it out. Are you giving up so close to the finishing line?"

Manas rose to his feet and wiped his eyes. "No. I made a promise and I intend to keep it if that's the last thing I do."

"So, stop whining about it and man up." Prateek leaned forward, supporting his head on his folded hands, and staring straight ahead. "Let's take it one step at a time."

Manas nodded curtly. "We know he is in a 7-8-kilometre radius from Pettah." He pulled out his mobile and opened the Google Maps.

The map of Trivandrum loaded on the screen. Manas pinched and swiped the screen to focus on Pettah. From the city, where his house was, Pettah was towards the sea. There was very little chance Alex took a detour and travelled back to the city and some other direction, especially with Shruti in the backseat. So, the general direction he was travelling in should remain the same.

Manas panned the map in all directions to account for all the directions the roads took. "There are only three directions which he would have taken- towards Veli, towards Shankumugham, and towards Kovalam."

"But we don't have that much time." Prateek stroked his chin, deep in thought. "Then there are the shoes with garbage stuck on the bottom."

"Garbage dumps are a dime a dozen. It could be from anyone of those."

"Hmmm... What about the photos he sent you? May be there is something there?"

"As hard as it was, I studied every pixel in those pictures. Only thing I figured out was that they are in some kind of abandoned building, may be an old factory."

"What about the phone calls you recorded?"

"What about them?"

"May be there is something in them? May be something in the background?"

"That's a long shot, Prateek."

"Not that long. Every area would have its own signature in sounds. If it was near the sea, the sound of waves crashing on the shore might be present. If it is close to a busy road, the honks and chatter of normal traffic might be present."

"Hmmm, OK. But I doubt if we can hear that much detail in the background. After all it's a recording of a phone call."

"You can ask your friend, Ravi. He is a sound engineer, right? Maybe he can help isolate the background sounds?"

Manas nodded his head. "We'll pay him a visit. I don't know how I'm gonna convince him to help out. He does owe me a bit, but now things are different. I'm a wanted man, a serial killer, and whatever else the media has already branded me."

"Cooperation can be extracted if you press the right levers, if you know what I mean," said Prateek, with an evil hook in his eyes and a twinkle in his eyes.

Manas chuckled at the comical face. "No, you will not do any such thing." Prateek had a way of getting him out of the dumps. "I'm not gonna torture my friend. Let's just go to his house and ask nicely."

"You suck the fun out of everything." Prateek pouted.

It was dark when they ventured out of the lodge and towards Ravi's apartment. The police hadn't released the news about Manas to the public, but they must have surely had lookouts scouring the city for him. They caught an autorickshaw and reached Ravi's apartment at around half-past eight. It wasn't far from Thampanoor, but then again, nothing in Trivandrum was far away.

They climbed out of the rickshaw and looked up at a low-rise apartment complex, smack in the middle of the city. Cracks spread out in an intricate web across the walls. Manas had dreaded convincing Ravi over the intercom. It was doubly hard to convince someone through the phone. But here, the security looked pretty lax. He sauntered in the entrance; head held high and purpose in his walk. Prateek followed the lead, and both of them passed the security guards. When Manas gave them a nod, they were deciding whether to pull out the register to make an entry, but by that time, Manas and Prateek were at the lift.

A few minutes of waiting for the lift, and listening to the classical lift music, they were in front of Ravi's apartment. It was a plain door with two holes where the nameplate used to hang. A cross hung from the top of the door, dust collecting at the crevices.

"His name is Ravi, right?" said Prateek, nodding towards the cross. "Renting it?"

"Yeah, he is. Moved to the city a few months ago."

Right then, the door swung open. Ravi appeared in the gap in dark blue shorts and a light brown T-shirt. His hair was tousled, and his eyes groggy; maybe he woke up from an afternoon nap. If there was even a bit of sleep lingering on his eyes, it was chased away by the immediate shock as he registered Manas. The subsequent transformation of his face and the apparent change in body language told Manas that the police had paid him a visit. That was not good news.

Ravi shifted his weight backwards and closed the door, but Manas reached out and held the door open with his muscular arms. "Ravi... please. Just listen to what I have to say."

The force on the door eased up for a moment but was restored with passion. Manas didn't blame him for that. This was the natural reaction when a murderer was at your door. But the momentary respite in the force told him one thing - there was doubt in his mind.

"You've known me for some time, right? Have I ever done something to upset you? Have I given you the impression that I am a dangerous man?"

The force reduced a bit more. Ravi got completely behind the door and said," No. But the police told me everything. I'm calling them right now."

"Hold on and listen to me. All I am asking is for you to hear me out. And then you can call the police. I swear I won't stop you."

"Just kick in the door and let me deal with him," Prateek whispered in Manas' ear.

Manas shook his head vehemently. "Ravi, please. I'm no longer the man the police told you about. Right now, I'm just a father, desperate to save my daughter. Shruti is in danger, and I need your help."

And without warning, the force of the door went away altogether, and Manas stumbled into the drawing room. He quickly regained his balance and scanned the room. It was a small hall with a couch, a beanbag, and a small television. A couple of feet away, behind the couch, Ravi stood with a baseball bat-shaped rod in his hand.

"If that-," Manas nodded towards the rod in Ravi's hand,"- gives you comfort, hold on to it."

"Yes, it does. And let me be clear. The only reason I've let you in is because the Manas I've known has been nothing but kind to me. But the moment I see you as the slightest threat, I'm using the rod." Ravi tightened the grip on the rod in his hand. "You've got ten minutes, Manas."

Manas took a deep breath and walked around the bean bag and planted his bottom on top of it. "I don't know what the police have told-"

"They've told me enough to make me scared for my life."

"Be that as it may, I am not here to confirm or dispute what they've told you. I'm here to ask you to help me find my daughter."

Ravi dipped his gaze and his brows eased up a bit at the mention of Shruti's name. "I heard about the… kidnapping. I'm sorry." He trained his eyes back on Manas and brought back the intensity. "But that doesn't change the fact that you are a murderer."

"I am the same person who invited you into his home, the same person who had your back and saved your job. And that same person is begging for your help. Don't do it for me, do it for Shruti."

Ravi stepped back and shook his head. "You're right. I owe you for saving my job, and being a mentor and an elder brother to me in this strange city. And I'm really sorry that your daughter was taken. But, how can I help? I'm sure the police are doing all they can to get your daughter back."

"It's... complicated, Ravi." Manas leaned forward in the chair and fixed Ravi in a hard stare. "I'll explain. It's a long shot, but I'm desperate. Will you help me save my little girl?"

Ravi loosened the grip on the rod in his hand it slid down and rested against his leg. "Yes, but only if it is not illegal. And you should know that I'll call the police right after."

That was music to Manas's ear. That was all he could ask for. A warm smile broke out and spread across his face. Prateek also relaxed visibly, as he leaned on the wall on the far corner of the room.

Ravi veins popped as he tightened his grip on the rod. "You really killed all those people?"

Manas stared at his feet, tracing the curvy lines on the dark carpet. "You know the story of the hare and turtle, right? The hare ran fast, put a lot of distance between him and the turtle, and foolishly thought he had the race in the bag. But you can't outrun your past. You just can't." He rose to his feet and took two slow steps towards Ravi. Ravi's knuckles went white as he gripped the rod harder. "Yes, I killed those people, but it was complicated. What I can tell you is that I left that life behind when I moved to Trivandrum twenty years ago."

Ravi closed the distance between them in short, unsure steps. "OK, tell me what you want my help with."

Manas fished out the mobile phone from his pocket and pulled up the recording app. "I have a few phone calls I've recorded and some other recordings which the man you know as "The Artist" sent me after taking Shruti. I think it may help me figure where he is keeping her." He extended the hand holding the mobile phone towards Ravi. "Maybe something in the background."

Ravi leaned in and grabbed the mobile phone from Manas' hands. His forehead wrinkled in thought as he fidgeted with the mobile phone, rotating, and revolving in his hands. The anticipation was as worse as the silence that prevailed. But relief washed over Manas when, at the end of a long pause, Ravi nodded his head and rose to his feet. Manas followed him to his computer and waited as he connected the phone to the USB port.

"Fair warning," said Manas. "Some content is quite graphic."

The mouse hovered over the folder for a brief second before double-clicking and opening it. "Let's see," said Ravi. He quickly copied the six files Manas pointed out to his computer.

The progress bar slowly filled in as the files were being copied. "It may take some time. Gotta run a spectral analysis and identify the different frequencies of the audio and then pass it through a notch filter to extract the different wavelengths."

Manas nodded his head. He didn't understand a word, but he trusted him. "I'll wait in the hall. Gimme a shout when you are done."

He walked into the hall and sunk into the couch. The comfort of the soft fabric and feathery cushion enveloped him as he closed his eyes. Manas dug through his memories for a happy one of his daughter. The bloody images and guttural screams he put himself thorough over and over again had taken its toll. Every time he closed his eyes, Shruti was there, screaming for her Dad, drenched in blood. He needed a happy memory; something to hold on it, something to keep him going.

His mind wandered into a breezy Sunday afternoon, not long ago. Shruti sat on the patio furniture on the terrace with a cup of coffee in her one hand and an open book in her other. Anu and Manas stood at the edge of the terrace, looking out onto the lines of houses that spread in front of them; he had his arms around Anu. It was such an idyllic memory that it felt alien now.

"It's done," called out Ravi from the other room, interrupting his train of thought. Manas wiped off the watery excess from his eyes and headed towards Ravi, who was sitting beside the laptop. He had lost a bit of colour and sweat beads clung to his forehead. Prateek, who had confined himself to a corner of the house, came back to look over Manas' shoulders.

"Did you find anything?" asked Manas.

"Yes, but don't know how useful it would be."

"Let's got through them one by one, oldest to latest." That way, he would not have to listen to Shruti screaming right at the start. He would not be able to think clearly after that.

"OK," said Ravi as he manoeuvred the mouse which hovered over a file named '20140530'. "This one has an interesting voice track behind the main one. Just listen."

The speaker hissed and crackled as it came to life, and then it started. An incessant pitter-patter of a sound.

"Rain," offered Manas. "I think it was raining at that time... But wait, there is something else also, isn't it?"

Ravi nodded his head. "A hollow metallic sound."

"Like rain hitting a metal sheet," said Manas. "Even the pictures he sent me also showed a metal wall."

"Pictures?" Ravi cocked his head ever so slightly to the left.

"Yeah, to prove a point," said Manas, biting back a sob. He cleared his throat and said, "Let's hear the next one."

"Didn't find anything interesting in the next one. But let's look at the one on May 3rd morning."

A barrage of damped barks, yelps and growls came through the speakers.

"Dogs," said Manas, stating the obvious.

"A lot of dogs," added Ravi. "Fighting among themselves. Usually around food or waste."

"Garbage," said Manas.

Prateek nodded his head and said, "The garbage on his shoes."

"Hmmm," said Manas. "Let's see the next one."

"Yes, the one later the same day has the most interesting sounds of all," said Ravi as he moved the mouse and clicked on the file. "There were two separate wavelengths... here is the first one."

The speakers came alive with distorted Islamic songs. The sound faded in and out as they progressed through the audio file.

"A Mosque?" asked Manas.

"Sounds like it," said Ravi. "It has a distortion which is typical to those loudspeakers Mosques usually have to announce Adhan."

"Awesome-"

"Wait, there is more." Ravi cut Manas off and played the next file.

Islamic songs or prayers came on the speaker again, but this time it wasn't that distorted. It was more like a chorus of a multitude of people intoning the prayers. A rhythmic bang of drums accompanied it.

"The amplitude of this wavelength was much higher than the other one. This was much closer."

"Sounds like a group of people chanting Islamic prayers or songs."

Ravi nodded his head. "It may be a procession because the amplitude fades out towards the end, indicating an increase in distance."

"This was on 3rd May, afternoon, isn't it?"

A spark ignited a few hundred neurons in his brain and the signal cascaded into a chain reaction which lit up his entire brain. In the haze of dopamine fuelled frenzy, Manas saw a glimmer of hope, a silver lining. He knew what that was.

Ravi whipped his head back to stare at Manas. "Yeah?"

"That's the Uroos."

"The what?"

An unexplained euphoria rose from Manas' stomach and bubbled up his throat. "The Uroos from Beemapally. The annual festival, which shuts down the whole city for half a day."

Ravi's eyes grew wider as realisation dawned on him. "Yes. It can be. But that passes through the entire city."

The euphoria exploded out of his mouth in a burst of maniacal laughter. "You are missing the other audio, my friend. Mosques don't usually play these songs all day. It's usually reserved for the call to prayer.

If this Mosque was playing it all day, it can only be the Mosque where the Uroos originates." And it fit the earlier deduction about the probable areas as well, Manas thought.

For the first time since they entered the house, Ravi smiled. But soon, a dark shadow dawned on his face. "I listened to the audio.... Almost didn't finish the process because of Shruti's screams. I can't imagine how hard it must have been for you."

The mere mention of his daughter's screams knocked down cold the euphoria that was coursing through his system.

"Let me ask you something, Manas."

Manas met Ravi's hard stare and gave him a nod to go ahead.

"In one of the recordings, he asked you to kill someone called Rajashekharan. That was the guy who was murdered yesterday, wasn't it? Was that you?"

Manas took a deep breath and turned away from Ravi. "Maybe you will understand when you have a kid of your own that you'll do anything to keep them safe."

Ravi rose to his feet and said, "I hope this helps you save your daughter." He pointed at the door, indicating an end to his hospitality. "Who are you, Manas? Are you the kind man I considered a mentor, or the cold-blooded killer the police told me about?"

Manas reached for a handshake, out of habit, but pulled back the last moment seeing Ravi flinch. "I wish I had an easy answer to that question," he said.

"But you do know that I'll have to call the police now," said Ravi. "I'll give you a ten-minute head start because I'm not sure what to make of you..."

Manas nodded his head as he disconnected his phone from the computer and pocketed it. "Thanks again, Ravi."

"What are you going to do?" asked Ravi.

"What needs to be done," said Manas, as he exited the door and closed it behind him.

Sonam

Tuesday, May 6, 2014

I didn't let you kiss me because you were my superior.
I did it because I like you.

Beethoven's Für Elise played through the tinny speakers of the phone, effectively destroying the composition. Sonam took the receiver off of her ear, offended at the way the masterpiece was massacred. She had been on hold at the labs for almost fifteen minutes now, but she was determined to hold on till hell freezes over.

At the end of what felt like an eternity, a sweet voice answered the phone. "Hi, thank you for holding the line. How can I help you today?"

"Good morning, Mrs. Chandni. It's Sonam." The fake politeness irked her. "It's the same thing I ask every day."

"Oh, yes, the soil analysis." Chandni had a phoney peppiness in her voice. Either she had been answering calls too long, or she was made for the job. "Just got to office. I'll check and let you know if the test is done. Can you call me in half an hour?"

"Can you just head down to the lab and check it right away?" said Sonam, regretting the touch of rudeness which crept into her tone. She would have gotten away with a guy on the other line. But women pick up on these quickly. "There is a little girl's life on the line," she offered. "Please try and understand the urgency of the matter."

There was a long pause on the other end as Sonam waited with bated breath.

A deep breath crackled through the telephone. "Yes, I will," said Chandni. "Please hold."

Sonam was so relieved that she was tempted to do a cartoonish 'phew', complete with the forehead wipe and whip of the hand. She put the phone on speaker and leaned back on her chair. It might be a long wait, she thought to herself before she drifted into one of the million thoughts running through her mind.

Pretty soon, it landed on the night when she and Nasir had kissed. It was perfect, or as perfect as it can get considering the circumstances.

She just wished it would not have ended so abruptly. Both had the right amount of liquor in their system - enough to dissolve the inhibitions, but not their sense of judgement. His lips surprised her. She didn't expect them to be this soft; he was a good kisser. There was warmth and safety in his thin, fine-boned arms. A soft sigh escaped her mouth.

It wasn't as weird as she expected when they had a brief ten minutes earlier in the day.

The team always caught breakfast together any time they were away from home, and there was strictly no talk about work during. It wasn't something written down or enforced, but a custom that evolved through time. It helped fill the void of being away from your family for extended periods of time and keep everyone from being overworked, stressed, or obsessed about any case.

As expected, Avinash led the meaningless banter race by a mile. He kept on unrolling anecdote after anecdote from his endless repertoire of stories. How he had so many stories or how many of them were true were questions that swam around in Sonam's mind. Nasir, usually, was an active participant in the friendly ribbing and was notorious for tongue-in-cheek one-liners which destroyed the target. But not that day. His eyes stuck to the plate, dipping the *dosa* in *sambar* longer than necessary; he was physically present, but far from there.

His hollow cheeks stuck to the bones as he chewed food half a second more than necessary. Nasir tried to keep up the charade for the team by occasionally laughing at Avinash's jokes. They lacked mirth.

But the team was too engrossed in what Avinash had to say to take notice. Not her. Soon, one by one, everyone finished up and left, leaving the two of them alone - Nasir and Sonam. She was sitting two chairs away, fiddling with the glass of water and Nasir was still chewing his food, lost in thought.

Sonam shifted next to him and said, "Hi."

Nasir looked up from his food and a smile pushed up the corners of his thin mouth. "Hey..." He broke eye contact and looked past Sonam and then focused them back on hers. "How are... you?"

"Well, I came over to ask you the same thing. You've been off all morning. Is it the case, or what happened that night?"

She had never seen Nasir flustered, but her direct question may have taken him off guard. "It's the case. Just wondering if I am making the right calls."

"Oh…," said Sonam.

"There are a few things the rest of you guys do not know."

"What things?"

"I'll tell you when it's all over."

Sonam took a sip of water from the glass she had been twirling in her hand all this time. An awkward silence ensued, which lasted almost a minute. In what felt like an eternity, Sonam began to wonder why Nasir just totally avoided the topic of what happened that night.

"Listen...," said Nasir, breaking the silence. "About... the other night..." He stared into his white plate, tracing the contours of the left over *dosa* with his fingers. "I don't know what got into me. You are my subordinate. I should never have misused my position like that. I'm sorry."

Ah! so he wasn't avoiding after all; just gathering courage to breach the matter. Sonam chuckled. "I didn't let you kiss me because you were my superior. I did it because I like you."

Nasir stole a quick glance at her and resumed his intent focus on the plate and the designs on it. "Still, it was wrong. If not the professional angle, there the age difference. I'm too old for you."

"Well, I'm old enough to decide what is good for me, aren't I? And about the work thing. I think we are professional enough not to let that interfere. Or we can establish ground rules from the beginning. There are ways, you know."

Nasir looked up and into Sonam's eyes. The gaze penetrated her like a laser beam. "That's not going to be easy. In our line of work, sooner or later, I will be in a position where I'll need to put you at risk; choose someone else's life over yours. And when that comes, I'm not sure if I'll be strong enough to do it."

"I know you will be. And even if you are not, I won't let that happen, not because of our relationship."

Nasir resumed his inspection of the plate of food with a shake of his head. "I need some time to think this over. Let all this boil down, and then we can talk again. OK?"

"That's probably not a bad idea," Sonam said, with a low chuckle. "Let's catch the bad guy first."

"Hello, Ms. Sonam, are you there?" crackled the speaker phone of the phone.

She jumped up and grabbed the phone from the table. "Yes, yes, I'm here. Tell me it's good news."

"Yes, it is."

Sonam practically jumped out of the seat. "It's done?" In her head, she heard how stupid she sounded, asking the same thing Chandni just said. But she just had to ask it.

"Yes, it is. I'm sending you the soft copy as we speak. The hard copy should reach your office in a couple of days."

"If you were here, I would have kissed you, Chandni."

An unusually high-pitched laughter erupted from the other side of the line. "Goodbye, Sonam," she said before disconnecting the call.

Sonam slammed the phone down, yanked open her laptop, and checked her email. The first email in the list was from the lab. She opened it and clicked print.

The printer whirred to life, traversing the paper, line by line, transferring the electronic information to the real world. It was the longest 30 seconds of her life. As soon as the printer churned out the last of the papers, she grabbed them and rushed to the conference room.

"I got it," said Sonam, as she burst into the room. Half the team, along with Nasir looked up from what they were doing and blinked.

"The soil analysis." Sonam waved the papers in front of her.

A smile formed on Nasir's thin face. His luminous, jet-black eyes sparkled with excitement. "It's about time. What does it say?"

Dammit. In the excitement of getting the report, she had forgotten to look at it. Heat rose in her cheeks. "Haven't read it myself. Just give a second."

She felt every eye in the room on her as she scanned the report. It was way too technical for anyone else in the team to understand. She skimmed through the composition analysis, both inorganic and organic, the bacterial analysis, geographical information system mapping, and Fourier transform infrared absorption spectrometry. Even though they took a long time to finish, the lab had done a thorough job.

Sonam finally looked up at the room and smiled. "They did a lot of really useful analysis on the samples we-"

"Samples," interrupted Avinash. "We just have the one sample from the shoe, right?"

"Yes, that was the test sample. We also sent them a couple of other samples to act as control so that they can baseline the samples and focus on the anomalies."

Avinash nodded his head, but his eyes were still a little confused.

"They have done separate analysis for inorganic and organic material," Sonam continued. "They have even gone ahead and done a Geographical Information System mapping of the soil sample from the results of the inorganic material analysis."

"Geographical-?" asked Salim.

"It's a method by which you map the type of soil on a map using the information from sensor satellites like ResourceSat-1, Cartosat-2, etc.," said Sonam. Observing Salim's blank face, she added," So, in short, we get a map with probable areas where the soil sample is present."

Avinash let out a low whistle. "That's awesome."

"Yes, it is, and useful too. Look at the map, it's not a lot of area as well." Sonam passed the map in the results around.

"What's more interesting is the organic analysis," Sonam continued. "The strong presence of faecal and vegetable matter in the sample stood out. Bacterial analysis was also off the charts. The sample is from a place where there is a lot of decaying organic material.

"Hmmm, like a graveyard?" offered Akshay.

"I would have said yes, but the composition of the materials is all wrong," said Sonam. "Human graveyards have a specific composition of minerals and this one does not have that. This is more like organic matter or even faecal matter."

"Maybe a waste dump?" Nasir spoke up for the first time, his eyes sharp as ever.

Sonam nodded her head. "Possible. In fact, that would explain the traces of plastic fragments and vegetable matter in the sample. But a garbage dump won't create such high levels of bacteria in the sample."

"Hmmm." Nasir rubbed his forehead.

"There was one other interesting observation," said Sonam. "High levels of heavy metals like Zinc and Nickel in the soil." She had a feeling she knew what that meant. But she had to be sure. Without saying a word, she headed over to the closest laptop and fired up Google. She felt the room close in on her as the tic-tac of the keyboard filled the room. The first link was a journal from *ScienceDirect* and another journal from *Springer* followed suit. She opened both and skimmed through the contents. *Yes*. She was right.

Sonam keyed in a new query in Google and looked up from the screen. "I just had to be sure. High levels of Zinc and Nickel are usually associated with sewage treatment. Or more specifically the disposal of treated water from sewage treatment plants." She glanced at the screen and clicked on a result from the maps. "And as it happens, I got two hits for 'sewage treatment plant in Trivandrum' in Google."

"Way to go, kiddo!" Avinash rose to his feet with excitement.

Although she didn't enjoy the title, that felt good. It was the best breakthrough they had ever since this thing started, and it came from her. She beamed at the room.

Nasir was still too preoccupied with his thought process to partake in the exhilaration sweeping the room. "Would that also explain the high levels of bacteria in the sample? Or the plastic and vegetable matter?"

"No," said Sonam. "But the area affected by the treated water is usually much larger area. May be there is a garbage dump in the area we ought to look for?"

"Akshay, can you double check the sewage treatment plant location with the local police?" asked Nasir. "Also ask them about any garbage dumps in the area. Official or un-official."

As Akshay grabbed his mobile phone from the desk and left the room, Nasir marched towards the whiteboard and flipped through the A3 sheets which hung from it until he reached the map of Trivandrum. The map had the area that they had to focus marked out, which basically a huge semi-circle with its centre at Pettah. He silently sketched in the area that the Geographical Information System analysis marked out. By the time he was done, the area on the map had reduced considerably.

The rest of the team crowded around the map, silently observing the pockets of red. It wasn't a lot of ground. Just then, Akshay walked back into the room and announced, "Local police confirmed. There is only one sewage treatment facility which caters to the whole city." He marched up to the map and drew a black cross smack in the middle of one of the red pockets.

"Excellent! Finally, we have something solid. We've got a location, but the area we need to cover is quite large. The good thing is that we've got the element of surprise." Nasir scanned the room and spotted Akshay. "Get in touch with the police and get all the necessary setup. I mean weapons, backup, the whole shebang. We would need a lot of manpower to set up a perimeter and comb the area. I don't want to take any chances this time. We head out at first light." He paused for a second and then added, "All of you get a good night's sleep 'cause tomorrow we nail the bastard."

Manas

Wednesday, May 7, 2014

Either way it ends today.

Blood whooshed through Manas' ears in a hurry. A drop of sweat trickled down his back, but it wasn't hot outside. The sun wasn't even out yet. An old, dilapidated building loomed in front of him. The pre-sunrise light cast an eerie halo around the structure. Prateek crouched beside him, like a coiled spring, waiting for his instructions. Manas gestured towards the left of the building, and they both darted across the clearing, keeping low and out of sight. As soon as he reached the building, Manas made himself flat against the walls, with Prateek following suit.

They were at the fourth place they checked out that day. Lying in bed last night, his mind had wandered through all the ways in which the next day could go. The positives balanced the negatives, and, in his mind, that was a huge win. But all the while, a part of his brain shouted at him to catch some sleep. He needed to be rested for the next day. But like a kid who can't sleep the night before the class tour, sleep evaded Manas.

At around four in the morning, he gave up his futile effort to woo sleep and kicked off the sheets. He sat at the edge of the bed, reached for his wallet, and flipped open to Shruti's photograph. The carefree laughter she had was contagious. A warm smile broke out on his face, which darkened soon enough as reality dawned.

Manas headed to the dingy bathroom, kicking Prateek awake on the way, and splashed some water on his face, washing away some of the tiredness. He pulled on a black polo T-shirt as soon as he got out of the bathroom.

"Get up. I wanna leave before light," said Manas.

Prateek rose to his feet, as fresh as ever. Manas slung the knapsack he had packed the day before. It had everything he needed for the day ahead.

They caught the first bus out of the main bus depot, which was just under half a kilometre walk from their place. Prateek was silent the entire bus ride, which served Manas well. He divided up the space around the

Mosque into sectors so that he could cover all of them and not miss anything.

The satellite view in Google Maps was nothing short of a blessing. The first area he eliminated was the area to the south of the mosque. It was sandwiched between the mosque and the sea and was a busy residential area. Alex can't really hide out for days in a densely populated area without drawing attention. Using the same logic, the sector to the west was also ruled out.

A sewage treatment facility and a compound of All India Radio occupied the sectors to the north and east, respectively. The compound of the All-India Radio station was a huge sprawling area with a whole lot of nothing and one building in the middle. A few trees peppered the predominantly brown landscape, with a couple of gigantic towers which broadcast the signal. Manas pinched the map to zoom in. There was no other building in the vicinity, and unless Alex was hiding in the trees around the radio station, there was no point searching there.

But the area with the sewage treatment facility seemed promising. A lot of isolated buildings and temporary sheds peppered the surrounding area. There were a lot of places someone could easily hide out without getting noticed. *This is it. Alex has got to be there.*

The bus was almost empty, except for a few early birds rushing to get the day started. The serenity and solitude of early morning were something Manas missed. He used to go for early morning runs when he was younger, but as age caught up with him his early mornings became as late as six or seven.

Prateek stared into the empty space right in front of him, his eyes unfocused, his mind far away. For a brief second of panic, Manas thought Prateek was on to his plan. But he dismissed the thought as soon as it formed. He had always been able to keep a thought private from Prateek if he wanted to. But every now and then, a few thoughts leak, but knowing Prateek, this wouldn't be the reaction if he figured it out.

It was a short walk from the bus stop to the sewage treatment plant. Pale blue light, the precursor to the rising sun, bathed the deserted streets. and the silence between them finally broke when Prateek said, "Let's teach the bastard a lesson." A crooked smile twisted his face into a familiar, cocky expression.

The next hour they spent in checking out different places, starting at the north end of the plant. There were many places which fit the bill - metal sheets for a roof. All three places they checked before were empty. Now they were crouched next to the entrance to the fourth place. Manas balled his hands into a fist as resolve filled his heart. If he had to knock on every single door in the area, he would do so. *Either way, it ends today.*

He leaned against the building with his ears flat against the cold, concrete wall. Nothing. All he could hear was his own heavy breathing. Manas crept towards the door, making as little noise as possible. The door had fallen off its hinges to make way for an elaborate spider web which sprawled across the entrance. Unless there was another entrance to the place, it didn't look occupied. But he didn't want to leave any stone unturned.

He slowly rose to his feet and brushed aside the web. The intricate trap crumbled around his fingers, clinging on to it. The spider ran up his hands, scrambling for safety. Manas crushed the arachnid without mercy and tossed the exoskeleton aside. With Prateek in tow, he stepped into the enclosure; yes, there was no better word to describe the place. It wasn't a building, but more like a space with four walls around it. The inside of the place was as dilapidated as the outside. It looked like some storage room of sorts. The floor was littered with garbage. Walls housed wooden shelves which were empty except for the dirt that had accumulated on it.

As he walked further into the enclosure, his disappointment came crashing down. But Manas dodged it with his nimble feet and rushed forward. There was no room for it, not when he was this close to the finishing line. He turned around and walked back out into the open. On his way, one of his steps sounded different.

"You hear that?" asked Prateek.

Manas nodded his head and retraced his steps. *There it was again.* A hollow thud as opposed to a crisp step on concrete. He dropped to his knees and felt around the garbage that covered the floor. As his hands ran along the floor, the cold, rough, concrete floor made way for a smooth, wooden warmth.

"There is a trap door here," said Manas. "And a latch," he added.

Prateek stepped closer, swiping away the garbage with his feet.

Manas pulled on the latch with all his might and it opened outward with a loud crank. He peered into the absolute darkness inside and the stairs which plunged into it.

"Looks like a cellar," said Prateek.

"Sure does. Can you hand me the flashlight, Prateek?"

Prateek extracted a flashlight from the knapsack and handed it to Manas. He switched on the flash-light and took the first step down into the darkness. The stairs creaked under his weight. Manas slowly made his way down into the darkness and scanned the area with his flashlight.

"Nothing, but more empty shelves mounted on the walls," Manas yelled up to Prateek. Even though he tried hard to keep disappointment out of his voice, he could hear it leak through.

They were back and out of the enclosure in a minute and on their way to the next building.

As he trudged his way to the next place, self-doubt seeped into his thoughts like a drop of black ink on blotting paper. Were they looking at the right place?

Prateek stopped abruptly, turned and looked at Manas. "We are at the right place. I know it."

"Mind getting out of my head?" words rolled off Manas' mouth faster than usual.

A low chuckle escaped Prateek. "I am in your head, remember? But you wanted me to hear that."

Manas shot a puff of air into the universe in irritation as he walked away. It always irritated him when Prateek read his mind. But he had a point. May be his sub-conscious leaked the thought because he needed some reassurance to keep going. "Thank you," he muttered over his shoulders at Prateek.

They circled the sewage treatment facility and reached the southern corner. Three rusty, abandoned single-storey warehouses rose from the brown earth, all at right angles to each other, forming a 'U'. Remnants of reddish-brown paint hung from the walls. They looked the farthest from inhabitable, but Manas decided to check them out anyway. *Leave no stones unturned.*

He crept closer, heading for the layered metal sheets masquerading as the wall; brown patches of rust carved out large sections of the sheets. The metal sheets which made up the roof were also at a dismal state of degradation. All three places had huge sections of the wall missing, and that made it easier to check them out. *Empty.*

Manas rose to his feet, planted them apart, and took in a deep breath. The rank mixture of sewage and chemical smell rushed up his nose. He had gotten used to it being in the vicinity since morning. But along with it, a rancid smell of rotting garbage tickled his olfactory senses. And out of nowhere, a pack of dogs erupted into an all-out gang war. Loud barks and yelps filled the serene silence of the morning. Manas glanced at Prateek, who met his gaze, understanding in his eyes. He knew the significance of what they just heard - garbage and a pack of dogs.

They crept towards the direction they heard the sound coming from. Around the corner, they came upon another building, much smaller than the other three, nestled behind the 'U', hidden from plain sight. It looked even more rusty and abandoned that the other three, but somehow the walls seemed to hold together. A blackened grey metal sheet acted as a functioning roof. And a quick glance told him that the walls had no gaping holes.

This was perfect. The three abandoned warehouses shielded it on one side and the line of trees that grew around it hid it from the other three sides. And the pile of garbage out front deters local miscreants who might stumble upon the place. Back in the days, he would have picked this place if he wanted privacy.

Manas' gut screamed; this is it. Staying close to the ground, he and Prateek sprinted across the clearing between the two buildings and came to a halt at the side of the building, kneeling in the mud. Manas shimmied his way to the corner and peeked to find a Maruti 800 parked at the far end of the building. The door to the building was between him and the car and there was a chain hanging from it with a lock at the end; unlocked.

Manas drew back and gestured Prateek to follow him, as he dropped to the ground. On his elbows, they crawled towards the building, like they do it in the military. When they reached the door, Manas reached over and tried it; it was open. He peeked inside, but it was dark inside. The windows were boarded up. He slowly rose to his feet, pulled open the door, and stepped inside the building.

Nasir

Wednesday, May 7, 2014

This is where the rabbit hole ends. Today The Artist ceases to exist, because dead men need no names.

The first rays of sunlight pierced through the mist and assaulted Nasir's eyes. He narrowed his eyes in response and scanned his surroundings. Akshay had parked the unmarked SUV on the east side of the plant, away from their area of search. He made his nose smaller, an automatic reaction to the smell of sewage.

His team gathered around him, every single one of them alert and on the edge. They were more than a team; they were his family.

"This is it," said Nasir. "This, here and now. This is where the rabbit hole ends. Today The Artist ceases to exist, because dead men need no names." He roamed his eyes, meeting eye to eye with each and every member of his family gathered around him. "Whatever happens today, Alex does not come out of this alive. There is no prison reserved for him, no appeals to the justice system, just the end of a smoking gun. But make sure you secure Shruti before that. And if the situation comes where you have to get that information out of him, do not hesitate to use whatever means necessary. We will get it out of him, one way or the other. And just remember, whatever happens, I've got your back."

Every head, even Sonam's, gathered around him nodded. "Yes, sir."

"OK. So, let's split into teams of two and do a preliminary recon. Keep the radio channels open and call in as soon as you see something. This is just a recon, do not, I repeat, do not engage."

"Yes, sir," the team chorused.

"OK, then, let's go get him."

Avinash paired with Salim and veered off in a direction away from the sewage treatment facility. Nasir felt Sonam's expectant eyes piercing through the back of his head. But no, he could not afford that distraction now. Soon enough Akshay and Sonam paired up and headed off to the right and Nasir headed to the left.

Nasir ran to the far-left side of the facility. He was out of breath by the time he reached the corner. Years of smoking had destroyed his lung capacity. No amount of exercise was going to recover that. Leaning on the wall, he peeked over the corner. There were very few buildings on this side and most of them looked like extensions of the plant.

The first one had a blue metal sheet roof, which was just gaining its colour in the morning light. He glanced at his watch; it was fifteen past five. There wasn't much time to lose. Nasir hurried over to the building. He wanted to get the recon done before the day was bright. The local police will reach the location with full force by seven.

A cursory check told him that the building was empty. Without losing momentum, he headed for the second one down the line, which turned out to be empty as well.

This continued for a while when he saw three rusty old warehouses arranged like an inverted 'U'. All three buildings had endured the wear and tear of time. Rust had eaten up most of the walls and even some parts of the roof. Nasir inspected the three buildings. Each one was worse than the other. They had bigger and bigger sections of walls missing.

But just as he was about to turn around and head back, a splash of rusty brown flashed through the gap between two of the old warehouses. It was another, much smaller warehouse, hidden behind the three big ones. Nasir crept forward in between the two warehouses and peeked over the corner. The smaller warehouse was in a much more advanced state of decay than the other three. Sunlight glinted off whatever small patch of grey was left on the rusty roof. Despite the decay and rot, the walls had no gaping holes, and the structure seemed to be stable.

The building was nestled in behind the larger warehouses and had a line of trees circling the other side. It was a good place to hide. Nasir retreated back the way he came from, slipped into the line of trees and circled his way around to the front of the building to get a better look. When he saw the garbage dump right in front of the abandoned building, his heart jumped to his throat. *This is it.*

With a sudden creak, the door in the front of the building flew open. Nasir dove to the ground to stay out of sight. He counted to three and peeked out. The door swung on its hinges, but there was no one in the doorway. But a little to the side, he spotted a man, leaning against the wall. A hoodie was drawn up over his head casting a dark shadow on his face. A deep orange eye burned bright, glowing in slow pulses as smoke swirled out of the darkness.

Nasir waited with bated breath. The man was Alex's height and the same body structure. He was eighty percent sure, but he wanted confirmation.

And so, he waited until the man finished smoking. Nasir dropped to the ground when the man threw away the butt of the cigarette and headed back in. He stuck to the ground till he heard the creak again and finally a soft thud of the door closing.

Nasir circled to the side of the building through the line of trees and dashed across the clearing, and skidded to a stop, crouching near the side wall. He spied a few windows, but all of them were boarded up. Just as he was about to give up, he stumbled upon a crack in the wall, covered up with a makeshift sheet of metal. Nasir picked up the sheet, taking care not to touch the walls around him, and moved it aside.

The man had his hoodie down over his shoulders and in the pale light of the early sun, he saw Alex. He scanned the area for signs of Shruti, but with no luck. Slowly replacing the makeshift covering back where it was, Nasir retreated his steps all the way to the southern corner of the sewage treatment facility. On the way, he radioed his team," Target acquired. Converge onto the south corner of the facility ASAP."

A string of affirmatives spluttered through the radio as the team abandoned their recon and converged to the location provided.

Nasir crouched near the walls of the facility and checked both sides for signs of his team. Nothing yet. He checked his watch again, just after half-past five. He didn't expect to find Alex so fast and that means he has to wait almost an hour and a half for the local police to show up. Taking him before that would be risky. With a team of five, they could technically cover all sides of the building, but it would stretch his team thin and that increased risk – the risk of Alex getting away and the risk of one of his team getting hurt.

The shuffle of footsteps announced the arrival of his team before he saw them. Avinash and Salim led the pack, their guns out, and pointed downwards, fingers off the trigger. Akshay and Sonam were right behind them, their holsters unbuckled. Nasir waved them towards him, and they joined him in the crouch. He quickly gave a run-down of all that went down and drew a small map of the place on the ground.

"This is where he is holed up," said Nasir, circling the smaller warehouse. "We're gonna split up and cover different exits and wait for the local police to show up. Avinash and Salim, you guys cover the far side." He pointed to the squiggly lines on the ground. "Take cover in the line of trees on this side. Akshay, there was a ditch on the east side of the building. You take position there. Me and Sonam will take the tree line to the west."

Without a word, everybody rose to their feet and fell in line behind Nasir. He led them, cutting the cold, crisp morning air, towards the 'U' shaped buildings. When they were at the edge of one of the buildings, Nasir held up a closed fist and the team stopped. Nasir pointed towards the building nestled behind the bigger warehouses and veered off to the tree line on the west. Sonam took the lead heading for the trees. They soon found a comfortable place in the trees. It hid them from view but was still able to keep an eye on the place. Nasir spotted Avinash and Salim slipping into the line of trees on the other side. They had circled around the building to stay out of sight.

Nasir touched his earpiece and said, "Eagle, in position."

"Mario, Luigi, in position," his radio responded as Avinash announced their status.

Nasir waited for a couple more minutes, and when Akshay reported back, he settled down to keep watch.

Fifteen minutes into the stakeout, a pack of dogs started a gang war in front of the building. The tribal nature of humans must have an evolutionary element to it, a stray gene imbibing the pack- behaviour. Humans took it and ran with it to a whole another level - packs based on geography, on religion, on caste; you name it and there is a pack for it. As he was lost in thought, absently watching the dogs fighting it out, Sonam poked him on his side and pointed towards the bigger warehouses.

A man crouched on the side of the building, the same place Nasir was a few minutes ago. It was hard to see his face, but he looked familiar. The man peeked out of his hiding place and ran to the building, keeping low. He paused to scan the surroundings, and then Nasir saw him. Manas? How did he get here?

Nasir pressed the transmitter on his radio. "I have eyes on Manas."

"Did you say Manas?" asked Avinash.

"I repeat. I have eyes on Manas. He is entering the building."

"New instructions?" asked Akshay.

"This doesn't change anything. Alex is our primary target and Shruti, the hostage. Everyone stays in position. I am going in to do a recce. Keep the channel clear and wait for my call."

Nasir slowly crept out of the trees, checked if the coast was clear, and made a beeline towards the building. Staying light on his feet, he made sure the angle between his and door was oblique enough to keep him hidden. He reached the edge of the, now open, door. The loud thuds of his heart beating rang in his ear. Nasir closed his eyes and took in a few deep breaths to control the wild rhythm of his heart. He inched closer to the door and peeked inside. The floor was a lot less cluttered than the other three places. The space inside was large enough for a small platoon. Huge, dusty machines, long metal poles, and shelves full of old cardboard boxes were scattered here and there as if somebody left the place in a hurry. But one of those areas was considerably less littered, as though it had been cleaned and tidied up. Nasir crept inside the space on all fours, slipped into the shadow of a huge machine, and slowly made his way towards the clearing.

As he zig-zagged from shadow to shadow and reached the periphery of the clearing, he spotted the silhouette of Manas moving towards the clearing from the other side. He made no effort to stay hidden, rather made slow measured steps towards the area, his eyes fixed on something Nasir could not see. Nasir changed the angle of his approach to see what Manas was focusing on. Because he had a feeling that it was exactly what he was also looking for. And then he saw it. Alex sat on top of a machine, his legs crossed, and eyes closed in a sagely fashion. *This was perfect.* Now he had both the killers in one room, but where was Shruti?

Nasir scanned the rest of the space. There was a pole to which a chain was tethered, but nobody at the end of it. A few clothes scattered on the ground, one of them red with blood. *Where was Shruti?*

As Manas got closer, Alex spoke up, "Didn't expect you so early." His voice sounded like it was coated with chocolate, but the poison underneath leaked through.

"I've done everything you've asked of me, haven't I? asked Manas.

Alex opened his eyes and uncrossed his legs. "Most definitely."

"Time to hold up your end of the deal."

Nasir stepped into the shadow of a bunch of metal poles, leaning against a pillar, and listened.

Alex jumped down from the machine and dusted his pants. "I've built up this moment in my head and this seems kind of anti-climactic. That's it? You come in, ask for your daughter, I give her to you, and you walk away?"

Manas' body went rigid in a second. "Choose your next words carefully."

"Oh, I have, Manas. I have."

"Hand over my daughter, right now."

Alex circled Manas, like a lion, sizing up his opponent. "What if I told you your daughter is not here?"

"That would be the biggest mistake you will ever make in your life." Manas bent his legs ever so slightly, lowering his centre of gravity, as he turned to keep Alex in front of his always.

Nasir couldn't let this go on for long. He wanted to try and get some information about Shruti, but Alex doesn't seem to be in the mood.

"Well, Shruti is not here. Let's talk for a while and maybe I'll take you to her."

The fire in Manas eyes bubbled up and exploded into a fiery volcano. "You have no idea what I am, *boy*." That last word had so much menace in it that it drove chills down Nasir's spine. It was getting out of hand. Nasir reached for his 9 mm automatic from his unbuckled shoulder holster. With the other hand he reached down his ankle and pulled out a 4.5 mm pistol.

"Guys, stand by. I'm engaging," he whispered into the radio.

With the guns pointed at Manas and Alex, Nasir slowly stepped out of the shadows.

"Hands behind your heads," he yelled.

With a sudden jerk, both heads turned his way. The deer caught in headlight expression on both faces was to die for.

"Come on now. Don't make it harder than what it must be. It's over."

Alex's face was red with anger. "You don't know what you are messing with," he shouted.

Manas slowly raised his hands behind his head. "Nasir, whatever you do, do not kill him. Shruti is not here."

"Shut up and raise your hands," Nasir barked.

"You are messing with God's plan, you puny servant of man." Alex had regained his composure, and the red of his face faded away.

Nasir's trigger finger itched. He could just pull the trigger and finish both if only he knew where Shruti was. "The only plan here is mine, and that involves sending both of you where you belong," said Nasir as he reached up to his ears and turned ever so slightly to the right to call for his team.

"I've got both of them," said Nasir. "Come fast."

Out of the corner of his eyes, he saw movement. A flash of red flying at him at full tilt. Nasir ducked, instinctively, and the brick flew past him. Alex and Manas dove to the ground.

Ha-ha, missed me, sucker.

But the brick landed on the pile of metal poles leaning on the pillar and it crashed down on him with a loud clatter.

Manas

Wednesday, May 7, 2014

Finish it.

Manas froze for a second; a million questions swimming in his head. How did Nasir figure out the place? Did he follow him? Does he know Shruti is not here? Will he shoot Alex? He slowly raised his hands behind his head and said, "Nasir, whatever you do, do not kill him. Shruti is not here."

"We gotta get out of here," Prateek said.

"I'm not going anywhere until I know where my daughter is," Manas whispered back.

"Shut up and raise your hands," Nasir barked.

"You are messing with God's plan, you a puny servant of man," Alex shouted as he edged backwards to the machine he was sitting on. His body was wound up like a spring, ready to unleash. He was up to something.

Nasir raised his thin wiry arm and touched his ear. "I've got them both. Come fast."

In the split second that Nasir took his eyes off them, Alex reached for something on top of the machine and threw it at Nasir. In that same split second, Manas decided to go for it and nodded at Prateek.

Alex was still gaining his balance back after throwing the brick when Prateek tackled him at full tilt. There was enough force to knock a man off his feet, but Alex and his 6"3' frame stayed put, albeit a little shocked. Prateek improvised without losing a step and ducked under Alex's outstretched arms, grabbing at air to regain balance. Prateek dropped to the ground and caught Alex around the waist from behind. With his hands firmly clasped around Alex, Prateek used his body weight to pull Alex down to the ground. On the way down, he rotated his body so that he came on top when they landed. The moment Alex landed on his back, Prateek landed two jabs on Alex's face.

Alex blinked, reeling from the assault. But Prateek was not giving him time to recover as punches landed one after the other. Manas looked around for Nasir. The brick Alex threw missed Nasir but landed on the bunch of metal poles which crashed on top of Nasir. He was trying to get out from under them, but there were too many poles. There wasn't a lot of time. Nasir would get out of it eventually and he could also hear footsteps coming around the building.

"Finish it," yelled Manas.

While Alex was catching his breath from the continuous assault, Prateek looped his right arm around Alex's neck and grabbed his left arm through the other side. He flexed his muscles and applied pressure over the carotid arteries on both sides of Alex's neck. Alex struggled a bit, but in five seconds the blood to his brain dried up and his body went limp.

"That should do it," said Manas.

Prateek released the choke hold, got on top of Alex, and swung his right arm in a massive hook to the top part of Alex's temple. His head flew to the side and recoiled like a ragdoll.

"*That* should be enough," said Prateek. "He'll be out for a while."

"We need to get out of here," said Manas as he nodded towards the back. The gap in the wall he had spotted earlier was perfect for getting away from here.

Prateek hooked his arms under Alex's shoulders and dragged the limp body towards the direction Manas showed. Just as they rounded a corner around a large machine, the footsteps grew louder and started to echo. *Nasir's backup was here.*

"Faster," whispered Manas. "They are going to go to Nasir first, but he will just point them in our direction."

"Over there," a deep voice shouted as the footsteps zeroed in towards the pile of metal poles and Nasir under it.

Prateek was almost at the gap in the wall when a couple of footsteps veered off towards them. The metal clink of hollow metal poles hitting the ground rang in the enclosed space.

Prateek was halfway through the gap when the footsteps grew louder, and closer.

"Prateek, get out now and head straight for the building with the underground cellar." And as soon as Alex's leg disappeared through the gap. Manas launched himself headfirst through the gap and out the other side.

Manas

Wednesday, May 7, 2014

Pain is a beautiful thing. It cleanses, it protects, it makes us remember, keeps us honest.

Pale fluorescent light of the emergency lamps bathed the dingy cellar in a light blue glow. Four lamps in Manas' bag were now perched on top of the shelves on all four sides of the room. The only other light came in from a small crack at the top corner, probably put in for air circulation. A chair Manas salvaged from the rubble above ground stood in the middle of the space, with Alex firmly tied to it. The yellow plastic rope which wound around Alex's hands and legs glowed in the pale light.

Alex was still out cold from the blow to his head. But Manas didn't have time to waste. He grabbed a bottle of water and threw half of it at Alex's face. The shock of cold water hurled at his face woke Alex up instantly. He gasped through the water running down his face and opened his eyes. In a moment of incomprehension, he struggled against the ropes which tied him down to the chair. But when his eyes found Manas's face, realization dawned, and he scrambled to put up an expression of composure on his face.

Manas leaned against one of the shelves with the emergency light behind him, casting his shadow on Alex. Prateek hung back in the shadows, waiting to be called upon. He didn't utter a word, but just stared at Alex.

Alex alternated between scanning his surroundings and glancing at Manas. It was absolute silence, except for the faint whir of the lights and weak creaks from the chair Alex was sitting on.

Alex broke the silence first, regaining his composure. "Well, well, well. Look what we have here... a torture chamber?"

Manas pushed off the wall and closed the distance between him and Alex in a few steps "The next words out of your mouth better be about Shruti, or..." He let his words hang in the silence, like a guillotine ready to slice heads at the drop of a hat.

Alex broke into a scornful laugh. "I'm not going to just tell you where she is." He waved at the room around him. "This tells me you know that as well."

"I just wanted to give you a chance to be a man and stand by your word."

Alex continued his laugh, now shaking his head. "Are you that naïve, Manas?" Prateek walked into the light towards Alex. But Manas stopped him with a casual raise of his hands.

Anger bubbled up inside Manas like a volcano. "Here is the run-down of what's going to happen. We are in the cellar of an abandoned warehouse, with a trap door which is practically hidden. It'll be at least four or five hours before anyone is going to find us."

"What—"

Manas cut Alex off. "You're tied up in a chair at my mercy and still being an ass?"

"I'll stop being an ass when you stop being a pussy."

Alex was wasting time he didn't have. A fuse inside Manas blew, and he saw red. He drew back his hand and slapped Alex across the face with the back of his hand. "Where is my daughter?"

Blood trickled out the side of Alex's mouth, but he was still laughing; his teeth, now stained with the blood leaking from his mouth. "That was a weak ass slap. Gotta try harder, Manas."

"Have it your way," said Manas, glancing at Prateek.

Prateek took slow measured steps towards Alex. In the pale fluorescent light, the darkness in his eyes showed through. "What do you know about pain, Alex?" He started circling Alex, still slow and deliberate.

"Pain has its uses," said Alex. "Like getting Amrita to talk about you. She must have loved you a lot, because it took me quite a while to get that information out of her."

Prateek chuckled hard. "You should really know who you are talking to, boy. That doesn't bother me at all." He glanced at Manas, who have him a nod ahead.

"Pain is a beautiful thing, don't you think? It cleanses, it protects, it makes us remember, keeps us honest. Pleasure on the other hand is irresponsible, carefree, and lives for the moment."

He stopped and grabbed Alex's face by the jaws. "Almost everybody in the world is searching for pleasure, all their life. 'Pursuit of Happiness', they call it. But a very few select have understood the intricate balance both pain and pleasure in our lives. They are not opposites; they are on both ends of a spectrum."

Prateek let Alex's face go and walked back to Manas' bag on the shelf and pulled out a knife from inside. "Masochism has its roots in the very same thought. They skirt the boundaries of pain and pleasure; they derive pleasure from pain inflicted upon themselves." He wiped the blade across his chest and tested the sharp end with the tip of his finger. "Knowingly or unknowingly, they have a higher level of consciousness. They know that pain and pleasure co-exist."

Prateek turned around and walked back to Alex, the knife in his hand shimmering in the pale blue light.

"But you and me. We fall into another category of people, don't we?"

Manas leaned against the wall in the shadows and observed Alex, whose eyes never left the shimmer of the knife. And for the first time since they met, Manas saw Alex flinch a little.

"Yes, we do," said Prateek. "We derive pleasure from inflicting pain on others. Some do it for the illusion of power it gives them, some do it for the sheer sadistic pleasure of watching somebody suffer. Which one are you, Alex?"

Alex opened his mouth to say something, then decided against it.

Prateek came to a stop right in front of Alex, a long metal knife quivered in his right hand.

"Even among those, there are an even smaller section of people who find their purpose in pain. They turn the instant gratification of pleasure through pain into something meaningful, something that will be remembered."

A slow smile grew on Alex's face. In the bluish light, Alex's eyes were more glassy than usual. "Yes, exactly," he said. "Thank you. It feels really good to hear you say that."

"What?" Prateek snapped. "I was talking about me. You are just a sick bastard who plays dress up with dead bodies. What do you know about purpose?"

Alex's nostrils flared and the glassy eyes narrowed. "A lot more than you think."

"Save it," Prateek snapped. "I'm not your shrink. Tell me where Shruti is. Are you gonna tell me or do I have to carve it out of you?"

"Purpose...," said Alex. "It's apt that you talk about purpose. You were right. I was lost in a sea of instant gratification, living from one artwork to another. But everything changed when I chanced upon Amrita. I found my way, found my purpose, which led me to this moment, right now."

Manas' ears perked up at the mention of Amrita. He glanced at his watch. The radium hands glowed at half-past six."

"I think I asked you a question," barked Prateek.

"Everything I have done after is to fulfil that purpose," Alex continued, ignoring Prateek. He paused for a second and let out a low chuckle. "Well, not everything. There were a few very pretty girls on the way."

In one swift motion, Prateek reached for Alex's little finger and swung it backwards. The crack of his bones echoed loud in the silence, which was drowned out by Alex's guttural scream.

"Pain...," said Prateek, as he let go of Alex's finger. It stuck out at an odd angle. "Beautiful isn't it?"

Alex bit back his screams and regained his composure faster than Manas expected. His chest rose and fell as his body coped with the sudden pain.

"Manas never lets me enjoy this, you know," said Prateek. "Always the righteous one, he wants to finish it as soon as possible. So, irritating." He grabbed Alex's hand and pinned it to the chair. With his index finger, he counted off the remaining four trembling fingers, playing *'eeny meeny miny moe'*. "But kudos. You pissed him off so much that he is OK with this."

Alex's eyes widened as he realised what was about to happen.

Prateek finger finished its little dance and landed on Alex's middle finger, which he grabbed in a fist and pushed it back. "You wanna tell me where Shruti is?"

Alex shook his head, biting back the pain from his twisted finger.

Prateek didn't wait to ask again. He jerked back the middle finger, breaking it.

Alex screamed, this time it was louder than before, just before he passed out.

Manas pushed off the wall and walked into the light. "Wake him up."

"You read my mind," chuckled Prateek. "I was just beginning to have fun."

"Cut the bullshit, Prateek. I want to save Shruti. That is our priority. Just get it out of him."

The hands on his Timex showed ten minutes to seven. They have been at it for almost half an hour, but not a step closer to finding Shruti.

Prateek dug out a bottle of water from the bag and splashed some of it on Alex's face.

Alex shuddered into consciousness. His eyes flew open, unfocused. Prateek drew his hands back and slapped Alex across his face.

"When you look at the human body, the anatomy, you'd think that it's just a fragile sack of organs, just waiting to give up at the slightest push. But they are astonishingly hard to kill. I'm sure you know that as well.

That's why there are set ways of killing someone – like sitting the throat, a bullet to the head, etc." Prateek rose to his feet and crossed over to the bag on the shelf. "On the flip side, it also means that there are a lot of ways not to kill someone. A stab or two missing the vital organs, important arteries; they are nothing. Of course, you'll be in a lot of pain, but you won't die." He pulled out a long knife from the bag and walked back towards Alex. "Over the years, I have acquired this skill, you know. I know how to miss them all."

Alex still reeled from the slap, his eyes trying hard to focus on something. The broken fingers stuck out at odd angles, trembling with each breath.

"Either you tell him what he wants to hear, or he is just gonna continue this until you do," said Manas, from the dark.

Alex opened his mouth to say something, but blood came out instead. He coughed for a few seconds and then said, "Go to hell."

"Have it your way," said Manas, nodding to Prateek.

Prateek shifted the grip on the knife and brought it down on Alex's stomach. It sliced open the skin and plunged into the body cavity. He struggled against the ropes tying him down as his body convulsed; a reflex action when you get stabbed.

Prateek twisted the knife ninety degrees. "Where...... is...... Shruti?" He pulled back the knife; blood oozed out of the puncture wound, soaking Alex's shirt, dripping on the floor. In the pale blue light of the lamps, the blood collected in a black pool under the chair.

Prateek smacked Alex across his face. "Where… the fuck… is Shruti?" He roared.

Alex barely managed to shake his head. But that was all Prateek needed. He drove the knife into Alex's palm, nailing it to the chair. The knife quivered on its end; blood flowed out, meandered through Alex's fingers, and joined the pool of blood under the chair.

"We can do this all day. Remember what Manas told you on the sea bridge? '*I'll make you wish I had killed you instead.*'." Prateek wiped off a few drops of blood on his face. "Listen, Manas wants to get his daughter back safely. So why don't you do us all a favour and tell us already?"

Alex grunted hard to control his screams. "Why do you…" - he gulped for air - "let yourself be controlled like this? You are better than this."

Prateek tugged on the handle of the knife and it swung back and forth, tearing into Alex's palms with each swing "You really don't know anything, boy. You think I'm a captive?"

Alex bit his teeth to suppress a scream of pain. "What's the time now?"

A shiver ran down Manas' spine. Something wasn't right. He checked his watch. "Ten minutes past seven."

Alex nodded his head and stared intently at Prateek. "You blabbed about purpose before, but what do you know about purpose? Didn't you leave it halfway through and fled to the other side of the country with your tails between your legs?"

Prateek pulled out the knife pinning Alex's palm to the chair and slammed it down on the other palm. Fresh spurts of blood joined the growing puddle at the foot of the chair.

Alex cried out in pain, breathing became shallow. "You can kill me if you want, but I'll die knowing I've fulfilled my purpose in life."

Manas shook his head slightly at Prateek. He needed Alex alive.

Alex stared intently at Prateek and said, "Manas had you captive for years, didn't he? And what made him release you?"

Prateek took two steps back and folded his hands.

"Me. I did that. And ever since I've been batting for your side, but you are still running behind the same guy who sent you to prison. Locked you up for years."

Prateek unfolded his hands and walked closer.

"God gave purpose – to free you from the prison Manas threw you in. And when I mean free you, it meant free you completely. That weak sack of flesh you call Manas was holding you back, keeping you on a leash. I had to get you back to your former glory. The three tasks, you know, was not random. They were specifically designed to set you free."

"You don't know me personally. How could you possibly know what I like, what I thrive on?"

Alex wiped the blood leaking out of his mouth on his shoulder. "An educated guess. Heard of the Macdonald's triad?"

Manas knew what that was. Reading up about dissociative identity disorder and serial killers was his coping mechanism. The more you understood something, the easier it was to avoid it. The Macdonald's triad was a set of three characteristics serial killers around the world has exhibited, even when they were kids – Cruelty to Animals, Arson, and Bed-wetting.

Alex chuckled, spitting out a few more shots of blood. "Don't you see?"

"Bella, Rajashekharan,..." Manas felt his legs become soft and lose their strength. He leaned on the wall to keep his balance.

Prateek closed the distance between him and Alex in a few long strides and grabbed the palm, which was pinned to the chair, now hanging limp, bleeding out. "I guess I should thank you, in one way. But you made one unforgivable mistake." He plunged his fingers into the open wound on Alex's palms and applied pressure. "Shruti is as much a daughter to me as she is to Manas. The moment you laid hands on her; your fate was sealed."

Alex let out a guttural scream which echoed in the small, dingy cellar.

"You tell us where Shruti is and there is still hope for you," said Manas.

Alex raised his eyes up from the ground and stared squarely at Manas. "She was never part of the plan, you know. All I wanted was to talk to you and get you to let the Butcher loose. But God works in mysterious ways. When you shooed me away, I was lost. But He showed me the way. Shruti and the game was nothing short of a divine interruption. And now, she is on the verge of being immortalized as my first live artwork."

The world collapsed around Manas as he stood rooted to the spot. He knew what Alex meant by 'artwork', but he also mentioned 'live' artwork. He pushed off the wall, marched over to Alex, and pulled out the knife pinning his palm to the chair.

"'Live' artwork?"

"Yeah, the first of my artwork to be displayed before they were dead."

"So, she is alive?"

"Not for long. The high tide is coming." Alex laughed a mirthless laugh. Blood spluttered out of his mouth, spraying everywhere.

Terror filled him up. It was not supposed to go down like this. Manas drew the knife back and buried it deep in Alex's right upper arm. It went in and struck against the bone, jarring in his hands. "Tell me her exact location... right now!" Manas roared into Alex's ears over the scream which filled the room.

"Valiyathura pier," Alex rasped. "Tied to one of the pillars of the pier, waiting for a salty watery death. At quarter to eight, she will be immortalised as the first and possibly the last live artwork."

Manas instinctively glanced at his watch. It showed half past seven and there was no way he was going to make it to the pier in time.

A weak chuckle escaped Alex, as the puddle at the foot of the chair grew bigger. "Why do you think I talked about her just now? She is as good as dead."

Manas' body convulsed into a spasm as a sob took shape at the bottom of his belly. "Why?" he cried. "Why did you have to drag her into this?"

"You would never… never let the Butcher free until she is alive."

A carnal desire to inflict pain rose in Manas. He yanked back the knife from Alex's upper arm and in one smooth motion slit his throat. The sharp knife cut through the soft flesh and cartilage like butter. Blood sprayed all over, soaking Manas' clothes, as Alex's head went sideways and hung limp.

Manas dropped the knife as we walked away. After everything, he didn't get to do the one thing he wanted to do, the one thing that he promised Anuradha - that he would get Shruti back home, safe and sound. He pulled out his phone, turned it on, and dialled Nasir.

"Who are you calling?" Prateek asked.

"Nasir. I want to save my daughter."

"The policeman? How do you have his number?"

"Shut up and let me do this."

Nasir picked it up on the third ring.

"Please save my daughter," Manas blurted out.

"Manas? Where are you?"

"Shruti is... where she is... I know... There is no time. Please save her."

"Calm down, Manas. And tell me where exactly she is."

"Tied to one of the pillars at the Valiyathura Pier. High tide is coming, and it would kill her in fifteen minutes."

"Oh, shit!" Nasir barked a few orders to someone.

"I've sent a few of my people, said Nasir. Don't worry, they will do everything to get her home, safely." After a brief pause, he added, "Alex?"

"No longer a problem for any of us." Manas wiped the blood dripping down his face with his hand. "I'm trusting you with my daughter's life. You are a good man and I know you will do everything in your power to save a life. And tell my wife I'm sorry." Manas hung up the phone and tossed it aside.

Prateek looked at him with an eyebrow raised.

"We'll never reach Shruti in time, not with the police hunting us anyway. This way, at least Shruti is safe."

"At least?"

Manas walked over to one of the lamps fighting off the engulfing darkness of the cellar. "Prateek, I wanna thank you, thank you for everything. Without you, I never would have gotten this close to getting my daughter free. Even now, it is because of you that we got a chance to save her. I'm grateful to have you, brother."

"We did it together, brother. But whatever I did, I know you would have done the same for me."

Manas let out a low chuckle, almost a growl. "You know what? Alex was right."

"His intentions were good, but he shouldn't have dragged Shruti into this," said Prateek.

"No, I mean the part about me imprisoning you and holding you back. I did all those for my selfish reasons."

Prateek nodded his head. "But it's OK. I'm glad that we have it behind us."

"No, you don't understand. I'm not the same person as before. I can't stand and watch you kill innocent people."

"Innocent?"

Manas raised his hands to stop the argument. "Listen to me. I'm not going to be a part of what you want to do, but I'm not gonna stop you either. The way I see it is that there is no going back to my old life. And I'm not petty enough to deny you the life you desire either. So, I'm gonna send myself into exile. There'll be no one holding you back anymore."

"No, wait!" said Prateek.

"This is goodbye, brother," said Manas flicking off the lamp and fading away from reality.

Sonam

Wednesday, May 7, 2014

Shruti, you are not dying on me. Not after all of this.

The SUV veered around a corner, narrowly missing a two-wheeler. Sonam grabbed her seat, her fingers digging into the cushion, as the vehicle zipped past blurry traffic. This was the fastest she had seen Akshay drive. Just as they got out of the curve, Akshay floored the accelerator; engine revved in response as the Scorpio pulled out of the corner. The incessant roar of the engine, the resounding police siren, and the blaring horn cleared the traffic up ahead.

Sonam tugged on her seat belt. "How long?"

"Ten minutes," said Akshay, never taking his eye off the road and the hand off the horn.

Sonam glanced at her watch. "We don't have ten minutes."

"I know," Akshay said as he swerved into oncoming traffic to get around a Maruti Swift which took a few more seconds than needed to respond to the siren. A truck rushed towards their Scorpio head long, honking. The driver was waving his hands to get out of the way. Akshay downshifted, stepped on the gas, and sped up towards the truck, overtaking the Swift. Sonam put her hands out and forced the Swift to slow down. Akshay ducked into the gap that ensued, missing the truck by a hair.

Sonam realised she was holding her breath and took two lungsful of air. Just then the radio crackled to life. "ETA?" Nasir barked.

"Five minutes," said Sonam.

"Get there faster. Radio me when you have the girl. We are going in."

The Scorpio took a violent turn into a muddy path which led up to the pier. The long, concrete pier extended into the sea, with several pillars holding up the structure. And there were a lot of pillars. *This was not good.*

Akshay slammed the brakes as the Scorpio skidded to a stop. Before the vehicle came to a stop, both the doors were open, and they jumped out. Sonam jumped a bit too early and landed on her feet with more momentum than she could handle. She lost her balance and tipped over.

The ground came rushing up, but her academy training kicked in at the last moment. She ducked into a ball and rolled off the fall and rose to her feet.

Akshay was running towards the pier, taking off the holster and throwing it to the ground. She climbed down the shallow end of the pier and rushed into the water.. Akshay jumped into the water from above, a few feet in front of her.

Sonam gestured right and veered off to scout the right side of the pier, and Akshay headed left.

"Shrutiii…." Sonam moved deeper into the water, each step cutting through the turbulent water resisting movement. The waves drenched her to her knees. Water was never her strong suit.

She waded deeper and deeper into the sea, but still no signs of Shruti. The sea water lapped her up to her hips now, tugging at her footholds, eroding the sand underneath. She held on to a pillar, and scanned ahead, but no signs of Shruti. Just the white bubbly water hitting the pillars and spraying salty water everywhere. Her legs locked in place, unable to move. She never learnt swimming until the academy. And that was one thing she barely got through. But Shruti…

Just then, she spied a flash of blue about twenty feet ahead. Not the blue of the sea, nor of the sky. This was different.

"Oi..." she shouted for Akshay. But the continuous roar of waves breaking against the pillars drowned it out.

Sonam wiped off the water that splashed on her face, clearing her eye. A long line of moss-covered, blackened concrete pillars extended all the way to the end of the pier. There it was again. The blue. It looked like a T-shirt.

Akshay had waded into deep water, swimming between pillars, but he didn't seem to have spotted the blue yet. "Akshayyy....," called out Sonam in a last-ditch effort to catch his attention but failed.

There wasn't time to waste. If the blue was Shruti's T-shirt, she was already skirting the surface of the sea. Sonam took a deep breath and started down deeper into the sea. Maybe she would be able to reach Shruti without swimming. She and Akshay were the little girl's last hope.

The sea rose quickly to her neck as she progressed. Small waves reached up and splashed salt water into her face and eyes. But she was still fifteen or twenty feet away. Akshay was nowhere to be seen, with the waves now rising up above her head.

Sonam held on to a pillar, thrusting her head above water. The next pillar was five feet ahead of her. She would have to swim. She barely knew how to swim in a swimming pool. It was a whole another story in the rough sea water. Sonam adjusted her position, planted her feet on the pillar and waited. When she saw one wave forming up and rising against the pillar, she took a deep breath and closed her eyes. The wave broke against Sonam, pinning her to the pillar and splashing water in her face. But as it receded. she pushed herself off the pillar and floated along with the retreating water to the next pillar, flailing her hands and legs to stay afloat. Salt water splashed across her face, entering her eyes. It burned, but she kept it open as her hands extended out to grab the next pillar. If she missed it, that was it.

When her fingers brushed against the cold hard concrete of the pillar, she grabbed it and held on to it, climbing higher. Her feet hung in the water with no foothold. It scared her, but there was no going back. Sonam counted the pillars she had to jump across. Four. That was a long way, but now she knew what to do.

Getting into position, she waited again for the next wave. She made good progress, and before you knew it, she just had one more jump to make. Holding to the pillar, she scanned ahead.

The blue was indeed Shruti. She was tied to the pillar, facing the sea. Her mouth was gagged, her right arm tied up at the pillar, and the other arm was submerged in water, probably tied to the pillar. She was struggling to break free, thrusting her head up and above the water which had reached her neck. Every time a wave came to shore, she would go underwater. There wasn't any time left. Sonam couldn't get her to shore, but if she could untie her, they could hold on to the pillar until help came.

Without thinking, she pushed off the pillar to the next pillar, mistiming the jump. Instead of using the momentum of the retreating wave, she hit it head-on. Although the retreating water did take her forward, her momentum wasn't enough to carry her all the way to the next pillar. Sonam was stranded a few feet from the pillar.

There was no momentum, and she felt the weight of her body pulling her down. She struggled against it and flailed her hands and legs, but all it did was break the water and splash some water. She still continued sinking, slowly but steadily.

Sonam caught the flash of blue through the blurry water. *No. This is not how it ends.* With a renewed spurt of energy, she clawed and kicked her way up. She broke the water and took a deep lungful of air.

"Do not panic", The voice of her instructor in the academy rang loud in her head.

Although analysts were not given full training in the physical aspects of the job, they still had basic training, more like a crash course on emergency procedures. One of those was 'drown proofing.' A technique for non-swimmers.

"Do not panic. Relax your body and stop struggling." There it was again. *"Believe in buoyancy. Use it. Make it your friend."*

Sonam did as she was told. She stopped struggling and re-positioned her body to be more vertical.

"Let your hands float slowly, elbows bent, hands in front of your shoulders," came the instructions.

Sonam followed it to the letter, and she felt her body rising. The dark underside of the pier became clearer and clearer as she approached the top. The moment she broke the surface of the water, she bent her head slightly forward and took a deep breath, filling her lungs with air.

"Do not try to bring your whole body above water. Relax and do not exert any force on the water. You will sink again, but rest assured. You will come right up."

Sonam believed those words completely; she had no other choice. The second time she surfaced, she tried to make small strokes towards the closest pillar. Before she went under again, she noticed the pillar was closer than before. The retreating waves must be pulling her into the sea, closer to the pillar.

The pier became blurry again, mixing with the greenish blue of the water, as she held her breath and waited for buoyancy to bring her back again. She felt the receding water tug her closer to the pillar. Just a little bit more, she willed the sea. A blurry blue shape emerged under water, tied to the pillar.

Pressure built up in her lungs. The rise to the top was slower than before. She resisted the urge to breathe underwater and held on.

As soon as she broke the surface, she looked around. The pillar with Shruti was closer, but water was at her chin now. Akshay was swimming towards her. Maybe he spotted Shruti?

Sonam couldn't fill her lungs as much as she would have liked before going under again. As she sunk down, she felt panic tickle the soles of her feet. Less air means less buoyancy and less time available. Sonam shut the voice up and calmed herself down. Panic would only use up more oxygen. She waited with her arms outstretched for buoyancy. The pressure crushed her lungs as her brain screamed for air. Just then her hands snagged on a loose piece of clothing, something blue. She tugged on it and got closer to Shruti's body underwater, and climbed up to the surface.

Sonam broke the surface with a huge gasp of air, calming her burning lungs. Shruti's face was barely above the water, her eyes closed. Shruti's face was strangely made up, almost like she had walked off a party. Water rolled off her face, unable to stick to it. *Waterproof makeup*, Sonam thought. *That was a strange thought to have. Maybe she was low on oxygen.*

Sonam cleared her head and took a deep breath. "Shruti?"

There was no answer and panic broke out, lowering her body temperature by a couple of degrees. She immediately checked her pulse. *Yes. She was alive, barely.* Shruti needed CPR as soon as possible and for that she had to get to the shore. But there was no way Sonam would be able to carry Shruti back to shore. Looking around, she saw Akshay swimming in her direction, getting closer every second. All she needed to do was to keep Shruti's head above water till he came closer.

The rope. Sonam pulled on the strings and worked the knots with her fingers. Being underwater for so long had made the synthetic rope knots a bit looser. She took a large breath and dived under the water, keeping a hand firmly on Shruti to avoid drifting off with the waves. There was a knot tying Shruti's legs to the pillar.

Increased water resistance made her movements slower, but thankfully the knot at her legs was loose. Maybe because Shruti had struggled so much already, all it took was a bit of tugging to come loose. She shot up to the surface, quickly shifting her hands along Shruti's body and broke the surface.

Akshay was closer. Maybe a minute away, maybe half a minute. It was really hard to tell with all the water in her eyes.

Sonam untied the last knot at Shruti's hands and she became free from the pillar, with all her weight now on Sonam's hands. But she held on to the pillar with one hand and held Shruti above the water with the other. Her hands strained against the pillar as wave after wave tried to pull both her and Shruti towards the shore. In the time between two waves, Sonam shifted her position, wrapped her legs around the pillar, and looped one of her hands around Shruti and settled into a firmer position. *That's better.*

Shruti's body was lifeless. Sonam remembered the weak pulse she had sensed earlier and the cold running down her spine came back with full force. Shruti was holding on to life by a thread. She frantically gestured to Akshay. He was almost there.

"Are you OK?" asked Akshay, as soon as he came closer.

"Take her… Take her to shore. She needs CPR," said Sonam.

Akshay hesitated for a second and then took Shruti in his arms, expertly arranging her so that her head stayed above water. "Can you hold on to the pillar till I come back?"

Sonam nodded vehemently. "I'll manage. Take her to shore."

Akshay pushed off the pillar with Shruti in tow. Sonam watched them bobbing up and down the water, heading towards the shore. *Were they too late?*

A few locals peered down from the pier above, probably to check what the ruckus was all about. She raised her hands and signalled for help.

Without delay, three bodies jumped down from above. They splashed and sunk into the sea only to resurface and swim towards her with the ease of swimming in a pool. They ducked under the waves and made their way to Sonam. Soon enough, she was dragged to shore, with someone holding up her head and pulling her along.

The moment her legs touched solid ground, she ran up the beach towards Akshay. Shruti lay beside him, eyes closed and motionless. *No, no, no.* Akshay was on his knees, his hands compressing Shruti's chest at regular intervals. Sonam's saviours also rushed forward to help.

"28...29....30," counted Akshay before pinching her nose and blowing through her mouth. Shruti's chest inflated and collapsed as soon as the pressure was eased.

This was not good. "Call an ambulance," Sonam shouted. One of the guys gathered around, pulled out a mobile phone and started dialling the number.

Sonam spotted the radio they discarded before jumping into the water and rushed to pick it up.

Akshay continued compression, making sure blood was pumped through Shruti's body. He bent down to inflate her lungs again. Shruti showed no signs of revival. Akshay eased backwards and stared at Shruti's lifeless body.

"No," Sonam said, and rushed to Akshay's side. He was tired from all the swimming and was struggling to keep up the compressions.

"Where is the ambulance?" she screamed as she took over the CPR. "Shruti, you are not dying on me. Not after all of this."

Prateek

Wednesday, May 7, 2014

Goodbye, Manas, I'll miss you.

"Manas....," called out Prateek.

Nothing. The silence of the dark, dingy room freaked him out. He paced the room like a caged animal, stepping on blood and splashing it all around. Alex's lifeless body was still tied to the chair. His head had fallen sideways, but his vacant eyes stared back at Prateek, accusing him, shocked by his betrayal.

"Manas.... come back."

"Come back, Manas. I swear we will do things your way." *Still nothing.*

Prateek slowed down to a stop near Alex's body, stepping in the puddle of blood underneath. His lifeless eyes burned with an intensity which freaked Prateek out. He reached and closed them. He didn't need it right now.

"This sucks, Manas. You suck." He was just beginning to enjoy the second chance at life, revelling in the camaraderie and slowly getting enough say to take control of his life. "Brothers, don't leave each other high and dry."

Manas just couldn't pick a better time than this. The whole city was looking for him, with the police just around the corner. He was counting on Manas to get him out of there, out of the mess they were in.

"Manas, come back." But by this time, he realised it was pointless. With or without Manas, he had to get out of there as soon as possible. In fact, he should get out of the city, move to someplace else and start afresh. A new chapter in the tales of the legendary "*Butcher of Bhalswa*."

He grabbed the knapsack off the shelf and fished for a towel and a change of clothes. Manas had been thorough in packing everything they might need. It was that level-headed planning that Prateek would miss. But that's something you can learn, isn't it? Put a process around it. If you take that out, Prateek was the heart and soul of the team, wasn't he? *Maybe he doesn't need Manas that much. All he did was hold him back.*

Prateek stripped down, casting the blood-soaked clothes to the side. With the towel, he wiped clean his body and face. He can't possibly walk around unnoticed with blood on his face, could he? He changed into new clothes, combed his hair, and zipped up the knapsack. *Time to get out of here.* He slung the knapsack over his shoulder and crept up the stairs.

His plan was straightforward - get out, find a car, and drive as far away from here as possible. As he reached the top, Prateek slowly pushed open the trap door a few millimetres. The light outside seeped in, blinding him for a few seconds. When his eyes adjusted and vision cleared, he scanned the building through the crack. *No one.*

He pushed up the door, and it opened with a creak. Dust rained down from the door. Prateek covered his nose and stepped out of the underground cellar.

The non-existent door made a large enough opening which lit up the entire space inside. The cobwebs on the door were just the way they left when he and Manas came in. *That was good news.*

Prateek ran towards the door, crouched behind it, and peeked outside. The coast looked clear. He might get out of this mess after all. *This was it. Get out of the building, find a car, and just drive.*

"Goodbye, Manas, I'll miss you," said Prateek before he got up and ran outside into the light, into freedom.

Nasir

Wednesday, May 7, 2014

There was no question in his mind, no moral dilemma.
Just pure clinical execution

Nasir unhooked the radio from his belt and called in the local police. "Altaf, come in."

Sharp at 7 am, a bus full of local police arrived. Nasir had asked them to conduct a grid search around the area where Manas and Alex slipped out of his hands. There was no news till now. Nasir kicked a stray stone with his shoes. It flew off in a hurry. *He had them at fucking gunpoint.* All he had to do was pull the trigger and finish it. If not for Shruti...

"Altaf here," crackled the radio. Altaf was their point of contact with the local police. Akshay insisted on having him from the time they worked together to sniff out Alex.

"We've got a tip-off about the location of the fugitive," said Nasir. "He is armed and dangerous. Call off the grid search and form a kilometre-wide perimeter around the sewage treatment plant. Nobody, and I mean nobody gets out."

"Got it," Altaf said.

Nasir twisted the knob to change the channels on his radio. "ETA?" he barked.

"Five minutes," said Sonam.

When Manas called him up and told him about Shruti, his first instinct was to dismiss it as a ruse to get him off the trail. But the pain in his voice got through. And it was that pain in his voice that made him decide to send Akshay and Sonam to the scene. Maybe he was telling the truth. Manas was an enigma that Nasir couldn't figure out yet. The mask he wears of a loving husband and a caring father seems real. But Nasir also knew what he was capable of. No matter how difficult it was to swallow, the explanation about dual personalities added up perfectly.

But even in the off chance that the multiple personalities story was a lie, the part about Shruti was right. He had no doubts about that. And so was the word he gave Manas. He intended to save that little girl, no matter what, even if it was at the cost of letting Manas slip through his fingers.

He had to save Shruti. Not just because it was his duty, but also because he is a man of his word. Manas delivered another piece of good news – about Alex. *Good riddance. One less encounter to fake.*

"Get there faster. Radio me when you have the girl. We are going in."

Avinash and Salim geared up for combat. They shrugged into their bulletproof vests, strapping and fastening them in place. Salim drew out the magazine and checked if it was empty before thrusting it back in place. Avinash strapped on the holster with his gun on to the vest. Nasir had pulled on his vest the moment Manas shared his live location through WhatsApp. He kept his promise.

Nasir switched back to the other channel. "Altaf, maintain the perimeter. Do not come in unless I or someone from my team gives the signal."

It was best to keep the local police at a distance. He had seen too many cases where criminals were let go or even sentenced to life imprisonment because the evidence wasn't airtight. There was no way The Butcher gets to spend the rest of his life in government protection, wasting the taxpayer's money. The fewer witnesses, the easier it is to brush it under the carpet.

Avinash and Salim gave a thumbs up, the signal that they were ready.

Nasir turned off and clipped the radio to his belt as he marched over to Avinash and Salim, falling behind them. In tactical situations, Avinash was the lead; it was always that way.

The three of them made a beeline towards the target building, keeping to the shadows as much as possible. But speed was the priority as they closed the distance as fast as possible. As they approached a corner of a building, Avinash held up his closed fist. Salim stopped behind Avinash, and so did Nasir.

Avinash crouched and peeked around the corner. He thrust his left arm perpendicular to his body, the fist closed and then pointed forward. Seamlessly they transitioned into a line-abreast formation and moved ahead. Avinash led the pack from the middle with lightning speed. Nasir and Salim took up each of the flanks, a few steps behind Avinash. At a compromise of stealth and exposure, the formation increased their combined field of vision, which was the need of the hour.

Soon enough, they reached another corner of another building and crouched behind it. Avinash brought two fingers to his eyes and then pointed beyond the corner. *The target building was in sight.*

On Avinash's *'go'*, the three of them rushed towards the target building, staying away from the line of sight from the door of the building. They halted at a side of the building with no windows and doors. Avinash pointed towards Salim and Nasir and then pushed his hands down, his palms facing downwards. The message was clear; Nasir and Salim stayed rooted to the spot as Avinash headed out for recce.

Nasir's fingers itched as he curled them around the trigger on his MP5. *This was it.* He was about to put an end to the case, which haunted him for decades. The case which almost derailed his life ruined his family, his career, everything. But somehow, it doesn't feel as satisfying as he thought. Manas wasn't what he expected when he pictured *The Butcher of Bhalswa*.

Avinash crept back as quietly as he left. He grabbed his own wrist forcefully as soon as he rounded the corner. He spotted the Butcher. And just then, a scurry of footsteps rang from inside the building. They stopped abruptly, paused for a second, and started again.

Nasir crept towards the edge and peeked out to see the Butcher running out of the building. He turned back and pointed towards Salim, the sharpshooter. "Take him out."

Without a blink, Salim holstered his MP5 and reached for the 7.62 1A1 rifle slung across his back. There was no question in his mind, no moral dilemma. Just pure clinical execution.

Salim rose to his feet and planted them apart, lowering his centre of gravity. He raised the rifle and aligned the gunsight with his eyes. The Butcher was getting farther and farther away, but he didn't panic. Salim clicked the safety off, breathed out, and took aim.

"Body shot," whispered Nasir. He wanted to talk to Manas before the end.

Salim squeezed the trigger with love, and the bullet left the rifle with a loud bang.

Prateek

Wednesday, May 7, 2014

His feet would carry him far away from here to a new life, a new place.

Prateek sped past the shrubs, growing on both sides of the pathway. Nature reclaiming its place in the world. Just like he was, he was getting away from here. Half the city was looking for him but let them. His feet would carry him far away from here to a new life, a new place. He didn't need Manas to craft a new life, and it might be even be better without Manas holding him back.

Something pushed him from behind with a loud crack. Prateek staggered, unable to hold his momentum. The legs didn't go as fast as he hoped, almost as if his brain was preoccupied with something more important, more imminent. Gravity took the better of him, and he fell face down in the dirt.

It was strange. His back was wet, but it wasn't raining. Prateek tried to push himself up, but his right hand was not moving as he wanted it to.

And then an unbearable burning kicked in from the back of his right shoulder. It spread through his body.

The crack. A push from behind. The pain.

Realisation dawned on him. Prateek heard footsteps fast approaching. What kind of cowards shoot someone from behind? He tried to turn back and look at the cowards rushing towards him, but he just could not. The initial numbness was fading away, and just behind the smoke screen, the real pain lay waiting to consume him.

As the pain sucked into his body, slowly swallowing him whole, his consciousness faded, and everything went dark.

Manas

Wednesday, May 7, 2014

Shruti?

Manas had watched Prateek making all the wrong moves from a silent corner of his mind. Like a toddler learning to walk, he bumbled his way through the warehouse, bumping into everything on the way. Even if Manas hadn't shared the location through WhatsApp, Nasir would have traced the call and figured it out. But Prateek never even thought of that possibility. Instead, he just ran out into the open and got shot.

And now all that was left was an ever-present burning in his core. *The bullet must be still inside.* But no sign of Prateek. For the tough guy he portrays himself to be, he is a wuss. The first sign of pain, and he was gone. Manas chuckled, and it sent shooters of pain all through his body.

The footsteps were getting closer. Manas pushed against the ground with his left hand and rolled over. Nasir was in full combat gear as he barrelled towards him with the two cronies in tow. *He could have just shot me in the head, but he didn't.* That gave him hope. Maybe Nasir had something to tell him. Manas hoped it wasn't to capture him alive, parade him in front of the country and make him go through the long-drawn process of justice. It would be a lot easier to just shoot him in the head; there was no point in living in a world where he could not be with Anu and Shruti.

Nasir came to a stop a few feet from him, his handgun already drawn and trained on Manas.

Manas blocked out the pain and asked, "Shruti?"

Nasir's face softened as he straightened, holstered his gun, and pulled out his radio. The two cronies had their guns pointed at Manas, their fingers on the trigger. Nasir turned on the radio and talked into it. Manas sharpened his ears to catch any news, but it wasn't clear. He caught words here and there - *high tide, compressions, drowned.*

Manas' heart fluttered in his chest, hitting against the rib cage, willing to let go so that it could fly to Shruti and check if she was all right. Something caught his chest, and he coughed it up and spat it out. Red streaks on his shirt told him it was blood.

Nasir hooked the radio to his belt and came closer. He crouched next to Manas and gave him a curt nod. "Our people got to her in time."

At that moment, all his pain, the burning hole in his back, everything faded away. All that mattered was that Shruti was safe.

As the burning pain receded, the world grew dark. He drifted in and out of consciousness. In brief flashes, he was aware of the movement in the real world; Nasir talked on the radio, the cronies came closer, and one of them checked his pulse.

But at the same time, he was with Anu and Shruti, back on his terrace. The sun had hung up his shoes for the day. The soft rays of light didn't have the intensity of the noon sun but managed to spread its fiery orange tint on everything it touched. A warm breeze swooshed across the terrace, caressing everything and everyone on its way. Manas, Anuradha and Shruti leaned back on three chairs with mugs of coffee in each of their hands. It was strange to see himself in the third person, but Manas was kind of used to it. After all, it was the way he used to see himself when Prateek took over.

The people on the terrace seemed happy and content. It was the kind of silence which only lives between people who feel at home with each other.

Was it an outtake from his past? Or a glimpse into the future? Or just a construct of his dying mind? He didn't care, but he wanted to be there. He was with his loving wife and daughter. There was no Alex to ruin the moment, no Nasir to capture him, just him, his family, and their love for each other. It was all he ever wanted.

But it didn't last long. The inevitable darkness started leaking into this idyllic place as well. It started with the sun, blocking it out and slowly spreading through everything like black paint on a canvas. Manas cried out in agony as it spread everywhere, devouring Anu, Shruti, his terrace, everything.

As everything faded to black, he hung in mid-air, darkness all around him. Although it didn't feel like air, it was colder. But even though that darkness, his mind found solace in the love for his family; Shruti's smile, Anuradha's laugh.

Manas was thinking about the quirk in Shruti's smile when he felt something beneath him. It was still darkness, but a darkness within darkness. Somehow different. It wasn't the cold darkness which invaded his mind, but a warmer, more comforting darkness. He could almost feel its calm quietness. All he had to do was let go and fall into its loving embrace.

Not yet. He didn't get to grow old with Anu, take long walks in the park with her, remind her about the tablets she should take, admonish her when she forgets to take some medicine, buy chocolates and spoil his grandchild. He didn't get to see Shruti become a successful scientist, scare her boyfriends into not breaking her heart, or give her hand in marriage to one of those boys she liked. There was so much left to do.

But the darkness beneath grew warmer and more inviting by the minute. It held the promise of a place where everything ceased to exist, a place where consciousness would melt away. A place where definitions of what is and what is not ceased to exist.

Manas knew the futility in holding on. The life he was holding on to didn't exist anymore. Out in the real world, the Pandora's box was open, and it was impossible to get back all the demons that escaped. The life that was waiting for him was one without his family, one in confinement.

In that moment of clarity, he let go. He let go of his dreams, his hopes, and plans and sunk into the warm darkness. It cradled him in its loving arms as he ceased to exist.

Epilogue

Saturday, May 10, 2014

He really didn't want the monster to be unleashed on the world again.

Rain streamed down in bucketfuls onto the windshield. The wiper didn't stand a chance. Nasir squinted his eyes and inched forward, following the brake lights of the car ahead of him. He checked his watch; there was time.

He woke up that morning to the rattle of rain on his windows, and it only got worse from then. By the time he got out of the guest house and into the car, it was pouring down like anything. The saving grace was Sonam waiting in the car with a warm smile. The rest of the team was still enjoying their break. Moreover, where they were going was more of a personal trip.

The last few days went by in a blur. Nasir and his team closed the case, celebrated for a night, and then took a well-deserved vacation. Nasir slept like a log for 16 hours straight. It was the best sleep he had in years. And he woke up with such clarity of thought that he picked up the phone and dialled Sonam. They had left so much hanging in the air; it needed to be addressed.

It wasn't the most comfortable conversation, with all the awkward pauses and silence. But they kept at it for hours; they talked about the age difference, the professional complications, their fears and insecurities. Nasir tried his best to convince Sonam that it was absurd to even think about a relationship. But behind that façade, he wanted it to happen. Sonam called his bluff and turned the tables around. She convinced him that it was crazy not to go for it. Nasir chuckled at the memory.

But Nasir managed to set some ground rules before caving in. Some really obvious things, like no relationship while in uniform, etc. And some counter-intuitive ones like `Sonam can't call Nasir her boyfriend' or 'no marriages'. She thought it was silly, but Nasir stood his ground. He was the farthest thing from a 'boy'. But he made it clear that although he said 'no marriages', he meant it in the traditional sense. It doesn't really affect the future of the relationship if it has any.

Finally, after much deliberation, they made it official. They broke the news to the team at a dinner the next day. As expected, Avinash and Salim roasted them with jokes about the age difference. But Nasir could see in their eyes that they were happy for him. Those two had seen him through his lows, been there when he went through the divorce, the alcohol addiction, everything. Akshay smiled and nodded in approval in that unassuming silent way only he could. And Sonam was giddy with joy; so was Nasir. For the first time in years, the world seemed colourful.

Nasir reached over and held Sonam's hand. They were warm and cold at the same time. A smile grew on her porcelain face as she brushed aside her bangs.

Nasir flipped on the left indicator as he prepared to make the turn. They were almost there. A beige building with large windows and two tall chimneys loomed ahead–the Electric Crematorium. There were just a couple of cars parked out front. Nasir pulled up alongside them. He pulled out an umbrella, stepped into the rain, and rounded to the other side of the car to get Sonam out. Together, they headed inside the building.

Anuradha stood tall in a crimson red kurta and blue denim, with her head held high, but her slightly ruined mascara told a different story. Shruti buried her face in Anuradha's shoulder and leaned on her. She had a bandage around her collarbone, and her right arm was in a sling. Being tied up in the rough sea during high tide really did a number on her arms. She was in the hospital till the day before, getting treated for the injuries she sustained.

There was hardly anybody else apart from these two. Who would come to the funeral of a notorious serial killer? The press lost interest and moved on to the next hot take.

Anuradha looked up at the entrance and smiled wanly at Nasir, and shifted her gaze back to the door of the furnace. He and Sonam walked towards them.

"Our condolences," he said.

Anuradha flicked her watery eyes towards Nasir for a split second and said, "Thank you."

"How are you feeling, Shruti?" asked Sonam.

Shruti got up from Anuradha's shoulder and wiped her eyes. "I'm okay. Have a few sprains and wounds, but nothing serious."

They relapsed into an awkward silence as they waited for Manas' body to be pushed into the furnace.

"There are no ceremonies?" asked Nasir to break the silence.

"He wouldn't have wanted those," said Anuradha, without looking at Nasir.

Nasir stared at the body, clad in white, on the roller at the entrance of the furnace. The handler was busy setting up the furnace and checking everything was all right.

"He was a good man, you know?" said Anuradha. Her voice wavered in the middle.

Nasir nodded his head. "The Manas you knew was an honourable man. Even on his last breath, his only thought was about Shruti."

"Shruti and I only knew one Manas. It doesn't matter what he was before we met him. Her father, my husband, was a loving, caring man. There was tenderness in him; respect, courage, and loyalty." Tears streamed down her face. "And now he will never get to see the woman Shruti will grow up to be. He really wanted that. I really wanted that."

Sonam leaned on his shoulder and wiped her eyes on his shirt. It was difficult for Nasir to separate The Butcher and Manas. But in those rare moments when he succeeded, he felt respect for Manas. He could have easily evaded capture, but he didn't. He really didn't want the monster to be unleashed on the world again.

The handler finally checked everything and pushed Manas' body into the yellow furnace. Anuradha and Shruti strained to catch one last glimpse of Manas before being incinerated. But both mother and daughter didn't break down; there were no wailing cries. But somehow, the silent tears that streamed down their faces were more heartbreaking. Nasir couldn't help but admire the strength and poise the two women displayed; they were going to do just fine without Manas.

The roller with the body clanked into place. The handler closed the furnace doors and turned on the furnace.

Outside, smoke rose out of the chimney, and blended into the air, becoming one with the nature.